SPRING BLOSSOMS AT MILL GRANGE

Autumn Leaves at Mill Grange
Christmas Wishes at Mill Grange
Summer Blossoms at Mill Grange
Winter Flowers at Mill Grange

ALSO BY JENNY KANE

Midsummer Dreams at Mill Grange
Autumn Leaves at Mill Grange
Spring Blossoms at Mill Grange
Winter Fires at Mill Grange

SPRING BLOSSOMS AT MILL GRANGE

Jenny Kane

An Aria Book

This edition first published in the United Kingdom in 2021 by Aria,
an imprint of Head of Zeus Ltd

Copyright © Jenny Kane, 2021

The moral right of Jenny Kane to be identified as the author
of this work has been asserted in accordance with the Copyright,
Designs and Patents Act of 1988.

A CIP catalogue record for this book is available from the
British Library.

E ISBN 9781838938130
PB ISBN 9781800246058

Cover design © Cherie Chapman

Typeset by Siliconchips Services Ltd UK

To secret benches and hidden doorways.

Prologue

Monday March 9th

Helen cradled the stone in her palm. The size of a cookie, grey in colour, it was jagged on one side and smooth on the other. Once upon a time it had been part of the bedrock; a tiny fragment of the geology that had formed the basis of the village of Upwich and its surrounds. Now, however, it felt like the most precious possession she'd ever owned.

She hadn't had the heart to tell Dylan that it wasn't an exciting find from the Roman fortlet they were excavating in Mill Grange's garden. The five-year-old had been so thrilled to be able to help his dad, Tom, when they'd peeled the tarpaulin off the archaeological site after a frosty winter, that when he'd picked up the stone and run to her, his face wide with pleasure, she'd held it with a reverence normally reserved for the crown jewels.

The boy's eyes had got wider and wider as she'd told him about the land beneath Exmoor, how it had formed, and how the stone he'd found was part of that.

Helen had been conscious of Tom's eyes on her as his son had sat on her knee and listened with rapt attention to every word she said.

Laying the stone back on her desk, tucked neatly in the corner of the store room, Helen sighed. She had come to Mill Grange to take a break from the pressures of her management job. She had not come to fall in love – especially not with Tom – a man with a horrendous track record with woman – and a son.

One

'Do you honestly think I'll need eighteen pairs of knickers? It's the Cotswolds, not the Kalahari.'

Thea scooped the entire contents of her underwear drawer onto the bed as Shaun flung open a suitcase.

'No, I think you'll need thirty pairs or more, but as you only have eighteen, then pack them.'

'Seriously?' Thea eyed some of her older undies with suspicion. The greying fabric had been consigned to the back of the drawer to be used in emergencies only, although now she thought about it, she wasn't sure what that emergency might be. An archaeological excavation in the middle of nowhere, perhaps?

'You know what it's like on a dig. Laundry facilities only happen to other people. A flushing toilet can be a luxury sometimes.'

'Won't the local village have a launderette?'

'It's the Cotswolds, Thea. The people who can afford to live there don't need launderettes.' Shaun winked. 'I tend to wring out my smalls in the nearest public toilet sink or a bucket of cold water.'

Thea laughed. 'I used to do that when I was a student on excavation.' Stuffing every pair of socks she owned into the suitcase, she added, 'Age has softened me!'

'You've got used to manor house living, that's what it is.' As Shaun threw a pile of t-shirts onto the bed, he caught a glimpse of anxiety crossing Thea's face. 'I was only joking. It's not like student times. We get a catering truck, posh tents and Portaloos. The only thing we don't have is regular access to a washing machine.'

Holding a thick jumper to her chest, Thea pulled a face. 'I'm not worried about knickers or having our own bathroom or anything like that. It's just... what if the show's new producer hates me? Phil gave me the job as co-host of *Landscape Treasures* because of the work I did for you in Cornwall, but the new guy... is it a guy?'

'It is. A bloke called Julian Blackwood. I've not worked with him before, but I've heard he's good.'

'Well, what if this Julian takes one look at me and decides to trade me in for a younger model? I'm thirty-three for goodness sake, that's ancient in female telly present land.'

'Then he'd be a fool. Anyway, that attitude, thank goodness, is gradually dying off. And if he was a "pretty young thing" bloke, rather than a "pretty thirty-something with experience and talent" type of chap, then he'd lose your skills and my respect. Which, as I'm the show's presenter, would be pretty stupid.'

'That's the other thing.'

'What is?' Shaun threw a mountain of socks into the

4

case, many of which, Thea was convinced she'd never seen before.

'I don't want the guest-presenter role just because I'm your partner. Some of the archaeologists are bound to think that's why I got it. If Phil only gave me the job because—'

Raising a hand to stop the fear he'd heard Thea utter at least once a week since *Landscape Treasures* had asked her to appear as their Roman expert for the next series' opening episode, Shaun said, 'You got the job because you are good at it. End of. Now, if you put all the clothes you want to take on the bed, I'll finish packing them so you can go and say goodbye to Tina and Helen. Go to Sybil's or something. It'll be a while before you have a scone as good as one from her café.'

'There is something rather delicious about sneaking off for morning coffee on a work day.' Tina raised her coffee cup in salute to Thea and Helen as they waited for Sybil to deliver a round of her famous cheese scones.

'I ought to be scraping a ton of mud off the shovels ready for the new guests this afternoon,' Helen dropped a sugar cube into her mug, 'but I can live with the guilt.'

Looking at her two friends across the Spode covered, table, Thea smiled. 'I'm going to miss you two.'

'You're only going for eight weeks. Anyway, you'll be far too busy being famous to miss the likes of us,' Helen gave her a friendly nudge, 'and too knackered from all the digging to notice the time passing.'

Thea laughed, 'The famous bit I doubt, the knackered bit

I can't argue with. I ache enough after a day helping you and Tom on our fortlet, these days. A full eight week dig with television cameras watching my every move is going to kill me.'

'Don't be daft.' Tina looked up as Sybil arrived at their table, 'I swear your scones smell more delicious every time we come in here.'

Sybil rolled her eyes, 'Praise indeed seeing as at least one of you – Thea – is here every other day testing the merchandise.'

Thea stuck out her tongue. 'Well, the chicken's eggs need delivering. It would be rude to walk all this way and not sample the goods.'

'It's a twenty-minute walk! You make it sound like you need Kendal Mint Cake and crampons!'

'I'm going to miss your cooking almost as much as I'll miss you, Sybil.'

Picking up a large paper bag from where she'd placed it on the next table, the café owner passed it to Thea. 'Well, these should keep you going for a while at least.'

Having peeped inside the top of the bag, Thea got up and gave Sybil a hug. 'Thank you.'

'I didn't want Shaun to go without my scones either.'

'Shaun?' Thea laughed. 'If you think a bag of your scones will last long enough to share with him, you are under a serious misconception!'

Watching Sybil skip off to her next customer, Thea was suddenly emotional. She was only going away to work for a while, and she was going with the man she loved, yet it felt as if she was leaving Mill Grange for good.

Cradling the warm paper bag, Thea realised with a start

that it had been almost a year since she'd first arrived at the manor house where she, Tina, Sam, Helen, Tom and Shaun – when he wasn't away filming – lived. Along with their friends, Mabel and Bert, they ran the manor as a retreat for former military personnel recovering from various injuries and debilitating experiences. Part of that recovery therapy included working on uncovering a Roman Fortlet that she and Shaun had found in the manor's garden.

The excavation, a rare find for Exmoor, an area of Britain which the Romans had hardly touched, was a popular choice of work for Mill Grange's visitors. In fact, it was so much in demand that, now the digging of the site was almost complete, they'd set up a fake dig so that their visitors could still learn archaeological techniques during their stay.

Having worked for years as an archaeologist and historian at the Roman Baths in Bath alongside Helen, Thea was finding the dual challenges of running a manor house, being host to guests, and co-managing a dig, immensely rewarding. *So why am I going to the Cotswolds to be a TV presenter?*

'Thea? Are you with us?' Tina pushed a plate in her friend's direction. 'Your scone has been sat in front of you for over thirty seconds and you haven't pounced.'

'I just realised it's a year since I first came to Mill Grange to help do the place up.'

'Oh my goodness! Already? We should celebrate!' Tina raised her cup in salute. 'So much has happened since then.'

'Including your engagement to Sam!' Thea cut her scone in half, inhaling the rich aroma of vintage cheese and cayenne pepper. 'I feel awful for not being around to help you arrange it.'

'Don't worry, Sam and I intend to keep things very simple.'

'Simple sounds good,' Thea tilted her head to one side, 'but is that what you want or what Sam wants? I remember a Tina Martin who wanted to get married in satin lace and diamonds at Westminster Abbey.'

'I wasn't quite that bad. I'd have settled for St Paul's Cathedral.'

Helen's eyebrows rose. 'I can't imagine you wanting an all-the-trimmings type wedding Tina.'

'Before I met Sam, I was a bit lost bloke wise. Couldn't see the kind hearts for the gold cufflinks.' Tina happily scooped up some extra butter. 'A marquee on the lawn at Mill Grange, with all our friends and Sam's family will suit us just fine.'

'With Sam's claustrophobia, that sounds wise. How is that now?' Thea dabbed up a stray scone crumb. 'I know he sleeps in the downstairs bedroom when we don't have guests with mobility issues, but is there any progress on him facing the stairs and the attics yet?'

Tina shook her head, her mouth too full to speak.

'He'll get there, you'll see.'

'He will,' Helen agreed. 'Got a date sorted for the wedding yet?'

'I wanted a May date so we can have a couple more months to concentrate on getting the retreat running on track, plus the gardens here look wonderful in late spring. The local registrar can do the sixteenth or twenty-third of May, so we've gone for the twenty-third. As it's a Saturday, we won't have guests in the manor to worry about at the same time.'

'Surely you'll close Mill Grange to visitors for a few days?' Helen poured everyone a top up of coffee from the pot. 'Or maybe not, it's a new business after all.'

'Precisely. We want to keep closed days to the minimum. Bookings have been improving steadily, but they are non-existent over the Easter period at the moment, so we will probably close that week in April. We can do most of our wedding planning then. Then we'll close the week of the actual wedding.'

Helen wiped a finger around her buttery plate. 'What week is Easter this year?'

'Works out from the eleventh to the twentieth, if you include weekends. It's a bit of a long time to be closed to be honest, but if we have no bookings then…'

Thea suddenly sat up straight. 'Helen, that's when your birthday is, you're going to be—'

'Yes. I know.' Waving her hand, as if to brush away the fact of another passing year, Helen asked, 'What time are you and Shaun leaving?'

'Oh no you don't. No sidestepping the issue, Helen Rogers!'

'What is it?' Tina asked.

'Helen's fortieth birthday is during the Easter break. The twelfth of April.'

Helen sighed. 'I was hoping it would go away if I didn't think about it.'

'But don't you want to celebrate?' Tina added a dollop of butter to her final mouthful of scone. 'We could have a party.'

'Hell no!' Helen looked horrified. 'I just want to crawl under the bed and forget about it. I'm going to be forty and I've done nothing with my life.'

'Apart from manage the Roman Baths for almost two decades and be one of the most respected Roman archaeologists and historians on the circuit!' Thea paused, before adding, 'I bet Tom will want to celebrate it. And let's not forget Dylan! Any chance for balloons and birthday cake.'

Guessing that Tom – and the fact he hadn't made any move on her despite obviously being besotted – was at the heart of Helen's discomfort over her forthcoming birthday, rather than the fact she was a year older, Thea let her off the hook. 'If you change your mind, let me know. I'd better get back. I've left Shaun packing our clothes.'

'Seriously?' This time it was Tina who looked horrified. 'If I left Sam packing for me, I'd end up with buckets of underwear and very little else.'

Thea laughed. 'Well that's young love for you. Makes you blind to the need for woolly jumpers, don't you think, Helen?'

She gave a brave smile. 'I wouldn't know.'

Two

Monday March 16th

As Shaun's car drove away, Thea waving madly through the passenger window, Tina threaded her arm through Sam's.

'I know it's only for a couple of months, but it's going to feel strange without Thea here.'

'It will.' Sam kissed the top of his fiancée's head. 'And even though Shaun's only here on and off, I've got used to him being around too.' He smiled at Helen and Tom, who were propped against the side of the manor. 'You guys up for a quick staff meeting? I've got a couple of things I'd like to discuss before today's guests arrive.'

'I'll go and put the kettle on.' Helen pulled herself away from the wall. 'Where do you want to meet?'

'The walled garden.' Sam grinned mischievously as he turned to Tom. 'Would you mind helping me carry a couple of trestle tables over?'

'No problem.'

Tina tilted her head to one side. 'What are you up to, Samuel Philips?'

'You'll see.' He winked. 'Fancy bringing one of your delicious lemon cakes? Oh, and some apple slices for the chickens? Gertrude and Mavis would never forgive us if we entered their domain without treats.'

Helen had been so caught up in her own thoughts that she hadn't heard the quiet sobs until her feet were almost on the kitchen's threshold.

Hovering in the corridor, unsure whether to move forward or leave Mabel in peace, Helen was relieved when Tina arrived at her side.

'You okay?'

Helen whispered, 'I think Mabel's crying.'

'What?'

'Listen.' As the sound of someone trying not to make a noise crying reached their ears, Helen mouthed, 'She's such a proud woman, I didn't know if my going in would be welcome, or if I'd embarrass her.'

Tina didn't hesitate. 'You put the kettle on and then phone Bert. He should be here if his wife's upset. I'll talk to Mabel.'

Wiping her hands down her side, Tina sat next to Mabel at the kitchen table. Easing the pen and shopping list pad out of the old lady's hand, she reached for the tissue box Helen had pushed in her direction when en route to the kettle.

'Mabel? Whatever is it? Do you feel unwell?'

Tina realised with a shock that, without her usual indomitable spirit, Mabel actually looked like what she was – a woman in her late seventies. She and her husband, Bert, always had so much energy; so much drive, that they always came across as being at least a decade younger than they were. Seeing Mill Grange's catering guru so distraught was both frightening and moving.

'It's Bert.'

'Bert?' Tina looked across to Helen, who immediately stopped her passage towards the manor's phone. 'What about Bert, Mabel?'

'All our lives we've been together. I can't remember a time without him.'

A sickening feeling grew in Tina's stomach as she took Mabel's hand. 'Is Bert poorly?'

'He says he's fine, but I know he's pretending. He's so damn stubborn. Won't even let me call the doctor.'

Not commenting on the irony of Mabel calling her placid husband stubborn, when she was the mistress of the art, Tina asked, 'Is he at home in bed?'

'Says it's just a touch of the cold, but he's eighty-two, Tina and...' Disappearing into a handful of tissues, Mabel gave her nose a blow. The act seemed to steady her, and Tina could feel her friend give herself a metaphorical shake. 'I'm sorry. I shouldn't burden you; especially not on a new guest day. Bert's probably right, it's just a cold.'

'Cold or not, I think he should see a doctor. How about I get Sam to talk to Bert?'

Mabel sniffed as she picked the pen and pad back up. 'I didn't like to ask Sam. I know Bert would like to see him, but, well...'

Tina immediately understood Mabel's reluctance. 'Bert's inside, in bed, and Sam still struggles to go indoors.'

'Exactly. I didn't want to put Sam in an awkward position.'

'Why don't we let Sam decide what he wants to do about that? Bert has done so much for him. If it wasn't for Bert, Sam would still be sleeping in his tent every night, rather than the downstairs bedroom. Well, when we don't have a guest in it.'

Mabel nodded as she wrote, 'order potatoes', on her pad. 'Has Sam got upstairs yet?'

'Halfway up the main staircase, but no further. The corridors upstairs are so narrow. Their enclosed nature is still a problem.'

'But he's getting there, and that's what counts.' Mabel's eyes flashed with pride, but whether that pride was for Sam or for Bert for helping him, Tina wasn't sure. Nor did she care. What mattered was getting a doctor to Bert as soon as possible. If Mabel was upset enough to show she was concerned, then something was terribly wrong.

'Here you go, Mabel.' Helen passed her a cup of tea. 'Why don't I go and get Tom and Sam?'

'Good idea.' Tina smiled. 'Thanks to Bert, Sam can join us at the kitchen table these days if we leave the backdoor open. We can have our meeting here rather than the garden.'

Mabel looked scandalised. 'Don't rearrange your day for me. You have to—'

'We have to make sure that *all* our valued members of staff are cared for.'

Mabel's wrinkled hands shook slightly as she asked, 'Have Thea and Shaun gone?'

Suddenly as concerned for Mabel as she was for Bert,

Tina said, 'About ten minutes ago. I thought they'd come in to say goodbye?'

'Oh yes, so they did.'

Swapping concerned glances with Helen as she left for the garden, Tina turned back to Mabel. 'Why don't you head home? I'll do the food today.'

Mabel stared at the pen in her hands. 'I'm better busy.'

'Okay. Then, let's get this week's meal list written.' Hoping she sounded stronger than she felt, Tina picked up the top piece of paper from an open box file on the table. 'Here's the dietary requirement list for this week's residents. We just have one vegetarian this time; and five guests over all. No allergies or intolerances.'

'That's nice and straightforward.' Mabel brushed invisible crumbs off her apron. 'I'm getting used to vegan meal and gluten free thinking, but I confess, it doesn't come easy at my time of life.'

Resisting the urge to hug the old lady, Tina said, 'I think you're a marvel.'

'Thank you.' Mabel stared blankly at the sheet of paper. 'So, I'll cook the meal tonight, and then provide lunches and the evening meal ingredients for the rest of the week as usual?'

'Yes. Apart from the bit where you cook tonight's welcome meal. Helen and I will do that. We aren't as good at it as you, but luckily the newcomers don't know how good a cook you are yet, so we won't have your high standards to live up to.'

'But—'

'Mabel. You have looked after the food here since before

we opened in October. You have been my right hand since I started here, long before Thea arrived to help restore Mill Grange. It's our turn to care for you. Please let us.'

Sam hadn't hung around for his tea. Having checked Mabel was being looked after by his friends, and that all preparations for the guest bedrooms and activities had been done, he ran the length of road from Mill Grange to Upwich village.

It was only now he stood on the drive of Mabel and Bert's home, Mabel's set of keys in his hand, that he faced the fact that he would have to go inside to see his friend.

The flashbacks to his time in the army didn't come as often as they used to. But they still came. '*But not now*. Not when Bert needs me, rather than the other way around.'

Sam spoke sternly to himself as he slid the key in the door, closing his mind to his memories of being cornered in a burning building – of being unable to save the people inside – of helplessness and... *No. Not now!*

Breathing slowly in the manner Bert had taught him, Sam muttered to himself as he pushed the door open.

'I've been in Bert's kitchen before. It's safe.' Keeping up his personal commentary, Sam ignored the perspiration that dotted his forehead. 'Bert might want tea.'

Telling himself he wasn't prevaricating, but was providing his friend with a drink, Sam went through the motions of beverage making, replaying Mabel's instructions on how to find Bert.

'Second room on the left.'

Armed with the mug of tea and his mobile phone, already

programmed with Bert's doctor's number, Sam took a deep breath and headed into the hallway.

The old man hadn't seemed that surprised to see Sam, but as he'd gone to speak a coughing fit had overtaken him. By the time it was past, there was a sheen of sweat on Bert's forehead and he was gasping for breath.

Heading to the bathroom to find a wet flannel to soothe Bert's brow, Sam forgot to be afraid of the roof falling on his head, and paused to phone the doctor. After a frustrating wait through a pointless answer phone message, telling the caller to only ring if they really needed an appointment, he eventually reached a human being. Having stressed that he was worried enough to have considered calling an ambulance, the receptionist promised an on-call doctor would be there before three o'clock that afternoon.

Texting Tina to tell her a doctor was due, Sam went back to the bedroom. His eyes landed on the breakfast Mabel had left for Bert. It was untouched.

'Right then, Bert, what's been going on here?'

'Just a cold. Been off for a few days. Tired today.'

'Then you are wise to have stayed in bed. I've called the doctor.'

Bert shook his head, 'No need, my boy, no—' Another coughing fit took over his protests as, wrestling a handful of tissues from the box by the bed, Bert spat out a mouthful of mucus.

'Okay mate, okay.' Sam wiped his forehead. 'You know this isn't a cold, come on, what aches and what doesn't?'

Resting his head back against his pillows, Bert released a painful sigh. 'Everything hurts, Sam. Everything.'

Three

'We have three hours before the guests arrive.' Tina checked her wristwatch as Sam addressed his colleagues. 'I know Mabel's friend Diane is with her, but I'd like at least one of us to be there when the doctor sees Bert, so let's crack on.'

Tom raised the outdoor to-do list he held. 'Beyond a little tool cleaning, Helen and I are as ready as we can be for the week ahead. Perhaps we could be of use in the house until then?'

Helen agreed. 'Absolutely. Why don't you and Tina go and check on Mabel while we start prepping tonight's dinner?'

'Would you mind?' Tina was itching to go and check on Bert.

'Of course we wouldn't.' Helen turned to Tom. 'I know the week's groceries were ordered on Friday. They're due between twelve and two. If you don't mind listening out for the van, I'll double check the bathrooms have loo roll

18

and clean towels, then we can start on whatever Mabel has decided is for dinner tonight.'

As Tom readily agreed, Sam got to his feet. 'I'll go and check on Mabel and Bert. Diane is a good friend to them, and very capable – she was one of the original team here when Mill Grange was under restoration so we got to know her quite well. If she's happy keeping Mabel's spirits up, then maybe, if you come up later, Tina, we can take it in turns to sit with Bert. Although we'll need to be back to greet the new guests at four.'

Tina gave a weak grin. 'If we didn't, Bert would give us a hard time for putting him before the business.'

'Aint' that the truth!'

Tom's insides clenched as he stepped out of Mill Grange's backdoor and saw his ex- girlfriend's Mini pull up outside of the old butler's quarters.

'Sue?'

Having expected the vehicle he'd heard, crawling up the drive, to be the supermarket delivery van, Tom experienced a sense of foreboding. Sue turning up unannounced anywhere was never good news. Unannounced on a week day, at a time when she was normally at work, was even worse.

'You've landed on your feet here, haven't you?' Sue slid out of the car and eyed the side of the manor house.

Biting the inside of his cheek to prevent himself saying something he'd regret, Tom peered over Sue's head, hoping the groceries would arrive, and therefore legitimately take him away from her. 'Why are you here? Is Dylan alright?'

'He's at school.'

'I didn't ask that, I asked if my son was alright.'

'Don't snap!' Sue tucked a strand of bright pink hair behind her ear. 'Dylan is fine.'

Exhaling with a rush of air, Tom dug his hands deep into his trouser pockets. 'I'm at work, Sue, what do you want?'

She gave him a dazzling smile that immediately put Tom even more on his guard. 'I thought you worked outside?'

'Your point is?'

'You were inside. I saw you come out of the backdoor.'

'I was doing some paperwork while waiting for a grocery delivery for our caterer, if you must know.'

Sue sneered. 'Hardly the hot shot archaeology tutor now then.'

'Oh for goodness sake, Sue. Just tell me what you want and go home.' He checked his watch. 'You'll need to get back to collect Dylan from school at three.'

'Three-fifteen, actually.'

'Sue!'

'Yeah, okay.' She shuffled her trainers on the gravel. 'I wanted to talk to you about Dylan.' She raised her hand fast to calm his repeated enquiry as to their son's welfare. 'He is fine, I promise. Whatever our differences, I've never for a moment doubted that you love our boy.'

Taken aback, Tom said, 'Right, well yes. Good. So, what about Dylan?'

'He's growing up fast. Every day he gets more inquisitive, brighter. He's a clever boy.'

Pride lit Tom's eyes. 'He is. We were talking about dinosaurs again on Sunday. I'm not sure there's anything he doesn't know about them.'

'Well that's just it you see.'

'Dinosaurs?'

'No! School. Look.' Sue opened the bag she'd slung over her shoulder and extracted a letter.

Reading it, Tom's face shone with pride. 'Accelerated reader's scheme? That's fantastic.'

'Honestly Tom, I had a little cry when Dylan wasn't looking. The thing is...'

Reeling from the fact his ex was admitting to having an emotional response to something, Tom pushed, 'What's the thing, Sue?'

'There's going to be a parent's evening at his school soon. Then there'll be loads of other things. Events that we haven't had to deal with before. School concerts, nativity plays, parent assemblies and all that.' Continuing to stare at her feet, rather than at him, Sue scuffed a line in the gravel with the toe of her trainer. 'I don't think you should miss out on those things just because we aren't together.'

'Really? You mean it?'

'Yes.' Sue checked her watch. 'Like you said, I can't hang about now, but I want to talk to you without Dylan being around. Do you think we could do a proper meeting? We've never talked about access and stuff.'

'I wanted to, but you—'

'I know.' Sue rolled her brightly painted fingernails into fists and pushed them into her jacket pockets. 'But if Dylan is going to have a better life than we've got, we need to start putting him first.' Catching one look at Tom's expression, she hastily added, '*I* need to start putting him first.'

Knowing how much it would have cost her to admit that she might not always have done so, Tom relented. 'He's at a decent school, he's settled in and doing well. You've got a nice home for him. Rents a bit steep but—'

'Yeah, sorry about that.'

'I don't mind as long as Dylan is happy. But I would like to see him more often, and I'd definitely appreciate you adding my number to the school contact list.'

'So, can we meet for a drink and a decision-making session soon?'

'Yes.'

Tom was about to ask about suitable times when the supermarket van lumbered into sight. 'I'm sorry, Sue, it's a bit all hands to the pump today. Our caterer's husband is sick and—'

But Sue had stopped listening. 'I must go. If I get stuck behind a tractor between Upwich and Tiverton, it could take an hour to get back. I'll text you.'

By the time the van driver had parked, Sue's Mini was hurtling away, leaving Tom torn between elation at the prospect of seeing his son more often, and suspicion that his ex was up to something.

Only a few months ago, Tina had experienced a hit of anxiety every time a new group of retreat guests arrived on a Monday afternoon. Today, as the five newcomers happily explored Mill Grange after listening to Sam's introductory talk, Tina realised that, although she'd been nervous, she wasn't her usual ball of tension.

'Maybe it's because I'm worrying about Bert instead.' She

passed Helen the tray of dirty cups and saucers to place in the dishwasher.

'Or, perhaps you're getting used to it.' Helen poked a fork into the lasagne bubbling inside the Aga to check the pasta was softening as per Mabel's very specific instructions.

'Possibly.' Tina checked her watch. 'Mabel hasn't called. Surely the doctor would have finished by now? It's gone five.'

'If there's been an emergency at the surgery, then the doctor could have been delayed.'

'Maybe.' Tina didn't look convinced.

'Why don't you head over there? I can hold the fort. There's still two hours until dinner.' Helen turned the heat of the Aga right down. 'I've only got this cooking early as Mabel said it tastes better if it's cooked and then reheated before serving.'

'I'm not sure.' Tina tugged at her pigtails. 'The first few hours with new guests can either be smooth, or full of trouble shooting. I don't see why you should have to do that.'

Helen smiled. 'I'm happy to, don't worry.'

'If only Thea was here as well! Talk about bad timing to be a set of hands down.'

Sam pressed the 'end call' function on his mobile's screen and looked up at Tina, who was sat close enough to him to have partially heard what had been said down the other end of the line, but she still sensed she only had half the story.

'So?'

'I'm afraid it's as I feared.'

Tina frowned. 'What was it you feared?'

'Bert has pneumonia.'

Sucking in a sharp intake of breath, Tina forced herself not to panic. 'That's potentially serious when you're Bert's age. You thought that's what he had?'

'I didn't say anything because I wanted to be wrong.'

'Is he in hospital?'

'No. His GP thinks they've caught it early enough for him to stay put. He has given Bert antibiotics and Mabel strict instructions to keep a close eye on him. The doctor's visiting again tomorrow.'

Tina exhaled slowly. 'That means it's not as serious as it might have been then, if he isn't in hospital.'

'It will depend if the antibiotics help. If they don't make a difference within three days, or if his temperature spikes further, or he gets diarrhoea or chest pain as he coughs, he'll have to be admitted.' Sam sighed. 'Plus, there's less chance of Bert being infected with other things if he stays at home.'

'Is Mabel okay?'

'She sounded shaky but her usual determined tone was back in evidence down the line.' Sam hugged Tina to his side. 'She told me in no uncertain terms to take care of you and this place and not bother about the likes of them.'

'That sounds like Mabel!' Tina laughed. 'I feel a bit better for knowing she got stern with you.'

'I know what you mean.' Sam pointed towards the kitchen door. 'All going okay here? Everyone happy?'

'Seem to be. All food has been consumed and rooms inspected.' Tina got to her feet. 'Helen and Tom are in the drawing room doing the rounds of tea and coffee.'

'Should we relieve them?' Sam looked across the garden.

'It's a nice evening, and we could take the guests over to the walled garden to meet the chickens.'

'Good idea.' Tina got to her feet. 'I thought maybe we could give Tom and Helen a night off. If Bert does end up in hospital, with Thea gone, time off is going to become a precious thing.'

'Excellent idea. They both work far longer hours than we pay them for anyway.'

Tina was halfway to the kitchen door when she suddenly remembered something. 'Before we heard about Bert, you were going to take us all into the walled garden to tell us about an idea you'd had.'

'So I was.'

'Aren't you going to tell me what it was?'

'Nope. Not yet.'

Four

Helen sipped her cider as Tom settled down in the chair opposite, a pint of the Stag and Hound's latest guest ale in his hand.

'It was all I could do not to ask Sue if she'd had a bump on the head.'

'Was it so out of character for her to offer to add you to the parent contact list at Dylan's primary school?'

'Completely. The Sue I know is selfish to the point of obsession. Although,' Tom placed his pint back on the table, 'I will admit she hasn't been so self-absorbed since her latest house move. She must have had a lobotomy at some point between leaving Swindon and coming to Tiverton.'

'She can't be that bad or you'd never have got together in the first place.'

Lifting his glass back up, Tom hid in his pint for a moment, unsure if he wanted to tell Helen why he'd originally dated Sue. Helen was so different. So separate from the life he was trying to leave behind him. He was tired of wishing

26

he didn't enjoy her company, of thinking about her when he woke up, and all the other signs he knew meant he'd fallen for her.

Helen deserves far better than me.

Tom stifled a sigh. He knew Helen felt the same about him, but neither of them mentioned it. They just carried on as if they were good friends who happened to work together.

Maybe if I tell her about Sue, Helen will see I'm no good for her?

'Meeting Sue was not my finest hour.'

'And yet you have Dylan, so don't tell me you wish her away.'

Smiling despite himself, Tom wiped some ale foam from his lips. 'There you have me. If Dylan hadn't come along, I'd have moved on and left my past behind as I always had before, but, as you say, I'd not be without my son.'

'And who's to say that, if you hadn't had Dylan, you'd have calmed down? You may not even have realised your passion for archaeology, but carried on moving from poorly paid job to poorly paid job, never finding your calling.'

'That's true.'

'And you wouldn't be here in this lovely pub, doing the best job in the world.'

Tom could feel the unspoken, 'and we'd never have met' hanging in the air as he said, 'I have a great deal to thank Dylan for.'

Helen grinned as she remembered the proud expression on Tom's face when he'd bounded into the kitchen with Mabel's groceries that afternoon. When he'd said Sue had been, her heart had stopped for a second – immediately assuming his good humour was because they were going to attempt reconciliation for their son's sake. Helen's moment of sadness, however, had been replaced with a rush of pride for Dylan, as Tom had told her about his reading prowess. 'I'm so pleased his talent for English has been noticed at school.'

'Me too. I can't wait to tell Bert and Mabel tomorrow. I'm hoping the news will cheer Bert up a bit.'

'Why didn't you tell Mabel earlier?'

'I wanted to tell you first.' Tom took another sip of beer, not looking at Helen as he realised what he'd said, hastily adding, 'All that reading you've done with Dylan when he's been here must have helped him.'

'I enjoy it. He's a great kid.' Helen smiled as she thought of the five-year-old's cheeky face.

'The thing is,' Tom's eyes dropped to the table as he spoke, 'Sue and I only stayed together beyond a drunken one-night stand because she got pregnant. It was a disaster from the start, but we tried, for Dylan's sake. The trouble is, the more we tried, the more we hated that we had to try. It soon disintegrated into resentment and hate. In the end…' Tom's eyes flicked to the empty fireplace, unsure if he should be as honest as he ought to be '… we both cheated on each other and the situation became insupportable.'

'I see.' Helen stared into the pale liquid remaining her glass.

Shifting uncomfortably in his seat, Tom moved the conversation on. 'When Sue moved to Tiverton, I wasn't that surprised. She was always relocating from one home to another, with whoever was the man of the moment.'

'Hence you giving up your job with the Wiltshire

Archaeology Trust and coming here. So you could be near Dylan.'

'Yes.' Tom risked a glimpse at Helen. A coil of red hair had flopped over her eyes as her unruly curls shone in the pub's low lighting. 'But this time it was different. Rather than leave Swindon to follow a man, she left to have a new, more independent, start. One where Dylan could settle at school and stay there until his education was complete.'

'I didn't believe Sue when she told me that at first. I assumed she was running away from something and using Dylan as an excuse. But then I saw how tidy their home is, rather than the usual bombsite, and how smart and clean Dylan's school uniform was and, well…'

'You think she really does want to give Dylan the secure start in life she didn't have?'

'What makes you think she didn't have one?'

'Educated guess.'

Tom drained the last few centimetres of ale. 'So, as I said, she wants to see me for a proper talk about Dylan's future, and me seeing more of him.'

'That's good.'

'It is.'

Helen's forehead crinkled. 'You don't sound sure.'

'I can't shift the feeling that, even though Sue has definitely changed of late, this is a roundabout way of getting something she wants.'

'Such as?' Helen's throat went dry. *She wants you back so you can be mum and dad to Dylan together.*

'I have to presume more money, but as I don't have any that isn't a wish I can grant – even if I wanted to.'

'It might not be that. Maybe Sue really has realised that Dylan would be better off having two hands-on parents, albeit living in different locations?'

'Perhaps.' Tom stood up with his empty glass in hand. 'Do you want another drink?'

Helen shook her head. 'I'm fine, thanks.'

Watching Tom's back while he chatted to Moira, the landlady, across the bar, Helen told herself off for jumping to conclusions. Although Tom was bound to be suspicious of his former partner, there was no reason for her to assume Sue wanted him back.

It's nothing to do with me. Tom and I are friends. End of. If he wanted me to be more than that, he'd have made a move by now.

Tom returned to the table and, with a feeling of sadness she couldn't shake, Helen asked, 'When's Dylan staying here again?'

'Weekend after next if Sue is sticking to the plan we currently have. Depends if we meet up before then and alter things.' Tom's belly gave a voluble growl. 'Oops, sorry!'

'You can't be hungry.' Helen laughed. 'You had more lasagne than anyone.'

'Are you implying I'm greedy, Miss Rogers?'

'No, I'm implying you have hollow legs! Where on earth do you put all that food you eat? There's nothing of you.'

'Fast metabolism. The calories don't have time to touch the sides!'

Helen patted her hips dramatically. 'Not a problem I have over here.'

'I hope you're not fishing for compliments!' Tom smirked.

'As if I would?' Helen laughed again, a tiny flicker of hope igniting inside her.

Spacious and yet cosy, The Carthorse pub, with its traditional thatched roof and Cotswold stone features, was exactly as Thea imagined it would be.

The bar was lined with taps dispensing a variety of local beers, while blackboards proclaimed a generous list of homemade meals, which were served in the bar or a small restaurant to the left-hand side. Two open fireplaces, lit for the tourists despite the nice weather outside, sat at opposite ends of the pub, between which, tables, chairs and a few sofas, jostled for room, among the large numbers of locals and visitors.

Thea was about to ask Shaun how he thought The Carthorse would cope with the additional daily influx of post dig archaeologists for the next few weeks, when a man she didn't recognise strolled through the crowd with easy confidence, and shook Shaun by the hand.

'Shaun, it's a pleasure to meet you. Julian. Julian Blackwood, Producer and Director.'

'It's good to meet you too.' Shaun reached a hand out to Thea, resting it on her shoulder. 'This is Thea Thomas, our guest expert.'

Julian immediately reoffered his hand, as Thea returned his greeting. 'Phil told me all about you before he left. Former Roman Baths' curator, no less. Impressive.'

'That makes it sounds far grander than it was. I was co-curator to an excellent manager.'

'Who couldn't have managed without you, I'm sure.'

Aware of Shaun clearing his throat, Thea turned to her boyfriend. He had an odd expression on his face. 'I expected Ajay, Andy and the others to be here. It's not like any of the *Landscape Treasures* crew to be within a mile of a pub after 7 p.m., and not have alcohol to hand.'

Julian gave a booming laugh that sounded like it belonged to a much bigger person. 'I was sent out here to find you both. The delicious Gina, landlady of this establishment, has opened up the function room for us. Providing there are no last-minute parties or wedding reception bookings, it is at our disposal.'

'That's great.' Shaun nodded. 'I'll just grab us some drinks and order some food. Do you want anything, Julian?'

'Only the privilege of escorting Miss Thomas into the other room. You can manage the order for you both, can't you, Shaun?'

Before Thea knew what was happening, she was being propelled away, while hearing all about how important Julian thought archaeology was to the nation's heritage and wellbeing, leaving a gaping Shaun by the bar, with no idea what she wanted to eat.

As they reached a wooden door at the far side of the pub, Thea wasn't sure if this counted as old fashioned gallantry or plain rudeness.

'Is he always like this?' Shaun muttered to Ajay as he half ate a pile of cheesy chips while he watched Julian talking to Thea at a table across the room.

'Apparently he's a great producer.' Ajay chewed a mouthful of garlic bread.

'That isn't what I asked.' Shaun's brow puckered as he observed Julian lean in rather closer to Thea than he would have liked.

Ajay shrugged. 'I don't know. I haven't worked with him before. He mostly does documentaries and travelogues rather than this sort of stuff.'

'If he gets any closer to Thea, he's going to be in her bloody blouse.'

'Chill, mate! He's probably just asking her about Roman stuff and ideas for the dig.'

'Maybe.' Shaun pushed away his food. 'He was a bit in my face personal space wise when we were in the pub's main room, now I think about it.'

Ajay stabbed a piece of tomato with his fork. 'That's probably it then. I used to have a kid like that in my class at school. Bloody big he was as well, so intimidating. He wasn't a bully or anything, just totally unaware of personal space issues.'

Realising he was in danger of becoming jealous for no reason, Shaun sighed. 'Ignore me, I'm sure Julian is fine. Phil suggested him for the job, so he'll be good at it.'

Glad not to have to reassure his friend any more, Ajay asked, 'You seen the tents yet?'

'No, we came straight here. I assumed Julian would want a meeting with me about starting tomorrow like Phil always did, but he doesn't seem bothered at all.'

'Well I can give you some good news about the accommodation at least.'

'Tents that don't leak?'

Ajay laughed, 'Not only that, but the stars of the show – that would be you and Thea, myself, Andy and the producer of course – have campervans.'

'Seriously?'

'Yep. We have one each. They're a bit small, but clean and dry.' Ajay laid his knife and fork down with an air of satisfaction. 'That's why Andy isn't here at the moment. He's making himself cosy in his wheeled mini mansion.'

'Wow. It'll be Winnebagos next.' Shaun raised his pint to his lips. 'I wonder what bought that on?'

Ajay gestured his empty glass in Julian's direction. 'I don't see him as a "sleep in a tent" sort of person, do you?'

'Possibly not.' Shaun grinned. 'At least Thea and I don't have to share an airbed. I'm heavier than her, which causes serious hassle with roll together.'

'I can imagine!'

'Shame this place doesn't have accommodation, although at least we are guaranteed a good meal and a beer.'

Getting to his feet to fetch another pint, Ajay smiled. 'I'll drink to that.'

Five

Shaun cursed as he rolled over, knocking his head on the cupboard that ran adjacent to the campervan bed in the process.

'You alright?' Thea rose up on her elbow, her muscles stiff from two of them trying to sleep in a single bed.

'No,' Shaun snapped, before apologising. 'Sorry, bad night. Did you get any sleep at all?'

'Think I drifted off at one point.' Thea rubbed her eyes. 'I hope I don't have to do any camera work today. I bet I look like death. Poor Hilda would have to use her entire supply of foundation on the bags under my eyes.'

Easing his legs to the floor, Shaun flicked on the travel kettle he'd taken the precaution of filling the night before. 'At least we've got electric, so we can have our morning coffee.'

'True.' Thea pulled on some clean underwear. 'And if it rains, we won't have to deal with soggy clothes in a damp tent and potentially wet bed linen.'

'It's just sleep we're going to be short of.' Shaun ruffled a hand through his hair as a giant yawn escaped from his lips. 'I can't imagine why we were allocated a single camper each, rather than a double between us. It's not as if they didn't know we're a couple.'

Thea suddenly stilled. 'You don't think that they forgot about me coming do you?'

'You know they didn't, Julian greeted you like royalty last night.'

'I'm not sure about royalty, but you're right. He knew I was coming.' She paused. 'But now I think about it... Does he know we're a couple? Did you tell him, or did you assume that he'd know because Phil would have told him?'

'I honestly don't remember if I said or not, but he has to know. Everyone on the team knows.' An unpleasant thought arrived in Shaun's head. 'Unless he knew, and decided to make life uncomfortable for us anyway.'

Thea pulled on her jeans. 'How do you mean?'

'He fancies you. Perhaps he wanted to make it too uncomfortable for us to share.'

'Oh don't be so ridiculous.' Thea couldn't believe what she was hearing. 'Firstly, he does not fancy me. Secondly, it wouldn't matter if he did because I am in love with you, and thirdly, he hadn't set eyes on me before last night and the accommodation would have been sorted out weeks ago.'

'Yes. Right.'

'We'll get used to sharing a single bed. If not, I'll move into the camper laid on for me and we can take it in turns to wake each other with morning coffee. It's not for long. Now, if you're a good boy, and stop being silly, I'll make bacon sandwiches for breakfast.'

'You remembered the bacon?' Shaun sidled around the side of the bed, his neck bent so he didn't hit it against the roof.

'I'd like to claim I did, but it was Mabel. She slipped it into the food supplies she packed for us.'

'That woman is a diamond.'

'Sam's back from seeing Bert. These are from Mabel.' Helen placed three wedding magazines on the kitchen table.

Tina's eyebrows rose in surprise. 'When on earth did Mabel find time to go shopping for those?'

'Apparently, she was going out of her mind sitting in with Bert all day, so Diane sent her to the newsagents. She didn't need anything for herself, so she got these for you instead.'

'That's so kind.' Tina flicked through the copy of *Wedding Dreams*. 'Hang on, did you say she's going out of her mind being at home all day already? Bert was only taken ill yesterday.'

'Doesn't bode well, does it?' Helen smiled. 'I haven't known Mabel as long as you, but I quickly grasped that she's not one for sitting still.'

'How is Bert today, did Sam say?'

'No worse, no better.'

'Bit soon for the antibiotics to start working I suppose.' Tina put the magazine down. 'I better not sit with those now or I'll waste the morning away.' She shook her head. 'It's a weird thing. I have no time for magazines as a rule, but now I have a wedding to plan, I can't get enough of them. Although, how anyone can afford anything that's advertised in these things is beyond me.'

Helen reached for the kettle. 'I suppose people see things they like and adapt them into what they can afford.'

'There'll be a lot of that going on for us.' Tina's face glowed as her eyes flicked back to Mabel's thoughtful gift. 'We're so lucky to be able to get married here. Saves a fortune.'

'I hadn't realised Mill Grange had a marriage licence.'

'It was one of the many things Thea looked into when she was restoring the place while hunting for ways for the house to earn its own keep. All the paperwork is in place. All Sam had to do was send it to be processed.'

'Will you open it as a venue for weddings in general?'

Tina opened the dishwasher, unloading the latest batch of clean mugs, plates and cutlery. 'Maybe. If the retreat side of things flounders.' Straightening up, Tina caught the wistful look in Helen's eye. 'Would you fancy it then, getting married here, I mean?'

'It's a beautiful place.' Helen switched her attention to the tea bag pot. 'Not really something I need to worry about. Do you want a cuppa? I'm taking a load to Tom and the team. All five guests are with us morning, so I'd better get back.'

'I'm good, thanks.'

As Tina watched Helen balance seven mugs precariously on a tray she swore she was okay carrying, Tina cursed her thoughtlessness. She'd been so wrapped up in her own wedding, that she had been tactless. It was so obvious Helen was in love with Tom. If the pair of them didn't sort themselves out soon, she was going to have to talk to Thea about staging an intervention.

★

There was no doubt that the site was a fascinating one. As Shaun looked over the geophysics results that Ajay and Andy, affectionately known as the AA, had already compiled, he could tell that the villa had been impressive. Seeing it stood proudly in the middle of a Romano-British landscape must have been something special.

Making notes about where he thought the opening test investigation pits should go, Shaun glanced over to where Thea was doing her first piece to camera. It was a simple introduction to the history of the villa to England. Despite her fears of looking zombie-like through the lens, Thea shone as she explained the evolution of the most famous of all Roman accommodation types.

'Here you go, mate.' Andy dropped a file in front of Shaun. 'The updated scripts for today.'

'Updated?' Shaun flicked open the file. 'I haven't done anything beyond the episode's introduction yet.'

'Apparently Julian has lots of ideas.'

'I bet he does,' Shaun muttered as he scanned through the papers.

Returning to the geophysics plans that he and Ajay had been particularly excited about, Andy asked, 'What do you think? Private bath house for the villa's owner and guests?'

'What?'

'Are you with me, Shaun?' Andy tapped a finger on the plans. 'Possible bath house?'

'Yeah. Very probably.'

'I bet Thea will be keen on that.'

Tearing his eyes away from where his girlfriend was working, Shaun sighed. 'Sorry mate. Yes, bath house. Thea will be extremely interested.'

'Julian obviously thinks it is too, look.' Andy turned a page over in the script folder. 'He's got her talking about bathing ritual and routines for quite a while.'

'So he has.' Shaun's mouth went dry.

'You might actually get to do some proper archaeology this time. Looks like Thea has most of the screen time. Julian must have been impressed by the bits and pieces she did to camera for the Mill Grange Christmas episode.'

'Of course!' Shaun groaned at his own stupidity. 'He's seen her before, but she hadn't seen him.'

'You've lost me, mate.'

'Julian, did he know Thea and I were a couple?'

'Sure.' Andy fired up his laptop ready to process some more results. 'Ajay and I told him when we arrived yesterday. I got the impression he already knew though. I assumed you, Thea, or Phil would have told him.'

'Right.'

'You okay?'

'Didn't get much sleep.'

'Lucky devil.' Andy winked as he clicked through to the page on his computer he wanted.

Shaun mumbled, 'Not really, mate.'

Lady Bea oozed excitement down the phone line as she reacted to Sam telling her they'd set the wedding date for May 23rd.

'May is a wonderful month to marry in. I can just picture Tina standing in the hallway in a gorgeous dress waiting to be escorted to the church. Perhaps she could go by horse and carriage! Now we have a solid date to work with, I can give the vicar a call. I'll do it as soon as I'm off the phone. He gets booked up, especially in early summer. And then…'

Sam's heart sank. His mother was talking ten-to-the dozen. Her joy radiated down the line. Trying hard to cut into her stream of words, hating that he was about to crush her dream, Sam knew he had to finish telling her about the rest of their wedding plans before she put her preconceptions in motion.

'Mum!'

'Sorry, Sam. I'm just so excited. I can't wait. It's been years since Malvern House saw a wedding and—'

'Mum!' Sam realised he'd shouted, and lowered his tone. 'Sorry, I didn't mean to yell, but you're getting a bit carried away.'

'I am, aren't I?'

Sam could picture Lady Bea on the other end of the line. She'd be perched on the Chesterfield that had been known as the telephone chair ever since he was little boy.

'I'm glad you're excited, Mum. Tina and I are too, but, the thing is—'

'What? What's the thing? Is everything okay? I know Tina hasn't got any parents of her own so, we thought that…'

Sam shook his head. His normal, calm, placid mother had turned into a mass of wedding anxiety, the likes of which neither he, nor Tina, had come anywhere near exhibiting.

'Please, Mum. Everything is alright. Tina's fine, I'm fine, but this is our wedding, and as you said, Tina hasn't got parents, but she *is* the bride-to-be. Old fashioned though it sounds, I want her to choose where to marry and what sort of wedding we have so—'

'You mean you might not marry here?' Lady Bea's

voice cracked, but Sam heard her quickly rally. 'I admit I'd assumed that you would, but... Could you ask her if that would be something she'd consider?'

'Alright, Mum, but to be honest, Tina is pretty set on marrying here. Our friends here are the closest thing she has to a family.'

'Well yes, I can see that, but we're your *actual* family Sam, and *we* have traditions.'

Surprised by how much like his father she suddenly sounded, Sam was lost for words as his mother added, 'I'm just asking that you explain to Tina that all your ancestors, male and female, have married at Malvern House in Worcestershire. We'd very much like you, as our third son, to continue that tradition.'

The line went silent. Sam was stunned. He'd never heard his mother sound so inflexible about anything before. Until Tina had come along, he'd been estranged from his parents, particularly his father. But Tina had fixed that, and over the past few months an increasingly relaxed relationship had existed between them.

It hadn't occurred to Sam that he'd be expected to marry at their home. He closed his eyes and counted to ten. When he opened them, the sunlight that poured through the roof of his tent in Mill Grange's gardens made him blink. Spring had arrived in earnest. Until his phone call, he'd been as optimistic as the budding daffodils that lined the driveway. Now he felt a sense of foreboding.

Did he upset the parents he'd only recently been reconciled with, or his future wife?

Six

Helen brushed the mud off her palms and straightened up from the trench in which she'd been kneeling. The retreat guest she was working with, a chirpy former Marine called Pete, smiled broadly as he shook his head.

'I could do this when I was digging on the pretend site. I'm all fingers and thumbs now it's for real.'

Helen was reassuring. 'Everyone's the same, don't worry.'

Shuffling backwards, Pete held his trowel out before him, gingerly resting its long side edge against the earth.

'That's it. Now if you keep the trowel at that angle, and ease it backwards you'll get a nice clean sweep. That way it takes just a fraction of soil away at a time, but isn't so slow as to be frustrating and make no impact.'

Pete steadily worked his arm backwards. 'I had no idea this would be so satisfying.'

'Amazing, isn't it? And if you find something, the sensation is incredible, especially the first time.'

'I can imagine.'

As Pete scraped back the earth, Tom wandered over. 'Good technique, mate.' He gave Helen a nod of acknowledgement. 'If our thinking is correct, you are on top of what was either a store room or possibly a private room for a senior guard. Obviously, we can't be exact yet. Any finds will help us work things out as we go.'

Leaving Pete to get on without them breathing down his neck, but with instructions to call if he was unsure about anything, Tom and Helen headed to the trestle table that acted as their daytime desk at the edge of the main site.

'How are your team getting on?'

'Really well.' Tom grinned. 'I'm so glad Shaun found this fortlet. I'm sure it would be good work therapy whatever type of site this was, but over the past few months I've heard lots of our guests comment on how they, as former soldiers, are working on the home of other former soldiers. It gives them a personal connection to the dig.'

'I've heard the same. It's rather nice.' Helen waved her clipboard. 'Did you want to look at the plans?'

'Sorry?'

'I got the impression you wanted something.'

'Oh yes, I had a message from Sam; he wants a brief staff meeting today. I'm imagining it's about whatever he was going to tell us before Bert was taken ill.'

'Any news on Bert?'

'Situation is the same: no worse, but no improvement either.'

'I suppose stable is good in the circumstances.' Helen picked up her trench plan. 'If Pete wants to, he could help me finish that trench this week, but only if he's keen. I'd

44

hate to stop him doing anything else he fancied. Should I ask him?'

'Both he, and one of the other chaps I have working at the moment, are good, and both seem keen to keep digging. If the three of you concentrated on the storeroom trench, as we've called it for now, it might even be open down to the bedrock by end of play tomorrow.'

Helen took a pen and circled the area they were working on. 'Once that's done, the fortlet will be almost completely open. The next stage will be to start to consolidate what's been found and preserve it as it stands in a more permanent way. I need to chat to Sam, Thea and Shaun about the best way to go about it.'

'All I know for sure is that Sam wants the fortlet left open.'

'Yes.' Helen was thoughtful. 'It isn't just the site I wanted to discuss. Look, do you have time for a drink after the guests have gone home tomorrow? There's something I'd like to pick your brain about.'

'Sure.' Tom looked over to where Pete was methodically working his way through the soil's stratigraphic layers. 'That would be good. As it'll be Friday night, shall we grab some dinner too? Maybe we could nip out of Upwich? I love Moira's cooking, but I'll be honest, I've been craving a decent curry. Sue told me there was a great Indian restaurant in Tiverton. Fancy it?'

Helen's pulse beat slightly faster than usual. *Is he asking me on a date, or does he just want a change of scene with poppadoms?* 'That sounds great. I haven't had naan bread in months.'

'I'll book a table for seven o'clock if that works for you?'
'Perfect.'

'Are you going to give me a clue as to what you wanted to talk about?'

'It's just a work thing. It'll keep. Be nice to get out of here for a while though.'

Tom could hear a voice at the back of his mind telling him to back track. *It sounds like a date. It isn't, it's just curry.* 'I'm looking forward to it. We could do with being somewhere without mud under our fingernails.'

'That's a brilliant idea! I love it.' Tina scribbled, "Buy Easter Eggs", on her ever-present list.

As the four friends sat around the trestle table Sam and Tom had erected a few days ago, Sam elaborated. 'As we've had no bookings for Easter week, I thought we'd see if Mill Grange could host an Easter egg hunt over Easter weekend. It will be hard work for us, but it should also be tremendous fun. I'm sure lots of locals will come. Obviously, as you, Helen and Tom, don't work weekends, it would be up to you if you want to join in or not.'

Tom laughed. 'Dylan would not be impressed if I didn't help the Easter Bunny out! Although, it will depend if it's my weekend with him or not. Sue and I are going to renegotiate when I take care of him, so I'm a bit up in the air on dates right now.'

Helen could just picture Dylan running around hunting for chocolate treats. 'I bet he'd enjoy helping to hide the eggs.'

'Easter is just over three weeks away, so if we start

advertising straight away, it should be worth doing.' Sam looked up at Tina. 'In Thea's absence, would you mind doing the press bit? Calling the local papers, designing a poster to take around the shops and so on?'

'No problem.'

'I expect I could ask them to put a poster up at Dylan's school. Be the right age demographic and all that.'

'That's great, thanks, Tom.'

Helen smiled. 'I can just imagine Dylan telling his friends all about it, and then proudly leading them around the house to hunt those chocolate beauties down.'

'Me too!' Tina laughed. 'How many eggs will we need do you think?'

'No idea, but better bulk buy. The village shop might help us out with that.'

Helen started to picture a few of the places they could hide eggs. 'How will we make sure people stay off the fortlet and the fake dig?'

Sam looked in the direction of the site. 'Good point. Can you and Tom liaise about how we can cordon the relevant areas off for a while?'

'Sure.' Helen made a note on her pad. 'How much are you going to charge for this?'

'I thought two pounds per child. Not too much then if you have four kids.' Sam looked up at his friends. 'The only problem is, what with Bert being unwell, we may have to ask someone other than Mabel to do tea and coffee.'

'She'll be gutted if we don't ask her to do them.' Tina sighed.

'It could be just what she needs to look forward to, to be honest,' Helen agreed. 'Mabel is one of life's doers. If she isn't helping someone, she won't feel like herself. I'm worried about Bert, but I'm just as worried about Mabel. Her mental health won't be in good shape if she doesn't do something constructive soon.'

'I suspect you're right.' Sam pulled a face. 'So, shall I ask her to help? Maybe she could start planning a few cakes to bake, etc? If we let everyone have free tea and coffee or juice, but charged for cakes then we should cover our costs. I was also thinking of offering half the proceeds to the Help for Heroes foundation. What do you think?'

'I think you're the nicest man in the world, and I'm glad I'm marrying you.' Tina leant forward and kissed Sam's cheek.

Tom and Helen exchanged glances. Each experienced a shimmer of attraction that they both stoically ignored.

Bringing the meeting back to order, Sam said, 'Thea and Shaun will be back here as they aren't filming over the Easter weekend. I hope they don't mind walking into a horde of children.'

'Thea did say she'd be back for...' Tina suddenly turned to Helen, 'Of course! I'd almost forgotten.'

'What?' Sam frowned, as if he suspected he had forgotten something important.

Helen wasn't quick enough. By the time she realised what Tina was going to say the words had already floated from her friend's mouth.

'It's Helen's birthday that weekend. Thea won't want to miss that.'

'Birthday?' A faint memory of the first proper conversation they'd had the previous autumn floated through Tom's mind. In a roundabout way she'd told him she was thirty-nine, which meant this next birthday was a milestone. One, he suspected, from Helen's expression, she'd rather not be facing.

'It's no big deal. I'm happy to enjoy the Easter egg hunt and forget the rest of that week.'

'But, you'll be...' Tina stopped talking as she registered the warning look on Helen's face. 'Okay, I'll drop it. But if you change your mind, just let me know, and we'll party.'

A black car drew away from Bert and Mabel's driveway as Sam approached their cottage on the edge of Upwich. Mabel was still on the doorstep, and waved as she saw Sam approach.

'Good news?'

Mabel blew her nose in a flurry of tissues, and Sam suspected if he hadn't turned up, she'd have allowed herself to indulge in some very un-British blubbing. 'The antibiotics are working. His temperature is down and the coughing no longer sounds as if he's trying to chew through hardboard.'

'That's fantastic. Is Bert up to a visitor, or has the doctor worn him out?'

'He's going nuts in there. A visitor would be welcome.'

Bert, tucked away in the cottage's spare room, presumably so he didn't wake Mabel with his coughing at night, looked much smaller than he had the week before. The room had a stuffy air of illness about it. Sam was desperate to open a window.

'You can open a window if you want.' Bert smiled as

Sam looked surprised. 'I know an escape hatch is always welcome. Besides the air is so stale in here. Mabel won't let me open it in case I get cold.'

'I can't blame her for that.'

'Please open it, Sam. I'm not doing so well being stuck inside for so long myself.'

Sam could see his friend's hands shaking. The old man, like him, had suffered severe claustrophobia years ago, and though he coped brilliantly, every now and then his enemy made its presence felt. *But if I open the window and Bert got cold...*

'The doctor told me I could have it open for a little while.'

'Promise?'

'Promise.' Bert grunted. 'But it will be best for both our sakes if you close it if you hear Mabel coming!'

'Wise!' Sam lifted the sash window a fraction, the action alone making him feel better.

'So, my boy, what's on your mind?'

'What makes you think there's something bothering me?'

'Call me psychic. Let's have it.'

'I'm here to make sure you're alright. Everyone's worried about you.'

Bert tapped his friend's arm. 'And while I believe that, and I'm grateful, I also can see there is something on your mind. Now, spit it out.'

Sam couldn't help but laugh. 'There are no flies on you, Bert!'

'Give me something to think about other than feeling ill. Tell me.'

'Okay. You asked for it! Tina has her heart set on getting married at Mill Grange and my parents are desperate for me to keep up the family tradition – which both my older brothers followed – of marrying at Malvern House. I don't want to let Tina down, nor do I want to upset my mother. Any and all ideas welcome!'

'Tomorrow night? Can't we do another night, Sue, I've got a work thing on.'

Tom closed his yes. He'd longed for the chance to talk to Sue in a civilised fashion about gaining more access to Dylan, and now she was offering him that chance, but it was tomorrow night, when he'd told Helen he'd take her for a curry.

'I thought your colleagues were your friends? They'll understand if you have to reschedule.'

'But why then, Sue? What's wrong with one night next week? Won't you need to look after Dylan?'

'I have a lot of extra work on next week, and tomorrow night I have access to a babysitter. I thought you wanted to get this sorted?'

Tom bit back the sense of frustration he always experienced when he spoke to Sue. 'Of course I do, I suppose I just assumed you'd want to see me in the day, rather than in the evening.'

'I told you, I'm busy next week. It's tomorrow night or not for ages. I've booked a table at the local Indian. Are you coming or not?'

Seven

Friday March 20th

'That's it. I give up!' Shaun rolled over, almost falling out of bed after another night of very little sleep. 'All I've done is lay in bed thinking about how badly I want to sleep, and how sick I am of Julian leering over you.'

The edges of Thea's temper began to fray. 'For the last time, Shaun, he isn't doing any such thing!'

'You seriously can't see it, can you?' Shaun scrubbed his knuckles across his bloodshot eyes.

'Because there is *nothing* to see!' Thea, her limbs heavy from her own lack of sleep, groaned as she got to her feet. 'You're beginning to sound like a stuck record. Worse! Like a prima donna who can't get a vegan snack in the middle of the jungle!'

'I knew this project was a voyage of discovery, but I didn't think the first thing I'd find out was that you're a very different person when deprived of sleep.' Thea sagged back against the side of the van as she clicked on the kettle. 'Whatever the situation, if you don't want me dozing off in the trench next to you tomorrow, I'll be sleeping in the other campervan tonight.'

Seeing Thea meant what she said, Shaun gave up. 'Okay, I guess we need some quality sleep.'

'Thank you!' She banged an empty coffee cup down in front of him, 'Now, I think we need caffeine. And fast.'

Shaun spoke into the camera, his presenter's smile firmly in place. 'The valley in which Birdlip Villa is set is simply outstanding. Do you think it was purely the desire for a nice view from the garden that led to it being built here, Thea, or was there more to it?'

Taking her cue from Shaun, Thea gestured into the distance, her arm sweeping across the camera, as if to encapsulate the open plain before them. 'While I'm sure the stunning vista had a lot to do with it, I have no doubt status played a part. Being able to afford to have such a vast home built here would have been solid proof of status in the Romano-British community. This villa is the period equivalent of a modern business man buying a mansion and putting a Jacuzzi, swimming pool and gym in the grounds.'

'You think the owner was a business man?'

Thea gave Shaun a dazzling grin. 'He could well have been, but more likely a politician of some sort. Quite possibly he was both.'

'And how about mosaics, Thea? It's early days yet, but what do you think the chances are of us finding mosaics on the floors?'

'I would love to say we will, but obviously I can't do that until the archaeology reaches floor level. Let's just say I'd be surprised if we didn't find any. As the geophysics results show, we are looking to uncover a decent sized dining area, or triclinium, and a bath house here. With Chedworth Roman Villa only fifteen miles away, we already know that the local people, at least those wealthy enough to afford it, had access to mosaic makers, who put together the pieces, or tesserae, into incredible geometric patterns and detailed pictures.'

'Let's hope we find some examples of their work.' Shaun turned away from Thea and spoke directly into the camera. 'It's time to see how our diggers are getting on.'

'Cut!' Julian rubbed his palms. 'Brilliant, Thea. Thank you. Shaun, can we do that last line to camera again? It was a bit flat. More excitement this time please.'

'More excitement!' Shaun growled under his breath as he spoke to Sam. 'Honest to God, I think this is the first time in my life I've actually pictured myself punching someone.'

'You really think he's trying to make you look bad in Thea's eyes by getting you to redo bits to camera that are perfectly alright?'

'It feels like it. Phil was picky, but this bloke...' Shaun puffed out a blast of pent-up tension down the phone line. 'Oh I don't know, Sam. Half the time I think I'm being paranoid. Thea certainly does.'

'Could you be?'

'Possibly.'

'Even if what you say is true, and this Julian does have a crush on Thea, so what?'

'How do you mean?'

'Don't be dim. Julian could have a major crush on Thea, but if she isn't interested, then it makes no difference. Remember how it was when you were in Cornwall, and that Sophie had a crush on you? Now the boot's on the other foot. Thea hasn't shown any signs of flirting with him, has she?'

'Well, no.'

'Stop being an arse then, mate. In fact, as Bert would say, apologise to Thea without delay.'

'He would, wouldn't he? I've been an idiot, haven't I?'

'Yep.'

Raking a hand through his hair, Shaun resolved to find Thea as soon as he'd finished talking to Sam. 'Anyway, enough of my moans. How's life at Mill Grange?'

'All good, thanks. The current guests are almost ready to leave. One of them has already rebooked with a mind to doing the archaeology certificate with Tom when it launches properly in July.'

'Excellent news.'

'Talking of news, what are you guys doing about Easter? Tina said you had the weekend off?'

'I'm hoping we'll get back to Mill Grange.'

'In that case, I should warn you that you will be driving into a whole world of chocolate.'

'Did you tell Shaun and Thea about Bert being ill?'

Tina passed Sam a slice of lemon cake and sat on the bench next to him, lifting her face to the sunshine that bathed the garden.

'No. Bert asked me not to. They'd only worry, and what

can they do? It's not like they can drop everything and come to see him.' Sam stretched out his legs and wrapped an arm around Tina's shoulders. He knew he ought to tell her about his conversation with his mother, but somehow he couldn't find a way to frame the words. And besides, she looked so happy. He didn't want to ruin the mood.

'I love this time of the week.' Tina laid a head on Sam's shoulder as she surveyed the sloping garden as it swept down to the woods that formed the borders of Mill Grange's land down to the River Barle, where it merged with Exmoor. 'One set of guests gone, and a whole hour before I need to start stripping the bed linen and you start cleaning the garden tools, and checking the walking equipment.'

'It wouldn't be the end of the world if you left the beds until this evening or tomorrow.' A hint of guilt edged into Sam's contentment. With Thea away and Mabel looking after Bert, Tina would end up doing the housework on her own. 'I'm sorry I haven't managed to go upstairs yet. I can do the downstairs bedroom and help in the kitchen, but—'

Tina placed a single finger over Sam's lips. 'You have plenty to do, and I'll be fine. Helen will help me as soon as she and Tom have finished recording the week's work on the fortlet.'

Filling Tina in on Shaun's insecurities in Gloucestershire, Sam found himself picturing his fiancée, complete in wedding dress, walking across the garden before him. His conscience pricked him for a second time.

And it's not just Tina. I want to get married here too. I want to be able to tell our children we got married in the garden they'll play in.

Taking a deep breath, Sam turned to Tina. 'I'm sorry to

ruin the moment, but there's something I need to talk to you about.'

Tom risked glancing at Helen. While her face wasn't etched with thunder, she certainly wasn't smiling. He hadn't realised how much he liked her smile until it wasn't there. He hated that he was responsible for taking it away.

He'd explained about Sue, and it being the only time she could meet him and talk about Dylan for at least a week. Helen had said all the right things, had claimed to understand, and said they could chat about what she wanted to discuss anytime. Then she'd taken up his offer of a coffee at Sybil's the following day, saying in the same breath that anything he had to do for Dylan's sake was important, and that the Indian restaurant would be there another time.

Tom hadn't told her he was still going to the restaurant. Just not with her.

'What are these for?' Thea cradled the bunch of spring flowers in her arms, 'and where did you get them?'

'There's a shop in Northleach that had flowers for sale alongside the groceries. I wanted to say sorry for being a jerk.'

Giving him a hug, Thea found a water jug in her van's tiny kitchen cupboard, and lowered the daffodils and crocuses inside. 'Not the most beautiful vase, but they do cheer the place up.'

'It'll be weird sleeping without you.' Shaun ran a finger across Thea's cheek.

'You're always sleeping without me.' She kissed his nose. 'You're away for at least half the year filming.'

'Which is why I begrudge a single night apart when we don't need to be.' Shaun held Thea tight. 'I've been a jealous idiot. Forgive me?'

'Forgiven.' She rested her head on his shoulder. 'Just don't do it again.'

They had changed the third set of bed linens before Tina realised that neither she nor Helen had spoken a word since they started work on the guest bedrooms. She knew why she was feeling subdued, but couldn't think why Helen was so quiet, especially after such a successful week on the dig.

'You alright?' Tina smoothed the corner of the duvet flat, and picked up a pile of towels to place on the end of the bed. 'You're very quiet.'

'I was just thinking the same about you.' Helen plumped up the pillow she'd just squeezed into a case.

'I'm fine. Just a few wedding glitches I hadn't foreseen.'

'Glitches?'

'Sam's mum wants us to marry at her place.'

'In Worcestershire?' Helen frowned. 'But you can't, can you? Don't you have to live in the area where you wish to marry and do complicated things with having the banns read – or is that just if it's a church do?'

'I don't know.' Tina shrugged. 'I'll find out. It would be very convenient if that was the case. Then I wouldn't have to feel bad about Sam breaking years of family tradition by marrying away from Malvern House.'

'What does Sam want?'

'He wants to marry here too, but obviously he doesn't want to upset his parents.' Tina resisted the urge to flop down onto the bed they'd just made. 'Why is everything always so complicated?'

'Wish I knew.' Helen gave a hollow laugh. 'Although it is odd. I mean, isn't it the bride that marries from home and not the groom?'

'Apparently not in Sam's family, although goodness knows why not. And it's not as if I have a parental home to marry from.' Tina pulled a face. 'Well that's my moan, what's stopping your usual smile in its tracks?'

Looking at the remaining pile of linen left to sort, Helen sighed. 'How about we leave this lot until the morning and skive off to the pub? I'll buy us a bottle of Pinot and we can have a mutual whinge.'

'Deal.'

Eight

Friday March 20th

Moira placed the bottle of Pinot in a bucket of ice and set it on the table between Helen and Tina. A minute later she came back with two bags of dry roasted peanuts.

'We didn't order these, Moira.' Tina poured out two glasses of wine.

'You didn't. But neither of you drink much. I thought the nuts might be needed to take the edge off. Put it down to landlady instinct.'

Helen laughed. 'An instinct which is spot on. Thank you, Moira.'

Tina took a mouthful of the deliciously chilled wine as Helen said, 'So, Sam's mum, she wants you to marry at the family manor in Worcestershire?'

'Family tradition for them, apparently. Both his elder brothers married there before they emigrated.' Tina heaved a sigh. 'I want to marry here and so does Sam, but he's obviously wary about upsetting his folks after so long without being part of their lives.'

'What will you do?'

'Stick to my guns and get married here and deal with the fallout.' Tina grimaced. 'So, what's your woe?'

Helen lifted her glass in salute to her friend's determination. 'Ah, well, unlike you, I have no right to feel put out, but I still do.'

'Are we going to need an interpreter for this conversation?' Tina was already lost.

Helen pulled a face. 'Between you and me, Tom and I were supposed to be going out tonight.' Before Tina could comment, she added, 'Not on a date. Just to talk over something work related. We thought it would be nice to get out of Upwich for a bit. There's a good Indian restaurant in Tiverton apparently. We were going there.'

'Are you sure it wasn't a date?' Tina refilled Helen's fast disappearing wine. 'It does sound like one.'

'It was just a change of scene. That's all.'

'But you're here with me, with the air of someone who's been let down, rather than looking like someone who's had a work chat cancelled.'

Helen couldn't help but chuckle. 'What on earth does acting like someone with the air of being let down look like?'

'Oh, I've no idea, but you know what I mean.' Tina tilted her head to one side. She knew Helen liked Tom, and she was pretty sure Tom reciprocated, yet nothing had happened. If tonight was his way of having a non-date-date, then something must have happened to stop him. Or his bottle had gone. 'I know Tom's gone out tonight, because his car's missing. So, what happened?'

'Sue happened.'

'Dylan's mum?' Tina was about to become indigent on Helen's behalf, when she realised. 'Dylan's okay, isn't he?'

'Yes. He's the reason Tom's gone out with Sue. She wants to discuss giving him more time with Dylan, add his name to the school contacts list and such like. That way Tom will be notified when there are parent's evenings and stuff.'

'Hence you saying you have no right to feel put out about Tom not being able to take you out.'

'Exactly.' Helen took a sip of drink as she watched the customers of the busy pub carrying on around them, exchanging friendly waves and chats with each other as they settled to their drinks and meals.

Tina put down her glass. 'It's just a hunch, but I suspect Tom isn't in a hurry to start another relationship, with such a messy one still hanging over him.'

'I know.' Helen popped the final peanut into her mouth. 'I wish to goodness I didn't like him, but I can't turn the feeling off. It's ridiculous at my age! I'm nearly... I'm thirty-nine for goodness sake.'

'It doesn't work like that.' Tina paused. 'You aren't really worried about turning forty, are you? I know loads of forty-somethings who say life gets better and better.'

'Me too, it's just...' Helen took a moment to think how to phrase her thoughts. 'Look, it isn't that I'm single. It isn't that I don't think my life is complete without a partner. Nor do I feel I haven't achieved anything with my life. I did think all those things for a while. Took each of those issues in turn and worried about them – but it isn't any of that... it's... I don't know...'

'Is that how you felt when you came to Mill Grange last September?'

'Pretty much. I was working through the, "I haven't achieved anything with my life because I've been in the same job for years and have no man," phase at that point. That passed when you and Thea made me see I'd been working too hard and simply needed a break. But then, just as I was chilling out, and wasn't constantly thinking about museum planning meetings and school trip quotas—'

'Tom came along, you realised you fancied him like crazy and now you're stuck with feelings you can't do a thing about.'

Helen ruffled her curls from her eyes. 'Hell! It is all so bloody cliché!'

'Everything about love is.'

'Love?' Helen dismissed the notion. 'I fancy him. Not the same thing. I'm sure if we could just be friends that—'

'Friends with benefits? Is that what you want?' Tina's eyebrows rose as she picked her wine back up.

'Best of both worlds.'

'If you say so.'

'I do say so.' Helen wasn't sure if she was as convinced by this argument as she sounded. 'Tom is absolutely the last sort of man I should fall for.'

'Because he has a past?'

'More because I don't. He has more baggage than a luggage shop, has fought with the army all over the world and has a son. I have a wide knowledge of Roman archaeology and can dig a decent hole.'

Sue was already waiting for Tom when he arrived at the Indian. Finding himself wondering if she was sat at the table he and Helen would have occupied if they'd come here together, Tom tried to rein in his thoughts.

It wasn't a date. Helen wanted to talk something work-ish through and you suggested a change of scene. That's all.

Sue's hair wasn't the same colour it had been on Monday. It was much quieter in tone now, a light brown rather than her usual jet black or bright pinks and purples. It was as if her hairstyle was reflecting the changes she was making in her life.

Waving when she spotted him, Tom realised he hadn't looked at Sue as anything other than someone who simply needed to be dealt with, an inconvenience on the way to his son, for years. He'd forgotten she was attractive, especially when she stopped trying to make herself look younger than she was.

Tonight, her usual teen fashion style had been replaced by a smart shirt and jacket. Her makeup was more subtle, and her fingernails, currently curled around the menu, were a regular pink, not all the colours of the rainbow, with weird patterns on every other one.

She's made an effort.

Tom looked down at his jeans and jumper. They were clean, but beyond that he'd made no effort. He thought about the shirt and new black jeans he'd been planning to wear if he'd come here with Helen. An image of him teasing out one of her long red curls, and watching it spring back into place filled his mind, only to be swept away as a waiter arrived with a bottle of alcohol-free lager and a menu.

'I assumed that's what you still drink when you're driving.' Sue flashed a smile.

'Yes, thank you.' Tom glanced around at the pristine

white table cloths and swan folded napkins. He suddenly wondered if Sue would expect him to pay for her meal. Helen he'd have paid for, if she'd let him, but Sue... *I suppose I'll pay for it somehow, whichever way we work it.*

'What do you think?' Sue asked as she placed her menu open on the table.

Not sure if she meant her appearance or the venue, Tom sat down. 'Sorry Sue, what do I think about what?'

'The restaurant. It's nice, isn't it?'

'Very.' Tom scanned his eye down the menu. 'I've no idea what to have. It's been years since I had anything I haven't cooked myself, that wasn't a takeaway or pub meal, or that Mabel or a guest cooked.'

'Mabel?' Sue's tone was suddenly sharper.

'The old lady I was waiting in for the groceries for the other day.'

'Oh. Oh yes.' Sue pointed at the menu. 'I can recommend nearly everything in here. Especially the aloo puri for starter.'

'You've been here before?' He didn't ask what he was thinking. *How could you afford that?*

'It's where we had our Christmas work do last year. And some of the girls have celebrated birthdays here.'

'Oh right, yes of course.'

'You look all put out.' She fluttered her eyelashes at him. 'You aren't jealous are you, darling?'

'Cut it out, Sue.' He returned to reading the menu. 'Apart from the aloo puri, any recommendations?'

'How about we share a couple of dishes? You'll be able to try more that way.'

'Well, umm—'

'Don't panic, that won't make this a date. We're here to talk about Dylan, remember?'

'Of course I remember. That's why I'm here with you and not—'

Sue pounced immediately, her expression curiously unreadable. 'And not what? With someone else? Oh my God, you didn't have a date, did you?'

'No. I told you, I had a work thing. It can be rescheduled.' Tom hid in his lager for a moment. 'Let's talk about what we are here for. How is Dylan, and more to the point, who's looking after him?'

'He's great,' Sue checked the time on her phone, 'and about now Harriet will be reading him a bedtime story.'

'Harriet?'

'The eighteen-year-old daughter of one of my work colleagues. She's a lovely girl and Dylan adores her.'

'Right. Okay.' Tom suddenly felt as though he knew nothing about his son's life at all, let alone Sue's.

Before he could ask more questions, a waiter arrived at their table and Sue ordered for them both.

'Was the food I chose okay for you?'

'Pardon?'

'Honestly, Tom.' Sue passed him a poppadom. 'Are you with me tonight?'

'Sorry.' Tom cracked his poppadom in two and dipped one half into some mango chutney. 'Look, Sue, it's just occurred to me that I know even less about yours and Dylan's daily lives than I thought I did. At the risk of making it sound like an inquisition, can I ask some questions before we do the rest of it?'

'Shoot.'

'Okay. So, your job. I know you work in the local supermarket.'

'Tesco.'

'And you are on the tills, yes?'

'Ah.' Sue shuffled uneasily, taking rather more time balancing some chutney on a small fragment of poppadom. 'I was, but I'm not now.'

Tom stopped eating and laid down his food. 'Sue, if your job changes, you're supposed to tell me. It affects how much maintenance I pay. And while I don't begrudge Dylan a penny, I'm not exactly affluent here.'

'Don't go arsy! Work is one of the things I wanted to talk about.'

'So, what's the job and how long have you had it?'

'In the admin office. Payroll Assistant.' Sue blushed. 'I thought I should train for something better, you know, for when Dylan is over eighteen and you don't have to help us anymore.'

Stunned, Tom repeated, 'When did you start?'

'Two months ago.' She crumbled a fragment of poppadom between her fingers. 'I should have said but—'

'But you didn't want me to pay you less each month!'

'No!' Sue looked around, aware that other diners were staring at them. 'It's more that, well... I didn't want to tell you and then find I was rubbish at it. I'd have been so embarrassed if I'd lost the job before I'd even finished the training.'

Being surprised by Sue was beginning to become a regular experience. 'Are you enjoying it?'

'I am. It's challenging. There's so much to remember, but if I can do it... I want Dylan to be proud of me. Do you think that's silly?'

'Not at all.' Tom hesitated before saying, 'You've changed so much, Sue. What brought this on, it can't just be Dylan?'

'Well it is. I want the best for him.' She took a deep draught of her glass of wine. 'Talking of which, I put you on the school list as promised, and, if you'd like to, I'd be open to you having Dylan 50 per cent of the time.'

Tom put his glass of lager down in slow motion. 'Did you really just say 50 per cent of the time? As in, split custody?'

'I did.'

Nine

Saturday March 21st

A ray of morning sun streamed through a gap in the curtains, waking Tom in his attic room. Blinking with a groan, he pulled his pillow over his head. It was becoming increasingly difficult to sleep in the bedroom next to Helen.

Last night, as he'd driven home from Tiverton to Upwich, he'd realised how ridiculous their situation had become. He knew she liked him, she knew he liked her. They were like a couple of teenagers who weren't quite brave enough to make the first move.

When he'd climbed up the servant stairs at just gone eleven the previous evening, Tom had been tempted to knock on Helen's door, but his hand hadn't quite connected with the wood. She'd probably have been asleep anyway.

'And what would I have said if she'd opened the door?' he muttered into his pillow. 'Hi, Helen, I'm pretty sure I'm falling in love with you, but I'm bad news on that front, but I'd love to sleep with you, so may I come in? Hardly!'

Daydreaming about Helen was one thing, and fantasising

about someone you fancy was normal, but today he decided he was going to be sensible about the situation that was building between them. Unless Helen had plans for the day, he'd ask her if she'd like to take a walk across Exmoor. They could discuss whatever it was she'd wanted to talk about last night, and he could tell her about having Dylan part time.

He'd been so thrilled at the thought of sharing parenting with Sue that the practicalities of achieving that had escaped him at first. That elation had died by the time he and Sue were eating the final mouthfuls of naan bread, and now they crowded in on him again. *How could he fit work around Dylan? What about school pick-up? Where would Dylan sleep?*

Leaving the warmth of his bed, which had once been used by one of the Victorian serving maids that had worked at Mill Grange, Tom flung opened the curtains. One glimpse of the view and his optimism returned. He would shower, dress and then see if Helen would like to walk over to the Tarr Steps. If she didn't, then he'd walk anyway, and try to work out how to fit his life at Mill Grange around Dylan. Then he'd start enquiring into how much it would be to rent a place with two bedrooms in or around the village.

As he grabbed a towel, Tom's insides clenched with nerves. After years of living in a self-imposed emotional wilderness he was contemplating a life with his own home, his son with him half the time and a proper girlfriend. 'I swear fighting the IRA was less frightening than this!'

Tina placed the empty notebook on the picnic bench outside the kitchen door and opened the first crisp page. Smoothing her palm across the cool lined paper she wrote, 'Guest List', at the top.

A smile crossed her face as she wrote down her friends' names. She knew she didn't need to add Thea, Shaun, Helena and Tom, but she did anyway. They might be automatic invitees, but apart from Sam, they were the most important people in her life.

Next to Thea's name, Tina added – 'ask to be bridesmaid'.

Since they'd first met at Durham University as archaeology students, Tina and Thea had been firm friends. While Thea had been a born archaeologist, Tina had enjoyed every second of her degree, but hadn't the love for the subject required to stay in the field. Instead she'd moved towards her own passion; heritage work. It was that, combined with her skill with numbers, which had led her to a career with the Exmoor Heritage Trust as their financial advisor and restoration co-ordinator – until Sam had come along just as the trust decided to sell Mill Grange. After that, everything had changed.

She hadn't asked Sam who he'd like to be best man, but assumed Shaun would be offered the role. Unless there was someone from his time in the forces that he hadn't mentioned before, that he'd like to perform the task.

A cloud blew in front of the sun, and with it, Tina's spirits dipped as she considered who would give her away. She'd been a teenager about to head to university when a car crash had taken her parents from her. It had been a long haul to get where she was now without them, but she'd done it. However, that didn't stop her wishing they were here. An image of her father walking down the aisle she and Sam intended to make with chairs and bands of willow, sent tears to the corner of her eyes. Pushing them away, Tina got up, clutched the notebook and pen to her chest and headed to the walled garden.

Gertrude and Mavis were strutting around the chicken coop with their usual air of nonchalance. Every now and then one of them would tilt their heads in the direction of Tony Stark, the cockerel, making sure they still held his affections.

'Good morning, ladies.' Tina leaned on the fence which Sam had built around the hen house. 'I'm in need of some chicken wisdom.'

As if on cue, Betty and a few more of the White Sussex hens popped their heads out of their house, and strolled across the coop towards Tina.

'I'm trying to organise mine and Sam's wedding. We want to marry here, but his parents want us to marry at Malvern House. What do you think?'

Gertrude gave Tina such an old-fashioned stare that she could help but laugh. 'You have strong views about us staying here, then?' Sitting down on a bench that overlooked the coop, Tina wondered why she was still debating the location of the wedding. It had to be at Mill Grange.

'But perhaps not in the main garden as we thought. Maybe in here.'

There was a general clucking of agreement from her feather companions.

Tina's gaze fell on the ruined Victorian greenhouse. Its spooky, almost gothic, splendour was something Sam had wanted to restore since he'd first purchased the manor. Although cost and time had prevented them doing anything more than a tidy up of the site, it still exuded a timeless beauty.

Putting down her notebook, Tina moved forward to stand on the square of grass between the chickens, and the vegetable garden beyond, and tried to work out how much space there was, and if the marquee they'd envisaged for the main garden, would fit in.

Suddenly she could see the greenhouse's skeleton bedecked in fairy lights, a stunning backdrop to their vows.

Running back to her pad, Tina scribbled down her idea. 'Do you think Dylan would like to help with the putting up the fairy lights, Gertrude?'

The responding clucks from the chief hen confirmed her suspicion that Tom's son would like that very much, but it might not be the safest venture for the boy. 'You're right of course.' Tina quickly added Dylan's name to the guest list as a potential page boy.

'How about you and Mr Stark give me away then, Gertrude? I'm sure you'd both be up to the task, and it's not as if…' Tina stopped talking and stared at the hens, who all stared back at her. 'I've been an idiot, girls. I've got to go. I'll be back later with some food.'

Clutching her notebook, Tina jogged across the garden. She'd expected to find Sam taking his habitual early morning stroll around the grounds, making sure his domain was as it should be. Instead she found him sat on the bench by the kitchen door, a mug of tea in his hand, with another next to him.

'Tea?' Sam smiled as he spotted the notebook Thea had given her as a present before she'd left for the Cotswolds. 'I was going to bring it over to the chickens, but then I heard the gate squeak, so I knew you were on your way.'

Tina laughed. 'Better get that oiled before the wedding.'

Sam pointed to the notebook. 'Is there room in there for a list of practical things, or is it just for the nice stuff?'

'Everything!' Tina opened to the back page. 'But boring stuff goes at the end!'

'Fair enough.' Sam took a sip of tea before asking, 'How far have you got?'

Tina flashed the only page of the book with anything written on it, under Sam's nose. 'Thea for bridesmaid and maybe Dylan as a pageboy. I sort of assumed Shaun would be your best man, but I didn't write it down. You might have someone else who—'

'Shaun. Definitely. If he wants to do it.' Sam nodded as Tina wrote down Shaun's name next to 'best man'.

'I was talking to the chickens just now.'

'And what genius did Gertrude and the gang deliver this morning?'

'Well.' Tina suddenly found her eyes pricked with tears. Thinking about who would attend her wedding in place of her parents was one thing, but actually saying it out loud was something entirely different.

Sam frowned, pulling her close to his side. 'What is it?'

'I've been thinking about who's going to give me away. The answer is obvious, but it means admitting my dad won't be doing it.' She wiped the back of a hand over her eyes. 'Silly, really, after all this time.'

'It's not silly, it's natural. I'd be worried if you didn't feel that way.' Sam kissed the top of her head, as Tina rested against his side.

'Do you think Bert would do it? He'll be well enough by then, won't he?'

Sam beamed. 'I hoped you'd ask him.'

'I'd like Mabel to be mother of the bride.' Tina smiled. 'I can just picture her in a hat Queen Elizabeth might wear.'

Sam laughed. 'Me too. Probably in lilac.' More serious for a moment, Sam checked his watch. 'It's still early, but in a couple of hours why don't we go and ask them? It might give Bert the extra oomph he needs to recover.'

'He is getting better, isn't he?' Tina's heart constricted. She couldn't bear to lose Bert as well.

'He is, but he's weak. Something positive to think about will help him recover all the quicker.'

Writing, 'Ask Bert and Mabel to be honorary father and mother of the bride' in her book, Tina said, 'I thought of something else when I was with the chickens.'

'Oh yes.'

'I know we were going to have the wedding on this bit of garden, with the house behind us, but how about having it in the walled garden, with the greenhouse behind us?'

'But the greenhouse is in ruin?'

'Yes, but it's very beautiful, and it means that Gertrude and crew could come to the wedding.'

'You're crackers.'

'Yes.' Tina sat up so she could drink her tea. 'I had another thought too. Why don't we invite your parents over for the weekend soon? If they saw this place, they might understand why we want to marry here.'

Ten

As they walked through Mill Grange's garden, down to the woods, and along the path that led from Sam's land towards the Tarr Steps and the open plains of Exmoor, Helen was reminded of the first time she'd met Tom on the manor's fortlet excavation.

The conversation then had veered between awkward small talk and no talk at all. Today, with the weight of their non-date hanging unspoken between them, Helen could feel the words no one was saying bouncing in the air, ricocheting off the trees, hitting them everywhere but their vocal chords.

Hitching her backpack higher onto her shoulder, Helen knew if Tom didn't break the silence soon, she'd have to, but a childish part of her didn't want to be the one who went first.

And whatever she thought of saying seemed to reflect on them as a couple – or more on them not being a couple.

Even mentioning that she and Tina had a good evening last night wasn't possible without bringing up why she'd been with Tina and not him.

But we did have a good night. Helen looked along the stretch of the River Barle as they wove along its banks. *Tina cheered me up, even though she made me see that I've been kidding myself.* Helen risked a glance at Tom, and immediately had a feeling he'd been glancing at her only a second before. *I don't just want this man to be a friend with benefits. I was just afraid of the alternative.* Helen swallowed. *I'm still afraid – and so is he.*

Tom stared at the path beneath his feet. This had felt like such a good idea earlier, but now, as each new step took them further from Mill Grange, and still neither of them had spoken, he was regretting his decision.

I could talk about Dylan. Ask Helen's opinion about him living at Mill Grange sometimes. I ought to ask what it was she wanted to talk about over dinner... but if that's us then...

'Oh, this is ridiculous!' Tom was surprised to hear himself say the words rather than think them as he stopped walking and dropped his rucksack to the ground.

Her heart beating fast, Helen stopped too. 'It is. Utterly ridiculous.'

'Yes, it is. We are.' Tom burst out laughing. He couldn't help it. 'Look at us! We're supposed to be grown-ups and we can't even have a conversation about why we aren't having a conversation.'

Helen's shoulders relaxed in relief. 'We're as bad as each other. I've been thinking about what to say, but it's all so trite. So corny!'

'Same here.' Tom looked over his shoulder to make sure they were alone. Not a soul was in sight. 'I want to tell you about last night, about Dylan, and I want to ask what you did, and about whatever you wanted to talk about and most of all, I want to kiss you. But I'm a nightmare with women, Helen. You deserve so much more, yet I can't offer you more. I wish I could but this is it. This is me. An ex-squaddie with more baggage than an airport.'

Stopping abruptly, Tom was out of breath. His words had tumbled out at such a pace that they'd left Helen open mouthed and temporarily speechless. A voice was yelling at the back of her head; telling her that if this was the movies they'd be kissing by now.

But this isn't the movies.

Instead, Helen reached down to the dropped bag and passed it back to Tom. 'How about you start by telling me what Sue wanted last night, and we walk as we talk? That was the plan today, wasn't it, for you and me to chat as we enjoyed the scenery?'

Tom simply nodded. He knew if Helen hadn't spoken he'd have tried to kiss her. Perhaps it was as well he didn't. As he'd said, she deserved better. Slinging his bag onto his back, he gestured forward. 'Then let's walk and talk.'

'What did your mum say?'

Tina paused in the act of baking a batch of muffins to be frozen and used for future guest breakfasts.

'That she and Father were delighted to be invited. They haven't confirmed a date yet though.'

Adding some sugar to her mix, Tina asked, 'Did either of you mention the wedding or where it would be held?'

'No. As Mum didn't, I didn't.'

'Ummm. Right.'

'That was a loaded ummm.'

'Perhaps they think we're inviting them here to discuss the wedding, and have assumed you'll cave and have it in Worcestershire.'

'Possibly, but I did say we were inviting them because we wanted to show them our home.'

Tina plugged the electric whisk into the wall. 'I'm glad they're coming. If they fall for the house, then it'll be much easier. I really don't want them to be at our wedding feeling hurt because we turned down the offer of their home as a venue.'

'Let's face it, it wasn't so much of an offer as a royal command – presumably from my father, even though Mum was the messenger. This has his stuffiness written all over it.' Sam sighed. 'But you're right. I don't want any sort of cloud hanging over the wedding.' He pointed to the muffin mixture. 'How long until you're done here?'

'About an hour, I've got a cake to do after these, then they have to bake.'

'Fancy heading into the village to see Bert and Mabel afterwards?'

'Via Sybil's to ask if she'll cater for the wedding tea?'

'Deal.'

★

'A book? That's fantastic!'

Helen wasn't so sure. 'I don't know. I mean, I've written countless papers and site reports and so on, but a book… I'm honestly not sure I have it in me. And I'm damn sure I have no idea where to start.'

'Of course you do! You just said, you've written papers, presumably on aspects of Roman Britain and Romano-British life. Just tackle each chapter as if it were a paper.'

'History books don't read like academic papers though, do they?'

'Well, no, okay, but if you had something down, then it would be easier to adapt into the style the publisher wanted.' Tom hung back so Helen could climb over a stile before him. 'It's really exciting. Who asked you to do this?'

'Batsford, they're—'

'The leading publishers of archaeological site-based history books. Wow. Go you!'

Helen shook her head. 'I think I'll have to say no, or at least see if Thea wants to be co-author with me; or maybe even do the whole thing instead of me. She knows as much about the subject as I do, and well… I'm not sure I'll have time with work as well.'

'But they asked *you*, not Thea.'

'The article I did for Currently Archaeology about the fortlet got noticed. If Thea had written it, she'd be the one with the book offer.'

'Or, perhaps, the paper wouldn't have been so good, and there wouldn't be an offer at all.'

'You're biased.'

'True.' Tom said nothing, before, without looking at her, he reached out and took Helen's hand.

Neither of them mentioned how right it felt as their fingers linked.

'When do you need to tell them if you're going to write it or not?'

'Next week.' Helen kept her eyes forward, despite her desire to glance down at their hands. 'If I agree, they want a chapter by chapter breakdown of the subject matter and a brief outline of how I'd tackle the book.'

'That sounds really professional.'

'It sounds really grown up and scary.' Helen risked a peep at Tom. His face was staring straight ahead, making her wonder if he was also not allowing himself to look at their entwined fingers. 'What chapters would I include?'

'An introduction, about how the site was found I suppose, then the site's chronological development, each chapter being about a new phase of the site and comparing them with other similar sites elsewhere in the UK. Maybe with separate chapters on Roman military life and why the fort would have been built at Upwich in the first place.'

Helen stopped walking and, squeezing his palm tighter, looked directly at him. 'That's it. How did you think of that, just like that?'

He gave a suggestive wink, sending a funny feeling through Helen's nervous system. 'I've read a lot of Batsford history books. It's how they're laid out.'

'I've been going around in mental circles thinking about it.' Helen stared out across the beautiful landscape. 'I should have just asked you in the first place. Maybe we should write this together.'

'Don't be daft, I'm dyslexic and failed my English GCSE with a style that would be the envy of none. Clever, I'm not.'

Swivelling on the spot, Helen met Tom's gaze, her expression serious. 'That's the first and last time you put yourself down like that. There are many different types of clever, and when the hell did being able to spell brilliantly have anything to do with cleverness anyway? It's just a skill like any other, but we're all good at different things in different measures. You had a rough start, you got through it, and you're here. Got it!'

Tom was too stunned to speak, as Helen pointed along the path. 'Yes, well. Enough said. The steps are only half a mile away. Come on, I could do with a sit down.'

Despite it being a Saturday, the prehistoric clapper bridge, known as the Tarr Steps, was fairly quiet. Helen could see a few families ahead of them, on the other side of the water. Several dog walkers passed them as they sat on the grass in the sunshine, looking at the ancient spectacle.

'I think Sam and Tina would be fine about Dylan staying at the manor for a while.' Helen unhooked her bag, and passed Tom a slice of cake left over from the previous week's guests. 'Here, Tina said it was still edible, although I can't vouch for that yet.'

Smiling into the sunshine, Tom took it. 'Tina's lemon cake is always edible. I can't believe there was some left to bring.' He held up a flask. 'Coffee?'

'Please.' Helen took a mouthful of cake, murmuring her approval as she chewed. 'It's perfect.'

'Do you think Mabel might like to help me find somewhere to rent?' He passed Helen a plastic mug of coffee. 'I'm not bailing on sorting it out myself. I just thought it would be good to give her something to do. She must be bored stiff at home with Bert.'

Helen tilted her head as she regarded Tom carefully.

'What is it?' Tom ran a hand over his face. 'Have I got mud on me or something?'

'No. I was just thinking that you're a lot nicer man than you think you are.' She looked away abruptly. 'I think Mabel would enjoy that. She'd feel part of things again. And let's face it, not only does Mabel love to help people, she also has local knowledge. There aren't many places around Upwich for let, but I bet Mabel knows everyone that owns rented property in the area.'

Tom thought of his small attic room. 'My bedroom at Mill Grange has two singles in it, so Dylan would be fine for now, assuming Sam was agreeable to him staying. But it's not a sound long term solution. Dylan has toys and clothes and it won't be long before he needs his own computer. Schools seem to run homework from them these days. And he'll want his own space, as will I.'

Helen didn't voice the thought that popped into her head. Telling him that Dylan could have his room, and he could sleep with her, would only have complicated things. Especially as they hadn't so much as hugged yet. 'It will be strange without you living in, although I suppose...'

'What?'

Helen checked the date on her phone. 'It depends on how soon Dylan is going to move in with you. What was the plan again, Wednesday to Saturday one week, and Sunday to Wednesday the next?'

'Yes, that was it.' Tom put down his empty cup. 'From the beginning of April. Seemed easiest to start at the beginning of the month.'

'In that case, you'd only have to share with Dylan for ten or so days before you could have a room each.'

'What do you mean?'

'My sabbatical ends on April 10th. I have a holiday off over Easter, but then I have to go back to the Roman Baths. That's why I'm worried about not having time to write the book. I won't be here to do it.'

Eleven

Saturday March 21st

Tina spotted the note sticky-taped to the front door of Mabel and Bert's cottage as she and Sam walked down the drive.

'Mabel must have gone out for a walk. Probably got a delivery coming or something and doesn't want Bert disturbed.'

'I didn't have Mabel down as an online shopper.' Sam fished in his pocket for his key ring. 'Don't worry, Bert gave me a spare key months ago in case of emergency. We can keep him company while Mabel's out.'

Tina froze as she got within reading distance of the front door. 'They're both out.' She reached out her arm and grabbed Sam. 'Oh god. The note's for us.'

Sam was already reading over Tina's shoulder. The handwriting was erratic, a far cry from Mabel's usual neat script.

Sam and Tina, Bert was rushed to Musgrove in night. Didn't want to call and wake you. M x

'In the Musgrove.' Sam slipped his keys back into his pocket and began to walk with purpose back to Mill Grange.

'But he was so much better yesterday. Why would Bert be in hospital now?' The clammy hand of fear gripped at Tina's dry throat.

'We'll drive to Taunton right now and find out.'

'But…' Tina had to jog to catch up with him. 'Sam, please! Stop a minute.'

He paused, holding Tina to his side. 'We must go and find them. Mabel will be in pieces if—'

'We aren't family. We'll have to wait until visiting hours, and then there's the other thing…' Tina hesitated, not sure if she should mention the thought that had crossed her mind or not.

'Other thing?'

'You're getting good at going inside downstairs in Mill Grange, and in Bert's cottage you're fine because it's become familiar, but—'

Sam's shoulders sagged in defeat as his old enemy reared its head. 'Damn!'

Tina jumped at the unexpected shout. 'I'm sorry, I just thought better to bring it up here, rather than you fainting in the hospital and becoming a patient too.'

'Bloody claustrophobia! How many more years will I have to cope with this damn thing!?' Sam's tone dropped to an apologetic mumble. 'Maybe I'd be okay.' But even as he said it, Sam could feel the images of the hospitals sterile whiteness closing in on him and a perspiration that was only partly down to his concern for Bert coated his back.

'We'll phone the hospital. Come on.' Tina gently tugged at Sam's hand to get him to move again. 'Hopefully, Bert will be in a ward on the ground floor and you can wave through the window.'

'Fat chance!' Sam wrapped an arm around her shoulder as they walked. 'Tina, he's been rushed into hospital with pneumonia. That's serious at any age, but Bert's… He might be in intensive care.'

Tina's pale face blanched. 'I know. I just didn't want to think about that. First my parents, and now—'

'Don't say it. Bert hasn't gone anywhere yet.'

'It can't be six months already?'

'It's nearly seven. My sabbatical has already been extended by a month. You know what they say about time flying when you're enjoying yourself.'

Tom picked up a stone from by his foot and threw it into the river, where it made a satisfying plop. 'And have you, enjoyed yourself?'

'You know I have.' Helen felt the awkwardness they'd managed to shake off start to descend again as she saw Tom fix his attention on a young family on the opposite side of the water. 'If it helps, I don't particularly want to go back.'

As Tom didn't look as if he was willing, or able, to reply, Helen kept talking, not wanting a new silence to fall between them.

'I hadn't realised how much I needed a break from work when I came to Mill Grange. Don't get me wrong, I love my job at the Roman Baths. It is hard work, demanding, and full on – but so rewarding. Have you ever been?'

'I took Dylan last year.'

Helen imagined the wonder on the little boy's face. 'He must have been four then. Already taking after his dad.'

'A week before he was five. It was his birthday treat. I'd read him a Ladybird book on the Romans I'd got from the library. The book was almost as old as the subject matter, but Dylan loved it. He said he could imagine the soldiers marching and getting cross when the roads weren't straight enough.'

Laughing, Helen could picture the lad saying so. 'Shame I didn't know you then. I'd have given him a behind the scenes tour. Loads more to see in the workshops and storerooms.'

'He'd have liked that.' Tom resumed his observation of the family opposite. The father was holding a young boy, of about three years old, over his head, whizzing him round like an aeroplane. 'So would I.'

'Maybe you could come. Both of you.' Helen found herself staring at her hands as they sat in her lap. 'There are some artefacts Dylan could help clean if he wanted to.'

'You know he'd want to.'

'Yes… He's good at it too. He's helped me before.' Helen winced at the stilted nature of their conversation. 'I'd like him to. I'd like you both to come and visit.'

'You or the Baths?'

'Both.' Helen reached for the flask, hoping there was some coffee left. 'It isn't that far to Bath. You could—'

'It's a two-hour drive.' Tom shook his head. 'Going once for a visit, I could do that with Dylan. But I have work here,

I have a son I'm finally getting to spend more time with and, let's be honest, next to no money to spend on petrol. I try very hard not to live beyond my means.'

'Right, yes, of course.' She stared into the plastic beaker in her hand.

'And how often do you have weekends off, Helen? Rarely, I imagine. And I *only* get weekends off and never week days, so—'

'Okay, I get it.' Pouring the dregs of the coffee between their cups, she passed one to Tom. 'What would you have me do, then? It's my job, and it's a good one. I have a home in Bath that will be goodness knows how deep in dust and cobwebs by now. And I have colleagues that are relying on me to come back. Plus, Sam and Tina only employed me until mid-April, and that time is almost up. They don't have the money to spend on me for any longer.'

'But with Thea away with Shaun, then…'

'Don't think I haven't thought about that. I know Mill Grange will be shorthanded for a while, but my bosses have already been more than generous with my sabbatical, I can't ask for another extension.'

'Would you stay if you could? If Sam offered you a job here?'

Placing a hand over his, Helen risked looking at Tom as he stared across the water. 'Would there be more than a job to stay for?'

'Your friends, your work here; the book you've been asked to write. Then there's—'

'Tom!' Helen put down her tepid coffee and took hold of his chin, gently turning him to face her. 'You know that isn't what I meant.'

His words came out as a whisper. 'But I'm a nightmare with women.'

'So you keep saying.' She placed a finger on Tom's lips. 'Maybe it's time you stopped judging the people of your future by the mistakes of your past.'

Lowering her hand from his face, Tom kept hold of it as he asked again, 'If Sam offers you the chance to stay would you take it?'

'If it's a permanent post and you and Dylan are here, yes.' Helen felt herself leaning in. *Please kiss me. Please. Now.*

'Right.' Looking away, Tom sounded determined. 'Come on.'

Disappointed, hoping her desire for him hadn't shown, Helen scrambled to her feet. 'Where are we going?'

'To stand on the clapper bridge.'

'Really?' Helen couldn't stop the nervous giggle that shot from her lips. 'Why?'

'Because our first kiss should happen somewhere amazing.' Tom took both her hands in his. Longing shone in his eyes as he returned Helen's suddenly shy smile. 'And as we're archaeologists, you can't get much more amazing than a prehistoric bridge.'

Twelve

'I can't believe we had to wait so long to see Bert. I did explain that we were virtually family, but apparently that isn't good enough!' Sam was still fuming as Tina drove him and Mabel to the hospital through the Sunday afternoon traffic.

Tina glanced in her rear-view mirror at Mabel in the back seat. The old woman had barely spoken since they'd picked her up from the cottage and driven from Upwich towards the Musgrove hospital on the outskirts of Taunton. She seemed shrunken somehow, as if without Bert to direct her boundless, forthright energy, she was rudderless.

Although she'd asked the question before, Tina spoke to Mabel, hoping to pull her out of her frightening silence. 'Which ward are we looking for when we get there?'

'Coleridge.' The word was barely a whisper. 'It's the one where you go if you can't breathe properly. Bert's on…' she licked her cracked lips '… he's on a ventilator.'

'Do you know how to find it, Mabel?' Sam leaned

forward to grab some change that Tina kept in the glove compartment for the car park.

'No, I...' Mabel kept her eyes fixed on the window to her side, blindly passing the rows of white and cream council houses that lined the road before they turned into the car park. 'There was a big lift that could fit Bert in on a trolley. The nurse was nice. He kept talking to me, keeping me going. I didn't notice how we got there.'

Tina slowed the car, ready to face the hunt for a precious parking space during visiting hours. 'It's okay, Mabel, there'll be a map, or we can ask at reception.'

Almost twenty minutes later, having circled the parking lot more times than they cared to remember, Sam waved frantically as a BMW ahead of them pulled out of a gap, and Tina drove into it.

Helping Mabel out, Sam mouthed to Tina as she went to pay for the ticket, 'I wish I could come in too.'

'I know, but it is best I check out the amount of space inside first.' She took the change from Sam's hand and whispered, 'I'll see how Bert is and, assuming I'm allowed, I'll text you. But I won't ask Bert about giving me away until we see him together.'

Staring after them as Tina guided Mabel through the glass doors and on into a stark wilderness hung with a dizzying array of blue and white signs, and heaving with people, Sam backed away. His legs felt shaky and his pulse was already racing.

Angry at himself for not being able to see his friend or support Tina and Mabel, Sam grabbed a coffee from an outside kiosk and moved around the side of the building, sitting on the first bank of grass he came to.

Watching cars moving around the car park opposite, he felt blissfully invisible. The flashbacks to his past, and the cause of his claustrophobia, didn't come as often since he'd settled with Tina at Mill Grange. But they still came. Sam managed to sleep in the downstairs bedroom, comfortingly near the front door to the Victorian manor house, fairly often now. But if that room was needed for a guest, or if he was having a bad spell, Sam would return to the tent in the garden to sleep. Tina usually moved outside with him, but if it was particularly cold or wet, he'd send her to the attic room she used to store her personal belongings, telling her repeatedly not to feel guilty for doing so.

Bert had told Sam the flashbacks would never truly leave, but they'd lessen month by month, year by year, and that the best way to deal with them was to accept they were part of him. He'd told Sam to use them as a yardstick for positive behaviour; that when he found himself reliving the hells he'd seen, it meant he was being frustrated while trying to do something good; probably for someone else. This, Bert had concluded, meant Sam was a decent person, and thus each flashback, although disturbing, was a mark of his kindness and progress as a human being. It was not a mark of a failure to move on.

He could hear Bert now. 'Some things you don't move on from, my boy, but you do learn to live with them.'

Sam loved Bert for that. For giving him a way to breathe through the terrors when they came.

It happened. I couldn't save them, but I tried. Other people are alive because of me.

Sam clutched his flimsy paper cup until the heat was almost unbearable and the contents were in danger of slopping over the sides, as the nightmare he'd sensed coming, arrived.

The building had burnt around him, but he'd stayed with his fellow squaddies, trying to get the locals out of their home. Sam shifted on the grass. He could smell the smoke, the choking charring stench of trapped, terrified, people. He knew what vision was coming next, and tried hard to relax his shoulder as the sound of crashing timbers and screams echoed through his mind, their horror foreign to the urgent, but relatively calm, bustle around him. Four men had gone into the building, but only Sam had come out again on that life-changing day.

Sam thought of Bert lying in a hospital bed, away from Mabel, frightened and yet still fighting.

It happened. I couldn't save them, but I tried. Other people are alive because of me.

Sipping his cooling drink, Sam wiped his sweat covered palms on the grass. At that moment he wasn't sure what scared him more, the nightmares of his past or the fact that Bert was inside the building behind him and he couldn't get to him.

'Everything he's done for me over the past year and I can't help at all.' Muttering to himself, Sam abruptly stopped talking, realising he was going around in circles and was in danger of feeling sorry for himself, which Bert would not approve of at all.

He checked his phone. There was still no text from Tina.

Mabel was shaking so much that Tina wasn't sure she'd get her to the nearest seat before she collapsed to the floor and ended up being admitted and put in the bed next to Bert.

As soon as Tina had guided them both through the main doors of the hospital, Mabel had stood up straight, her old self much more in evidence. Not wanting to be seen not to be coping Tina had assumed. Together they managed to navigate their way to Coleridge ward, where they'd waited with growing anxiety for the receptionist to finish dealing with some other visitors before attending to them.

When, at last, it had been their turn, Mabel explained who they were, and who they had come to see. When the receptionist looked puzzled, Mabel had added that this was where, when she'd been here the day before, Bert had been allocated a bed, but she wasn't sure where precisely she'd find him.

The receptionist's response was not helpful, and had led directly to Mabel's current shaken state.

'I'm sorry, Mrs Hastings, but your husband is no longer with us.'

The second she'd spoken the unwise words, and seen the devastating effect they'd had, the receptionist had blurted out apologies. 'That came out so wrong, I'm so sorry. I meant he's on a different ward now.'

Biting her tongue against what she'd like to say, Tina held Mabel close and sat her down, before asking, 'Where is Mr Hastings and is he alright?'

'He's on Eliot Ward. I'm so sorry, I...'

Once the receptionist had waffled another apology, Tina said, 'Perhaps you could look after Mrs Hastings while I try and find her husband. Visiting time will be over before he's had a single visitor, but I'm not sure Mabel should go anywhere for a second.'

'Look, I really am—'

Tina beckoned the receptionist away from Mabel's side. She looked exhausted. 'We all make mistakes, and I appreciate your apology. Could you just give me directions to Eliot Ward and perhaps loan me a wheelchair for Mabel? I honestly don't think she could walk far right now. Oh, and could you tell me what we can expect when we get there. Is it Intensive Care, is it a pneumonia ward?'

'Oh no, nothing like that.' The woman smiled, and Tina realised she was much younger than she'd first thought. 'Mr Hasting's breathing calmed within hours. He still needs the help of a mask, but nothing like the major equipment we have in here.'

Tina felt light headed as the news sank in. 'You mean he's alright?'

'All I can promise is that when I last saw Mr Hastings, he was telling the young porter pushing his trolley that if he wanted to colour his hair he should, because life was too short for regrets.'

A hysterical giggle escaped Tina's lips. 'How on earth did that conversation start?'

'I have no idea.' The receptionist waved to a colleague on the desk and asked if Jamie would come with a chair, and if he'd phone through to Eliot Ward to tell them that Mrs Hastings was on her way, and should be allowed an additional ten minutes to standard visiting hours.

'Thank you.' Tina nodded her gratitude.

'I'm sorry it's only ten minutes extra, but the drug rounds start then, and routine is so important in a place like this.'

'I quite understand.' Tina dashed back to explain the situation to Mabel, while they waited for the aforementioned Jamie to appear.

Jamie knew far more about Bert than the receptionist had. For a start, he knew that Bert favoured redheads to blondes, and when he was a lad, any female with ginger hair had, as he'd put it, "ticked his box".

Tina hadn't been sure how Mabel would respond to that, but as the old lady patted her own hair in self-satisfaction, Tina could only laugh. 'Those luscious locks were once red then, Mabel?'

'They were. Bert loved them.'

Jamie laughed. 'He still does.'

Tina was just wondering how Bert had managed to be so chatty when he was supposed to be having breathing difficulties and be wearing an oxygen mask, when Jamie explained what had happened after Mabel left.

'I was one of the porters who brought Bert up to Coleridge. I'm training as a nurse part time, so I'm a bit more aware of the medial lingo, and often help out with the small nursing jobs when things are busy.

'Bert was admitted because he couldn't catch his breath properly, something not uncommon in pneumonia. It's frightening for the patient, but often even more frightening for their loved ones to watch.'

'You can say that again.' Mabel gripped the arms of the wheelchair as they moved through the stark off-white corridor.

'Sometimes the episodes of breathing difficulties can be

very severe indeed, in other cases, an occasional period of shortness of breath is just a symptom of the whole illness, rather than the thing that takes over and becomes the issue around which the whole problem revolves – if that makes sense.'

Tina exhaled slowly. 'And Bert falls into the episodes of shortness of breath category?'

'He does.' Jamie smiled at Mabel as they pulled up in the reception of Eliot Ward. 'And while still a serious situation, it means Bert does not need heavy duty equipment to help him. Our aim now, or should I say, the nursing staff have the aim of keeping Bert at that level and improving, rather than these episodes increasing and having to take him back down the corridor again.'

Heading to reception, the porter went to report Mabel's arrival as Tina bent to her friend. 'Are you alright, Mabel? I'm sure you could stay in the chair if you'd rather.'

Mabel however, was already rising to her feet with a slow dignity. 'Bert is not seeing me in one of these things.' She held a hand out to Tina. 'You won't tell him I had to be pushed here, will you? I don't want him to worry.'

'Of course I won't.' Tina's heart constricted for the elderly couple as Jamie returned and held out both arms to Mabel and Tina.

'Shall I escort madam and mademoiselle to Mr Hastings' bedside?'

Mabel chuckled, her old self beginning to reassert itself in the face of the young man's good humour. 'We'd be delighted.'

Thirteen

Sunday March 22nd

Julian rubbed his hands as he watched Thea and Shaun work methodically across a small section of the bath house floor.

Shaun thought the producer looked like a cross between Ebenezer Scrooge and Fagin. There was something calculating about him; although Shaun was beginning to think he was the only one who saw it. Aware of the television cameras that were trained on them, Shaun laid down the trowel he'd been using and reached for a small soft brush to wipe away the grains of soil dotting the tiny section of mosaic that had been uncovered so far.

'Cut.' Julian nodded to the cameraman. 'Take a break, mate. We'll pick this up again once we've got a bit more on show.'

As the cameraman headed off for a late lunch, Thea smoothed her fingertips over the ten-centimetre-wide, metre long, rectangle of freshly exposed mosaic that would have once been the envy of many a merchant.

The bath house at Birdlip Villa, as they now called it, consisted of two sections; a small cold plunge pool, which was currently being dug by two members of *Landscape Treasures* regular team of archaeologists, and the main bath which, if the geophysics and test trenches could be believed, was going to rival the one at Chedworth Roman Villa in size.

Thea was about to ask Shaun what he thought the pattern might ultimately reveal itself to be, when Julian crouched on his haunches at the side of the dig, next to her shoulder.

'After lunch, I thought we'd do the scheduled piece about the bath house and its potential with you, Thea, talking straight to camera. We don't need it to be a discussion with you, Shaun, as it's clear you know the answers to each other's questions already.' Julian turned to his lead presenter. 'Best not to patronise the audience, don't you think?'

Giving Thea an, "I told you so look", Shaun climbed from the trench. 'Whatever you say, Julian.'

'But I haven't rehearsed it on my own.' Thea panicked. 'I'm not sure what to say?'

Julian brushed the matter aside as a mere formality. 'You can look at the script notes over lunch. You'll be brilliant, won't she, Shaun?'

'She will.' Shaun reached out a hand to Thea, pointedly keeping hold of her palm after he'd helped pull her from the trench.

'How long have we got until you need me?' The buzz of nerves Thea associated with the camera being trained on her fizzed in her stomach. She wasn't sure she'd be able to eat until her next piece of commentary was done.

'Only half an hour, so make the most of it.'

The moment Julian was out of earshot, Thea turned to Shaun. 'I know what you're going to say, but I still think you're wrong. He's right; it is obvious we know what the other is thinking. We really don't want to talk down to the audience.'

'Funny how that's never occurred to any of the other producers we've had on the show when I've interviewed guests in the past.'

Thea groaned. 'Shaun, please, this can't go on. We have to work with this guy, and I could do with your help if I have to perform solo without preparation time.'

Shaun hugged her close. 'Sorry, love. Green eyed monster.'

'Well get rid of the damn thing! There is no need to be jealous, but there's every need for strong coffee and script practice.'

'And a bacon roll.' Shaun kissed the top of her head. 'I don't know about you, but I *really* miss Mabel's bacon rolls.'

Sam pulled the car into the car park of The Exeter Arms between Tiverton and Upwich, and leapt out to open the door for Mabel.

'Come on, it's a lovely sunny afternoon. Let's have a drink and a late lunch, or early dinner. I'm not sure which, hospital time always throws me.'

Mabel took Sam's hand as he helped her from the backseat. 'That would be lovely. I couldn't eat a thing before we saw Bert. I'm rather peckish now.'

Tina pointed to a large picnic bench in the sunshine. 'You two get settled, I'll fetch some tea, coffee and menus, unless you want a stronger drink, Mabel?'

'I'm tempted to have gin! But actually, a cup of tea sounds heavenly. And don't worry about a menu Tina, love. Just grab me anything straightforward. Scampi and chips, lasagne, something simple.'

'Sam?'

'Yep, coffee and whatever Mabel's having food wise.'

Mabel watched as Tina headed into the pub. 'You've got a good lass there.'

'Don't I know it!' Sam shifted awkwardly. 'You think I'd be used to her having to go into pubs and stuff and do the ordering, but it still feels wrong.'

'That's because you're a gentleman. I used to have to do the same for Bert. You can imagine how that went down in the 1940s and 50s! Bert was teased constantly for it. Drove him mad. Still…'

Sam could well imagine. Not for the first time was grateful that, if he had to have seen hell, he'd witnessed it in the twenty-first century not the twentieth. 'So, how is the old boy? I couldn't hear much of what I was told in the car.'

While Tina was busy ordering, Mabel explained to Sam about Bert not being in the Coleridge ward after all, and how Jamie had taken care of them before going off home at the end of what they'd discovered was a twelve-hour shift.

'You'd never have known; the lad was as lively as anything.'

Sam laughed. 'So was I when I worked twelve hours at a time when I was young. Not so good at it now!'

'Why do you think Bert and I nap in the afternoons between helping with lunch and dinner at the manor?' Mabel smiled, but the sigh that escaped her was unmissable.

Sam gave her hand a supportive squeeze. 'But Bert was in

good spirits? His breathing an occasional issue rather than a crisis?'

'The problem is that they're concerned it might get worse not better. That's why he's staying in hospital, so if he does have a bad moment like he did on Friday night, then they can help him instantly. Although he's upbeat, you can tell it costs Bert to speak for too long. Not that it stops him of course!'

Tina returned with a tray laden with cutlery and drinks. 'We timed that well. Worst of lunch rush is over and the diners for evening meals aren't here yet.' She slid the tray onto the table. 'I ordered ham, egg and chips all round. Hope that's alright.'

'Perfect.' Mabel picked up her tea and cradled it to her chest. 'Thank you both. I don't know what I'd have done about seeing Bert today if you weren't here.'

'Our pleasure.' Sam looked at Tina, who immediately inclined her head; agreeing with what she was sure Sam was about to say.

'One of us will get you over to see Bert every day until he's home.'

'But you can't. I mean, thank you, but Mill Grange needs you. The next round of visitors arrives tomorrow. I couldn't ask you to interrupt the business for me. Bert wouldn't like that either.'

'You didn't ask,' Sam passed the cutlery around the table, 'we offered. If Tina or I can't bring you, then Tom or Helen will. We can all drive and we all adore you and Bert.'

'But—'

Mabel's objections were interrupted by the arrival of their food. After which Tina said, 'Did you tell Sam about Bert trying to chat up the old dear in the bed next to him?'

Chuckling, Mabel speared a chip. 'Made my day that did. The old fool is still after the redheads!'

'But it was *dyed* – and a ghastly shade of red at that. It clashed alarmingly with her white wrinkled skin.'

'She was laughing when we left her though, and she wasn't when we arrived.' Mabel looked proudly across at Tina. 'My Bert did that.'

'Unlike the public baths in many Roman towns, the bath suite at Birdlip would have been an exclusive place for specifically invited guests of high social status. We think of social networking as a new idea, but the Romans knew the value of it centuries ago. Bathing with your peers in places such as this, would have been an essential part of that networking process, enhancing business opportunities and improving personal status.

'This area is part of the later phase of the villa's development. We are looking at workmanship from the fourth century, whereas over there,' Thea waved a hand to the left, 'the earlier phases of the sites can be seen, with the outhouses and, what we expect, are servant's quarters.'

Thea knelt to the tiny section of mosaic, picking up a soft brush and sweeping it over the tiles. 'As you can see, Shaun and I have had the privilege of uncovering the first few rows of mosaic tesserae, or tiles, and I'm pleased to report that, so far, they are largely intact. Naturally, it is too soon to guess what pattern might be revealed, or indeed if we're going to be lucky and have an undisturbed mosaic beneath us, but we *could* ultimately be looking at something in the same style as at Chedworth. If that's the case, it may even have been created by the same artist.' Thea looked directly into the camera, 'Although, I'm getting ahead of myself. Let's get back to the digging, and see what appears next.'

'And cut!'

Before Julian could tell Thea how fantastic she was, Shaun stepped down into the bath house, next to her and engulfed her in a hug. 'That was brilliant. Well done, love.'

'Yes indeed.' Julian brushed his hands together briskly. 'Right then, if you could just put our guest historian down, Shaun, I need you to crack on. Let's get some more hands in here and get this mosaic opened to the eyes of the world.'

Twisting on the balls of his feet, Julian suddenly looked back at the two archaeologists. 'Drinks on me tonight, Thea. You deserve a treat after doing such a flawless job today.'

Fourteen

Tuesday March 24th

Holding the plans of the Roman fortlet before her, Helen stood at the head of the site and examined its layout. The publishers needed to know if she was going to write the book, or not, soon. But apart from Tom, she still hadn't told anyone about the offer.

Tom.

The smile that had more or less lived on her face for the past few days widened as Helen twisted her stance. She could see him and his companions working across the fake trench on the other side of the site.

Helen knew Sam and Tina had noticed her new contentment, but she and Tom had agreed to say nothing about their walk on Saturday, nor the kiss that had followed on the clapper bridge. Gentle at first, tentative, it had quickly turned into something urgent and charged with passion. A kiss that had lasted so long, a rather embarrassed dog walker had been obliged to loudly cough at them, so they would stop and let him cross the river.

With the arrival of the new guests yesterday and being short staffed, they'd had little time alone since then. But that was alright. Now they'd finally admitted how they felt, time was on their side.

Except, it wasn't.

When she'd first taken her sabbatical, seven months had felt an age, now the days towards her departure date were ebbing away. Soon, she'd have to depart for Bath, ready to resume her post after the Easter weekend.

Two hours away. As she thought about how far she was going to be from Mill Grange, and how long the working hours she was returning to were, Helen wondered why she hadn't just dragged Tom into bed with her on Saturday night. The attic had been empty but for them. No one would have known, and she'd certainly wanted to, but her insecurities had stopped her. No man had seen her body in years. What if he hated what he saw when – if – the moment came?

'Cupid, if you're listening out there, I think it's high time you thought about the consequences of your actions!' Muttering as she tried to concentrate on the job in hand, Helen found herself smiling again. It might feel like she was freefalling without a parachute, but she still felt more alive than she had in years.

'Focus, woman!' Helen pulled her phone from her pocket. Knowing she should have spoken to Sam and Tina about the book offer already, she sent Sam a quick text asking for a meeting when he was back from seeing Bert. Then she sent Thea a text asking if she could call when it was safe to talk away from the cameras.

She was about to start a list of ideas for the book based on what she'd discussed with Tom, when he appeared with one of the guests. Cherry, Helen thought her name was. There were three women staying at Mill Grange that week, all with the same hairstyles and uniform of jeans and t-shirts. To her shame, Helen was having trouble remembering which was which.

'Helen.' Tom raised a hand in greeting. 'Cherry is proving a natural at this archaeology lark. Anything she could do up on the real site?'

'Certainly is.' Helen got up, gesturing to the far side of the fortlet. 'Come on, let's take a look.'

Helen tried not to mind the flirty thank you Cherry offered Tom before he returned to his other charges. *You have to accept he's a good-looking man. People are going to find him attractive.*

Ten minutes later, as she knelt next to Cherry in a trench on the outer edge of the site, Helen's phone buzzed with the arrival of a text. Expecting it to be Thea or Sam, Helen mumbled an apology, and checking Cherry was happy with what she was doing, stepped away to check her message.

It was from Tom.

I really fancy you. Just saying. Tom x

Ajay jabbed a fork towards the note stuck up on the wall.
'Have you seen this, Shaun?'

Picking up his pint, Shaun joined his friend on the far side of The Carthorse's function room. The hastily put together poster, written on a page ripped from a notebook, announced that Julian had arranged a meal for the main presenters on Friday night.

'Just the main presenters?' Shaun frowned. 'And this was the man who didn't want me and Thea to chat on telly together in case it patronised the viewers! What about the archaeologists? They're the ones that do most of the work around here.'

Sharing his indignation Ajay ran a finger over the words, main presenters. 'I'd like to know what *main* actually means. Is it Julian, you and Thea, or is it me and Andy too?'

Shaun grunted. 'It means you two as well. At least it ought to. But I have a feeling Julian would prefer it if you weren't there, or me for that matter.'

'You still think he's after Thea?'

'If he isn't, then he's got a funny way of showing it.'

'Mabel, how wonderful to see you!' Helen came in through the kitchen door, Cherry at her side. 'Cherry, meet Mabel, preparer of the finest lunches in all of England.'

'Daft girl.' Mabel swatted away the compliment. 'Bacon rolls are almost ready and there's fresh coffee in the pot.' She paused when she saw the state of the new arrivals' hands. 'For those who have scrubbed enough mud off their hands!'

Cherry laughed as Helen pointed the way through the kitchen to the downstairs washroom. Waiting while her charge got cleaned up, Helen asked, 'How was Bert this morning?'

'Much the same.' Mabel turned away from the Aga. 'His main problem is boredom. He isn't one to sit and do nothing, but every time he tries to move, he starts coughing and that makes his breathing tricky.'

'Which makes him weaker?'

Mabel nodded. 'I hate seeing him in that horrid mask.'

'I'm down to take you to the hospital tomorrow. Would you like me to come in with you? I'd like to see him. Your conversation must be running a bit dry by now.'

'Would you?' Mabel sat at the kitchen table. She looked worn out.

'Of course.' Helen held her hands up, so she didn't drop mud on the table. 'Forgive me saying so, but should you be here, Mabel? You seem tired.'

'I am.' Mabel twisted her wedding ring around her finger. 'But sitting around at home all day, just waiting... Waiting for the hospital to call, waiting for the next trip to the hospital, and then not knowing what to say when I get there... Here, at least, I'm useful.'

Hearing Cherry's footsteps along the corridor, Helen quickly said, 'I'm glad you're here, and not just because of your delicious bacon sandwiches.'

'Thank you,' Mabel whispered into Helen's ear. 'Good to see that you and Tom have sorted yourselves out at last.'

'How did you know? We haven't told anyone.' Helen blushed bright red.

'I'm old, not blind.'

'We aren't ready to tell anyone yet. Would you mind not...?'

Mabel winked. 'Don't worry, my lips are sealed.'

Getting to her feet as Cherry came in, Mabel busied herself into hostess mode, as Helen retreated to the bathroom.

Making sure his workforce was happily tucking into their lunch, Tom hailed Sam as he saw him leaving the walled garden, an empty sack of chicken feed in one hand, and a clipboard and pen in the other.

'Gertrude and co. alright today?'

Sam shook out the empty sack. 'Wondering why they don't get fed more often and insisting on front row seats at the wedding. Usual stuff.'

'Sounds about right.' Tom grinned as he gestured to the kitchen. 'Bacon sandwich and coffee? Or are you in a tea mood?'

'Tea would be great thanks. The sandwich goes without saying.' Sam gestured to the nearest picnic bench. 'I've got time for that chat now if you have?'

Having collected their lunches, Tom headed to the table. Until now it hadn't occurred to him that Sam might say no to Dylan staying at Mill Grange until he'd found somewhere to rent. Now the chat he'd asked for was about to start, Tom realised he'd taken it for granted Sam would be okay with it. He hadn't even got round to asking Mabel about good letting agents.

'So, how can I help?'

Tom passed Sam his sandwich and decided to dive straight in with his request. 'I'm after a favour. A big one.'

'Go on.'

'Sue has agreed I should have joint custody of Dylan.'

'That's brilliant news. I'm so chuffed for you.' Sam patted his friend on the back. 'How can I help?'

'It's a case of living arrangements. I'll need to find a place to rent for the two of us, but until then…'

'Until then you'll need to have Dylan with you here, is that it?'

Tom took sanctuary in his sandwich for a moment, before saying, 'I know it's a hell of a cheek, but what do you think? If you'd allow me to have Dylan here for half the week, would it work? The house isn't designed for children, and although he is used to the place from his visits, it would mean me having to fetch him from school during the afternoon, which means finishing work early some days, or at least breaking off from it for a while. Then Dylan would need watching while I am working and...'

As he heard his own words, the reality of the situation he'd agreed to with Sue sank in properly for the first time. This wasn't just a question of Dylan sleeping in the spare twin bed in his room now and then. This would affect his whole life and work, and therefore the running of Mill Grange. He found himself holding his breath as he waited for Sam to speak.

'When does this arrangement with Sue start?'

'April the fifth.' Tom didn't dare meet Sam's eyes.

'In theory I'm in favour. We'd need to work out how to make sure the archaeological training wasn't interrupted, so let's have a group meeting. Helen can stand in for Thea. I owe her a meeting as she asked for a chat this morning as well.'

Tom had stopped listening to Sam as he repeated, 'Stand in for Thea?'

'Well yes, we only have Helen for a few more weeks. Once Thea is back, she'll be the one who covers the trenches while you do the school run.'

'Of course.' Tom's insides clenched. *She really is leaving soon.*

'You alright, mate?'

Tom picked up his coffee mug. 'To tell you the truth, I feel guilty for putting this on you, especially when we're short-handed and you have a wedding to organise.'

'Not a bit of it. We all love Dylan. Anyway,' Sam peered over his shoulder to make sure they weren't being overheard, 'it isn't just the wedding we have to organise. I have something else in mind, and I'm going to need your help.'

Fifteen

Friday March 27th

Mabel engulfed Dylan's hand in hers as they walked through the clinical corridors, with Tom right behind them.

'I've never been to a hospital before.' Dylan stayed close to Mabel as they wove their way through the corridors towards the wards for afternoon visiting.

Tom laughed. 'You have, but you won't remember.'

'Have I?'

'Of course. You were born in a hospital.'

'This one, Dad?'

'No, but they all look pretty much the same. You were born in Swindon.' Tom ruffled his son's hair. 'Best day of my life.'

'Why, what happened?'

Mabel laughed despite the cluster of nervous apprehension gathering in her gut as they approached Bert's ward. 'Because you were born, Dylan.'

'Oh. That's nice.' He looked at his dad. 'Are we almost there yet?'

'Next corridor.'

'It's a long walk.' Mabel looked apologetically at Tom. 'Like I said in the car, I don't think they'll let all three of us see Bert. They're strict about the two at the bedside rule.'

'It's fine. You can give Bert my love and I'll go and find us some coffee for afterwards.'

'Coffee! Yuk.' Dylan pulled a face. 'Can I have orange juice? Mum forgot to put one in my school lunch today.'

'Did she?' Tom frowned. 'Did you find a drink alright?'

'There's always water.'

'Right. Okay, coffee and orange juice.'

'Thanks, Dad.'

'We'll ask though, just in case we can all go in.' Mabel smiled. 'I'm looking forward to seeing my old boy's face when he sees you, young fella.'

Dylan tugged anxiously at Mabel's arm. 'Bert will be okay, won't he? He's my friend.'

Looking helplessly at Tom, Mabel opened her mouth, but no words would come out. How could she make a promise it wasn't in her power to keep?

Seeing the emotions battle on her face, Tom picked up Dylan. 'Why don't you go and book in at reception, Mabel? We'll wait here.'

As the relieved old lady joined the short queue, Tom sat on a plastic chair and took a deep breath. 'Bert is going to be pleased to see you, Dylan, but you must remember he is very poorly. His voice might sound a bit strange. He might even be wearing a special mask to help him breathe.'

Dylan's usual red cheeks paled. 'Mabel said he was tired a lot.'

'That's because all of his energy's going into getting better.' Tom held his son close. 'You remember when you had a cold last year, and you wanted to sleep all the time?'

'Yes. I felt yucky.'

'Well Bert feels like that, but much worse.'

Dylan was quiet for a while before he said, 'We need to buy him some soup and chocolate.'

Tom laughed. 'Do we?'

'Yes. Harriet said her dad always gives her soup for a bad throat and chocolate for getting better energy.'

'Does she?' A stab of jealousy hit Tom that he told himself he had no reason to feel. 'You like Harriet looking after you when Mum's busy?'

'She's fun.' Dylan looked over at Mabel. 'Will it be alright, Dad? Does Bert's mask look scary?'

'A bit, but it's helping him.'

As Mabel joined them, she stretched out a hand for Dylan to take. 'Sorry, Tom, I couldn't persuade them that Dylan was only little, so didn't count as a whole person.'

Tom laughed at Dylan's expression. 'I am a whole person!'

'Mabel meant you didn't take up much room,' Tom said with a wink. 'Now, Dylan, I want you to take care of Mabel. Make sure she behaves herself. Okay?'

Bert's expression changed from sombre to overjoyed, as he saw Dylan towing Mabel along behind him.

'Well here's a sight for sore eyes! An afterschool visitor.' Bert patted the side of the bed, as Dylan let go of Mabel's hand and scooted forward. 'Quick, lad, climb up for a cuddle before the nurse spots us and I get told off for allowing you to crease the linen.'

Dylan giggled as he cuddled up to Bert. 'You won't really get told off, will you?'

'Nah.' Warmth seeped into Bert's bones as Mabel sat beside him.

'No mask today then, I was about to warn Dylan that you might look like Darth Vader.'

'Ohh! Did you really look like him, Bert?'

'Sort of, but my mask is white. See?' Bert pointed to the machine behind his head. 'It makes me sound a bit like him.' Enjoying Dylan's giggles, Bert said, 'I want to hear all about school and Mill—' He broke off suddenly. A sharp rattling cough took him unawares, making him shudder.

'Bert?' Dylan turned to Mabel, jumping off the bed and into her arms.

'It's alright. That's what pneumonia does, it makes your breathing weird and sometimes you cough. Sounds worse than it is.'

'Okay.' Dylan didn't look convinced as the old lady held him tight.

Mabel wasn't convinced either, but as she held both the young boy's and the old man's hands, she prayed she was right. 'Why don't you tell Bert your good news while he's getting his breath back?'

Trying to smile through his wheezing, Bert concentrated on the boy's voice, determined not to have to use the mask.

Shyly, not sure Bert would hear him properly, Dylan said, 'I'm going to be living at Mill Grange sometimes. I'll be with Mum half the time and Dad half the time. I'm so excited. I'll be sharing a room with Dad until Helen goes back to Bath, then I'll have her room until we can find a home nearby. Can you imagine, Bert? I'm going to sleep in a room that's ancient! People used to sleep in there before even you and Mabel were born.'

As Mabel chuckled at the boy's concept of ancient history, Bert squeezed Dylan's free hand. A little husky at first, he mastered his voice. 'That's wonderful.'

'I'm glad you're pleased. Dad said if I was a good boy and asked nicely, you might read me a bedtime story sometimes.'

Bert took his time, before saying, 'That's something worth getting better fast for.' He beamed at Mabel, who was looking at the child sat between them as if he was a miracle of hope.

'Seems to me, Dylan, that I need some magic medicine to get me better fast.'

'Oh I can sort that out for you easily, Bert.' Dylan's expression became endearingly serious as he said, 'Soup and bars of chocolate. They always make everything better. Harriet's dad says so. Shall I ask the nurse to fetch you some?'

'How was Bert?'

Sam was washing down wheelbarrows outside the tool store when Tom parked in Mill Grange's driveway.

'I didn't get to see him myself. They're strict on the visitor numbers. I thought he'd enjoy Dylan's company more than mine.'

'Where is Dylan?' Sam gestured towards the empty car seat.

'I dropped him off at Sue's and then I took Mabel home too. She was worn out, bless her.'

Sam nodded. 'She fell asleep on the way back from the Musgrove with Tina yesterday.'

Tom smiled. 'I can report however, that according to my son, who did not stop talking about Bert all the way home, he's on good form. Still having coughing attacks, but not so bad or so often. He sounds like Darth Vader on occasion apparently.'

'Is that so?' Sam peered around the door to the store, to make sure Helen wasn't there. 'You know I asked for your help on a secret matter the other day?'

'Yes. I've looked into some of that by the way. It's possible but pricy.'

'Right.' Sam rubbed his hands together. 'Well, there's something else I'd like us to plot and plan.'

Tom's eyebrows rose. 'I'm beginning to think you're missing your undercover work in the forces more than you realise!'

'On this occasion, I'm less confident my idea will be well received. I need to talk to Thea about it really, but as you and Helen get on well and work together, I thought you'd have more insight than me.'

On hearing himself mentioned in the same breath as Helen, Tom's stomach gave a light jolt. He hoped he wouldn't give his feelings away. 'What's this all about then?'

'You know Helen is leaving us on the tenth, well, it's her birthday on the twelfth. Her fortieth. Tina thinks Helen would secretly like to celebrate, but at the same time, she'd like to hide under a stone and pretend it isn't happening.'

'Right, so…?'

'So, if we are going to arrange a party we need to get on and do it, or it'll get lost in the wedding plans that somehow aren't quite being made, what with one thing and another.'

Tom ran a hand over his mouth as he tried to work out if Sam was merely asking his opinion as to whether Helen would like a party, or if he was being asked to do the organising. Buying thinking time, he said, 'That reminds me, I measured the plot between the chickens and the greenhouse, I scribbled the figures down and posted the piece of paper into your tent before I collected Mabel and Dylan. It should be big enough for a marquee.'

'Fantastic, thanks, Tom.' Sam looked thrilled. 'Tina wants to get married where the chickens can watch.'

'Seriously?'

'Yep.' Sam laughed at Tom's expression. 'We got to know each other while we built the chicken coop for Gertrude and her pals. Seems only right they should be there.'

'Can't argue with that.' Tom laughed. 'So is marquee hiring next on the to-do list?'

'It is.' Sam's eyes fell to the clipboard of lists propped up against the side of the store. 'We had a guy here last year who supplied them for the open day. Nice and local, so I'd like to use him again.'

'Do you want me to call him, or do you have it covered?'

'Thanks, Tom, but I'm okay on that.' Sam upturned the final wheelbarrow needing to be washed down. 'Anyway, about Helen. I'm going to talk to her about the excavation in a minute. It's only a fortnight until she goes. I want everything labelled and written up, so we know where we're at until Thea comes home.'

Tom looked out across the garden. 'It'll be strange without her here.'

'It will.' Sam hesitated as he noted a hint of wistfulness in Tom's voice, and for the first time wondered if Tina's conviction that he and Helen should be a couple was correct. 'Her arrival was unexpected, but I'm honestly not sure we'd have managed so well without her.'

'Then maybe you should ask her to stay?'

Sixteen

Friday March 27th

It didn't feel right sitting in the back room of The Carthorse, tucking into something off the gastro pub's a la carte menu, when the rest of the workforce were stuffed into the bar and pub's small restaurant on a busy Friday night. Catching Shaun's eye as she lifted a forkful of perfectly cooked Beef Wellington to her lips, Thea could see he wasn't happy about it either.

Shaun hasn't been happy about much since we got here.

Thea's sigh merged into a suppressed giggle as she saw Ajay and Andy turn away from the table for a second and roll their eyes at each other, as Julian started talking about the show's ratings. It had been a relief to find the geophysics boys had been invited as well. Shaun had been convinced it would just be himself, Julian and Thea; and that Julian would insist on sitting next to Thea. When she'd explained that, as the tables in the function room were circular, and that, if there were just three of them, she'd have to sit next to Julian, Shaun had gone quiet on the subject.

Thea, on the other hand, had been sure the AA would be invited. It would have looked odd if they'd been excluded. Ajay and Andy had been with *Landscape Treasures* from the start, and were household names within the show's fan base.

Julian was tucking into his chilli roasted salmon with gusto, talking between each mouthful about his plans for the show now they'd uncovered a mosaic every bit as impressive as those in Chedworth and Cirencester. His words, all revolving around how much kudos the find would bring *Landscape Treasures*, were becoming white noise. Thea was happily zoning out, when she suddenly heard her name mentioned.

'Have you ever uncovered a mosaic as impressive as the one we have here, Thea?'

'I have actually. I was part of a team that excavated one in Africa when I was a student. That was equally stunning, but different of course. Cultural influences can often be seen within mosaic designs. It was in a mausoleum on the edge of a—'

Interrupting, Julian flapped away the idea that the mosaic could have been anything like as good as this one. 'Impressive it may well have been, but I bet the design wasn't as good. A dolphin, splashed right across the bath floor – if you'll excuse the pun! And made from locally sourced stone tiles as well. What were the chances?'

Thea didn't answer. She had a feeling Julian wouldn't want to hear that local stone was the obvious source for the tiles, nor would he want to hear that a dolphin design had been used on similar mosaics before, although not on such a scale.

As Julian waffled on, Thea found herself wondering if Shaun had been right about him all along. Not concerning his feelings for her, that was old fashioned jealousy as far as she was concerned. But, despite the impression he'd first given her on meeting, the fact Julian didn't care about the archaeology was becoming clearer all the time. He was here to advance his career. Organising the television coverage of the discovery of one of the most important mosaic finds in decades would do him no harm whatsoever. One glance at her friends told her they felt the same.

'Where in Africa, Thea?' Ajay asked, in an attempt to stop Julian's monologue.

'Lepti Minus. It's near Sousse in Tunisia. Well, near-ish.' Raising her wine glass to her lips, Thea added, 'Incredible place. I was lucky enough to be part of a team working on an entire Romano-African city, rather than a single building complex. There were baths, and villas and a forum and—'

'Yes, that sounds great, Thea.' Julian laid down his knife and fork and immediately picked up the dessert menu. 'But your work ten years or so ago isn't going to make any impression on our ratings now. They aren't bad, but they could be better.' Julian sat back with a self-satisfied belch. 'No, this mosaic couldn't have popped up at a better time, and it's all thanks to you, Thea.'

'Hardly.' Thea's palms tingled with unease. 'I opened the first section with Shaun.' She turned and toasted her colleagues. 'It was the AA here, who confirmed its whereabouts with the geophysics.'

'And the farmer who rang the show and told us about the finds he'd been ploughing up might have helped,' Andy muttered.

'Not to mention the aerial photograph of the place taken in 1976!' Ajay threw in. 'And the team from Cotswold Archaeology, who did the initial assessment and have been helping us ever since.'

Shaun nodded. 'And while we're at it, Julian, Thea and I may have taken back the first layers of the bath house, but it was the guys crammed into the other room, getting in the way of the locals, who did most of the work. So why the hell aren't they in here too?' He shook his head. 'Phil had his faults as a producer, but he never put us, or himself, above the team.'

'Okay, okay!' Julian held up his hands. 'Give me a break, guys! This was supposed to be a treat from me, to say thanks for all your hard work. A pat on the back.'

'Pat on the back?' Shaun bit back his temper. 'We're doing our job, Julian. That's it. Yes, it would be great to celebrate when the dig is done. To raise a pint with all the people involved, but most of those people aren't here. What did you really want to talk to us about that couldn't be shared with the rest of the workforce?'

'Well, I—'

'We are a team, Julian.' Shaun lowered his voice as Thea rested a supportive hand on his thigh. 'That's what makes *Landscape Treasures* work, why we're asked to keep coming back by the television company year after year. Nothing lasts forever, and one day we'll be axed, but while…' He trailed off. 'Hang on, you were talking about the show's ratings just now. Is that what this is all about, buttering us up before you tell us this is the final series?'

The AA lowered their pints as one.

'I can assure you that it is not.' Julian smiled, but Thea noticed that it failed to reach his eyes.

'But you do have a reason?' she asked, 'For this get together including just us, I mean. After all, I'm only a guest expert. If you need to talk about the show's future, maybe I ought to leave you to it?'

As Thea pushed her chair back to go, Julian's hand shot out and briefly held hers against the table, before letting go and tapping it lightly with his fingertips. 'Not at all. You should stay.'

Glad to see Thea remove her hand with speed, Shaun asked, 'So what did you want to tell us?'

Lowering his glass, Julian leaned forward. 'The word on the wire is that our main rival, *Treasure Hunters*, is out to recruit a new lead presenter.'

'So?' Shaun looked at the others, who all shrugged.

'*Treasure Hunters* are looking for someone to rival you, Shaun.' Julian refilled his glass, 'Doesn't that bother any of you?'

Ajay, Shaun, and Andy shook their heads as Thea asked, 'Why should that worry them, Julian? They don't work for *Treasure Hunters*. And everyone knows *Treasure Hunters* is the show that is trying to be *Landscape Treasures*, but without the budget.'

Shaun nodded as he remembered their brush with *Treasure Hunters'* dodgy excavation acquirement tactics in the summer. 'We've dealt with them before. Our ratings knock them under the table, and they aren't on such a well-watched or funded channel.'

Julian rested back in his chair. 'Well, I wouldn't be quite

so relaxed about that if I were you. Word is that along with the new presenter, they're switching to a better channel.'

Shaun sat forward a little. 'Which one?'

'I don't know, but there are rumours of Channel Four, or even BBC Two.'

Ajay winced. 'Okay, so that's more serious.'

Andy wiped a piece of bread around the gravy left on his plate. 'Good thing we've found an incredibly important mosaic then, isn't it?'

Not wanting to be on her own, but not sure she could face being cooped up in Shaun's campervan with him, when he was bound to want to rant about Julian, Thea suggested a walk around Birdlip village. She slipped her palm into Shaun's as they strolled past the pub and along the main street, between picture book Cotswolds cottages, complete with thatched roofs and stone walled gardens.

'I know you can't stand the man, but try not to let Julian get under your skin.'

'Difficult not to.' Shaun raked his free hand through his hair as they walked, turning the gesture into a wave, as someone spotted Shaun Cowlson 'off the telly' passing their garden. 'Did you see how he patted your hand?'

Thea shuddered. 'It was like being licked by a wet haddock.'

Shaun laughed, as he put his arm around Thea. 'I've been an idiot about him on that score, haven't I?'

'At last, the penny drops!' She hugged him close as they walked through a narrow pathway, leading to a duck pond. 'Do you think what he said about *Treasure Hunters* is true?'

'Can't see why he'd make it up.' Shaun scowled. 'They put together a good show. Okay, *Treasure Hunters* don't have the budget, but they are all good archaeologists. I wonder why the current presenter is leaving? Gareth, his name is. Nice bloke.'

'Maybe he isn't leaving so much as being replaced. New format, new channel, etc. You know, like they did for *The Great British Bake Off.*'

'Possible.'

Shaun led them to a seat by the pond. It was an almost classic circle, with reeds and lily pads tastefully growing to one side, as if whoever built it wanted the pond to look like a children's drawing. The ducks were all grouped beneath the reeds, clearly surprised to have late night visitors, but not intrigued enough to bother dabbling over in the hope of being fed.

'What I don't understand, is why Julian thought only the four of us should hear about *Treasure Hunter's* plans?'

'Perhaps it's not public knowledge yet?' Thea laid her head on his shoulder. 'We hadn't heard had we?'

'No, but we're on a dig in the middle of the countryside with little Wi-Fi.'

'Fair enough.' Thea watched the water ripple as a fish brushed the surface before descending to its nightly rest. 'Providing *Landscape Treasure* isn't axed, I can't see the problem.'

'And if it is, I'll come to Mill Grange and be your right-hand man.'

Thea smiled. 'Would you now?'

'Absolutely. Perhaps it's time I gave it up anyway? I'm not exactly a youngster, and telly companies prefer women presenters now.'

Sitting up, Thea studied Shaun's face. 'You don't want to give it up though, do you? I thought you loved your job.'

'I do. It's the best job ever, but I can't see myself working with Julian for long. I've never wanted to punch anyone so much in my life.'

'He does invite that feeling.'

Shaun kissed her forehead. 'Shall we change the subject?'

'Yes!'

Shaun laughed. 'Looking forward to going back to Mill Grange for Easter?'

'Hugely! We'll be able to sleep together in a proper bed for a start.'

'And then there's Mabel's bacon rolls.'

'You are obsessed with those!'

'True.' Shaun poked her ribs. 'How long after we're back do you think it'll be before you, Tina and Helen disappear to Sybil's for a cheese scone or seven?'

'Ohh, maybe half an hour?'

Seventeen

Friday March 27th

'And how would it work exactly?

Sam looked almost as proud as Tom had done when Helen'd told him about the offer to write a book.

'To begin with, it's a case of working out how to best structure the book, something Tom's already made a few suggestions about.' Helen face coloured. 'I hope you don't mind that I spoke to Tom first. I wasn't convinced I was capable of writing one in the first place, and you have so much on your plate at the moment. I didn't want to bother you with it until I knew what needed doing.'

'I'm glad Tom helped you decide to write it. It's a great idea and, thinking with my business head on, it would be fantastic for Mill Grange. Not to mention your career.' Sam beamed. 'Have you spoken to Thea about it?'

'I sent a text asking what she thought of the idea, but I haven't heard back yet.'

'Probably the mobile signal issue. I haven't had a reply from Shaun about a few ideas I've had for this place either.'

Not wanting to elaborate, Sam said, 'If you're sure you have time, then I'd be delighted for you to do it, which brings me nicely onto something I'd like to discuss with you.'

'Go on?'

'Your time with us is almost up.'

Helen raised her eyes from the cup of coffee she was holding to the excavation they were sat next to. 'It's gone so fast. I'll be sorry to leave.'

'And we'll be sorry to lose you.' Getting up, Sam beckoned for Helen to join him on the fortlet's west side. 'Just look at this. We'd never have got so far without you. The book you're going to write will be quite a story.'

'You get that it'll be non-fiction, right?'

'Figure of speech.' Sam looked beyond Upwich Fortlet to the false dig on the other side of the site. 'Tom tells me he's bringing at least one guest over to dig with you each day now.'

'I've had three today. One, Cherry, would like to come back to learn more. What with Pete from last week, and that deaf chap the week before – sorry his name escapes me.'

'Ian.'

'Yes, Ian. We're averaging a very good rebooking rate.'

'Assuming they do rebook.'

'Well, yes.' Helen scanned the view before her, taking in the row of trestle tables covered in buckets and bowls for cleaning finds, and the piles of clipboards for recording information. 'I'm going to miss getting my hands dirty.'

'Not relishing going back to sitting in an office all day?'

'It'll be great to see the staff and the Baths themselves. It's such a stunning place. You only have to be away a short time before you see a difference in it, even though, quintessentially, it doesn't change.'

Not missing the sigh that Helen tried to hide, Sam pushed a little further. 'And you'll be looking forward to going back to your own home.'

'More of my own space will be nice, no offence to your good self.'

'None taken.' Sam headed back to the bench and sat down, picking up his mug of tea as he did so. 'This book, I'm assuming there's a deadline?'

'They want the first draft by Christmas; which seems frighteningly soon.'

'Which begs another question, when will you find the time to write it? Your hours at the Baths are longer than those here, aren't they?'

'Well yes, although I don't suppose we're off duty much here when we have guests.'

'That's true.' Sam grinned. 'Next week we'll have two vegans with us. Mabel's going to wish she hadn't come back to do the lunches.'

Helen laughed. 'She does have a bit of a thing about vegans. I've noticed her tut rate increases when she can't use cheese or butter in the meals.'

'It'll help keep her mind off Bert.' Sam took a sip of tea. 'Helen, I'm going to ask you a question, and I want you to promise me to think about it, okay?'

'Okay.' Helen clutched her cup tighter, she had a feeling she knew what he was going to ask, and had no idea how she'd answer.

'I was talking with Tom and—'

'Tom?'

'Yes, is that alright? He is your colleague.'

'Sorry, of course it is. I shouldn't have interrupted. What did you want to ask me?'

'Would you like to stay?' Sam held up a hand before Helen could give any sort of answer. 'Sooner or later the dig here will be finished. Then there'll be work to do on preserving it and, ultimately, opening it to the public. Tom will need help running the test site, and he'll need someone to secure him placements on real digs for those who decide to do the archaeology certificate scheme we intend to run. It'll be great for those guests who want to take the skills they have developed here to the next level. We've had plenty of interest, and once the wedding is over, I intend to advertise it properly. So we'll need tutors. Tom won't be able to do it all.'

'I don't know what to say. I'd like to stay obviously, but—'

'I can't pay you as much as the Baths plus, you have a home and life in Bath to consider. That's why I said I didn't expect an answer now.'

Taking a large mouthful of coffee, Helen let it ease her throat. 'Does anyone else know about your offer?'

'Just Tina.'

'Not Tom or Thea and Shaun?'

'No. Tom brought the subject up, but that was after Tina and I had discussed it.'

'It wasn't his idea then?'

'I suppose he had the idea, but so did we – independently of him. Is that a problem?'

'Not at all. I'm flattered you want me to stay.' Helen's cheeks went beetroot. 'Sam, would you mind if we kept this secret for now? Just between you, Tina and me while I think about it.'

'Certainly.'

Hoping Sam wouldn't ask why she didn't want Tom to know he'd asked her to stay, Helen changed the subject. 'How are the wedding plans going?'

Saturday March 28ᵗʰ

'Why don't you come with me?' Tom murmured into Helen's ear as he kissed the side of her neck.

Suppressing the feeling that she'd love to come and collect Dylan from Tiverton, Helen murmured as Tom hands ran down her arms, 'Because Sue wouldn't like it.'

'She probably wouldn't know. She never comes out of the house with Dylan. Anyway, our friendship isn't a secret.'

Helen took his hands, halting their journey towards her chest. 'Unlike snogging in the store room when no one's looking.'

'If we don't stop soon, I can't vouch for that being all we do.'

'Is that so?'

'And don't pretend you don't want to, Miss Rodgers, you give yourself away,' Tom murmured into her ear. 'Honestly, woman, it's only been two hours since we made love. No one told me Roman historians could be so wanton.'

'We aren't, unless under the influence of former squaddies.'

'Is that so, and how many former squaddies do you know?'

Helen stuck out her tongue in lieu of a reply before reluctantly pulling away from Tom 'There's something I meant to tell you last night – and then again this morning, before we got, umm... distracted. Mabel knows. She guessed.'

'Oh.'

'Don't worry, she said she'd keep it under her hat.' Helen stroked a finger over Tom's chin. 'I feel awkward not telling people, but...'

'It's okay. I'm not ready to tell people either. I'm enjoying having you all to myself.'

Helen wrapped her arms around him, before forcing herself away. 'I'm glad you feel the same. Although, if Mabel guessed, the others might.'

'We'll cope with that if it happens.' Tom planted a kiss on the end of her nose. 'Well, if you won't come to Tiverton with me, will you join Dylan and me for scones at Sybil's? I've reserved a table.'

'For two?'

'Three, actually.' Tom ran his hands down her sides. 'Dylan has already asked me to invite you.'

A tender glow inflamed the heat that Tom had already started in her chest. 'Did he?'

'He likes you very much.'

'I like him too.'

'Good, because when we're ready to tell him, I really want us to be—'

The sound of a vehicle coming up the driveway and passing the store made them jump away from each other.

'We aren't expecting a delivery, are we?' Helen checked her clothing was in order as Tom headed for the door.

'Mabel didn't say so.' As he swung the stores double doors wide, Tom's face creased into panic. 'Sue!'

He was already running the short distance to where his ex had parked, before Helen had registered who'd arrived.

'Sue? What's going on? Has something happened to Dylan?'

His frantic enquiry was answered by the wave of a little hand out of the car's open back window. 'Hi, Dad!'

As Sue climbed out of the Mini, Helen stepped back into the shadows of the store-come-office, her heart thudding in her chest. She wasn't sure exactly what she'd expected Sue to look like, but the woman she could see standing in front of Tom was nothing like her preconceptions.

Rather than being a bit wild looking, with ripped jeans, piercings, and tattoos up her arms, Sue was tastefully turned out in a white shirt, black denims and a pair of new looking trainers. Her hair, which Tom had told her could be any colour under the sun, depending on her mood, was currently an ordinary deep brown, cut into a stylish bob. The only gesture towards any sort of outrageous behaviour was on the tips of her fingernails, which were painted bright orange.

Tom had described Sue as a woman who went from man to man, sponging her way along. That image didn't fit with the together looking female stood on the drive with their son.

Their son.

Reminding herself that Tom had said Sue had changed a lot lately, and was making more effort for their child, Helen took a deep breath. Tom hadn't lied to her. She'd made assumptions about the woman and been wrong. Helen attempted to quieten the sound of her racing pulse so she could hear what was going on outside.

'What are you doing here? I was about to leave to come and fetch Dylan.'

Scooping his son into his arms, Tom wondered if Helen was alright, and if she could hear them.

'We have some news don't we, Dylan? And we wanted to tell you together.'

'Yeah, Dad. I told Mum about those lovely scones. Can we take her for one, Dad? We could tell you our news then.'

'Well I don't know, I—'

'Aww, please, Dad. You did say we could go to Sybil's today.'

'Yes, I did, but…'

Sue looked up at the manor. 'Will you be sorry to leave here once you have custody of Dylan?'

'Custody?' Tom jumped on the word, as Sue hastily added, 'I meant partial custody.'

'Of course.' Tom followed Sue's eye line up to the manor's slate roof. 'I will, although we have been offered two bedrooms here while I hunt for somewhere suitable.'

Sue sniffed. 'I bet you haven't even started looking.'

'Always so ready to dismiss my efforts before you know what they are.'

Noting the fall of Dylan's smile, Sue shifted her feet. 'Sorry. Old habits.' She brushed her hands together. 'Will you take us for this scone then? Dylan has hardly stopped talking about them on the trip over. I think we owe him some proper family time, don't you?'

'Right,' Tom lowered Dylan to the ground, 'I just need to talk to someone first.'

Helen was ready for him when he arrived. Even before he'd opened his lips she whispered, 'Your son has something he wants to talk to his mum and dad about, you must go.'

Tom kissed her gently. 'You are something very special, Helen Rogers.'

As she watched them walk away, Helen picked up the stone Dylan had given her and squeezed it in her palm. The little boy was between his parents, each holding a hand so they could swing him along the road. Helen felt tears coat her eyes.

'Not that special, Tom. Dylan just forgot all about me.'

Eighteen

Saturday March 28th

Ajay leaned against the side of the catering truck next to Shaun, his arms folded across his chest, as they watched the local news reporter brief Thea.

'That should be you, mate.'

'Thea is our guest expert. She knows a lot more about Roman archaeology than me.'

Ajay glanced at Shaun. 'If that was the criteria, then it should be someone from Cotswold Archaeology stood there. The mosaic was made from local stone, very probably by a local artisan.'

'The Roman Baths aren't exactly miles away, Ajay.' Shaun dug his hands deep into his pockets. 'If Thea was still working there, the chances are that we would have been asking her, as a local expert, to come and look at the bath house anyway.'

'Maybe.' Ajay don't look convinced. 'I can't help thinking this is Julian pulling strings though.'

'But what for? Thea isn't interested in him and I've promised her I'll drop the subject.'

'Ummm.' Ajay switched his gaze to their producer, who was standing close to the news show's director. 'Julian doesn't strike me as a man who lets something like that get in the way... unless...'

'You left that hanging in the air.'

'Unless that isn't what he wants Thea for. Perhaps he has an eye on her for a completely different reason?'

'What reason?' Shaun ran a hand through his hair, ruffling his fringe. 'Getting her to talk more than me on camera might bruise my ego if it was anyone but Thea I suppose, but...' Shaun stopped talking and turned to face Ajay, an uncomfortable notion forming in his mind. 'You don't think...?'

Ajay was already nodding. '*Treasure Hunters* are getting a new look and a new presenter.'

'You think our TV company will want us to do the same?' Shaun's chest tightened. Chatting casually with Thea about not minding if he had to give up and work at Mill Grange was one thing, but being replaced by his girlfriend as head presenter was something else entirely.

He watched as the news show's makeup artist dabbed some powder over Thea's cheeks. Was that what Julian was planning? If so, what would be the point of working back at Mill Grange, if Thea wasn't there too?

Wiping her hands down her trousers, hoping her nerves didn't show on her face, Thea watched the director as the show's reporter spoke into the camera. Seconds later, he turned to face her, his microphone held out before him.

'I'm pleased to introduce Thea Thomas, guest expert at the latest *Landscape Treasures* dig to be filmed in the Cotswolds. As you will have heard from the main bulletin, the Roman villa at Birdlip, being excavated by the award-winning archaeology show, is proving to be one of the region's most important discoveries to date, not least because of the stunning mosaic uncovered in the villa's bath house. Before I ask about that in particular, Thea, can you tell us a little about mosaics in general?'

'Certainly.' Thea smiled into the camera as the late morning sunshine bathed her face. 'As you'll know, mosaics are made up of thousands of individual tiles, known as tesserae. These pieces, usually cube shaped, about a centimetre square each, would have been hand cut from local stone or marble, or even glass or baked clay. The practice of laying floors in this way began around the second century BC. The art of designing and laying a mosaic was a specialised one, and such artisans would have been highly prized...'

Sybil raised an eyebrow as she saw Tom and his son come in with someone who was certainly not Helen.

'Dylan, how wonderful to see you.' Sybil watched as the lad clutched a menu, doing his best to read as much as he could. 'Let me guess, either a strawberry milkshake and a great big cheese scone, or an orange juice and a great big cheese scone.'

Almost bouncing on his chair with pleasure, Dylan asked, 'Can I have the orange juice please?'

Sybil pretended to look shocked. 'No scone? Dylan, are you ill?'

Giggling, Dylan shook his head fast. 'And the greatest biggest cheese scone ever please.'

'Thank goodness for that!' Sybil winked. 'I was worried for a second.'

Still laughing, Dylan turned to the lady sat to his left. 'See, Mum, I told you Sybil would know what I wanted.'

'I'm Sue, pleased to meet you.'

Sybil shook the offered hand politely. 'Can I tempt you to anything?'

'Just a black coffee thanks.' Sue patted her non-existent waist. 'I have to be *so* careful.'

'How tiresome for you.' Sybil turned from the person sat in Helen's seat. 'Tom, usual?'

'Please.' He hadn't missed that Sue had offended Sybil by not wanting to eat. 'Could we have a pot of coffee like you do when I visit with Helen, please?'

'Of course.' Biting back the urge to ask where Helen was, Sybil was saved the bother by Sue.

'Who's Helen?'

Dylan came to Tom's rescue. 'I've told you about Helen, Mum. She works on the dig with Dad. She's really nice. Knows about the Romans and dinosaurs.'

Keeping her eyes fixed on Tom, Sue sounded suspicious. 'A work colleague then?'

'And a friend.' Feeling increasingly uncomfortable that Sue was here and Helen wasn't, Tom changed the subject. 'I believe you had something exciting to tell me?'

'Can I tell him, Mum?'

'Go for it.'

'Next week it's my very first parent's evening at school. Will you come Dad? Will you? Pleeeeease.'

As Dylan wriggled off his seat and scrambled onto his dad's lap, Tom felt his heart burst with love for his son. 'I wouldn't miss it for the world.' He looked up as Sue, who was looking at him oddly. 'What time is it?'

'Four o'clock. Will that be okay for you?'

'Blimey, I was expecting an evening appointment. I'm sure my parents, when they bothered to go to such things, dragged me back into school after seven.'

'I expect they did, but this is a new century. Anyway, I needed to book an early timeslot, as I'm going out afterwards.'

'So you chose four o'clock to suit you, even though you knew I don't finish work until six?'

'Well, I...'

Catching the worried expression on Dylan's face, Tom gave his son a smile. 'I will be there. I'll talk to Sam the minute we get back. I'm sure he won't mind.'

'You can meet my teacher! And you'll get to see my work. I've got a picture on the wall over the art table. But I'm not going to tell you what it's of. It's a surprise!'

'Are you alright?' Thea locked the inside of the campervan door, and slid into bed next to Shaun. 'Got the guilts for sneaking off to bed with your temporary co-host in the middle of the afternoon?'

'Hardly! It's our day off anyway, apart from the news

thing. No, it was something Ajay said. It made me think.' Shaun tucked his arm around Thea's shoulder. 'If we hadn't met before, you and I might have met today for the first time.'

'How did you work that out?'

'It's not unusual for the local news crew to visit us when we're on site. They often invite an expert on the period in question, Saxon, Tudor, whatever.'

'So?'

'So, if life had been different, and you hadn't gone to work at Mill Grange, you may well have been the local expert, drafted in from the Roman Baths, so we'd have met today, and I'd have asked you on a date.'

Laughing, Thea kissed him hard. 'You old romantic you.'

'Well, it could have happened.'

'It could.' Rolling onto her side gingerly, so as not to fall out of the narrow bed, Thea slid a hand down under the covers. 'Or it could have been the bloke who runs the museum in Cirencester or the lass who manages Chedworth Villa.'

Shaun groaned gently as Thea's fingers found what they were looking for. 'Nah, it would have been the hot girl from the back room in the Roman Baths. No question.'

Nineteen

Saturday March 28th

Helen's legs ached more than they had any right to, considering how much physical work she'd done over the last six months. It wasn't as if the walk from where she'd parked her Land Rover at Exford, to Landacre Bridge was that far. The three and half miles of moorland terrain wasn't even tough going. It was the fact she'd marched there at an incredible speed, trying to outpace her thinking that caused her muscles to twinge.

Even the climb up Chibbet Hill, which was the steepest part of the walk, shouldn't have done more than increase her pulse. Today, however, as Helen sank down onto the grass next to the pretty bridge, and surveyed the wonder of Exmoor, she felt as if she'd like to borrow Bert's oxygen tank.

Not wanting to spend the day wandering about Mill Grange on her own, when there was a high chance that Tina would take one look at her expression and ask her what was wrong, Helen had packed a rucksack with food and drink, grabbed a notebook and pen, and grabbed her car keys. She hadn't known she was heading to Landacre, but now she was here, she was glad she'd come.

'I'll start planning the book,' Helen told a passing rabbit.

Resting against the dry-stone wall behind her, she stretched her legs out and tried to visualise the chapter headings she'd need to encompass everything a potential reader would wish to know about Upwich Fortlet. She grabbed her notebook and listed the headings, 'Introduction' and 'The Romans in South West England', before the picture she'd been trying to suppress floated to the front of her mind, obscuring her work-based thoughts.

Helen wondered if Dylan had stuck to orange juice or if he'd finally been brave and opted for the strawberry milkshake he always said he fancied, but never tried. Tom would have black coffee. *How many cupfuls has he drunk by now?* She couldn't imagine Sue eating scones, but maybe she was wrong. 'Or maybe you don't want her to eat them, because that's what you and Tom do when you go to Sybil's.'

I think we owe him some proper family time, don't you?

The memory of Sue's words made Helen feel cold as she leafed through her empty notebook. She tried to imagine all the pages filled with the notes she'd need to make if she was going to write about the fortlet's history, rather than picturing Tom, Sue and Dylan playing happy families.

You know that Tom was put in an impossible situation and he went with Sue and not you because it was the right thing to do for Dylan.

Helen forced herself to consider a more pressing problem. What would she do about her job?

'That's the only *real* problem,' she muttered to herself as she pulled a flask of coffee from her bag. 'I need to choose between working with my friends at Mill Grange or going back to working with my colleagues in Bath. The insecurity I feel towards Sue is a failing, not a problem.'

A memory of Tom's fingers running across the front of her t-shirt that morning sent a frisson of pleasure shooting through her, despite her self-imposed gloom. Finding herself suddenly smiling, Helen gave herself a mental shake, and checking no one was around, started to talk herself through her feelings as she used to do when working out tricky business issues back in Bath.

'One: Sue is Dylan's mum, so Tom will see her. Two: if Tom is going to have joint custody, then they're going to have to meet more often to sort out how it'll work. Three: You have no right, or reason, to feel excluded. You were not part of Tom's life when Dylan came along.' Rechecking no one was listening as she told herself off, Helen kept going. 'More to the point, no one knows you are part of his life now; a mutual decision based on common sense as we live and work in the same place and because we have Dylan to consider.

'Four: I wouldn't begrudge Dylan a moment of happiness with his parents. So, in conclusion, I've been feeling like a slighted teenager for no reason.'

Helen looked down at the notebook in her lap. 'Luckily, no one knows I stormed off in a huff, so no harm done.'

Picking up her pen, she added, 'The Romans on Exmoor', to her list of chapter headings.

*

Waving at Tom, Tina headed to the table for two she'd reserved. Situated on the opposite side of the café, she was out of earshot of the small family group, deep in animated conversation, near the garden door.

Sybil appeared at her side, a pot of tea in one hand and a pot of coffee in the other. 'Mabel almost with you, Tina, or should I make her a fresh pot in a while?'

'She's on her way. The hospital phoned as we were leaving her cottage. After I got the thumbs up telling me Bert was alright, I was ushered out to make sure we didn't lose the reservation.'

'As if I'd let anyone else sit at Mabel's favourite table.' Sybil laughed. 'How's she coping without Bert?'

Tina pulled a face. 'It's hard to tell. She's back doing lunches at the manor, so she's keeping busy, but she isn't the same.'

'That's what I thought when I saw her a couple of days ago. I'm not sure she's eating properly. She's lost weight, and she wasn't big to start with.'

'I don't think she's sleeping much either.' Tina looked out of the window in time to see Mabel crossing the road towards them. 'That's why I've invited her here this morning, to get some food into her while I distract her with wedding talk.'

Sybil added a handful of serviettes to the wooden dispenser on the neighbouring table. 'I'll assume three cheese scones between two, unless you come and tell me otherwise.'

'Perfect. Thanks Sybil.'

*

Dylan was having trouble sitting still. His scone and orange juice were long gone, but his parents were being extremely slow about drinking their coffee, despite having finished talking about school ages ago. When he saw Tina come in, Dylan put down the book he was reading and tugged his dad's sleeve.

'Look, it's Tina, can I go and say hello?'

Sue shook her head before Tom had time to answer. 'I don't think it would be a good idea to bother one of your dad's employers.'

Tom laid a hand on his son's leg. 'Tina's as much a friend as an employer, and I know she wouldn't mind, but perhaps you could just say hello on the way out, Dylan.'

'Okay.' Dylan lifted his book back up, only to drop it again when he saw Mabel. 'Look, Dad. It's Mabel! She's not an employ person, Mum. She's my friend. Can I go?'

Sue was surprised. 'That old lady is your friend?'

'And one of the nicest people you'd ever wish to meet.' Tom suddenly found himself having to pick his words with care so he didn't lose his temper. 'Of course you can, Dylan. But walk and be careful of Sybil moving around with hot food and drink.'

As Dylan shot off like a rocket trying very hard to move in slow motion, Tom hissed under his breath. 'That woman, in fact, those women, have been incredibly kind to your son. Don't you *ever* make them sound as if they are not worthy of his attention again.'

Sue's eyebrows shot up, as she looked over to where Dylan was being scooped up onto Mabel's lap and held as if he was visiting a grandparent. 'Don't tell me you have a thing for your boss?'

'I beg your pardon?' Tom leaned forward so he didn't have to raise his voice. 'I assume your implying a fling with Tina rather than Mabel?'

'Well—'

'What is wrong with you, Sue? We were having a lovely morning. Dylan was happy, we had things to look forward to, and then you go and say something like that?'

'Well, I—'

'You're jealous.'

Sue crashed her coffee cup down onto her saucer, causing half of the café's occupants to turn and look at her. 'Why the hell would I be jealous of a wrinkly old lady and a woman who hasn't grown out of having her hair in pigtails?'

'You are jealous of the way Dylan's face lit up when he saw them, that's what.' Tom shook his head. 'What's going on with you, Sue? I thought you were happy with your new job and new life and so on.'

'I am.'

'So what's with the barbs?'

Sue continued to watch Dylan. She couldn't hear what was being said but she could see he was giggling and she sighed. 'I suppose I wish he'd act like that around my friends.'

'I doubt they spoil him rotten and read him bedtime stories, though, do they?' Tom forced a smile, while wondering who these friends were. 'He likes Harriet though, she reads to him too.'

Sue ignored the question. 'Perhaps we should go. Dylan's probably disturbed them for quite long enough.'

Hastily leaving some cash on the table to pay the bill, Tom followed as Sue got up and headed across the café at a speed she'd have disapproved of if Dylan had adopted it.

'Hello, I'm Sue, Dylan's *mum*.'

Tom winced as he heard the stress Sue put on her role in Dylan's life. He felt embarrassed for his son, as recognising the tone his mother used as one to be wary of, he slid off Mabel's lap.

Mabel's face adopted an expression not dissimilar to the one she used when being told a vegan was coming to dinner. 'I'm Mrs Hastings, and this is my friend, Miss Martin.' She turned to Dylan, and winked playfully. 'I'll tell Bert I've seen you. Now be a good boy and we'll have another chat soon.'

With an apologetic flash of his eyes, Tom ushered Sue and Dylan out of the café as fast as he could.

'*Mrs* Hastings and *Miss* Martin,' Sue scoffed as Dylan ran ahead of them along the quiet pavement. 'Stuck up old biddy.'

Grabbing her elbow, Tom spun Sue around so she was looking right at him. 'Now you listen to me, Mabel is of a time where manners earned respect. If you think you acted like someone who deserved to be introduced on a first name basis, then you are delusional.'

'She's stuck in a time warp.'

'Better that than dismissing your son's friends as worthless right in front of him! Thank goodness he's too young to understand quite how rude you were. Don't forget, if you want me to be there to pick Dylan up from school sometimes, and skip off work so I can do parent's evenings and such like, they're the people who'll be covering for me!'

*

'She's just as I imagined, but without pink hair.'

Having dismissed Sue in one sentence, Mabel raised her teacup to her lips. 'So, Tina love, wedding plans. Tell me everything you've sorted out so far.'

'Very little.' Tina pulled her wedding planning notebook from her bag. 'The venue is sorted, but then again, it isn't.'

'I don't understand?'

Tina poured herself another cup of coffee as she told Mabel about Sam's parents' wish that they marry at Malvern House. 'We've told them we want to marry here, and that we'd love them to come and see the place, but it's been very quiet ever since.'

'I see.' Mabel lifted her teacup to her lips, hovering it there as she listened.

'I want to marry at Mill Grange, we've even worked out that we can put a marquee over the ground between the chickens and the greenhouse, so we can have the ceremony in the walled garden, and then a couple of small marquees on the main lawn for the reception.'

Finally taking a drink, Mabel said, 'I can just see that. I bet the old greenhouse would look beautiful with fairy lights all over its old frame.'

'You don't think I'm mean asking Sam to break with family tradition and marry here then?'

'No, and I doubt Sam does either. This is more than your home. This is where you met and where Sam began to recover from his claustrophobia. Anyway, you're the bride! Tradition *usually* dictates you get to marry from home.'

'I'm not sure Sam's family do *usual*. Sam is convinced his father is behind this, even though his mother was the messenger.'

'From what I've heard of the earl, he does seem to take tradition very seriously.'

Tina twiddled a teaspoon through her fingers and shrugged. 'Oh well, I'm sure we'll work it out.'

'To change the subject a moment, I have news.' Mabel's eyes suddenly twinkled, and she put her cup down with a clatter. 'I was going to tell you straight away, but then I thought I'd wait until we were back at Mill Grange, to tell everyone together, but I can't wait!'

'What is it?'

'Bert's coming home tomorrow!'

'Oh my God, that's fantastic! What a relief.'

'I thought Sam should be with us when I told you, but, well... I'm so excited, Tina! I know he'll have to stay at home and just sit around, and I'll probably get irritated with him. But I'm looking forward to that so much!'

'Getting irritated with him?' Tina laughed as Mabel rubbed her hands in delight.

'Yes. I've really missed it.'

Twenty

Saturday March 28th

Telling herself she needed to make a trip to see the remains of Rainsbury Roman fort and Martinshoe fortlet, the only other Roman military installations found on Exmoor so far, in the very near future, Helen sat back on her bed. Her notebook was almost half full. Lists of points to consider, academic papers she had to read, as well as ideas for the data she needed to accumulate from the fortlet itself, from precise measurements to photographs of the best finds.

She knew Tom was back. She could hear Dylan's voice faintly through the wall as he made the appropriate roaring noises while his dad read him his favourite dinosaur story before bed.

Closing the notebook, Helen stretched out her tired legs and looked around the little room. Its whitewashed walls helped give it a sense of space, even though there wasn't much. The built-in cupboard, which had been acting as Helen's wardrobe for half the year, was so crammed full of jumpers, jeans and dungarees that it didn't shut properly. There was a heap of trainers and walking shoes by the bedroom door. Her coat hung next to the old hoodie she'd been using as a dressing gown since she came to Mill Grange. Helen considered her wardrobe and chest of drawers in her two-bed terrace. They didn't hold much more in the way of variety when it came to her clothes, apart from her office clothes and the one dress she kept just in case she needed it.

Continuing with her survey of her attic space, seeing how the light from the small window reflected across the room, how the rag mat had been stuck down so you didn't skid across the polished floor boards, she tried to picture her bedroom at home.

It was twice as big as the old servant quarters she was in now, with soft, blue carpet, which meant you could cross the room without getting cold feet or being in danger of slipping unless you donned rubber soled slippers.

Helen sat up, running a hand over the wooden bed head she'd been resting against. It was hard and unforgiving without pillows to cushion it. At home she had a pine bedstead, which wasn't much more comfortable, now she thought about it. That bed was a double though. A fact she often considered ironic, as no one had ever shared it with her. But after squeezing her curves into a narrow single bed for weeks, she had to concede it would feel like bliss to have space to rollover in the night.

Or will it?

The dinosaur roaring had stopped next door. Helen wondered if Dylan was asleep, or if he and Tom were lying in their separate beds reading their own books. She hadn't heard the door open, so she knew Tom was still there.

Trying not to picture Tom in her double bed in Bath, Helen suddenly sat upright.

In Bath.

'I thought, in Bath, not at home.' She shut her eyes again and forced herself to move her mind from room to room of her home in the beautiful Georgian city.

The kitchen was a muddle, but a muddle she liked. Messy but hygienic. Small, with only three cupboards and a larder, it had a scrubbed oak table in one corner. A poor cousin to the one in Mill Grange's kitchen, but every bit as loved. Helen wasn't sure how much paperwork, books, bills, unopened letters and academic papers she'd left strewn on it when, on September 8th last year, she'd simply got up and decided that she wasn't going to work that day, instead heading for the wilds of Exmoor to visit her former colleague and good friend, Thea Thomas, and the fortlet she thought she'd found.

Apart from quick trip to grab a rucksack of clothes and to throw away the milk in the fridge, she hadn't been back since.

Her mind drifted on, seeing the hundreds of books that lined the library-like shelves in her living room, and on to the landslide of DVD's on the floor by the out-of-date television and the forever dusty CD player. The squashed leather sofa and the wing backed armchair that had once belonged to her grandfather.

Do I miss any of that?

She looked at the pile of novels sat on the chair that doubled as her bedside table. Taken from the rows of bookshelves that lined the corridors of Mill Grange's second floor, she was never without reading material, and although there was a television room, Helen hadn't watched it since the last episode of *Landscape Treasures* had aired at Christmas.

The notion that perhaps Bath wouldn't feel like home when she returned gnawed at her.

If I go back, will I have time to write the book?

How much will have changed at the Baths?

Will whoever's been doing my job, want me back? Will they resent me sweeping back in and taking over?

Helen knew there was an email in her inbox from the museum board; she suspected it was intended to bring her up to date on developments there. Although it was the weekend, and she wasn't technically at work, it was unusual for her not to respond to an email straight away. She knew the board would have noticed that too.

Her stomach rumbled. Not in the mood to be sociable when she'd got home from her walk, Helen had snuck up to her room, and not ventured down for dinner. But it was now eight o'clock, and she knew if she didn't get some food, she wouldn't sleep properly.

Glad to be distracted, albeit only briefly, from her struggle to decide whether to stay at Mill Grange or not, Helen was just admitting to herself that she did miss takeaways, when there was a knock at her door.

Startled by the sound after the silence of her thoughts, she called, 'It's open.'

'Can I come in?'

Helen hadn't realised she'd been holding her breath until Tom's head peeped around the door.

'Is Dylan asleep?'

'Sound. Lots of fresh air and too many scones.'

Not wanting to dwell on her absence from the scone consumption, Helen asked, 'Did you go for a walk?'

'The Tarr Steps. It's fast becoming one of Dylan's favourite places.'

Having convinced herself that it was perfectly reasonable for Tom to spend time with Sue and Dylan, she hadn't expected to feel so winded when he told her that he'd taken his ex to the very place they'd become a couple. Her lips opened to say something about Dylan having fun on the bridge, but all that came out was a quiet, 'Oh.'

'Yes.' Tom frowned. 'I'd thought we might find you there. When we got back to the house after being at Sybil's, Mabel said she'd seen you head off with your walking rucksack.'

'I went to Landacre Bridge.'

'Right.' Tom shut the door behind him, and hesitated, not sure if he should cross the room to sit next to Helen or not. 'Nice spot.'

She picked up her notebook and waved it in his direction. 'I was planning for the book.'

'Good idea. How's it going?' Tom rested his back against the closed door, the three strides between them feeling miles wide.

'I'm getting there. The chapter headings are sorted and I've sketched a few rough plans of the site to develop on the computer for their graphics team to adapt.'

'You're going to write it then?'

'Yes.' Helen found she meant it as she held the book to her chest. 'That's the one decision I have managed today.'

'And what's the other you should have made?' Tom felt uneasy as he wondered what else Helen had been planning.

'Oh, nothing really.' Cursing herself for her slip of the tongue, Helen asked, 'Did Sue like the Tarr Steps?'

'Sue?' Tom looked puzzled. 'I wouldn't take Sue there. That's our place. I told you, I thought Dylan and I might find you there.'

'Just you two?' Helen's face flushed. 'I assumed…'

Crossing the room as her words trailed off, Tom sat next to her on the bed and grabbed both her palms. 'That Sue and I would spend quality time together after coffee?'

'Something like that.'

'Sybil's scones are good, but as yet I don't think they have miracle working qualities, and it would take that before I spent longer with Sue than I need to.' Tom smiled. 'I know I'm rubbish with women, but even I'm not so low as to take my ex to the place where I first kissed my new partner!'

'Sorry, Tom,' Helen sighed, 'you looked so happy when you headed off to the café. Like a proper family, and what with Dylan… I'm sorry I jumped to conclusions.'

'What with Dylan what?'

'It doesn't matter.'

'Come on. Give.'

'Okay, but it's me being silly, and I've since given myself a firm talking to about it so it isn't important. Okay?'

'Okay.'

'I felt as if Dylan had forgotten about me. You'd just told me he was keen for me to come for scones, and then, minutes later, I'd been replaced at the café by his mother.'

Tom groaned. 'He's only five, he'd never…'

'I know.' Helen placed a hand on his knee. 'As I said, I worked it all out as I walked. You might be rubbish with women, but I'm so inexperienced with men that I haven't even had time to work out if I'm rubbish or not.'

Tom shifted uncomfortably. 'These beds are ridiculously small. Can you budge up a bit?'

'Only if one buttock hangs off the bed.'

'How about you budge up, and we each hang one buttock off each side of the bed?'

'As romantic gestures goes, that's a good 'un.' Feeling the tension that had built between them disperse, Helen tapped the space next to her on the bed.

Tom moved with more speed than dignity, his head resting next to Helen's.

'Good job you're so slim.' Helen kept her eyes focused on the window across the room. If she looked at Tom now, she wasn't sure she could stop what might happen next.

'Are you saying you wouldn't have sacrificed buttock space for me if I was bigger?'

Helen laughed, but rather than reply she asked how the meeting with Sue went.

'Apart from Sue offending Sybil, Tina and Mabel, it was a huge hit.'

'She didn't?' Helen turned to face him. 'How?'

'Do you mind if I tell you later?' Tom ran a hand over Helen's cheek, before taking a single red ringlet, pulled it gently and watched it bounce back into place. 'You have the most erotic hair in the world.'

'Do I?' Rather breathless, Helen found herself picturing her double bed in Bath again as Tom continued to run his fingertips through her curls.

'Oh yes.'

'I've never thought of my hair as sexy before.'

Tom, suddenly hoarse, whispered, 'You're the sexiest woman I've ever met.'

'I bet you say that to all—'

He placed a finger over her lips and shook his head. 'No. I've never said that before, not to anyone. I promise.'

Tears filmed over Helen's eyes as she whispered, 'Stay.'

Twenty-one

Sunday March 29th

A warm smile lit Helen's face as she read the note on the chair next to her bed.

I haven't 'gone' – but I didn't want Dylan to wake up and wonder where I was. Come for a walk with us today? PTO.

Wiping the sleep from her eyes, Helen raised herself up on one elbow as she turned the small piece of paper over.

I think I love you – no – I know I do. Hope that's OK. xx

Sitting up properly, Helen clutched the note to her chest, before reading it again, just to make sure she hadn't imagined it.

'He loves me.'

She spoke the words shyly. They felt good on her tongue.

The sun shone through the ill-fitting curtains as Helen placed the note back on the table. She felt different.

Lifting her hands up before her, she turned them over, looking at them properly for the first time in years. Far from smooth, they were archaeologists' hands, with blister marks, permanent calluses and rough skin. The nails were blunt and unpainted.

Helen found herself blushing like a self-conscious teenager as she thought about where those hands had been last night. Then, she found herself lifting the blankets up from the bed, and peering down at the length of her body.

She couldn't remember the last time she'd done more than glance at her naked form. Even in a shower or bath, Helen simply ignored herself, concentrating instead on the act of getting clean. Her lumps, bumps, curves and wobbly bits were, in her mind, not dissimilar to a cut through diagram of the Himalayas. Tom had disagreed.

Helen's body glowed as she remembered exactly how he'd disagreed, and his delight at exploration. He'd made it very clear when she'd told him to prepare himself for disappointment, that he'd been to the Himalayas, and she was even more beautiful than they were.

She was surprised she'd slept. It seemed impossible that she hadn't lain awake in a mist of heady bliss. Helen blushed again as she lowered the blankets. They'd been energetic to say the least. It was no wonder she'd slept.

A deep growl of her belly reminded Helen she hadn't eaten for a long time. Leaping out of bed, she gathered the clothes Tom had disposed of with lightning speed, hugging each one to herself, while tutting at herself for being so sentimental.

'A shower, clean clothes, food and then a walk with my two favourite men.'

Helen picked the note back up. By the time she'd dressed, she'd read it eight times.

The ambulance car had been kitted out with so many pills and potions that Mabel felt rather daunted as she led Bert into their cottage. A feeling that increased as the paramedic issued a list of instructions a mile long.

It wasn't until the paramedic had gone that Bert rested his head back on the cushions and exhaled in relief. Patting the place next to him for Mabel to sit down, he cupped her hand in his.

'Now before you start, listen to me, my girl. I can tell just by looking at you that you're worn out. And it's no wonder, visiting me every day, working at the manor and then keeping that lot going.' He pointed to a pile of open files on the dining room table, which made up all the committees and clubs that Mabel ran or took minutes for.

'You'd rather I'd sat here pining for you? Well, let me tell you, Bert Hastings, it's not easy sitting here, day after day, scared stiff that...'

Mabel broke off. Weeks of emotion and fear catching up with her as she sobbed, 'I was so looking forward to you coming home, and now you're here, I just want to sleep.'

'There, there lass.' Bert wiped a tear from her face. 'I've been desperate to get home too. I'm also shattered.'

Mabel gave a weak smile. 'A doze on the sofa then?'

'A doze on the sofa with my favourite girl.'

Nestling her head on Bert's shoulder, Mabel had just got

comfortable, when she sat bolt upright. 'Sybil sent over fresh scones. I forgot. They were a surprise for you, do you want—'

'Later.' Bert stifled a cough, the effort making him yawn. 'Sybil's scones are always worth waiting for.'

'Of course.' Mabel's head was only just back on his shoulder when she jolted up again. 'But what if we sleep through when you next pills are due and—'

'Whoa, there.' Bert shifted within his cocoon of cushions so he met his anxious wife's eyes. 'I'm not due more medicine until four.'

'Oh yes, right. Of course.' Mabel checked her watch, it was eleven o'clock. She settled back against Bert, only to sit back up for a third time. 'But Tina and Sam said they'd pop over. If they come and we don't hear them, they'll worry.'

'No they won't.' Bert tapped his shoulder, and Mabel rested back against him. 'They'll assume we're having a nap and come back later or tomorrow.'

He was about to tell her he was glad she was still the same overactive Mabel he'd left behind when he'd gone into hospital, but she was already fast asleep. Soft, hedgehog-like snores, which she'd later claim she hadn't made, ricocheted around the living room.

'Looking forward to heading back to Mill Grange for Easter, Thea?'

Ajay passed her a glass of white wine as they sat in the sunshine in The Carthorse's beer garden.

'Very much. I know it's only been a few weeks, but it feels ages.'

'Time not flying while you're having fun then?' Andy swung his legs over the wooden bench to sit down, as he joined Thea, Shaun and Ajay for a pub lunch.

'I'm having a great time dig wise, but there's only so long a girl can go without one of Sybil's scones.'

'Or how long a boy can go without Mabel's bacon...'

'Sandwiches,' his friends chorused as Shaun poked at his inferior BLT.

He laughed. 'I've mentioned I like them then?'

'Having tasted both of those culinary delights, I can understand the hurry to get back.' Andy nodded into his pint.

'I think work might be waiting for me when I get back.' Thea gestured to her phone. 'A heap of texts arrived this morning from Helen.'

'Where were you standing when they arrived?' Ajay asked eagerly, before changing his mind. 'Actually, don't tell me. If I know, I'll feel obliged to go there, and I'm quite enjoying not being bombarded with notifications.'

'Very wise.' Thea turned to Shaun. 'Helen's been asked to write a book about the fortlet.'

'That's great. Will she do it?' Thea held her phone up so Shaun could read the texts from Helen. 'Ah, so she's still thinking it over, but this was sent a few days back.'

'I know. I thought I'd take a walk and get enough signal to phone.'

'Or you could get really modern, and use the call box in the hall.' Andy waved a hand towards the pub.

'I hadn't realised there was one. Whereabouts is it?'

'Hidden right at the far end, opposite the gent's loo. It's

more or less underneath the coat racks, so it's no wonder you didn't know it was there.'

Taking a sip of her wine, Thea got to her feet. 'Thanks, Andy, I'll go now. That way, I'll miss Shaun bemoaning the inferior taste of bacon and bread combinations outside of the Upwich area.'

If it hadn't been for the sight of two legs sticking out under a mound of coats, Thea wouldn't have seen where the public phone was.

Shielded from view by – what she assumed – were the staff's jackets, all she could see of the person currently engaged in a muted conversation at the other end of the narrow corridor, was a pair of blue jeans. The way they were positioned suggested that their owner was resting with his back against the wall as he spoke down the line.

Not surprised to find the phone in use, when the signal for mobiles was so unreliable, Thea realised she might need change or a phone card to make the call, and headed to the bar to enquire how the phone was paid for.

Five minutes later, a fully charged phone card to hand, Thea returned to see the same pair of legs in situ. Not sure if she should wait nearer, so the caller knew someone was queuing for the phone, or stay where she was, so they could finish their call in private, Thea hovered in the passageway until she had to move to let someone by to reach the toilets.

Moving forwards, so she wouldn't be constantly in the way of the cloakrooms, Thea came to rest on the other side of the coat rack, close enough to hear the conversation, but shielded from the caller by the coats. Wondering what advice she could give Helen, if any, she suddenly recognised the shoes at the same time as she registered who the voice belonged to.

Julian was talking as if afraid of being overheard. There was definitely something covert about his tone. Thea had the strangest notion that if the coats hadn't been there to hide him, he'd have been wearing a disguise. Finding herself picturing the producer in a beige overcoat and trilby, she tried not to listen, but now she knew who was speaking, Thea found her curiosity getting the better of her.

Anyway, how I'm supposed to avoid hearing him?

'... so I manoeuvred the right person into doing the interview... Yes, it worked a treat. The production team were impressed... Absolutely, a private word in the right ear and all that...'

Thea winced as Julian gave a muted laugh of self-congratulation before carrying on his conversation.

'... you could say they'll soon be seen in action on a wider stage.'

There was a lengthy pause as Julian listened to whoever he was talking to. Thea's palms prickled. There was no reason to think he was up to something, yet the more time she'd spent in Julian's company of late, the more she was inclined to agree with Shaun and the AA. He might well be good at his job, but when it came down to it, that was all he cared about. Thea suspected he wouldn't care who got trampled on his path to the top.

'She's a natural. I'm telling you... yes...' Julian's voice dropped so he was almost whispering. 'A shake up of the team is inevitable. If we want to be seen to be keeping up, we'll need someone at the helm of the ship who is professional, likeable and, let's be honest, easy on the eye.'

She? Team shake up?

Thea backed silently away from the coats. Glad no one was around to see her, she tiptoed away, heading for the sanctuary of the ladies' bathroom.

Was that what Julian had been not quite telling them the other evening over food? That *Landscape Treasures'* line-up was going to be changed to try and compete with the new look *Treasure Hunters?*

Splashing her face with cold water from the tap, Thea stared into the mirror as the obvious conclusion arrived in her mind.

I'm the only one he's arranged to be interviewed on camera over the last few weeks. Surely he can't mean that he wants me to take over from Shaun?

Feeling nauseas, Thea took a deep breath.

You only heard half the conversation. You could be wrong. But what if I'm not? Poor Shaun. He'd be crushed if Julian offered me his job.

By the time she'd left the bathroom and seen that the phone was now free, Thea had convinced herself she was imagining things.

Of course you're wrong. Why would anyone in their right mind break up one of the most successful teams in recent television history?

Twenty-two

Monday March 30th

Helen hummed happily as she tidied her desk in the corner of the store room. If she was going to stay at Mill Grange permanently, she'd need to ask Sam and Tina about having a little more working space.

'If I rent out my place in Bath, then I can rent somewhere small here. All I need is a one- or two-bedroom place.'

Helen sat down, her mind a happy haze of memories that the last twenty-four hours had given her.

Being with Tom, walking around Haddon Hill, while he and Dylan ran in all directions chasing butterflies and hunting for Exmoor ponies, had been so much fun. They'd snuck kisses when the boy wasn't looking and soaked in the sunshine while Dylan told her about school and his friends. Later that day, Helen had passed Tom a note saying that she loved him. The expression on his face as he'd read her words, a heady mix of relief and desire, would stay with her forever.

They'd discussed their mutual notes on the drive home

from Tiverton, after dropping Dylan back to Sue's, before giving into passion the second they got home, and waking up together that morning, wrapped in a knot of linen on the tiny bed.

Muttering contentedly to herself as she collected the guest list for the week that Tina had left on her desk, Helen noted that, once again, every one of the six men booked in had elected to do archaeology training as part of their week of respite after years of forces' service.

'Sam's right, once we start advertising the certificate, this place is going to need another tutor.' Still at her desk, Helen pulled a piece of scrap paper from a pile in the corner and scribbled down some thoughts.

'So, rent the house in Bath and find a little place here, or nearby at least,' Helen mumbled as she wrote, 'Tiverton or maybe Bampton or Taunton?' Then she crossed out Tiverton. She didn't fancy bumping into Sue in the supermarket.

'I must find out how much agencies charge to rent out houses in Bath, or should I rent it out myself.' Helen's hand paused, before she added, 'research agencies' to her random list.

Her pulse beat fast as she read back what she'd written. 'Am I really going to do this? Am I going to leave a well-paid job I love, for a less well paid job I love – and a man?'

Picking up the paper, she balled it up and threw it into her recycling bin.

'At the end of the week you can write the list. It's only been a few days since Tom and I got together.'

Checking the time, and seeing she had three hours until the new guests were due to arrive, Helen headed for the fortlet.

She could see Tom in the distance, sweeping mud from the edges of the fake dig. His black combats were speckled with mud; his slim muscular arms were pushing the broom as if he was in a race against time.

'Hello,' Helen called as she approached. 'You're an urgent sweeper this morning.'

Tom beamed as he saw her, before checking over his shoulder to make sure no one was around. 'Come here, quick.'

Helen felt oddly vulnerable as he kissed her over the dig site, and found herself dissolving into a giggle.

'That funny?'

'Sorry, I feel like a kid not wanting to be caught snogging behind the bike sheds.'

Tom wiggled his eyebrows suggestively. 'Did a lot of that did you, Miss Rodgers?'

'Not once.' Helen slipped her hand into his. 'I was fat and clever. Fatal combination at a comprehensive in the 80s.'

'They didn't know what they were missing.' He winked. 'Come on, help me out and this'll be finished long before lunch.'

'And what makes you think I'd want to do that?' Helen pointed towards the main excavation. 'I might have things to do.'

'True, but if we finish here early, we can sneak back upstairs for a pre-lunch, umm… meeting.'

Helen looked across the lawns, expecting to see Sam or Tina, but no one was in sight. 'A meeting? And what might that be about?'

'I realised at about half past nine this morning that my extensive research of the Himalayas remains lacking in certain areas. I'd hate to disappoint, should I ever be quizzed on its undulations.'

As her body reacted to his suggestion, Helen whispered, 'And what about work?'

'You wouldn't be out here if you hadn't finished prepping inside. I'll help you with the fortlet after lunch.'

'And what if Sam or Tina need us?'

'I just saw them heading off to see Bert and Mabel. We've got at least an hour to ourselves.'

'Oh, now that is sneaky.'

'Only a bit.' Tom gestured towards the manor. 'Shall we?'

Tina bustled around Mabel's kitchen, following Sam's directions in her hunt for tea and coffee while he unpacked the care package of scones that Sybil had sent over first thing that morning.

Not wanting Bert and Mabel to hear from the adjoining living room, Tina spoke under her breath, 'How do you think he is, *really*?'

'Exhausted, but on the mend.' Sam fetched the butter from the fridge.

'Should we save our question for another time?'

'No.' Sam put the sugar bowl on the tea tray. 'It'll give him something else to get better for. But we won't hang around afterwards.'

'We can't anyway.' Tina glanced at the kitchen clock. 'It's coming up to lunchtime already, and I've got lots to do before the guests arrive at four.'

As Sam picked up the tray, and headed towards the lounge, Tina hung back.

She hadn't said a word when Sam had walked through the cottage door without breaking a sweat. Now he was strolling into the small living room without batting an eyelid.

Afraid that if she mentioned it, Sam would realise how enclosed he was and rush outside, Tina hurried through to join their friends.

Having updated Bert on life at Mill Grange, and confirming that next week Dylan was moving into the manor part time until Tom found a place to rent, the conversation had drifted onto the surprising upturn in the quality of hospital food – but Tina couldn't wait any longer. She was sure that, any minute now, Sam would realise how long he'd been indoors and the moment would be lost.

'Actually, as well as seeing that you'd been returned to us in one piece, Bert,' Tina looked to Sam, who tilted his head in encouragement, 'we have an ulterior motive for our visit.'

Bert chuckled. 'Sounds intriguing.'

'The thing is,' Tina took Sam's hand, 'as you both know, my parents died when I was in my teens. I don't have anyone to give me away at the wedding, so, we wondered…'

Emotion caught in Tina's throat and she turned to Sam, silently asking him to finish the sentence for her.

'Bert, Tina would very much like you to be father of the bride at our forthcoming wedding. And Mabel, would you do us the honour of standing in for Tina's mother?'

Sat side by side, the elderly couple looked at each other. Mouths open, simultaneously speechless for the first time in their lives.

Slowly, Bert took Mabel's hands. Cradling them gently,

he was the first to speak. 'I would be delighted. Honoured and delighted. Thank you.' His words choked as he smiled.

Mabel was nodding fast now. 'Yes, and I would. We... we never thought we'd ever be...'

The old lady lapsed into silence and a tear sprang to the corner of Tina's eyes. *They haven't got children. They never thought they'd do this.*

'That's wonderful. Thank you so much. Our day wouldn't be the same without you two, would it, Sam? We—'

Sam's mobile burst into life, interrupting Tina. 'Rats! Sorry. I only left it on in case a guest had last minute travel issues.' He hooked his phone from his pocket. 'Oh, it's my mum. I'll tell her I'll call her back.'

'Don't be daft, you can take it in the garden. Off you go.'

As Sam followed Mabel's instructions, Tina couldn't help but sigh.

'I take it the issue of where to get married is rumbling on?' Mabel asked, as Tina rested back against the armchair's cushions.

'Afraid so.'

Bert cleared his throat, a short cough escaping as he did so. 'Sam should invite...'

He coughed again, making Mabel turn to him. 'Steady now. Take your time.'

Tina gave Bert's arm a gentle pat. 'We should leave you in peace. We just wanted to make sure you were okay, and ask if you'd give me away of course.'

Already on her feet, Mabel ushered Tina back to her seat. 'We're delighted to see you and of course we'll stand in for your parents, but what about this wedding? It has to be at Mill Grange, so how will you tackle the location issue?'

Relieved Mabel had reverted to type, and all signs of emotional simmering had evaporated, Tina explained, 'Sam invited them to come and visit the house ages ago. We hoped they'd come to see why we love it so much, but the invite hasn't been taken up.'

'Maybe that's why Her Ladyship is calling now.'

'Maybe.' Tina doubted it. 'I really liked Lady Bea when we visited Malvern House in the autumn. And Sam's father, even though he's a bit stuffy.'

'Aren't earls *supposed* to be stuffy?' Bert chipped in.

'A bit, but Lord Malvern could win prizes.'

Mabel crossed her arms. 'I'm not sure I could like anyone who puts tradition before their child's happiness.'

Bert's eyebrows raised, but he wisely said nothing about how addicted to doing things the traditional way Mabel was.

'As much as I want to marry here, I'd hate Sam and his parents to fall out over this. They've only just healed the rift after six years of being estranged.'

Mabel patted Tina's hand. 'If that happens, it won't be anyone's fault but theirs. Now then,' she brushed her hands together as if the matter was solved, 'tell me, have you got a dress yet?'

'Beyond flicking through those magazines you sent me, I haven't so much as chosen a style, let alone the actual dress.'

Looking scandalised, Mabel's eyes darted to the calendar on the wall, and then back again. 'May's not that far away, Tina. And you'll need to have fittings and stuff and—'

'Until we have the venue sorted properly, there didn't seem much point.'

'Not much point?' Mabel shook her head. 'Wherever you wed, you'll need a frock.'

'I know, but there's so much to do, the days seem to fly by. Even with me working full time at Mill Grange now, I never seem to have a minute.' Tina glanced up at Mabel. 'I was going to ask if you'd come with me? It's so hard to know what really suits, and whether to believe what the shop assistant says suits you, because they might be trying to shift a dress no one wants.'

'Me?'

'Yes. Umm… you're my friend and well, my mum would have come and…' Tina was alarmed to see tears glisten in Mabel's eyes again. 'Did I say something wrong?'

'No. I'd love to. I just never thought you'd ask me.' Mabel wiped her eyes and gripped hold of Tina's hand. 'Thank you.'

Sam arrived back in the room in time to see Tina giving Mabel a hug. 'Everyone alright in here?'

'Mabel's agreed to go wedding dress shopping with me.'

'Fantastic. Thanks, Mabel.' Sam grabbed his cold cup of tea. 'But not this weekend if that's okay?'

'Absolutely,' Tina pointed to the calendar, 'because Dylan's moving in on Sunday. We'll be child proofing the house on Saturday.'

'Oh hell, I forgot about that!' Sam groaned. 'I've just told my parents they could come this weekend to see the house!'

Twenty-three

Thursday April 2nd

'**A** re you sure you don't mind?'

Tom passed Sam his semi completed to-do list for the day, rubbing a dirty hand down his combats as he did so.

'I'd have said if I did.' Sam gestured his clipboard towards the house. 'Go and get changed, or you'll never get to Tiverton in time.'

'Thanks, mate.'

Tom tried not to glance back at Helen as he strode toward the house. He knew she was watching him; he could feel the heat of her emerald eyes on his back.

They'd have to tell people soon. It was getting increasingly difficult not to take her hand whenever they stood near each other or hug her before leaving the site for a while.

People are going to think we've fallen out. We hardly look at each other for fear of people guessing.

Resolving to talk to Helen about the issue after they'd

come off guest care duty that evening, Tom made a beeline for the shower, to scrub away as much of the site mud and dust as possible before heading to Dylan's school.

He tried not to think about the preconceptions Dylan's teacher might have of him or what light Sue had painted him in.

Sue's changed. She's putting Dylan first. She won't have said anything bad about me.

Putting on a shirt and his only pair of smart trousers, Tom grabbed his car keys and ran down all three sets of stairs and out to the driveway.

'I thought I'd come and wish you luck.'

As Helen leaned against his old Fiesta, nerves fluttered in Tom's chest. 'Is Sam with the guests?'

'We'd reached a good place to stop for the day, so Sam's taken them for a walk in the woods.'

'Good timing.' Tom checked the coast was clear, before giving her a cuddle. 'That's better. I can't believe how nervous I am.'

'I wish I was coming with you.'

'So do I!' Tom unlocked the car and wound down the window to let some air into the stuffy interior. 'Actually, I wanted to talk to you about that later.'

'About me coming to the school?'

'No. Well, sort of, I suppose. About us being an official couple. That way, I get to hug you more often, and you'd be able to come to these events with me.'

Helen's smile creased the freckles on her cheeks. 'I'd like that. Although maybe not a parent's evening – that's Sue's. I wouldn't want to intrude.'

'Okay, maybe not those, but nativity plays and stuff.'

'You're sure?' Helen was already picturing Dylan decked out as a shepherd with a tea towel on his head.

'I'm sure. I also think we should tell everyone. I know we said we'd wait, but I'm beginning to wonder what we're waiting for.'

'Me too.' Helen grinned. 'We'll tell people once you're back.'

Driving away, Tom felt more contented than he had in years. He was looking forward to telling everyone Helen was in his life. Especially Dylan. He'd be delighted.

There was no doubt it was a dolphin. The mosaic artist had even managed to capture its joy at curling through the sea. Which, Thea mused to herself, was remarkable as he'd probably never seen a dolphin, or even the sea, in his life.

Standing back from the bath house, allowing the latest round of local newspaper reporters to get as many pictures as they could, Thea let out an exhalation of air she hadn't realised she'd been holding in.

'You okay?' Shaun muttered so that neither the reporters nor Julian could hear him.

'Relieved the mosaic really is made from local stone.' Thea grimaced. 'Can you imagine the reports if, after I'd said it was probably going to be locally sourced on telly, the test results came back with a different story?'

'That wouldn't have been your fault.'

Taking a step back, the knowledge of the conversation she'd overheard weighed on Thea's mind as she watched Julian chatting to the reporter, his chest so puffed out with pride, it was as if he'd built the villa himself. 'I meant to ask, has Julian said anything else about *Treasure Hunters*?'

'Not a word. Why?'

'With the dig nearly being over, and us having a weekend break soon, I wondered if he would say anything else about the future of the show.'

'Our show or *Treasure Hunters*?'

'Ours. The more I think about what he was saying over dinner the other week, the more I think he knows something we don't.'

Shaun shook his head. 'If the TV company wanted to make a change of presenter, they'd have to tell me. I can't see it happening. *Landscape Treasures* gets great ratings. And even if *Treasure Hunters* is upgraded, so what? Why can't people enjoy both shows?'

'You're probably right.'

'Julian's not been near me beyond work requirements since that meal.' Shaun stared towards the producer. 'Now I think about it, he hasn't been around much at all lately.'

'Can't say I miss him in the pub in the evenings.' Thea watched as Julian turned his charm on the female reporter. 'Where does he go instead?'

'Haven't a clue.' Shaun pointed to the site. 'I think they're done. Come on, they could have more questions for us.'

Thea's palms prickled as they walked back to the bath house. She'd hoped Shaun would know of an innocent reason why Julian had stopped socialising with them after work. She had a horrible suspicion that it was because he'd got whatever it was he wanted, and no longer felt he had to try and impress the team. *Or me.*

*

Tom held the painting in his hands as carefully as if it had been painted by Renoir. A lump came to his throat as Mrs Harley explained why his son's artwork was on display.

The painting was of Mill Grange. The brown square with extra painted squares to the side, which Tom guessed represented the kitchen and the storeroom, had three out of proportion figures stood before it. A man, a woman with a boy between them.

That's Helen. Will Sue realise?

Mrs Harley was talking about composition and how hard Dylan had concentrated on the painting. Sue meanwhile, was saying nothing. Her smile had become tight.

Plus, that's not her and Dylan's home. It's Mill Grange.

'Do you like it, Dad?' Dylan was sounding anxious, and Tom was suddenly aware he'd been quiet for a long time.

'I love it!' He gave his son a hug. 'That's the kitchen, isn't it?'

'Yes,' Dylan nodded, 'and that's the bench we sit on for lunch.'

Passing the work of art back to Mrs Harley, Tom held Dylan's hand. 'I can't wait to tell everyone about it.'

'You can take a photograph of it, if you like, Mr Harris.' Mrs Harley gestured for Dylan to lay the picture flat on the art table. 'It'll be a few weeks before that display comes down and Dylan can take the picture home.'

As her son and ex-partner shot into action with Tom's phone's camera, Sue tartly asked, 'And how's his maths and English? Rather more important than art, don't you think?'

★

'Would you like to join us for dinner?' Sue hovered on the doorstep. 'I'm sure Dylan would like that.'

Tom could see his son at the far end of the narrow hallway, stacking his trainers onto the shoe rack. 'I'd like that too, but I promised I'd be on hand tonight, to help with the guests. Making up for time off this afternoon.'

'Yes, of course.' Sue turned her face away.

'Anyway,' Tom said, 'I thought you booked an early slot at school because you were going out tonight.'

'What? Oh yes, well, I am.'

'Sue?'

'I am! But not until eight. It's only five now. Plenty of time for you to share fish finger sandwiches and oven chips with Dylan.'

'You said, join *us* for dinner, not just Dylan.'

'Same thing!' Sue glowered. 'What's with the questioning?'

'Forget it.' Tom shook his head. 'As long as I'm not letting Dylan down by not staying, I'd better get back. Don't want to use up all Sam and Tina's goodwill before Dylan's even moved in.'

'He said he'll have his own room soon because your friend Helen is leaving.'

'Yes.' Tom kept his gaze focused on the house. 'She works at the Roman Baths. Mill Grange was a sabbatical.'

'You'll miss her.'

It was a statement, not a question, but Sue still managed to sound as if she was sucking a lemon as she spoke.

'Of course I will. We've worked together for six months.'

Tom turned away with a wave to Dylan. 'I should go. Thanks for inviting me along. I'm so proud of Dylan.'

'Me too.' Sue quickly added, 'You know I want the best for him, don't you? Whatever I do, it's because I love Dylan.'

'Of course it is.' Unease made Tom look Sue straight in the eye. 'Is everything alright?'

'I'm fine, it's just… that painting. It wasn't here and it wasn't me. It was of your house and one of your friends. Helen, I suspect.'

'I know. I'm sorry.'

Twenty-four

Thursday April 2nd

They were the last people left in the drawing room. The guests had turned in, tired after a week of open air and physical exercise, all bemoaning that they'd have to leave in the morning, with calls of "the week's gone so fast" and "we must come again".

Sam and Tina had gone to bed and the fire had been dampened down for the night.

Getting up from her armchair, Helen joined Tom on the sofa. Beyond a brief thumbs up, to let her know it had gone well at school, they hadn't had a minute alone since Tom had returned to Mill Grange.

'So, how was it?'

'Amazing. Dylan has settled in really well. His maths and English are good for a lad of his age, and you already know his reading is good.'

'Was his teacher alright with you?' Helen laid her head on his shoulder as Tom's hand automatically sought out her curls, teasing them between his fingers. 'Sue hadn't said anything bad about you?'

'Mrs Harley was very nice. All she said was that she hoped I'd settled into my new job, and that she'd arranged for all the correspondence Sue gets, to come to me too.'

'Sounds good.'

'Umm...' Tom laid a hand on Helen's denim-covered legs. 'I'm sure Dylan will tell you about it tomorrow.'

Helen's body melted under Tom's touch as she battled to stay focused. 'Should we tell everyone about us before Dylan arrives tomorrow, or once he's settled in?'

'Maybe we should tell Dylan first. But we have to tell everyone soon! Sitting across the room from you and not touching you is driving me nuts.'

Helen laughed. 'And there I was thinking army boys were taught patience and self-restraint.'

'Only when there's a possibility of being shot. Rest of the time, we're as impatient as the next man... especially when sat next to someone we have the serious hots for.'

Returning Tom's kiss, Helen caught sight of a child's reading book out of the corner of her eye. It was one of Dylan's. 'He will be okay with it, won't he?'

'You and me, you mean?'

'Well, umm... if you are in my room with me sometimes, won't he want to come in and stuff?' She blushed at the thought of them being interrupted, 'I adore Dylan, but I'd hate to embarrass him or...'

'For him to catch us in flagrante delicto?'

'Well, yes.' Even Helen's freckles blushed at the thought.

'Umm...' Tom pulled a curl out, curious to see how far it would straighten before pinging back into a tight spiral.

'Are you with me, Tom?'

'Oh God, yes.'

Helen gulped as she saw the lust in his eyes. 'Tom, I was talking about not compromising your son!'

'Sorry, yes. Of course.' Letting go of the curl, Tom gave himself a shake. 'That settles it, we need to tell Dylan and everyone tomorrow, and see if there is a key that fits your bedroom door.'

Helen's already red face lit up like a beacon. 'No way! They'll all know why we want to lock the door.'

'But they'll know we're having sex anyway.'

'Yes, but—'

Tom reached out a hand. 'It's okay, I get it. Them knowing is one thing, but advertising the fact is something else entirely.'

'Yeah.' Helen took his hand as they stood up, 'I did wonder... I mean, not if you don't want to or anything, but...'

'What?' Tom wrapped her close. 'What is it, love?'

'Well, if you wanted, just while I'm here, umm...'

'Umm?'

'You could share with me. If you wanted... I mean, I don't mind if you don't want to and...'

Silencing her with a kiss, Tom whispered, 'I want to. Very much.'

'And Dylan, he won't mind? I mean—'

'For such a confident woman in the workplace, you're adorably shy when it comes to, what my nan called, "shenanigans".'

Helen gave him a playful shove. 'I told you, I'm out of practice.'

'Then let's practice some more.'

Friday April 3rd

The Mill Grange team waved enthusiastically as the people carrier, taking the week's guests back to Tiverton Parkway, wound its way down the drive.

Sam nodded in satisfaction. 'Another good week. Thanks everyone.'

Spinning around to the house, ready for a debriefing session, Tina gestured towards the backdoor. 'I'll grab some hot drinks and cake. See you in the garden?'

'I thought we'd aim for the bench by the fortlet if that's okay.' Sam turned to Helen. 'It would be good to have a report on progress. After all, it isn't long until you leave us.'

Feeling guilty that she hadn't told Sam if she was staying or not, Helen led the way across the gardens. As she walked, a voice at the back of her head asked why she hadn't said anything to Tom about Sam's offer to stay yet.

What are you waiting for? Last night you asked Tom to move into your room, so why haven't you said you'll stay at Mill Grange?

She thought again about the job she was contemplating giving up, her house in Bath and all the people she knew there.

But they're just people I know. Here I have friends.

Another thought collided with the others as she caught Tom's eye.

If we tell everyone we're a couple, Sam will assume I'm staying anyway.

Pulled from her introspection by their arrival at the bench, Helen saw Tom pat the seat next to him, so they should sit together. Sam hadn't appeared to notice, or if he had, hadn't thought anything of the gesture.

'How's the book thinking coming on, Helen?' Sam slid into his seat, laying his ever-present clipboard of lists and notes on the table between them.

'The chapter headings are planned. I've sent an outline sketch to the publisher. If they okay it, then it's just a case of gluing my butt to a chair and writing it.'

Tom looked at her proudly. 'Of course they'll like it. It's going to be amazing.'

'I agree.' Tina smiled as she lay down the tray of refreshments.

'Thanks.' Helen tried not to meet Tina's eyes, which plainly stated that if Tom hadn't declared himself, he was a fool because it was damn obvious he was in love with her.

Tina knows. We're going to have to tell Dylan soon.

Oblivious to the subtext going on around him, Sam pulled a piece of paper from his notes. 'I hope you don't mind, but there is so much happening at the moment, I've prepared some formal minutes for this meeting, rather than the usual catch up and check in.'

'Good job I brought cake then.' Tina sliced up some lemon cake as Sam made a start.

'We have had some excellent feedback from the week's guests once again.' Sam held up the questionnaires they asked each guest to complete before they left and passed them to Tina. 'Once again we have some wonderful endorsements we can add to the website, and we've had more interest in the archaeology skills certificate we're running from next July.'

'Is *Landscape Treasures* still up for sponsoring that?' Tom pulled his notebook from his jacket pocket.

'Absolutely. Once Shaun has finished in the Cotswolds, he has a month before filming again. He's agreed to use that time to work out the requirements with you Tom, and Thea of course.'

Helen shifted on her seat. She could feel the words 'but not with Helen', hanging unspoken over the bench. *She'd have to give Sam an answer soon. Why haven't I? What's bothering me?*

Sam picked up his mug of tea and raised it towards Helen. 'How's progress fortlet wise?'

Relieved to be on safe ground, Helen slipped into professional archaeologist mode. 'If you look at the original geophysics plans that Ajay and Andy did for Shaun when the site was first discovered, you'll see that we have almost opened each point of interest.'

Laying out the original plan and placing her own working dig plan next to it, Helen pointed out each room that had been opened, each corridor, store and courtyard. She talked of sleeping quarters for the small household of soldiers and how they were probably supporting themselves from the land with the help of supplies from nearby rural settlements. Her finger ran across the plans as she spoke of supply routes and journey times to Exeter and the nearest main fort at Rainsbury. By the time she'd stopped speaking, Sam and Tina were looking very impressed.

'Well no wonder you've been asked to write about this place.' Tina dabbed up some cake crumbs with her finger. 'You know it inside out. I've no idea how we'll—'

Helen cut across her friend, not wanting the fact of her

leaving mentioned. 'As soon as Thea is here tomorrow, I'll give her the full rundown on the dig, so she knows where I'm at. I don't think it will take much more than a month to finish uncovering everything. Then it'll just be a case of solidifying what we have.'

Sam nodded. 'Which brings me to the next point. Thea and Shaun should be back late tomorrow. While it will be fantastic to see them, and have a few more hands on deck, we are without paying guests now until April twentieth.'

Helen doodled on her pad as she asked, 'But bookings are good for the week of the twentieth, Tina?'

'Fully booked that week, and every week until September. Then things trail off rather.'

'Which is why,' Sam flapped his to-do list before him, 'I thought we'd open the house and gardens for Easter.'

There were general murmurs of approval as Tina said, 'I've got two hundred small Easter eggs ordered from the village shop. I wondered if Dylan would help plan where to hide them Tom, or do you think he'd rather not know, and enjoy hunting them down himself?'

'He'll love hiding them.'

'Excellent.' Tina scribbled a note on her pad. 'Maybe you could help Dylan with that, Helen? We'll hide them around the house and grounds on Easter Sunday.'

'How much are we charging, did you decide to stick to £2 per child?' Tom asked. 'I'm still happy to take posters to Dylan's school.'

'Thanks, Tom.' Tina scribbled, 'do poster' on her list. 'And it will be £5 per person to go into the house. I'm hoping Mabel will still help do tea and coffee.'

'I'm sure she will. Especially now Bert's home again.'

Helen felt herself relax now the emphasis was off her role at Mill Grange. 'Will Thea do a guided tour? She told me she led them during your Opening Day back in July.'

'I haven't asked her.' Sam turned to Tina. 'Have you, love?'

'Not yet, but I'm rather hoping she will. I have a few wedding things I want to ask her about, so I'll mention doing tours at the same time.'

Sam smiled. 'After bribing her with Sybil's scones?'

'Naturally.' Tina laughed. 'You'll come too, won't you, Helen? I need all the help I can get on the wedding front.'

'Well, yes. If you'd like me to.'

Not leaving anyone time to ask if Helen would still be around by then, Sam ploughed on. 'I want to take this fortnight to crack on with future plans and wedding plans. As you know, we intend to marry here, but my parents wish us to marry in Malvern. So we've invited them here in the hope they fall in love with the place. They are due tomorrow.'

'Tomorrow? But that's when Dylan comes?' Tom looked panicked.

'Don't worry, we haven't forgotten. My parents are just coming to see the house. I can't imagine they'll be here for more than a few hours. Dylan's presence won't be a problem.'

Tina nodded. 'He might even help. Look how quickly he won a place in Bert and Mabel's hearts.'

Sam, who thought his parents a very different kettle of fish to Mabel and Bert, glanced up at Mill Grange. It was a far cry from his parents' Queen Anne mansion, but he'd get them to see its charms if it was the last thing he did.

'We should crack on. Beyond our usual Friday tasks, there is a great deal of housework to do. I'm sure you'll have lots to do to get your room ready for Dylan, Tom. Is there anything else you need? An extra chest of drawers or a little desk, or anything?'

'Thank you, perhaps a little table for Dylan to draw at, but otherwise we'll be fine.' He glanced at Helen. 'Because, the thing is—'

'The thing is,' Helen interrupted, 'I've said Tom can take my desk for Dylan. Be easier than lugging extra furniture up there this weekend.'

Not glancing at Tom, Helen stared at an increasingly suspicious looking Tina. 'Would you like me to change the bed linen, Tina, so you can get a few of your cakes made to wow Lord and Lady Malvern?'

Twenty-five

Friday April 3rd

D on't panic. I haven't changed my mind. I just thought we should tell Dylan first as agreed – and soon – I think Tina has guessed. Hope you understand. H xx

We'll tell him tomorrow. T xx

Thanks for understanding. I'll make it up to you. H xx

Looking forward to that! T xx

Helen blushed and her chest tightened as she read Tom's last text. Relief mixed with guilt as she pulled an armful of linen out of the cupboard, ready to make up the rooms that had been occupied all week.

With a nagging feeling that she didn't understand why she'd used Dylan as an excuse not to tell everyone about her and Tom yet, Helen hoped Tina wouldn't want to talk about her leaving for Bath.

'There's something rather lovely about the smell of newly laundered sheets, don't you think?'

Tina flapped an Egyptian cotton sheet towards Helen, who waited on the opposite side of the bed in the manor's main bedroom.

'Absolutely.' Helen inhaled the scent of fresh air and cotton as they smoothed the sheet into place. 'I assume we're making up this room in case Sam's parents decide to stay overnight?'

'They haven't mentioned staying. I just want everything to look perfect while they're here. Is that daft?' Tina reached for a pile of pillow cases, passing two to Helen.

'Not at all. And it makes it look as if you hoped they'd stay. That can't be a bad thing, can it?'

'True. Although whether they'll come round to our way of thinking about the wedding venue…'

Helen sighed. 'Look, Tina, this is your home and Sam's home. It's also your wedding day. That makes it *your* choice. I know tradition can be hard to budge in ancestral families, but it isn't as if Sam's the heir to the estate – so stand firm. You're feeling guilty, but you haven't done anything wrong.'

'It's obvious I'm feeling guilty about holding out for what I want, then?'

'Not to anyone who doesn't know you.' Helen gave her a kind smile. 'It's allowed, you know, for the bride to have what she wants on her wedding day. Sam's parents know that. They're just battling with their expectations.'

'You may be right.'

'I am right.' Helen plumped the last pillow into a fresh case and went to open the window. 'It's stuffy today. I wouldn't be surprised if we had a burst of spring sunshine.'

'That would be good this weekend. Mill Grange looks even more beautiful when the sun shines.'

'Umm.' Helen mumbled her agreement as she spotted Tom and Sam heading towards the walled garden. Her insides gave an involuntary clench at the sight of her boyfriend.

Why haven't I told Sam and Tina I'm not leaving?

As if reading her friend's mind, Tina said, 'Sam told me he'd asked you if you'd like to stay. I don't want to hassle you or anything, but the tenth of April is less than a week away and—'

'And you could do with knowing if you're going to be another member of staff down when the place reopens on the twentieth.' Helen dug her hands deep into her jeans pockets. 'I should have said before, I'm sorry. It's just, I'm—'

'Spending a lot of time thinking about a tall slim archaeologist with piercing green eyes?' For a split-second Helen thought about denying it, but then realised there was no point. Tina wouldn't be fooled. If Thea was there, the two of them would probably be plying her with scones and portable thumbscrews, in a kindly, but unstoppable hunt for information about her love life.

'Perhaps.'

'You two have obviously been getting closer. You'd have to be blind not to notice the glances that pass between you when you think no one's looking.'

'I suspected you'd guessed.' Helen kept her gaze fixed on the garden. The men had disappeared from view, but she could see the impressive sweep of the garden as it blended with the woodland, and beyond into the heart of Exmoor. 'At first we weren't ready to share, and then we thought we should tell Dylan first.'

'Of course you should. I won't say anything. How long have you been a couple now, if you don't mind me asking?'

'Thirteen days.' As Helen spoke, the words *unlucky for some*, taunted her thoughts.

'And now his son is moving in, and you have a job to go back to and everything is moving just a bit too fast.'

'Yes.' Helen turned around. 'How did you know?'

'It was all rather a whirlwind with me and Sam. I knew what I wanted to do, but wasn't sure I was ready, or if it was the right thing to do.'

'That's it, you see.' Helen was amazed. 'Two weeks ago, I was just an archaeologist who fancied a nice man, but never thought anything would happen. And as I was leaving soon anyway... But then...'

'Then Tom realised he felt the same and now you're torn.'

'I really want to stay, but it just isn't that straightforward.'

'Because of the job in Bath or because of Dylan?'

Helen shrugged. 'Both.'

'Look, why don't we work and talk. Being busy often helps put things in perspective.'

Helen laughed. 'And there's heaps to do and no time for moping?'

Tina grinned. 'There's that as well.'

Tom threw the chickens a generous handful of pepper slices before joining Sam in front of the greenhouse.

'Tell me honestly, do you think the two of us can do this?' Sam studied the old structure, its glass panes gone, its framework intact, but battered by years of neglect, it still held a gothic beauty.

'I'd be lying if I claimed to know the answer to that, although I'm more than willing to have a go.' Tom passed Sam a list of the supplies they'd need to renovate the greenhouse. 'I got all the information you asked for, and this is what we'd need if we did the job ourselves. But I'll be honest, mate, I can't see how we'd ever manage to do it up without Tina noticing.'

'Maybe I should just do it up a bit and string up some fairy lights for the big day as Tina suggested in the first place?'

Tom checked back over his figures. 'The cheapest quote I found you wasn't cheap – if someone else did the work, that is. It would take him a week – if not more. I'm sorry, Sam, but unless you can take Tina away on holiday for a fortnight, this is one secret that would leak out in seconds.'

'As opposed to the secret that you and Helen are now a couple, you mean?'

'What?' Tom dug his hands deep into his pockets. 'Not as subtle as we thought then?'

'Nope.' Sam winked. 'I'm pleased for you.'

'Thanks.' Not sure if he should ask again, but asking anyway, Tom said, 'Did you think about inviting Helen to stay on?'

Surprised Tom didn't know about him asking Helen, and remembering his promise to say nothing, Sam felt rather awkward. 'It's a question of finances, Tom. But I do intend to discuss the matter with Helen before she goes. I'm sorry I can't promise more.'

'Pros and cons then.'

Helen threw Tina a couple of toilet rolls to put on the cistern of the main bathroom. 'Are you reducing my love life to a list?'

'Two lists actually.'

'Right.' As she hung fresh towels on the rail by the claw toed bath, Helen licked her lips. 'Pros are easy. Tom is a good man. I feel great when we're together and I love his son very much.'

'And he loves you. Tom, I mean. Dylan has always adored you. But his dad loves you.'

'Yes.'

'And you love him.'

'I think so. Yes.'

Tina kept her tone matter of fact, knowing that was how Helen would prefer thing. 'And you have similar interests and enough differences to keep things fresh.'

Helen couldn't help but smile. 'It sounds as if you've made this inventory before.'

'Once or twice.' Tina grabbed another handful of towels as she followed Helen to the next bathroom. 'And the cons?'

'I love this job, but I love the one in Bath too and...'

'It pays a lot better and you have a home there.'

'Sorry, but yes.'

'No need to be sorry. So, do you want to go back to the

Baths or stay working here? If you can answer that, then you'll be halfway there.'

'That's just it though, Tina,' Helen added a toilet roll to the empty dispenser, 'I can't answer that because it is so connected with Tom. Bath is a two-hour drive from here, so we couldn't see each other every day, or even every week as I often work weekends in Bath. Then there's Dylan; I adore him, but Tom and I would never have time alone if I were to move back to Bath. Our relationship could simply fizzle out.'

'At the risk of stating the obvious, then why not stay?'

'Because...' Helen paused, her hand on the side of the roll-top bath as she tried to form her fragmented thoughts into words. 'Because if it went wrong with Tom, I'd have nowhere to go and no job to go back to. And because I'm scared.'

Tina put down her pile of towels and moved to Helen's side. 'Of course you're scared. You're in love, and the thought of not being in love again is horrid. Suddenly life feels different. You feel different! Inside I mean. And you really want to eat chocolate, but maybe you shouldn't because you might not fit into your jeans next week and all that crap. Yes?'

'Yes.'

'So, whatever happens, whether you stay or go, you'll lose out on something, but if you want to give a future with Tom a chance, then you should.'

'But I can only do that if I stay.'

'No. You can do that whatever happens. It'll just be easier if you stay.'

Twenty-six

Friday April 3rd

The four security vans circled on the far side of the dig site as if they were cowboys arriving on a ranch.

Thea watched them vie for the best parking spot as she paused in the act of directing the tucking up of the dolphin mosaic under a series of tarpaulins. Flexing her back, she gave her team of helpers leave to grab a drink from the catering truck. The sun was beating down on their back and shoulders, and although it was only April, summer felt as if it had arrived in the Cotswolds via an accelerated fast track scheme.

She could see Shaun and the AA in conversation with Julian over by the truck which doubled as the show's technical hub. The discussion didn't look heated, yet she couldn't help but feel a prickle of suspicion as she saw Julian's arms gesticulating all over the place.

Glad they were to head back to Mill Grange soon, Thea wiped her forehead with her arm. The open land, on which the villa had been built, had neither shade nor shelter. While that gave her another insight into why the original owner positioned his home in such a suntrap, it didn't help her or her colleagues as they laboured in the stunning early spring sunshine.

Deciding to take a break herself, Thea headed to the refreshment van. Borrowing a tray, and collecting five cups of lemonade, she strolled over to the men, wondering if she was finally about to learn what Julian was up to. Whatever it was, Thea had a feeling they'd all be wishing that she was bringing them something far stronger than fizzy pop.

'Thea! And drinks. How thoughtful.' Julian beamed as he took his lemonade. 'How is putting the mosaic to bed going?'

'We're almost there. I'd like to add one more layer of covers, just to be on the safe side.' She gestured to the security team who were now queuing for drinks. 'They do know how important the site is, don't they?'

'I only employ the best.' Julian's smile became condescending. 'Which is why I employ you.' His focus remained on Thea for a split second, before he swept an arm around the group, as if to indicate his last remark was levelled at all of them.

Not giving anyone time to comment, Julian went on, 'The site will close completely when the light fails tonight. I'd like you, Shaun and Thea, to do a piece to camera as that happens.'

'Good idea.' Thea was surprised to hear Shaun agreeing with Julian. 'That's an angle we've never covered before. It will give our viewers something a little different.'

'Thank you, Shaun.' Julian flicked through the file he held, before pulling out a sheet upon which he'd scribbled some notes. 'Here's a rough idea of what I thought you could say.'

Thea wrapped her arm around Shaun's waist as they read from the script outline. It only took a quick scan of the sheet to see that she had very little to say. To her relief, Shaun was going to be in the driving seat for this piece to camera.

Maybe I got the wrong end of the stick? Perhaps Julian was talking about another show entirely on the phone?

'And you'd like this to form the episode's closing address?' Shaun asked as he reread the outline.

'With some additional words added in by your good self,' Julian said. 'That's only a hasty jotting of ideas.'

Thea didn't miss the looks the AA gave each other at Julian's unusually deferential tone.

'Thanks, Julian.' Shaun hooked a pen out of his pocket and turned to Thea. 'We'd better get this sorted and practiced.'

'Good idea,' she downed her lemonade and held up the empty cup, 'but I think I'll get us some refills first.'

Ajay picked up the other empty cups and the tray. 'I'll come with you. It's hot in the truck, and we need to get packed up too.'

As they strolled over to the catering van, tagging onto the short queue of security men and archaeologists, Ajay asked, 'I take it Shaun had the most to say in the closing speech?'

'Which is how it should be.'

'But not how it's been for the remainder of the episode.' Ajay's eyes narrowed as he looked back to where Julian was sitting. 'It's been you all the way. Why's he suddenly changed tack?'

'I don't know, but I'm glad.' Reassured to hear Ajay voice her own thoughts, but not wanting to fan the flames of his gossipy imagination, Thea added, 'It's Shaun's show. The viewers would be disappointed if he wasn't heading it.'

'Umm.'

'That was a loaded "umm".'

'I wish I could shift the feeling that our producer is up to something. Ever since that dinner we had, he's been acting as if he knows something we don't. It makes me uncomfortable.'

Part of the phone conversation Thea had overheard flashed through her mind. *A shake up of the team is inevitable. If we want to be seen to be keeping up, then we need someone at the helm of the ship who is professional and likeable and, let's be honest, easy on the eye.*

Ajay shuffled forward as they got closer to the front of the queue, his voice little more than a whisper. 'It might just be that he's a game player. Someone who likes to make people think he knows more than they do.'

'That would certainly fit his persona.' Thea sighed. 'Perhaps it's alright though. For the past few days, he's been less, what's the word?'

'Creepy?'

'I was thinking, "in your face".'

'A much more professional way of putting it.' Ajay grinned. As Thea reached her turn in the queue, he changed the subject. 'So, you're Mill Grange bound, then? Swapping one Roman excavation for another.'

'Yep.' Thea looked back to where Julian was now tapping furiously at his laptop. 'I can't wait.'

✶

The villa was swathed in a sea of blue. The heavy-duty tarpaulins, weighted down and neatly pegged in place, covered all but one last trench on the far right of the site. Here, three archaeologists swept away the final dustpans of loose earth as Shaun and Thea got ready to do their last piece to camera before Easter.

'It's looks so peaceful.' Thea surveyed the scene as the tarpaulins rippled gently in the soft breeze. 'Hard to imagine that there's thousands of years of history hidden beneath.'

Shaun slipped a hand into hers. 'I haven't seen a site put to bed like this for a long time.'

'Really?'

'We don't normally get breaks in the middle of a dig. We plough on through, Easter break or no Easter break. At least that's one thing we can thank Julian for.'

Thea turned the lock in her camper's door and picked up her rucksack and laptop case, ready to head across the grass to where Shaun had parked his car. She could see him throwing his own stuff into the boot as he chatted to Andy.

'Thea, I'm glad I caught you.'

'Julian! You made me jump.' Thea automatically took a step backwards as the producer appeared from around the side of the campervan, making her wonder how long he'd been stood there.

'Sorry, Thea. I needed a quick word before we go our separate ways.'

'Sure.' Hoping she sounded less uneasy than she was,

Thea pointed towards the car park. 'Shall we walk and talk?'

'Here would be better.' Julian tilted his head. 'I'm going to pop back to the site to have a final chat with the security team before I go.'

'Right.' Thea hugged her laptop to her chest. 'How can I help?'

'Just wanted you to know that the broadcast you did to the local news team went down very well with the chaps at head office.'

'Oh, thanks.'

Julian twisted his stance so he could follow the line of Thea's gaze, towards Shaun. 'Yes. Very well indeed. They congratulated me on getting you in action on a wider stage.'

Thea stiffened as Julian's phone conversation ran through her head once more. '... *they will soon be seen in action on a wider stage...*'

Julian kept his eyes on Shaun and Andy as he added, 'They were so impressed in fact, that they asked me to enquire if you'd ever considered doing more presenting?'

'Me?' Thea palms were suddenly sweaty. 'Phil asked me if I'd like to do more, and I'm here, doing just that. But beyond this, no, not really.'

'Nonetheless, I'd like you to think about it.' Julian turned to face the path back to the excavation. 'But, for now, keep this conversation to yourself.'

'Not tell Shaun, you mean?' Thea frowned.

'The conversation I had with the television company was confidential. I'd ask you to respect that.'

'Well I—'

'When you get back next week for the final mosaic shots, I'd like a meeting. Just us, please. To discuss where your career could go from here.'

'But I already have a good career.'

'So do I, but it doesn't mean we can't have better ones.'

Twenty-seven

Saturday April 4th

The aroma of strong fresh coffee teased Thea's senses as she sat across the immaculately set breakfast table from Shaun. Tucked into the hotel's bay window, they looked out over a pristine garden as a smartly aproned waitress delivered a mountain of croissants and Danish pastries.

'Is that a camomile lawn, do you think?' Thea poured some more coffee as she relaxed in her snugly padded wicker seat.

'I wouldn't be at all surprised.'

Thea watched a robin hop territorially around the nearest section of flower bed. 'I'm so glad we booked a night here on the way home. It's so peaceful.'

'I hoped you'd like it.'

'You've stayed here before?'

'Once, on the way to a conference. I hated being in those big beds and having no one to roll around with.'

Thea blushed, glad their early start meant they were the only ones in the breakfast room.

Since they'd got into Shaun's car the previous evening and driven to the nearby hotel in Stow-on-the-Wold, Thea had vowed to leave all thinking about what Julian had said until they were back at Mill Grange. Now, as they ate, she squashed the flutter of guilt she felt at keeping a secret from Shaun. The evening before, the night, and now their shared breakfast, had all been so perfect, she didn't want to ruin a second of it.

'I'm looking forward to being back at Mill Grange, but it would be nice to stay here longer and hide from the world for a while.' Thea brushed croissant crumbs from her cleavage.

'I was thinking the same.' Shaun checked to make sure they weren't overheard by the few diners that had started to arrive. 'In the meantime, I've secured a late check out, so I'd be obliged if you'd leave a few of those crumbs for me to find later.'

Thea's eyebrows rose. 'Perhaps I should have ordered more pastries and no fry up.'

Shaun winked as a rack of toast was delivered to the table. 'Toast crumbs work for me too.'

The staircase hadn't gleamed as brightly since Mill Grange had held an Open Day the previous July. Tina had buffed and polished it so much, it was a wonder you couldn't see your reflection in the wood. The paintings hanging in the main corridor had been straightened and re-straightened, and the usual pile of muddy shoes by the front door was conspicuous by its absence.

Helen, having expected to find Tina in the kitchen

making coffee in readiness for her future in-laws arrival, had tracked her to the hallway by following the scent of beeswax.

'If you polish that door any more, it'll gleam.'

Focusing all of her nervous energy on the duster she was working over the door's oak panels, Tina sagged. 'Do you think the house looks okay, Helen?'

'I thought it looked okay when you asked me last night, and again at eight o'clock this morning.' Taking the duster firmly but politely from Tina's hand, Helen steered her towards the kitchen. 'If you don't sit down soon, you'll have no energy left for when they get here.'

'But what if they don't like the house?'

'Then taking off non-existent layers of dust won't make any difference.' Helen led her to where Mabel was waiting with a mug of coffee and a plate of biscuits.

Allowing herself to be sat down, Tina picked up a cookie. 'Thanks, Mabel. Anyone know where Sam is?'

'In his tent getting changed.'

Tina jumped back to her feet, and stared down as her outfit. 'I was so busy making sure Mill Grange was perfect, I forgot about changing!'

Mabel placed a gentle hand on Tina's shoulder, and persuaded her to sit down again. 'Drink your coffee, have some food and then go. They won't be here for at least another hour.'

'But what if they're early?'

'Sam had a call about half an hour ago; they are running late. Heavy traffic on the motorway.'

'I wish he'd told me.'

'He was helping Tom move some furniture around upstairs so that Dylan's got a table in his bedroom.'

'Oh yes. I remember him saying now.' Tina picked up her coffee, looked at her friends. 'I'm flapping, aren't I?'

'You are. Which is perfectly understandable.' Mabel took a cloth and wiped away a few crumbs Tina had spilt. 'But this isn't a snap army inspection. They are visiting you and their son because they haven't seen the house before. Don't think of it as more than that.'

'I'm trying not to.'

'But it's hard not to worry at the same time.' Helen sat down and took a biscuit of her own. 'Do we know what time Thea and Shaun are due back?'

'Late afternoon.' Tina sipped at her coffee, enjoying its comforting warmth. 'It'll be good to all be together again. Seems ages.'

'If Lord and Lady Malvern stay for dinner, at least Shaun will be able to regale them with tales from *Landscape Treasures*.'

Tina's coffee cup met the table with a thud. 'Stay for dinner?' Oh my God. What if they do? They said they were coming for the day. So, lunch is sorted, but we assumed they'd go about four. You don't think they'll stay do you?'

'Whoa.' Helen took Tina's arm. 'If they were going to stay, they'd have said.'

'I wish I hadn't mentioned it now,' Mabel looked pale, 'but if they do – which they probably won't – I'll do my lasagne.'

'But, Mabel, that's kind and everything, but what about Bert?'

'He can have some too.'

'No, I meant, what about Bert being left on his own all day when he's ill.'

Mabel headed to the fridge to fetch milk and cheese. 'He sent me out this morning with strict instructions to enjoy the day.'

Tina couldn't help but smile. She could just imagine Bert understanding how much Mabel would want to meet Sam's parents. She also wondered if, now he was beginning to feel a little better, he was looking forward to a whole day of peace and quiet.

'Well I'm glad you're here. All reinforcements welcome today.' Tina suddenly registered what Mabel was doing. 'Are you making cheese sauce?'

'Lasagne. Might as well bake a couple while we wait. They smell amazing while they cook, so that won't hurt once your guests arrive, and then we can either freeze them, or you can eat them tonight.'

Tina got up again and hugged Mabel. 'I honestly don't know what we'd do without you.'

'Just think of it as me taking my mother of the bride duties seriously. Can't have you in a flap just because your in-laws are coming.'

Sam and Tom sat on the wall which joined the house's driveway to the road to Upwich, anticipating the arrival of Lord Malvern's car.

'How's your room looking now Dylan's desk is in place? I'm sorry I couldn't stay and move things round once I'd moved it out of Helen's room.'

'Don't worry. You've got a lot on today.' Tom gestured down the empty road to emphasise the forthcoming arrival of Sam's parents. 'The room is fine, thank you.'

Sam grinned. 'Does that really mean, "it's great, thanks, but hellish cramped for two"?'

'I'd be lying if I said it was spacious, but it won't be for long. I've signed on with some rental agencies, so it's just a case of waiting to see what turns up and keeping my eyes open now.'

'And you can have Helen's room too, soon.'

'Yes.' Tom was about to ask again if Sam had thought more about her staying, when a navy-blue Bentley appeared from around the corner. It was being driven at about five miles an hour as the driver edged along the narrow lane. 'Your folks, I think.'

'Oh hell, they brought the tank! I warned them the road was narrow.' Sam blew out an exhalation of breath.

Tom gave his friend a pat on the shoulder before darting up to the house to alert Tina to the arrival, leaving Sam to guide Lord and Lady Malvern up the drive to his home.

Mabel gave Tina a reassuring hug. 'You look lovely. Off you go.'

'Why am I so nervous? I've met them before.'

'Because it's important to you that they're happy here. Not just because of the wedding, but because you're a nice person and you want them to feel at home.'

'Thanks, Mabel.' Having lost her trademark pigtails in honour of the occasion, Tina anxiously brushed her fingers through her hair.

Tom echoed Mabel's sentiments as he filled the kettle. 'Just relax and have a good day. Imagine you're simply showing guests around the manor. It'll be good practice for open house on Easter Sunday.'

Tina was far from convinced as she hurried off in Sam's direction. She'd just got to the door, when she spun back round. 'Are you sure you don't mind bringing tea and cake into the garden, Mabel? I hate making you look like a servant!'

'Sshh with you, child. Now, off you go.'

'Tina! How lovely to see you.' Sam's mother, bedecked in a bright floral dress and knee length chocolate brown jacket, held out her hand, before changing her mind and giving her future daughter-in-law a hug. 'I'm so excited to see your home.'

Taken aback, having expected to have to justify every stone and floor tile, Tina found herself in her third hug of the hour, her nervous smile changing into a real one.

'We're just so glad you could both come, Lady Malvern.'

'Now, I told you before, call me Bea.'

Tina stepped back and turned to Lord Malvern. His expression was as sombre as ever; she wasn't sure if she was supposed to shake his hand or not. Attempting a hug would, she knew, be serious overkill. Sam came to her rescue.

'We thought you'd like a cuppa before we gave you the tour.' He stretched an arm towards the side of the house.

'That sounds lovely.' Bea looked up at the granite building, whose stones shone as, with perfect timing, the sun came out from behind a cloud.

'Outside?' Lord Malvern gave his son an appraising stare.

Not taking the bait, Sam merely nodded. 'There is a stunning view over the garden, and it's such a lovely day.'

'Quite right.' Bea gave her husband a stern look, before turning back to Tina. 'Could I trouble you for the bathroom first?'

'Yes of course.' Tina was suddenly flustered. In the rehearsal of this meeting, which had occupied most of her restless night, she'd offered Lady Bea the chance to freshen up as soon as she'd arrived, but in glow of relief that one of their guests looked happy, she'd forgotten all about her intentions.

Giving Tina's arm a reassuring squeeze, Sam said, 'Come on, Father, let's go and admire the view while we're waiting.'

Looping her arm through Tina's, Bea watched the men go. 'How's Sam doing? Has he been inside yet?'

Surprised by the familiarity of the gesture, Tina led her companion in through the main door. 'Yes. He's getting quite good at downstairs. Upstairs hasn't happened yet, but we'll get there.'

Lady Malvern stopped walking as they reached the porch, tears shone in her eyes. 'You're telling me my son is getting better?'

'Yes.' Tina felt awkward in the face of unexpected aristocratic emotion. 'He's working really hard. He still uses the tent to sleep at night if the downstairs bedroom is needed by a guest, but otherwise, the claustrophobia is definitely – slowly – being shown its place.'

Fishing a neatly folded cotton handkerchief from her long woollen jacket pocket, Bea dabbed at her eyes. 'Forgive me, Tina, but that's such good news. I'd begun to think he'd never get better.'

'He's had a lot of help from Bert of course. You remember us telling you about him when we came to stay?'

'The elderly gentleman who had been through something similar?'

'That's him.' Tina led the way through the hall, and towards the staircase. 'And his work here has helped. Sharing his time with so many veterans who've suffered in the defence of their country, it focuses the mind.'

'I don't doubt it.' Bea paused at the foot of the stairs. The scent of beeswax hung in the air; the paintings, while a million miles from her own collection of old masters, were fascinatingly eclectic. The light from the window on the landing bathed the hallway in a golden glow.

Hoping her guest approved of the view, Tina stepped onto the first stair. 'I've laid out a bathroom for you. It's just up here, to the left.'

Smiling by way of thanks, Bea ran her palm up the smooth banister, her eyes taking in everything around her as Tina walked nervously by her side, feeling as though she was waiting for a verdict from a court cased.

Lady Bea had almost reached the top of the stairs, when she stopped and inhaled. 'What's that wonderful smell?'

'The wood polish?'

'No, it smells like someone's cooking.'

'That's Mabel. Well, the smell isn't Mabel, it's lasagne.' Tina shook her head and started again, 'What I mean is, Mabel is in the kitchen cooking lasagne.'

'Mabel is Bert's wife?'

'Yes.' Pleased Bea had remembered, Tina was taken back when her guest turned around.

'To tell you the truth, Tina. I don't need the bathroom. I was just dying to see inside the house. Shall we go to the kitchen? It's the heart of a house, don't you think?'

Twenty-eight

Saturday April 4th

'**O**h, it's perfect,' Lady Malvern muttered as she stood at the threshold to the kitchen, blocking Tina's path so she couldn't dart through and warn Mabel, who was deep in concentration, that she was being watched.

Bea's eyes shone with delight as she ran her gaze from the Aga to the dresser, and on to the little old lady sat at the wooden table, umpteen recipe books laid open before her. 'You must be the inestimable Mrs Hastings. I'm delighted to meet you. Sam and Tina told us all about you when they came to Malvern. They owe you so much, and so, therefore, do my husband and I.'

Mabel jumped to her feet in surprise and wavered. Tina could see she was unsure if she should curtsey, and was relieved when her friend settled for holding her hand out in greeting.

'That's most kind of you, my Lady.' Mabel's eyes darted in alarm to the dishes waiting to go in the dishwasher and the empty coffee mug by her side. 'You must excuse the mess. I wasn't expecting you to come in here.'

Flapping the apology away, Bea sat down opposite Mabel. 'I love a kitchen, Mrs Hastings. You can learn more about a home and its household from a kitchen than anywhere else, don't you think?'

'I most certainly do.' Mabel was in full agreement. 'I was about to make up a tray of coffee and cake. Do you still want it outside, Tina?' Mabel glanced at the kitchen clock. 'Or would you like lunch? Time seems to be galloping away this morning.'

'I think coffee and tea to start with.' Tina headed to the coffee maker. 'But I'll do it. You two look comfortable.'

Lady Malvern was already leafing through the nearest cookery book. 'Your lasagne smells incredible. Is it your own recipe?'

'More a combination of other peoples, from which I've created my own.' Mabel took a piece of paper from her ever present list pad. 'Would you like me to write it down for you?'

'I'd love it. Thank you. Charles is most partial to Italian food. I'll pass it onto Karen. She's our cook at the moment. Brilliant girl. Doing a Physics PhD.'

Feeling she ought to contribute to the conversation, Tina said. 'Lord and Lady Malvern employ post grad students, so they can earn while they learn.'

'What an excellent idea.' Mabel got up from her seat and fetched a cake tin from the cupboard. 'That must be where Sam gets his goodness from. You should see him with the guests here. He coaxes them out of themselves without them even noticing.'

Placing cups onto the tray, Tina smiled. 'I'm so proud of him. Although, I must say, the whole team here are excellent.'

'They are,' Mabel concurred. 'Tom and Helen, they run the archaeological dig and the training that goes with it. They're so skilled, and the guests love them. Then there's Thea and Shaun of course. They're away filming on *Landscape Treasures*, would you believe! When she's here, Thea helps Sam and Tina run the place.'

'Sam told us all about you having a celebrity in your midst. I must say, I love *Landscape Treasures*!'

'Shaun and Thea should be here this afternoon; you'd be welcome to stay and say hello.' Tina, who'd previously wanted to get their visitors in and out of the house as soon as possible, found herself hoping Bea would stay.

'That would be lovely. I can't wait to tell the ladies at bridge club that I met Shaun Cowlson. Several of them have a serious crush in that direction.'

'Really?' Tina wondered how Shaun would feel about having a team of aging groupies, when she suddenly realised he was probably used to it. 'Both Thea and Shaun will help with the dig once Helen leaves next week.'

'You're losing a staff member. That's a shame.'

'It is.' Tina – who hadn't given up hope that Helen would decide to stay – was afraid Bea would think there was a sinister reason for her leaving, so quickly added, 'She was only here on sabbatical. Helen runs the Roman Baths in Bath.'

'Goodness. Now that's a job and a half I'm sure.' Bea got to her feet and headed to a chest of drawers. 'Cutlery in here? Shall I dig out the forks for that delicious cake?'

'Thank you, Lady Malvern.' Tina saw Mabel's eyebrows rise. Helping out in the kitchen obviously did not fit with her picture of how the aristocracy should behave.

'My pleasure, and please, you must both call me Bea. Having a title does rather get in the way of relaxed friendships. Sometimes I do wish I was plain Mrs Philips.'

'Then you must call me Mabel.'

'Thank you, Mabel. I can't tell you how tired I get of formality. It's important to keep up standards of course, but with family... well, I'd love it if we could just relax.' Bea straightened up, her shoulders losing their previous rigid uprightness. 'So, tell me, Mabel, what would your go-to cake recipe be? I just love a Victoria sponge. Traditional maybe, but when done right – perfection!'

'You are so right, Bea. My mother made the lightest sponge you can ever imagine.' Mabel smiled wider than ever. 'For me however, it has to be a Swiss roll. A home made one, rolled in a tea towel. My grandmother taught me how to make them.'

'You know the old-fashioned cakes are often the best.' Bea reached for the nearest recipe book and began to flick through the pages,

Exchanging glances with Mabel, Tina's eyes darted back to the kitchen clock, prompting the older woman to say, 'You know, it really is nearly lunch time. How about we get some soup going?'

Finding themselves ably assisted by Bea as they stirred soup and heated crusty rolls in the Aga, Tina suddenly said, 'Do you think I should tell Sam what we're up to? He'll think we've got lost on the way to the loo.'

'Don't worry, it'll do them good to have a talk on their

own. Anyway, Charles won't be interested in wedding stuff, and I'm dying to ask, have you got a dress? And if you have, can I have a peep?'

'I haven't, but if I had, you could certainly have a peep.' Tina found herself relaxing further as Sam's mum licked stray butter from her fingers. 'Mabel is going to help me look for one.'

Mabel beamed. 'Tina has asked Bert and me to be father and mother of the bride. I tell you, we fair near popped with pride.'

'How wonderful!' Bea clapped with enthusiasm. 'I hope we'll get to meet Bert. I've heard so much about him.'

As a slight cloud passed over Mabel's face, Tina explained about Bert recovering from pneumonia, and being house bound for the time being.

'Then I must go and visit him.' Bea spoke as if it was a done deal. 'I owe your husband for saving my son's life.'

Not having anticipated being left alone with his father, Sam dug his hands into his pockets as he led the way around the side of the manor. 'Do you think they'll be long, Father? I'd rather like your opinion on something while Tina isn't with us.'

Lord Malvern snorted. 'If I know your mother, she had no need for the bathroom at all, but wanted an excuse to be nosey.'

Sam smiled. 'In that case, would you mind a quick trip into the walled garden?'

'Lead on.' Lord Malvern surveyed the scene before him. 'You weren't exaggerating about the view over the gardens.

It is quite something. Goes right down to Exmoor, am I right?'

'It does.' Wondering if his mother had given his father a stern talking to about being nice, Sam pushed open the gate to the walled garden. 'It was the first thing I fell in love with at Mill Grange.'

'And Tina was the second.'

'Yes.' Sam wasn't sure how else to respond, so he shut the gate behind them and pointed to the far end of the garden. 'Do you remember me telling you about our greenhouse when we visited Malvern House?'

'Indeed. It was just after I'd had our orangery done up for your mother.' Charles strode on, his head moving from side to side as he took in the rows of neat vegetable patches and the large chicken run.

'I'd like to do ours up as a surprise for Tina. I've had some quotes done, but they were astronomical, so if possible, I'd like to do it up myself. I'd value your thoughts.'

'Certainly.'

Coming to a stop before the tumbledown structure, Lord Malvern regarded it carefully. 'A lot of work. Do you have the skills to set the panes of glass and so forth?'

'Not yet. But I'm willing to learn.'

'The wedding isn't far off, even if you got a professional in. It's unlikely you'd get the greenhouse ready before the end of May.' Lord Malvern paused. 'I'm assuming that was your plan?'

Sam sighed. 'It was, but I'm having a rethink. What with work and everything, I haven't even made a start on sourcing new glass, and neither Tom nor I can work out how to get the place done up secretly. There's no way Tina would stay out of the walled garden for long enough. She loves the hens far too much.'

'You couldn't take her away on holiday before the wedding?'

'Not a hope.' Sam swallowed. 'And there's the other thing.'

'Other thing?' Lord Malvern sat on the bench by the chicken run and studied the greenhouse, his forehead creased in thought.

Sam took a deep breath. 'Tina and I want to get married here, but—'

Charles's placid demeanour disappeared and his shoulder's stiffened. 'Well if neither of you are worried about family or your mother's feelings, then that is what you must do.'

Twenty-nine

Saturday April 4th

As they turned off the link road that led from the motorway towards Tiverton, Shaun pulled the car into the nearest lay-by.

Thea looked around in surprise. 'Why have we stopped? Are you alright?'

'I am, but I wasn't sure if you were. The closer we've got to Upwich, the quieter you've become.'

Thea licked her lips, not wanting to ruin the day by telling him about the text message that had arrived on her phone shortly after they'd crossed the border from Gloucestershire into Somerset. It had been short and to the point; enforcing Julian's offer of future presenting work and reminding her to keep the offer a secret.

'I'm fine. Just enjoying the scenery.' She smiled. 'It's been a lovely day.'

'It has.' Shaun picked up his phone, only to lower it again. 'Do you have a phone signal here?'

Thea picked up her mobile. Three bars lit up her screen.

She hesitated, not wanting to loan Shaun her phone in case another message from Julian arrived while he was using it. 'Sorry, no. Did you want to call ahead for them to put the kettle on?'

'No. I wanted to call that hotel and book us a room for the night on the way back to the dig.'

Guilt twisted in Thea's stomach. 'For a pre campervan cuddle?'

'For a pre campervan toast crumb hunt.'

Sam had felt as if he was walking on eggshells ever since he'd followed Lord Malvern out of the walled garden. Guilt hung heavily on his shoulders throughout lunch, as he watched his mum and Tina chat about the house in general. He hadn't had a chance to talk to Tina about his father's reaction to them marrying at home, which, he thought, was perhaps just as well.

As Tina finished expounding the virtues of the manor's interior, Sam piled their soup bowls onto the tray.

'Would you like to see inside, Father?'

'As we're here, I suppose that would be sensible.'

'Honestly, Charles, try and sound a little bit enthusiastic!' Bea rolled her eyes. 'Come on.' She got to her feet, picking up some empty coffee cups as she did so. 'I've only seen the kitchen properly so far. I'd love to explore the rest of the house.'

Giving his wife an indulgent look, Charles got to his feet. 'What will you do while we look inside, Sam?'

'I'll come with you, downstairs anyway. Tina will have to take you upstairs though.'

Tina enjoyed watching Lord Malvern's eyes widen. 'You can come inside, and stay inside, now, Sam?'

'Yes.'

Tina slipped a hand in Sam's. 'I told your mum about the efforts you and Bert have been making, and how they've been paying off.'

'Good for you, Sam.' Charles's smile returned, lingering at the corners of his mouth. 'Shall we go in?'

Leading the way, Tina could hear Bea behind her, telling her husband what a treasure Mabel was.

'Mabel will have gone home to check on Bert, I'm afraid, but I'm sure she'll be back later if you'd like to meet her.'

Bea placed the cups on the table as Charles surveyed his surroundings, his expression unreadable, although Tina couldn't help but notice he spent as much time observing his son in an indoor setting as the setting itself.

'Charles, I think I must visit Mr Hastings before we go home. He has done so much for Sam. He'll be giving Tina away at the wedding.'

'Will he now.' Charles head titled upwards. 'Then indeed he must be visited.'

Seeing his mother rolling up her sleeves, looking like a woman who had every intention of washing up, Sam tugged Tina gently to one side and whispered, 'Should we ask them to stay for dinner? It's almost three. Thea and Shaun will be here soon.'

Opening the large china cupboards doors, so their faces were hidden while in hushed conversation, Tina said, 'I think your mother's already assumed they're staying. She made a big fuss over the lasagne earlier.'

'Right.' Sam nodded. 'My father was a bit prickly about

the venue thing when we were in the garden. How's it going with Mum?'

'Hard to tell. She's thrilled that you're able to come inside. She got quite chocked when she realised how much progress you'd made. We've talked about the wedding, but not where it'll happen.' Tina grimaced. 'They seem to love the house. We can win them round, can't we?'

'Miracles do happen.' Sam winked before closing the cupboard again.

Tom pushed a chair under the desk and stood back to examine the affect. 'What do you think?'

'I think it's a good job you two sharing one room is a short-term thing.' Helen felt awkward. She knew that if they'd told Sam and Tina they were a couple when they'd originally planned to, then Dylan would have this room to himself already. And although Tina had guessed, she'd promised not to tell Sam until Dylan knew.

'At least I won't have many of his belongings to store until I find somewhere to rent. Sue's only bringing the essentials over with Dylan tomorrow.'

Helen pointed to the deep windowsill. 'Dylan could use that as his shelf for a while.'

'His shelf?'

'He's bound to have books and cuddly toys that he views as essentials, even if they're only weekend essentials.'

'You're right. I hadn't thought of that.' Moving forward to swipe a jumble of books and papers off the window sill, Tom peered into the garden. 'Sam and Tina aren't at the picnic table by the kitchen anymore. I hope it's going alright for them.'

'They spent long enough having lunch. The lack of raised voices has to be a good sign.' Glad they'd had the foresight to bring their own lunch up to her room, Helen said, 'Tina was hoping to do a tour of the house after they'd eaten. Perhaps we should slip outside and leave them undisturbed in case the attics are included in the itinerary?'

'Good idea.' Tom pushed his armful of possessions under the bed. 'There's nothing else we could do now until Dylan is here. Let's go and see the fortlet.'

Face to face with the fortlet, the weight of their unspoken conversation about her immediate future rested on Helen's shoulders.

'I want to get it under a few layers of protection before the public come in for the Easter egg hunt. We could get the covers ready to put it into sleep mode.'

'I'll help you put them on now if you like.' Tom bent down to lift a few blown in branches from the floor of, what was once, a Roman walkway.

'I wasn't sure if Sam would want to show his parents.' Helen's eyes flicked towards the house. 'I hope they can win them over. It would be so wrong for Sam and Tina to marry anywhere but here.'

'Yes.' Tom paused, sensing Helen's growing discomfort. They couldn't avoid the elephant in the room any longer. 'When you're back in Bath, you will visit won't you, when you can, I mean? Dylan will miss you. And I will too, obviously.'

Helen's heart thudded faster as she risked a glimpse at

Tom's face. He was staring at his feet, his expression torn between hope and fear.

She found her mind zipping back to the earlier part of that day, when he'd made love to her as if she was the most precious creature that had ever lived. Her thoughts rewound across the weeks they'd worked side by side, helping others to learn to love their heritage as they strove to improve their personal futures. She thought on, picturing Dylan, who'd lightened her life in a way she hadn't imagined possible, and suddenly she couldn't think what it was that had been stopping her making a decision about her future.

Taking Tom's hand, without a word, Helen walked them both into the woods that sheltered the far side of the excavation area.

Following her lead as she sat on the dry ground, her back resting against a hefty oak tree, Tom whispered, 'Helen?'

'I wanted us to tell everyone about us being together when we first planned to, I really did. But I got scared.' Helen shoved a ringlet behind her right ear. 'Although, I genuinely do think we ought to tell Dylan first.'

Tom wrapped her hand tighter in his, homing in on the first part of her statement. 'Scared in what way?'

'The enormity of it all. It's happened so fast. To go from us getting together, to basically living together so Dylan can have some space of his own. I know it isn't living together in the conventional sense, but it felt so huge.'

Not daring to speak for fear of saying the wrong thing, Tom squeezed her palm as he listened.

'... and to give up my job in Bath and move here. I suppose I panicked.'

'That I understand.' Tom squashed up against her side. 'I'm not asking you to give up your life in Bath. You love that job. I can't ask you to gamble on me. That's why I just asked if you'd come to see us once you were back there.'

'Of course I would, and I hope you'd come to see me. I know it is two hours away, and with Dylan with you every other weekend it's a big ask, but even if you were only there for when I got home from work...' She tousled a hand through her hair, making her fringe bounce across her forehead. 'But then I got to thinking that if we dated long distance for a while it would be less frightening, because if we missed each other we'd know for sure that we were meant to be together.'

'If that's what you want to do.' Tom forced himself not to adjust her fringe. A single curl was hovering between her eyebrows in a seductive manner that she was oblivious to.

'But that's just it. I don't know what I want. *Didn't know*. It's all been so jumbled in my head.'

'But now you do know? What you want, I mean.'

'Yes.' Helen shuffled around so she was facing Tom, holding his green gaze. 'Just then, as we stood by the old walkway the soldiers used to patrol the area, when you asked me about coming to visit. That's when I knew. I don't want you to come and visit Tom, because I don't want to leave Mill Grange in the first place.'

'You want to stay here?'

'Yes.'

'With me?'

'With you.' She went to push the curl out of her eyes, but Tom's hand darted forward and stopped her.

'No, let me do that.'

Thirty

Saturday April 4th

'Wow, now that's a car.'
As Shaun pulled up next to the old-style Bentley,
Thea admired the navy bodywork. 'Sam's parents must still
be here.'

'Does that mean we should make ourselves scarce, or do
you think it's okay to go inside?'

Thea swung her car door open and hopped out, stretching
her legs. 'I'm sure it's fine to go in, which is just as well,
because I'm bursting for a pee.'

Smiling as Thea darted towards the backdoor, Shaun
unlocked the car boot just as Tom and Helen appeared from
around the side of the house.

'Need help with your luggage?'

'Thanks, Tom.' Shaun's eyes widened as he noticed they
were holding hands. 'Looks like a lot's been happening in
our absence.'

Helen glanced at their hands self-consciously. 'Oh you
know life at Mill Grange, nothing stays the same for long.'

'Yep, nothing like a historical house for constant change.' Shaun laughed as he shook Tom's hand.

Grinning, Helen said, 'Actually, we didn't think anyone would be around. We haven't told anyone yet, so…'

'So mum's the word for now.'

'Although,' Tom exchanged glances with Helen as he said, 'Tina and Mabel both guessed, so it's not like no one knows, we just aren't broadcasting until we've spoken to Dylan.'

'Got it.' Shaun nodded. 'I'm delighted for the pair of you. Thea will be too. She's just dashed in to the loo. She told me you two had the hots for each other, as she put it, the day you arrived, Tom.'

Helen's eyes widened. 'Did she?'

'Yep.' Hauling a pair of overstuffed rucksacks from the boot of the car, Shaun paused. 'Now I think about it, she was convinced that Tina and Sam would get together long before they did too.'

'Spooky.' Tom let go of Helen's hand so he could take one of the heavy holdalls from Shaun. 'Secret witchcraft?'

Helen pulled a bag of walking boots from the boot. 'More likely she's been talking to Minerva again.'

'Sorry?' Tom looked confused.

'I'd almost forgotten she did that.' Shaun smiled. 'I haven't heard Thea talk to Minerva for ages.'

Helen followed the men towards the house, explaining the Minerva situation to Tom. 'Thea had a statute of the Goddess of Wisdom in the corner of her office when she worked at the Roman Baths. I often came in and found her in conversation with it.'

'There are worse things to take advice from I guess.' Tom's eyebrows rose. 'Perhaps I should get us a statue, then the next time we're in a dither about what to do, we can ask it for guidance.'

Helen laughed. 'That's not a bad idea, although you do have to listen really really hard for an answer.'

'Always a catch.'

Shaun pushed open the backdoor with his foot and checked along the corridor. 'Should we dump our things and then get out of Sam's way?'

Helen headed for the back stairs. 'We were just considering heading to the pub.'

'A plan with no drawbacks.' Shaun took Helen's bag from her. 'Can you stay here and wait for Thea while we run stuff upstairs?'

'Sure.' As Shaun and Tom disappeared from view, Helen's heart soared. She'd made her decision, and seeing Shaun's delighted expression at their being a couple, she knew it was the right one.

Hovering outside the bathroom, Helen called through the door. 'Thea, are you in there?'

'Helen! Yes, won't be a minute.'

Seconds later Thea threw open the door. 'Sorry, it was so hot in the car. I grabbed the chance for a quick wash. It's so good to see you.' Engulfing her friend in a hug, Thea stood back and regarded her shrewdly. 'Something's happened. Tom?'

Helen burst out laughing. 'You really are spooky.'

'Sorry?'

Explaining about the Minerva conversation she'd just had, Helen told Thea they were all off to the pub.

'Excellent. I've missed wandering into Upwich. We should leave a note so Tina and Sam know where we are.'

Heading into the kitchen, Helen fished a pen from her trouser pocket to jot a note down, when she saw one already in place on the table. 'They aren't here. Good lord!'

'What is it?'

'They've taken Lord and Lady Malvern to meet Bert.'

Sam stood by the door to the ruined mill and waited for his father to come out. The building, for which Mill Grange was named, had once been a thriving woollen mill, providing the Victorian community with employment. It had been the heart of Upwich until more advanced machinery at rival mills had put it out of action.

However much progress he was making with his claustrophobia, Sam still couldn't force his feet to cross the mill's threshold. He'd been in before. Just once, the previous June, to help Shaun rescue Thea and Tina when they'd been locked inside while fire blazed around them.

Lingering by the open double doors, Sam could smell the acrid aroma of smoke and burnt walls and floor. At least he thought he could. He knew he couldn't trust his senses when it came to the after scent of fire. Wiping perspiration from his palms, Sam wished his father would hurry up.

Having thanked Bert heartily for helping his son, in a manner of humility Sam hadn't realised his father had in him, Bert, sensing a wedding conversation was on the cards between their better halves, had suggested that Sam show his father the mill site.

The initial panic at Bert's suggestion had quickly been quelled as Lord Malvern said, 'I'd like to see the space. You could wait outside while I look. Do you have the keys on you, Sam?'

Now, as he wondered if he'd ever be able to go inside the building again, Sam found himself breathing deeply, using the mantra Bert had taught him to keep calm. Looking from left to right, making sure no one was watching him pacing anxiously up and down, he stopped as he saw, not just Tom and Helen walking towards him, but Thea and Shaun as well.

'What a lovely surprise.' Sam rubbed his sweaty palms on his trousers. 'Great to see you both.'

'Likewise.' Shaun gestured to the mill. 'We thought you were with Bert and Mabel.'

'Tina and Mum are. My father's inside, taking a look.'

'Right.' Shaun gestured to the door. 'Would you like me to go inside and make sure he's alright?'

'Would you mind? He's been in there a while.'

As Shaun headed inside, calling out to Lord Charles as he went, Thea said, 'we were on the way to the pub, but we can head to Mabel's if you like.'

'I'm sure she'd be glad to see you, but Bert's turned in. I think he's finding too much company very tiring right now.'

Thea was puzzled. 'Bert never has too much company.'

Sam exchanged anxious glances with Tom and Helen. 'I was going to tell you as soon as you got back, but then my folks came and—'

'Tell us what?' Thea frowned.

'He's had pneumonia.' Helen put an arm around Thea's shoulders. 'He's very much better, but he's still in recovery.'

'Oh God. We *have* to go and see him! Why didn't you tell us?'

'He wouldn't let us.' Helen shrugged. 'You know Bert. He didn't want you to be distracted from the dig. If things had got really bad, we'd have ignored him and told you, but luckily that didn't happen.'

'I'd still like to check on him and see Mabel. Do you think they'd mind if I gate-crashed their wedding talk?'

Sam smiled. 'Now what makes you think they're talking weddings?'

'Hunch.'

'My mother would be delighted to meet you. Why don't you go, I'll fill Shaun in.'

'I'll come with you.' Helen, keen to talk to her friend about Tom and her decision to stay, agreed. 'We'll catch up later. Enjoy the pub.'

'It's such a shame Mabel couldn't join us for dinner, especially as she cooked it.' Bea looked approvingly at her fast disappearing food.

As everyone else had their mouths full, Thea said, 'She wanted to get back to Bert. I can't believe he's been so ill.'

'He was quite firm about not worrying you two while you were filming.' Sam refilled his empty glass.

Bea picked up her wine as if to toast Bert. 'Having met that gentleman today, I can believe he's the sort of chap who wouldn't want to cause a fuss. An old school gentleman.'

Charles agreed. 'His suggestion that Sam showed me the mill was a good one, and once we met Tom and you Shaun of course, we got rather caught up in plans for the old mill over a pint. So much potential there.'

'I'm looking forward to hearing all about it.' Tina speared

some pasta with her fork. 'We had a nice time with Mabel. She's so excited about helping with the wedding.'

'Quite right too.' Bea lay down her cutlery. 'With Mabel at the helm, you have one wedding planner for whom the sun won't dare not shine.'

As everyone laughed good naturedly at Mabel's organisational abilities, Bea turned to Shaun. 'I've been dying to ask, where have you been filming *Landscape Treasures*? Can you tell us, or is it top secret?'

Thea looked across at Shaun. 'Are we allowed to say? It's been on the local news up in Gloucestershire.'

'We can say, within reason. Sam tells me you enjoy the show.'

'Oh yes, I'm quite a fan.'

Lord Malvern snorted. 'Make that massive fan. Never misses an episode.'

'I'm glad you like it.' Shaun gave her what Thea recognised as his television presenter smile. 'Our loyal viewers are what keep the show going.'

'Did you see the episode set here last Christmas?' Tina watched the exchange with a growing sense of hope. If they could keep up the positive talk about the manor, perhaps Sam's father would come round to the idea of the wedding being at Mill Grange.

Bea's nodded eagerly. 'We most certainly did. You should have seen the expressions of the ladies at the bridge club. Some of them looked as if they'd sucked on lemons, they were so envious. I don't think I've ever been prouder of you, Sam.'

'But I didn't really do anything.'

To everyone's surprise, it was Lord Charles who spoke

through the muttered protests that came from all sides. 'You sat inside to be filmed. *Inside!* And look at you now. Sat at your own dining room table.'

'With all the doors wide open and next to an open window.' Sam tried not to notice that all of his friends were eating with jackets on. 'And let's not forget Dylan's role in getting me inside.'

'Dylan?'

'My son.' Tom cradled his wine glass. 'He sat on Sam's lap keeping him distracted until the cameras rolled.'

'Another person to thank then.' Bea turned to Tom. 'How old is Dylan?'

'Five.' Tom, unsure how Sam's parents would react to his personal situation, was glad that Helen was sat next to him. 'I share custody with his mother.'

'He's one of the nicest children you'll ever meet.' Helen jumped in, meeting Tom's eye with a look that Bea didn't miss.

'Anyone who has helped Sam battle his condition is a hero in my book.'

'I'm not sure I'd ever have got in here without Dylan, Mum.' Sam looked around him. Talking about his claustrophobia was making him edgy.

Recognising the signs of Sam's unease, Tina laid a hand on his leg under the table. 'You are here now and you were then. No need to be so hard on yourself.'

'Well said.' Bea nodded. 'This place has been good to you, Sam. Investing in it was a very sensible move, not just for your health, but for a lot of other people's wellbeing too.'

'And for the village as a whole,' Thea added. 'The pub,

cafe and village shop are benefitting from the additional flow of visitors to the area.'

Feeling everyone was laying it on a bit thick, and suspecting it was in the hope of persuading his mother to come around to the idea of him marrying there, Sam raised a hand. 'That's very kind, but I'm simply fighting my own demons while helping others to do the same. Although,' he looked around the dining room he'd feared he'd never be able to set foot in, 'finding Mill Grange, and Tina, has made my rehabilitation much easier.'

'Which is why you should get married here.'

Tina dropped her fork as Lady Bea's words floated across the table. 'But? But you said that Malvern House... you wanted us to...'

Bea held up her hand, her eyes meeting Charles's. 'While it *is* tradition for all members of our family to marry at Malvern House, that isn't important. We thought – no, *I* thought – that your childhood home would feel more secure to you. Safer.'

'Safer?' Sam's forehead creased in confusion.

'You went into the kitchen, albeit briefly, when you visited so I thought—'

Sam, whose mouth had been opening and closing in surprise, was no longer listening. 'It was you, *not* Father who was insisting we didn't marry here? But—'

'Your mother was worried for you, son.' Lord Malvern reached a hand out to his wife. 'And weddings are such complex, unpredictable, affairs. You might well need the run of the house if the weather turns bad, marquees or not. She thought – and I agreed – that you'd be less likely to have a major episode of claustrophobia if you were on childhood territory. Ground that you knew before the forces.'

Tina gripped hold of Sam's hand as she made sure she understood what she was hearing. 'You were insisting on us marrying in Worcestershire because you were worried about Sam, not because you didn't want to break with family practice?'

Lord Malvern smiled. 'He's our son.'

'We didn't want his claustrophobia to have even the slightest chance of ruining your day, Tina.' Bea looked a bit embarrassed. 'I'm sorry if we were a bit clumsy in our approach, but we didn't want to say it out loud – you know, make the claustrophobia a big issue when you have so much else to think about.'

Sam and Tina looked blankly at each other before Sam muttered, 'So, we can marry here with your blessing? You'll come to the wedding and not hold it against us that we aren't at Malvern House?'

'Oh course we'll be there.' Bea looked at her son. 'I'm so proud of you.'

'We both are.' Charles patted his wife's palm before sitting up a little straighter. 'Now that's that sorted.'

Bea burst out laughing. 'Well there we are! Something for you six young things to remember. First rule in making any sort relationship work, whether between partners or parents and children: proper communication avoids misunderstandings.'

'Quite right.' Charles grunted. 'If you'd let me ask the boy how he was doing with this claustrophobia business in the first place—'

'But I didn't want to upset him, Charles, or—'

'Mum! Dad!' Sam rolled his eyes as his parents bickered. 'It's okay. While your concern is hugely appreciated, I'm not the fragile man I once was.' He looked lovingly at Tina. 'We're just thrilled you're going to be here on our big day.'

'As if we'd miss it!' Bea gave a sheepish smile.

'Let's change the subject.' Lord Malvern picked up his wine glass and turned to Shaun. 'Now, tell us about this dig. The Cotswolds, wasn't it?'

Thirty-one

Saturday April 4th

Squealing with excitement, Dylan gave his mum a quick hug before running, dinosaur rucksack in one hand and matching wellington boots in the other, to a waiting Mabel, who ushered him into the kitchen.

Tom smiled in his son's wake. 'Thanks for saving me the trip to collect him, Sue.'

'I owed you one after picking an awkward time for parent's eve.' Sue pointed to the Bentley she'd parked next to. 'Posh guests?'

'Sam's parents.'

'Isn't he the lucky one? Big house, posh parents—'

'Stop with the envy, Sue.'

With a curt nod of compliance, Sue tucked a hair behind her ear as she opened the boot of her Mini. It was packed solid.

'Blimey. I know that isn't the biggest car boot, Sue, but that's a lot of stuff for a weekend.'

'If Dylan's moving in, he'll need his things.'

'He's only half moving in. I thought he was going to keep just a few bits here until I find a house.' Tom stepped nearer the car. The front passenger seat was piled high with bags and boxes. 'What's all that lot?'

'Books, toys, shoes.' Sue waved at the bags and boxes. 'The other half of Dylan's stuff is still at my place.'

Tom took a deep breath, not wanting their conversation to dissolve into a row. 'I get that we'll need all this in time, but I did explain, Dylan hasn't got this own room here. The one we're sharing isn't very big. I've nowhere to put this lot.'

'Rubbish! Look at the size of this place. It's a mansion.'

'Which *isn't* mine.' Biting his lips, not sure what it was about this situation Sue didn't get, Tom added, 'I'm just an employee.'

'Of a very wealthy man. I'm sure he can stand the loss of an extra bedroom for a week, especially as this place is closed for Easter.'

'One: Sam is not wealthy. Nor would you be if you owned this place. Two: how did you know we were closed to guests?'

'The Easter egg hunt and Easter Sunday open house posters. Dylan's been showing everyone.'

'Oh, right, yes.' Tom fished his car keys from his pocket. 'Some of this can come inside. I'll see if Helen would mind storing a bit in her room. The rest will have to go in my car, at least until tomorrow.'

'Why until tomorrow?'

'I told you!' Tom rolled his eyes. 'Sam's parents are here.

It's not a good time to be traipsing loads of boxes through the house.'

'God, you're acting as if they're bloody royalty or something.'

'Sue, are you deliberately trying to provoke me into an argument?'

'Why would I do that?'

'I have no idea, and yet you do it so often!' Tom lifted a bag of Dylan's shoes out of the Sue's care and into his own. 'If you must know, Sam's folk are Lord and Lady Malvern, and right now, they're talking wedding plans with their son and future daughter-in-law. I'd rather not upset any of them.'

'Lord and Lady? You've got to be kidding me?'

'Nope.'

Sue lifted out a box of books and placed it on the floor by Tom's car. 'Then we'd better hurry up and I'll leave you to your hobnobbing.'

Working in silence, they emptied the Mini, leaving a fortlet of boxes and bags next to his car, no less impressive than the one Tom had been excavating.

'Look, I'm sorry.' Sue gave him a sudden smile, adjusting her hair as she did so in a manner that could easily be described as flirty. 'I just want Dylan to be surrounded by his things. At the moment he's excited about living in a big house, but when he hasn't been back to his usual bedroom for a while, he might start to miss his stuff.'

'I know. I am going to let him make his space his own as soon as I find a house to rent.'

Climbing into her car, Sue waggled her fingers at him as

she shut the door and rolled down the window. 'At least he has a *whole* week to settle in.'

'A whole week?' Tom put a hand on the Mini's roof. 'No, we agreed to split the weeks, and this one falls so that he is with me from today until Wednesday.'

'No darling, I said you could have Dylan for Easter.'

'But I meant Easter weekend.'

'Well yes, but there's no point in him coming home for two days and then coming back here is there?'

'But, Sue, you can't just—'

'I'm going away.' She pouted. 'I thought you'd be pleased to spend more time with Dylan. Going for walks and stuff.'

'Of course I am, but he's your *son*, not a dog you can drop off at a kennels for walkies!'

'Oh don't be so melodramatic!'

Sue had started the engine and was backing out of her parking space before Tom had realised that his ex had manoeuvred him into taking Dylan full time during the first week of his official relationship with Helen.

Just when I thought Sue was finally developing maternal instincts.

Tom stared at his son's possessions strewn about the driveway. *At least I'll have more time to tell him about me and Helen.*

Sunday April 5th

As the Bentley disappeared from view, Tina and Sam linked arms and headed to the kitchen.

'If you'd told me two days ago that my father would be

joining me in a pub with my friends, I'd have dismissed the idea as madness.'

'I'm so glad your parents stayed over. They're so different when they're out of their home environment.'

'You mean Father's less stuffy.'

'Well yes, but your mum too.' Tina thought of Mabel and Bea chatting at the kitchen table. 'It's like they can relax. Here they don't have to be *seen* to be lord and lady of the manor. It must be exhausting having to keep up appearances all the time.'

'I hadn't thought about it like that.' Sam grimaced. 'Thank goodness we don't have to live like that.' He reached for the empty sugar bowl and passed it to Tina. 'I was actually sorry to see them leave.'

'I think they'd have stayed if they hadn't got that charity event to open this afternoon. At least they had a good night's sleep. I thought we could give them the same bed when they come for the wedding.'

'Sounds good.' Sam scooped the last of the dirty mugs off the table. 'Changing the subject for a moment, has Helen said anything to you about staying now she and Tom are an item?'

'No, but to be fair, we haven't had a minute on our own to talk about anything. The focus at Mabel's yesterday was very much wedding related.'

'Oh yes?' Sam grinned. 'Anything I should know?'

'Not unless you want to hear about the vast differences in wedding dress style preferences between Mabel, your mum and me.'

'I can imagine! I certainly don't want to jinx things by hearing about – or seeing – your dress before the day.'

Tina shut the dishwasher door with a flourish. 'I never thought you'd be superstitious like that.'

'I'm not, but I'd like it to be a surprise on the day.'

Throwing her arms around Sam, Tina gave him a big kiss. 'We're really getting married *here*, aren't we?'

'We are,' Sam played with her golden pigtails as he glanced towards the calendar, 'in just under two months.'

'Two months!' Tina pulled away in panic. 'But that's not long enough!'

Sam's forehead creased as he stroked her worried face. 'But you knew it was in two months.'

'Well, yes I did, but you saying it out loud... I've been so focused on worrying about not upsetting your parents, that I haven't actually done anything more than think about what the wedding will be like. I've booked nothing! I don't even have a wedding dress shop in mind to go to. It can take *weeks* to find a dress – months even! And what about the food and my hair and the chickens, your clothes and—'

'The chickens?' Wrapping her in a soothing hug Sam shook his head. 'You don't expect me to provide them with little dresses do you? Although Tony Stark could probably rock a rooster sized tuxedo.'

Tina giggled into his shoulder. 'I can see him now.'

'Don't worry, love. The marquee is ordered for the ceremony. Tom's been helping me on that front.'

Tina pulled away in surprise. 'But we only just found out we were getting married here.'

'We were *always* going to get married here, but now we can with my parent's blessing.'

'But what about food?'

'I'm sure Sybil will step up with some afternoon teas. Are we, or are we not, the team that turned the restoration of Mill Grange around in a matter of weeks, against all odds?'

'We most certainly are!' Mabel appeared in the doorway, her arms wrapped around a large folder, which appeared to be stuffed full. 'You are not to fret about *anything*, Tina. Not a thing!'

Thirty-two

Thea read the email on her laptop. It echoed the text Julian had sent as she'd travelled home from the Cotswolds.

Thea,

I trust you are taking time to think things over regarding doing more television presenting. As you haven't replied to my text, I have to assume it never reached you. (I recall Shaun complaining that the Wi-Fi reception in Upwich is poor.)

This email is to ensure you that I am serious about your future prospects in the business.

I have booked a private meeting room in the conference suite of The Harborough Hotel, Northleach, not far from Birdlip. Unless I hear in the negative, I will expect to see you there at six pm on Tuesday 14th April.

Regards,

Julian.

Wishing she'd told Shaun about the overheard phone conversation and Julian cornering her as they left the dig straight away, Thea sighed. She'd hoped Julian would give up and go away if she ignored him for long enough. It appeared that this was not going to be the case.

Thea mumbled at the screen before her. 'How do I even start a conversation that will end with, "Julian asked me not to say anything about this, and oh, by the way, I suspect it's your job he wants me to have, Shaun"?'

Hearing footsteps echoing along the corridor outside, Thea shut the email down as Sam poked his head around the door.

'You alright? You look a bit pink?'

'Bit tired. I'm fine.'

'I wondered if you had a few minutes to save Tina.'

'Always. But from whom?'

'Mabel.' Sam rested against the doorframe. 'Now we're all steam ahead for holding the wedding here, it's hit us how little time we have. Mabel has stepped up as wedding planner extraordinaire. She's fab, and what she's saying is all good. But Mabel's in her element and Tina needs back up. We both do if I'm honest. It's a bit overwhelming.'

'No problem. Why not call an impromptu staff meeting,

that way we can talk about other things as well? I could do with being brought up to speed on the dig.'

'Good idea, although I think Helen and Tom had plans with Dylan today.'

'That might be as well. I was going to ask about Helen's birthday. Are we doing anything for that?'

'I rather assumed Tom would sort it out. I'll try and catch him on his own later.'

Thea smiled. 'You know that won't be easy now Dylan's here.'

'It is going to make life more difficult,' Sam agreed. 'There are going to be times when we'll need a full staff meeting. What will Tom do with Dylan then?'

'Perhaps we could organise the main ones when Sue has him, and keep all others short. Dylan could easily sit at the table with us. Maybe he can draw or read while we talk?'

'Maybe.'

'You don't sound sure.' Thea tilted her head to one side. 'Are you regretting your decision to let Dylan stay?'

'Not at all, I was just thinking how different everything will be here when Tina and I have a family.'

Thea grinned. 'That's something worth changing things for though.'

'Oh yes.' Sam looked around the scullery that Thea and Tina had been using as their office since he bought Mill Grange. 'Even though you showed me this room via video call, now I'm able to come in here, I am always surprised by how big it is.'

'Scullery maids needed plenty of elbow room.' Getting

up, Thea dropped her pen. 'I could do with a stretch. Shall I find Shaun and head to the kitchen?'

'Walled garden would be better if that's okay.'

'Perfect.'

Dylan proudly read out each title as he lined his books up on the window sill. Every now and then he'd look at Tom and Helen through his fringe, as if asking if it really was okay to put them there.

Sensing his excitement had morphed into insecurity; Helen patted the bag that was slung over her shoulder as she watched Dylan from the doorway. 'I have something you can use as a bookend if you like.'

'What's a bookend?'

'Something that holds your books in place on a shelf.' Helen opened the bag. 'Would you like to fetch it?'

Tom laughed as Dylan rocketed forwards, his hands inside the bag in seconds. 'It's so heavy!'

'It has to be, or your books will fall over. Careful now.' Helen held out a hand, ready to catch in case Dylan dropped his prize.

'Wow! It's a fozzel!'

Helen couldn't help but smile. 'Yes, a fossil. Put it on the bed a minute.'

Dylan stroked the stone in delight. 'Look, Dad, it's like a swirly snail.'

'It's an ammonite.' Tom looked at Helen in amazement. He'd seen the fossil in her room. It was the only unnecessary possession she'd brought with her from Bath – and now she was giving it to his son.

Is this the moment we should tell Dylan we're a couple?

'What's an ammmonbite?'

'Ammonite.' Helen ruffled the lad's hair. 'Tricky word to say, isn't it? They were ancestors of octopuses and squids. Lived in the sea between 400 and 66 million years ago.'

'Million!'

'Yes. That fossil is even older than Bert.'

Dylan giggled as he carried it to the window. 'Thank you, Helen.'

'You're welcome. You gave me a lovely stone, now you have one too.'

Helen felt choked with emotion as Dylan asked, 'Where did it come from?'

Hoping Tom would help her out, Helen pulled a handkerchief from her pocket; watching Dylan trace a finger over the lumps and bumps that formed an echo of the long dead creature.

'Helen found it.' Tom crouched down next to his son. 'It's from Lyme Regis, that's in Dorset. It was dug out of a cliff. That's what fossil means, "to be dug up from the soil".'

'*You* found this, Helen?' Dylan's eyes widened in awe.

'When I was a student. A long time ago.'

'But not millions of years?' Dylan's open expression reminded her of his father.

'Not quite.'

'Can I really keep it? Even when we live somewhere else?'

'Even then.'

As the fossil sat in place, propping up an Enid Blyton collection, Tom gave Helen's hand a secret squeeze. 'What would you like to do on your first day as part of the Mill Grange household, Dylan?'

'Can I choose?'

'You can.' Tom picked up Dylan's favourite teddy bear and placed him on the pillow of his son's bed. 'A walk, a picnic, lunch out and explore in the woods, a paddle in the river?'

'Well, umm.' Dylan suddenly looked shy. 'Could I have a go on the fortlet? Could I do archaeology?'

Butterflies danced around the trailing apple trees climbing the walls on either side of the garden. Sam joined his friends at the trestle table he'd set up for the meeting. 'If I'm any judge, the apple blossom will be out just before the wedding. Let's hope it stays.'

Thea smiled at Tina. 'It'll be like extra confetti if the wind blows.'

Mabel nodded approvingly. 'Better than real confetti, that would do the chickens no good at all if it blew into their coop. I've written it down here.' She lifted up a huge list, upon which she'd put, in capital letters, NO CONFETTI IN WALLED GARDEN.

Feeling a little intimidated as she clutched her own wedding notebook, Tina said, 'That's quite a list, Mabel. We only want a little wedding. Is there really that much to do?'

Catching Tina's troubled expression, Mabel patted her hand across the table. 'It looks worse than it is. It's the smallest things that often take the time, but fear not. I'll sort everything.'

Seeing that Mabel was in danger of giving Tina the wedding she'd have wanted for a daughter if she and Bert had been blessed with children, rather than the one she actually wanted, Sam spoke more firmly than he normally would. 'With Tina's help, Mabel.'

Ruffling through her papers, to hide her sudden embarrassed blush, Mabel opened her folder at a page covered in lists of wedding dress shops. 'So, Tina, I know from our chat with Lady Bea what sort of dresses you favour. I've taken the liberty of researching which local shops sell the sort of thing you're after. I hope that's okay?'

Getting up, Tina threw her arms around Mabel's shoulders. 'That's very okay. That's the sort of thing that's been panicking me. It's not the getting things sorted so much as the time it takes to source everything before we can get things sorted.'

Mabel patted the folder. 'That's what this is, potential outlets, people to ask for help and stuff.' She looked up from her planning Bible. 'I've been in Upwich a while, I know pretty much everyone.'

Thea pointed towards the list of dress retailers. 'Which is the closest, Mabel?'

'There are three in Taunton, and several in Exeter. But there are also two local boutique bridal shops. One in Bampton and one in Wiveliscombe.'

'So there is!' Tina clapped her hands together, reminding herself of Sam's mother as she did so. 'I've driven past both shops heaps of times. I forgot all about them.'

'Bridal shops are like that though.' Thea recalled the boutique in the corner of the Bampton's high street. 'You only need one when you need one – if you see what I mean.'

'I like to support local, but wouldn't a boutique be much more expensive than a department store in Taunton or Exeter?'

'Almost certainly.' Mabel tapped her pen against the list of shops. 'Also, the larger stores would probably have something off the peg you could take within a few days. We might already have left it too late for a specialist shop to get you a bespoke dress ready.'

Seeing the light in her friend's eyes dim with a disappointment, Thea was reminded of the Tina she knew before Sam had come along. The girl who was going to marry with all the trimmings, wearing a diamond tiara and a mile-long train. Suddenly, she was determined that, even if the rest of the wedding was on a budget, Tina would get the dress she wanted – and on time. 'Why don't we call them? The boutiques, I mean. Find out the availability of time slots for trying on and their estimated turn round time on outfits.'

'But if I fall in love with a dress and they can't make it on time that would be awful.' Tina looked at Sam. 'I think I'd better stick to the department stores.'

'And I think you should do what you want for once, and not what you think you ought to do.' Sam beamed at his future bride. 'Mabel, would you call the local shops, just on the off chance that our schedule doesn't daunt them?'

'My pleasure.'

'Now I have a question for you, Shaun.' Sam swallowed. 'With all the to-ing and fro-ing lately, I haven't had a chance to ask. I wondered if you'd do me the honour of being my best man.'

'I'd be delighted.' Shaun shook his friend's hand across the table as Tina turned to Thea.

'Obviously I want you to be my bridesmaid, Thea. And Helen as well, if she wants to. You will do it, won't you?'

'Of course!' Thea smirked. 'As long as you don't make us wear pink or peach. I'd look awful, and Helen's red hair would clash with it something awful!'

'Talking of Helen,' Sam gestured towards Mabel's folder, 'I don't suppose there's a spare piece of paper in there to plan something for her fortieth. What with the Easter egg hunt and open house on the same day, it's been rather forgotten about.'

'She might prefer it forgotten.' Thea wrinkled her nose. 'She's got a bit of a thing about turning forty.'

'Might be different now she's with Tom.' Sam tapped his pen against the table. 'Either way, we can't let the day go unmarked.'

Mabel turned to the back of the folder and wrote, 'Helen's Birthday', at the top of the page.

'Sorry about that.'

Tom pocketed his phone as he strode back to where Helen was showing Dylan how to hold a trowel in the test trench. 'Your mum was just checking on you, Dylan.'

'That's nice.' Dylan didn't look up, his concentration set on the task in hand.

'She's bound to be concerned about him settling in.' Keeping an eye on Dylan, Helen came to join Tom at the corner of the trench.

Tom lowered his voice. 'I can't work Sue out. One minute she's dumping her son for a week without warning – not that I mind having him, but it's the principle of the thing – and then she's fussing over him settling in. It isn't like he hasn't stayed here before.'

'Where has she gone on her break?'

'No idea.'

Dylan looked up, 'Mum's with her job friends. Harriet told me.'

'Your babysitter?'

'I'm not a *baby*, Dad!'

'Okay, your child sitter then.'

'Yeah. Harriet looks after me when Mum's out.'

Unease tripped down Tom's spine. 'Mum doesn't go out much though, does she?'

'Loads.' Dylan placed the edge of the trowel against the loose soil, and pulled it neatly back. 'Did I do it right, Helen?'

Puzzled as to why Tom was pulling his phone back from his pocket, Helen joined Dylan in the trench. 'That was perfect. You're going to make a fine archaeologist when you grow up.'

'I want to dig up dinosaurs.'

'And fossils?'

'Yes! Big ones like your anonnon... nnomite.'

'Good for you.' Helen looked up to see Tom scowling down the phone.

'Mum likes her work friends now she has a new job.'

'That's nice.'

'Harriet thinks Mum wants a proper family for me. She talks about that *a lot*.' Dylan rolled his eyes in a way that made Helen think he was copying it from someone, probably Harriet. 'I'd *much* rather talk about dinosaurs or Romans, wouldn't you?'

Thirty-three

Helen stared out of the window as Tina drove her, Thea and Mabel to the wedding boutique for their first dress trying session.

Dylan's first day at Mill Grange had gone well, but the little boy's comments about Sue wanting him to be part of a family had hit home. And what with Tom's popping off to the office to make calls or answer emails every hour or so, none of which he seemed to have a convincing reason for making, Helen had ended the day feeling confused rather than euphoric.

After a day of digging, by the time Dylan went to bed he was exhausted, and the chance to tell him about their relationship had slipped away. Tom had taken his son off for a bedtime story, and hadn't come back out of the room again.

Over breakfast, Helen had discovered that Tom had fallen asleep next to Dylan. But that information had come too late to stop her having a broken night's sleep, wondering if Dylan had told Tom that his mum wanted them to be a family again. All night she'd agonised over if that had a bearing on Tom not coming to share her bed.

Tom still hadn't told her who'd been calling him on and off all day yesterday, but then she hadn't asked. She hadn't wanted to. She supposed it was Sue checking up on Dylan or Tom quizzing Sue on just how often her son was left alone with Harriet. *Sometimes she hardly seems to care about Dylan – then others...*

A small groan escaped Helen's lips, causing Thea, sat next to her on the backseat of the car, to turn towards her. 'You okay? You and Tom told Dylan the good news yet?'

'No. Yesterday disappeared somehow.' Not wanting to talk about her unease, which she wasn't sure she understood anyway, Helen called into the front of the car as Tina pulled into a layby near Bampton's wedding boutique. 'Tina, are you sure you want me to be a bridesmaid? Thea would be fine without me. I'm not really a dress kind of person.'

Reversing a fraction, Tina made sure the car was tucked away from the road. 'You'll look amazing, and yes, of course I want you.'

'And I don't want to stand behind Tina and Sam on my own!' Thea gave Helen an anxious smile. 'I'll be less nervous if you're there too.'

'Right. Okay.' Helen exhaled a breath.

Unlocking her seatbelt, Mabel picked up her bag containing the huge wedding planning folder. 'The owner sounded lovely on the phone. She totally understands we are simply browsing and getting style ideas today. Come on, girls, no need for nerves.'

Thea and Helen climbed out of the car, but Tina remained where she was.

'You coming, Tina?' Thea opened the driver's door. 'We can't do this without you.'

Tina's hands remained on the steering wheel. 'What if she does try to sell me something I don't want, though? You know what I'm like. I'll find myself buying a dress because she thinks I should have it because I'm rubbish at saying no if I think it might offend someone.'

'Well, umm…' Thea floundered, knowing she'd probably have similar trouble in the face of a determined dress saleswoman.

Mabel tapped her folder thoughtfully. 'If you feel yourself being polite, rather than saying no thank you over a dress, signal me with a fake cough.'

'A fake cough?' Tina frowned.

'If you do that, then I'll know you need rescuing.'

Helen grinned at the old lady. 'You really have thought of everything.'

As Mabel and Helen crossed the road to the shop before them, a flutter of butterflies stirred in Tina's stomach as she turned to Thea. 'I've looked forward to this all my life, one way or another, so why am I so nervous?'

'Because you've been waiting for it all your life.' Thea linked arms with Tina. 'Come on, if I know Mabel, she'll have arranged for Bucks Fizz to be sipped during the trying on.'

'But what if they don't have anything I like?'

'Didn't you look at their range online?' Thea was surprised.

'I know it sounds daft, but I didn't dare. Mabel had already booked the appointment. I was worried I might not like anything I saw online.'

'Well I did look.' Thea gave her friend a hug. 'I promise you're going to love everything – well, nearly everything. There was one very meringue-ish construction which you'll want us all to give a very wide berth!'

Thea had been right about the Bucks Fizz, although Mabel swore it hadn't been her doing. After trying on two dresses, one for each glass of heavily diluted champagne she'd had, Tina realised she'd better abandon her drink or she'd be unable to drive home.

'You looked fantastic in both of them.' Thea realised her input wasn't terribly helpful. 'How many others have you lined up to try before you start ruling frocks out?'

'Three.' Tina gestured to the huge changing room behind her where the boutique owner was calmly and without fuss helping her in and out of each gown in turn. 'I just needed a break. It takes an age to get into the simplest frock, and to be honest, I'm falling in love with all of them!'

'I can imagine. At least you taking your time means I have longer to choose something. I hadn't realised how hard it would be. I usually just grab the first vaguely suitable dress and go with it.'

Tina laughed, 'Have you and Helen decided on a colour?'

'That at least has been sorted. Mabel was very firm on the matter, she...' Thea looked around. 'Where is Mabel?'

'She's in the changing room.'

'In with you?' Thea tilted her head to one side, not sure if this was an agreeable situation or not.

'She's taking her mother of the bride role seriously.'

'Is that okay?' Thea lowered her voice, not wanting to offend the old lady should she come out of the changing area.

'It is. She's being really helpful. Well, except for one thing.'

'One thing?'

'She keeps blubbing. Apparently, I look like the most beautiful woman in the world every time.'

'Oh bless her!' Thea experienced a stab of sadness for her friend. 'She and Bert would have made fabulous parents.'

Tina pulled a random bridesmaid's dress from the rack in front of her. 'This might suit you, Thea.'

'Maybe. I have no idea what suits me, to be honest, so I'm aiming to try a range once Helen's done.'

'Is Helen okay?'

'I think so, but now you mention it, she's been in the changing room for absolutely ages.'

Helen stared at herself in the mirror. Mabel had been right about the colour, but she wasn't sure about the dress. Or rather she was sure – and that made her feel even worse.

She looked good. She knew she did. *But I never look good in dresses.* She remembered Tom's expression of disbelief when they'd spoken before she'd joined Tina and the others for their shopping expedition. He'd dismissed her claim that she looked awful in anything that showed her legs, telling her she'd look good in a bin bag. She flushed at the memory of Tom picking a roll of bin bags off the store room shelf and suggesting she put the theory to the test for him later.

Is he going to see me wear this?

Helen knew, if she did attend the wedding, it would be in this dress. She didn't need to try on anything else.

Midnight blue, it made her eyes shine, complimented her hair and her colouring. With a corset top, it magically pulled her in at the waist, while the skirt slimmed her thighs; giving her a hint of sophistication, with just a touch of medieval serving wench thrown in.

Tom would love it.

'Tom.' She whispered his name as she turned to examine her side view for the fourth time. 'I'll have to go away. If Dylan wants them to be a family again...' She couldn't finish the sentence, and was somewhat relieved when she heard Thea calling to her from other side of the closed dressing room door.

'You okay in there, Helen? Can I come in?'

Quickly adding a smile to her appearance, Helen pulled back the curtain to the changing room. 'What do you think? I rather like it – and believe me, I'd never thought I'd say that about any sort of posh frock.'

'Oh my God! You look incredible. It's that dress. It has to be that one.' Tina came forward to hug Helen, but then stopped. 'Actually, I'd better not rumple you!'

Thea was already backing out of the changing room. 'I'll fetch Mabel, she *has* to see how fab you look. Is there one like that in my size do you think? It would be great if we matched style as well as colour.'

*

Having pronounced Helen, 'eye-wateringly beautiful', Mabel had secured the shop assistant's help, and within half an hour, Thea was wearing a dress of the same style and colour.

'Is it okay? If I don't look as good as Helen does, then I'll go with a completely different style, but keep the colour.'

Tears welled up in Tina's eyes as her bridesmaids stood side by side. 'You both look incredible. Don't you think so, Mabel?'

'I think Shaun and Tom are going to have a great deal of difficulty keeping their hands to themselves!'

'Mabel!' Tina giggled as Thea burst out laughing. 'I never thought I'd hear such innuendo from your lips.'

As Mabel winked, a single tear rolled down Helen's cheek. She wiped it away hurriedly, hoping that if the others had noticed, they'd put it down to the emotion of the occasion.

Thirty-four

Tuesday April 7th

Thea and Helen stared at the pile of boxes before them. Brightly coloured, they were stacked almost floor to ceiling in the storeroom of Upwich's village shop.

'So that's what two hundred Easter eggs looks like!' Thea could hear the activity in the shop; as ever it was busy.

'I should have asked Dylan to help us.' Helen flapped open the first of the eight giant sized shopping bags she'd brought with her. 'He'd be in heaven just looking at this lot.'

'Poor lad would think the Easter Bunny had gone on strike, leaving his entire haul here.'

'Thank goodness we came in the Land Rover rather than walked.' Helen gestured to the chocolate hoard. 'It's going to take two, maybe three trips back and forth with this lot.'

Grabbing a pair of scissors from a desk in the corner of the room, Thea cut open the plastic wrapping that bundled the first fifty chocolate eggs together. 'I was going to suggest we keep these in the scullery, but thinking about it, there's no way I can be surrounded by this much chocolate and resist temptation until Sunday!'

Stacking the first half dozen into a bag, Helen knew she was supposed to laugh, but the sound wouldn't come out. Instead she said, 'We can't put them in the store room in case the mice find them. Maybe the downstairs bedroom?'

'I'm not sure Tina and Sam would be thrilled about that.' Thea began to fill another bag.

'The drawing room?'

'Probably best. That way, at least everyone will have to be strong and not nibble the chocolate early, and not just me.' Thea paused. 'Unless you and Tom don't want Dylan to see them.'

You and Tom. Thea's already seeing us as being jointly responsible for Dylan. 'It's okay, Tom's told him that this is extra. Not real Easter Bunny stuff. He's excited about helping us hide them for the guests.'

'I hope we get enough visitors, or we'll all be eating Easter egg chocolate until Christmas.' Thea patted her hips. 'Which, frankly, would suit me under normal circumstances, but know we've found dresses we like for the wedding, I'm not sure Tina would be overly thrilled if we didn't fit in them. Nor do I want to have to go dress shopping again.'

Helen pushed one more Easter egg box into her bag and flapped open a new one. 'Didn't you enjoy yesterday? You looked like you did.'

'I was pretending at first, for Tina's sake. She's always liked clothes shopping. Before Sam came along, she was very particular about her appearance. Not that I'm saying she is scruffy now, but she's more relaxed about herself. But once I saw you in that dress, I got into it and started to have fun. But, I'll be honest, I wasn't sure I'd be able to match up to you, and I really wanted to.'

'You wanted to look like me?' Helen paused in the act of reaching for an egg. 'But I'm all lumpy.'

'Don't be ridiculous. You're gorgeous. Every time I see Tom look at you, I can see how much he thinks so too.'

Helen went back to the task in hand, twisting slightly so Thea couldn't see the cloud that had crossed her face. Last night she'd half expected Tom to turn up with a bin bag for her to model, but he hadn't. He'd read Dylan a bedtime story, then she'd read one too. It had been lovely. The three of them squashed together, either side of Dylan as he sat up in his little bed, but then Tom had told her he needed to make a few calls, and he'd be back later.

Midnight had come and gone before Helen had finally fallen asleep, but there had been no visit from Tom, and another day had passed by without the time being right to talk to Dylan about them.

Not wanting to dwell, Helen asked, 'Where is Tina anyway? I thought she was going to help with the egg heist.'

'Mabel fixed it so she could have a dress fitting this morning. Not one for letting the grass grow is our Mabel.'

'Tina looked amazing.' Afraid that she might have sounded wistful, Helen changed the subject. 'You haven't said much about the Cotswold dig. What's it like being a celebrity?'

'Actually, I wondered if I could have a word with you about that.' Making sure that no one in the shop could overhear them, Thea moved closer to Helen. She was about to confide her concerns about Julian when she suddenly registered what they were doing. 'But first, can you tell me why on earth we are filling all these bags, when we could have just carried a tray of fifty eggs at a time to the Land Rover?!'

'Stupidity?'

Thea laughed. 'That'll be it.'

Dylan scrambled onto the sofa next to Bert, holding out the bag of freshly cooked cheese scones. 'Sybil said to say these would get you better faster than chicken soup.'

Bert gave a throaty giggle as Tom took the bag from his son. 'Would you like one, Bert, or did Mabel stuff you with a full English breakfast before she went off with Tina?'

'I'd love one, but best not tell Mabel! She's worried I won't get in my suit for the wedding. Bless her, she's already clucking about the fact I'm not in a position to go shopping for a new one.'

Tom saw the glint dip from Bert's eyes and saw he was disappointed about that too. He could picture him in an old-fashioned gent's outfitters, proudly chatting away about being father of the bride by proxy.

'Forgive me, Bert, but I think you ought to be putting weight on if you want the suit to fit.'

'Me too young fella, so let's get eating! After so long without an appetite, now I have it back, I'm constantly peckish.'

As Tom disappeared into the kitchen to find plates, Bert put his arm around Dylan. 'Now, you will look after me at the wedding, won't you?'

'Me look after you?' Dylan's round eyes widened. 'I'm only little.'

'But growing all the time. I'm much better now, Dylan, but I get tired quickly. If I need things fetching, like one of Sybil's scones, will you be my wedding helper?'

'Course.' Dylan opened his dinosaur rucksack. 'I've got my school stuff. Do you want to see?'

The Land Rover bumped along Mill Grange's driveway, back towards Upwich for the second round of Easter egg collection. Thea had told Helen all about the dolphin mosaic and the villa's location, how the work was satisfying and that the archaeologists were fun to be with.

'It sounds fantastic, yet I can feel a "but" coming on.' Helen sent up a silent thank you to whichever god was passing by, that the parking space outside the village shop was still vacant.

'How did you know there was a but?'

'Because I've worked in the industry all my life. It doesn't matter how good it looks from the outside, there's always a niggle under the surface. A problem the public never get to see. A breach of health and safety that results in the need to fill in a million forms, or a measurement that was out, so all the plans need redrawing. You know the sort of thing.'

Thea snorted. 'I do indeed, but this time, so far at least, we've escaped those issues.' She stayed in the passenger seat, watching the village around her, many of the locals waving as they passed by. 'This time, as they say, it's personal.'

'Go on.'

'The producer. Julian. Shaun was convinced he had a thing for me at first. I didn't see it, and it took a while to convince Shaun he was mistaken. Finally, he accepted he'd just been jealous and that was that.'

'So, what's the problem?'

'Julian wants me to consider presenting on television as a career.'

Helen gave a puzzled smile. 'But that's wonderful. Congratulations.'

Shaking her head, Thea sighed. 'The thing is, from what Julian has implied, it isn't that he wants me to present alongside Shaun. I think he wants me to take over from him.'

'Oh my God!'

'Exactly.'

'What does Shaun say about this?'

'I haven't told him. How can I? Where do I even begin that conversation? And anyhow, Julian has asked me to keep quiet about his offer.' Thea looked longingly across the road at Sybil's Tea Rooms. 'So far, I haven't answered Julian's emails, but he's arranged a meeting about my future. A meeting in a local hotel. Just the two of us.'

'Ah.' Helen saw the problem straightaway. 'So you think this Julian wants you to be the show's new presenter, hence wanting to talk to you away from the team.'

'I feel awful. Poor Shaun. He loves his job so much.' Thea scrubbed her palms over her face. 'What do I do?'

'You have to tell him. Start with explaining why you didn't tell him straight away – not wanting to hurt his feelings, respecting your producer's confidences etc. But you have to tell Shaun, because if he finds out by accident, he'll think he was right about Julian's crush, and that you fancy Julian right back.'

'I know.'

'Remember how hurt you were when you thought Shaun had his eye on that Sophie in Cornwall. If Shaun finds out about this from someone else, he could jump to the same conclusions you did.'

Opening the door, Thea swung her legs out of the Land Rover. 'I wish I'd told him instantly, but I thought Julian would get fed up and try someone else if I ignored him. If Shaun's days as host on *Landscape Treasures* are numbered, I don't want them to be numbered because of me!'

'Come on.' Helen locked the vehicle. 'Sod the dresses fitting. We need scones.'

'That was delicious.' Bert put his plate down with a flourish. 'Now you two, what else have you been up to apart from young Dylan here moving in?'

'We've been plotting, haven't we, Dad?'

'Plotting? That sounds very secretive.'

Tom cradled his mug of coffee between his palms. 'As well as the Easter egg hunt, I've been helping Sam's parents sort a wedding present for the happy couple, as well as trying to organise my old army uniform to come out of storage in time for the wedding. It hadn't occurred to me I'd have a role, but they want me to be the usher. The phone calls and emails have hardly stopped over the past few days. Plus, it's Helen's birthday on Sunday. Her fortieth.'

'So it is. I'd clean forgotten. Are you planning a party?'

'The thing is, Helen has made it plain she doesn't want

her fortieth marked, but Thea and Tina think she's just saying that, and that secretly she'd like a bit of a fuss made of her.'

Bert chuckled. 'Ah, so middle ground is the way forward then.'

'Middle ground?'

'A nice present from you, naturally.'

Dylan joined in. 'I'm going to make her a card, aren't I, Dad?'

'You are. She'll love it.' Wondering if this was the time to tell Dylan why he wanted this to be an extra special birthday for Helen, but remembering he'd promised they'd tell Dylan about their relationship together, Tom looked at Bert. 'I'm not sure she is a party type person.'

'I know!' Dylan bounced on the sofa. 'One of Sam's bonfire dinners with jacket potatoes and stuff. They're fab.'

'Not a bad idea.' Bert ruffled Dylan's hair. 'But with champers rather than tea and coffee.'

'And balloons, Dad. Harriet says you *have* to have balloons at a party.'

Thirty-five

As Mabel twirled in a skirt, top and jacket that would have been the envy of any mother of the bride, Tina couldn't help but wonder what her mum would have worn if she'd been there. She hoped she'd have approved of the soft lilac ensemble Mabel was parading before her.

Guessing what was going on in her friend's mind, Mabel picked up a nearby box of tissues and sat next to Tina.

'I never had the honour of knowing your parents, but I'm sure they'd be very proud of you and I have no doubt at all they'd have approved of Sam.'

'Thanks, Mabel.' Tina sniffed into a tissue. 'How did you know I was thinking about them?'

'Who else would you think about at this time?' She patted Tina's knee. 'Now, if this outfit is okay with you, I think I'll add it to the tally.'

'You look wonderful.'

'Thank you.' Mabel clambered back to her feet. 'Now it's just Bert, Shaun and Dylan to worry about suit wise.'

'And Sam and Tom.' Tina escorted Mabel back to the changing room.

'No dear, they were in the forces. They'll have dress uniforms.'

Tina stopped moving. 'I wondered why Sam changed the subject when I mentioned him getting a suit this morning. He mumbled something about booking a fitting in Taunton, but I didn't know how, when he's unlikely to want to go into the shop. Perhaps that's what was on his mind? His uniform, I mean. It hadn't occurred to me he'd want to wear it after all he went through. I don't even know where it is.'

'He must do what feels best for him. Shame though,' Mabel smirked, 'Bert used to look a regular bobby dazzler in uniform.'

The far corner of the drawing room resembled a chocoholic's heaven. Thea could smell the enticing aroma of chocolate hanging in the air as Helen added the final box to the castle-like construction.

'Now all we need is a sunny day.' Thea looked across to Helen. 'I'm sorry Easter Sunday falls on your birthday, and you have to work that day.'

'I'd rather work to be honest. Keep my mind off the big four-oh.'

'You still bothered about that?' Thea dropped onto the nearest sofa with a soft thump. 'I thought you'd be looking forward to it, now you have someone to spoil you rotten.'

'He hasn't mentioned it, and I don't like to, especially as I told him a few weeks ago that I didn't want to celebrate it.

'But you weren't together then. Surely now—'

Helen sat down with a groan. 'Would you mind if we didn't talk about it?'

Thea frowned. 'You two are okay, aren't you?'

'Sure.' Helen's eyes ran over the chocolate mountain as she switched the focus back to Thea. 'You need to talk to Shaun before he finds out about Julian's proposal and everything gets ruined.'

Respecting Helen's need to change the subject, but wondering if the 'everything getting ruined' comment referred to Helen and Tom as well as, potentially, her and Shaun, Thea agreed, 'I'll do it today.' She gestured to the eggs. 'We need to decide where these are going to be hidden first.'

'Dylan is going to help with that.'

'Excellent.' Thea smiled.

'We could draw up egg hiding treasure maps of the house and garden. In the meantime, I ought to crack on with the book.'

'I meant to ask how that's going.'

'Somewhere between slowly and stopped. I've made a lot of notes, but no actual words have happened.'

'They'll come.'

'Soon, hopefully.' Helen looked out through the drawing room window. 'Because I have a feeling that time is running out.'

Sam greeted Tina and Mabel as the car pulled onto the drive.

'Judging by those grins, you two have had a successful morning.'

Tina threw her arms around Sam. 'We have. Your fiancée

has a dress that has been fully fitted, while Mabel is the proud owner of an outfit so stunning, the Queen herself would be envious.'

'Excellent.' Sam rubbed his dirty hands down his trousers. 'Anything you need me to carry inside?'

'It's all being kept at the boutique for now, thanks. Which is just as well with your grubby mitts!'

'I've just finished giving the chicken coop a spring clean. I can't say Gertrude and co were enamoured to have me fussing around them, but it's a lot cleaner and cosier in there now.'

Mabel clucked in a manner not unlike Gertrude. 'Talking of spring cleaning, time we were all rolling our sleeves up if you want Mill Grange to look its best on Sunday. Come on, no time like the present.'

'Hang on, Mabel! Lunch first, I'm famished.' Tina rested a hand on her friend's arm. 'And don't you want to go and see Bert?'

'Oh yes, you're probably right.' She looked sheepish. 'I was getting a bit carried away again. Sorry. I've just had such a nice few days, I wanted to help to say thank you.'

'You've been amazing, and we would love your help later, but right now, I'm pooped, so you must be too.'

'I am a bit,' Mabel admitted. 'But as soon as you need me, I'll be ready.'

'Are you sure I can't I offer you a lift home, Mabel?' Tina gestured to the car they'd just climbed out of.

'Some fresh air will do me good.' Mabel waved as she walked away. 'I'll see you both tomorrow.'

As Mabel disappeared from view, Sam kissed the top of Tina's head. 'The frocks are sorted then?'

'One more fitting for Thea and Helen, and that's it.' Tilting her head to one side, Tina asked, 'Did you make your appointment to hire a suit?'

'Umm, no. I keep getting sidetracked. It's not like what I wear is important. Everyone will be looking at you.'

'But Sam, it isn't long now.' Tina felt bad about what she was about to say, but knew if couldn't be avoided. 'You don't have to go into the shop. You can order one online and stuff.'

'I know.' Sam played one of her pigtails through his fingers. 'It isn't my claustrophobia that's the problem this time.'

'Tell me?'

'They'll expect me to wear my uniform.'

'Your parents?' Tina slipped her palm into his and towed Sam towards the kitchen.

'Not just them. Bert and Mabel. And probably Tom as well. He told me he's trying to get his out of storage.'

'And you think if Tom's in his uniform, then you should be too?'

'Something like that.'

Flicking the kettle on at the switch, Tina smiled. 'I won't pretend I wouldn't like to see you in uniform, because I know you'd look mouth-watering, but I want you to stand at the head of the aisle feeling relaxed and happy. If an army uniform is going to give you flashbacks then don't wear it. You'll look great in a suit too.'

Sam kissed her again. 'Thank you.'

'What for?'

'For saying what I needed to hear.' Sam unhooked two

mugs from the rack. 'Don't tell Helen about Tom looking for his uniform. He wants it to be a surprise.'

'I bet she'll love that.' Tina paused. 'She's been very quiet lately. I hope they're alright.'

'Probably a bit low because she's leaving.' Sam headed to the fridge for some milk. 'I'm assuming she is going. She's not told me she's staying.'

'Come to think of it, Helen hasn't said much about anything lately.' Tina mused. 'She was quiet at the dress fitting, although she looked stunning. With her in that dress and Tom in uniform, I'd be putting money on another wedding being just around the corner if I was a gambling sort of girl. Do you know where Helen is?'

'Thea told me she was planning to write some of her book.'

Tina cradled her newly poured coffee. 'That's probably on her mind too. It's a great idea to have a book about the fortlet, but how people get all those words from their heads onto paper to turn them into a book worth reading, I'll never know.'

Helen tapped *Chapter One: Exmoor and the Romans* onto the screen of her laptop and stared at it for a long time. Then she deleted it and tried again. *Chapter One: The Romans on Exmoor.*

'Better.' She absentmindedly picked up the stone Dylan had given her and played it around her palm.

'Think of it like writing a load of papers. That's what Tom said.' She turned the pages of her notebook over to see the copious lists of information she needed to include and double check, not to mention the list of references she'd need to put in the bibliography at the back of the book. 'If there ever is a book.'

Slamming her notebook shut, Helen looked at the stone in her hand. 'This is ridiculous. I'm feeling sorry for myself and I don't even know if I have anything to feel sorry about. Perhaps I'm making assumptions. Dylan's only five, maybe he got it wrong – and even if he didn't, Sue might want them to be a family, but that doesn't mean Tom does.' She focused on Dylan's stone. *But if them being together makes Dylan happy, then Tom will go back to Sue. He'd do anything to make his son happy.* Helen's throat closed in on itself. *And so would I.*

As if conjured by her thoughts, Helen heard the sound of running wellies across the gravel outside the storeroom. Hastily patting her damp eyes with a tissue, she saw a small round face peer around the door.

'Dad said if you were busy, I should leave you alone. Are you busy, Helen?'

Helen's heart melted on the spot. Even if she had been in the middle of the most productive writing session of all time, she'd have claimed otherwise. 'I'm not, and as it happens, I wondered if you'd help me with something.'

'Yes, please!' Dylan ran on into the storeroom. 'Oh, you're holding my stone. Do you still love it?'

Helen glanced at her hand. She hadn't realised she was still holding it. 'I love it very much.'

Thirty-six

Tuesday April 7th

Shaun's mouth dropped open as Thea led him into the drawing room. 'That is a serious chocolate haul.'

'Great, isn't it?' Thea smiled. 'Helen and Dylan are in the garden, drawing up plans where to hide them.'

'How many are being hidden at once?'

'Two hundred, with Dylan on duty replacing the ones that have been found.'

'He'll love that.'

'I suspect Helen's secretly hoping the running around will wear him out so he falls asleep early. She hasn't said anything, but I think Dylan being here twenty-four-seven is denting her alone time with Tom more than they expected.'

'Hardly surprising.' Shaun looped an arm around Thea's waist. 'So, what was it you wanted to talk about? You made it sound serious.'

Thea sat on the sofa and patted the seat next to her. 'Will you promise to let me finish speaking before you get cross?'

Shaun's forehead creased. 'Why would I get cross?'

'Because this concerns an email I received from Julian, and I would rather you didn't jump to conclusions about him fancying me. *Because he doesn't.*'

Looking far from reassured, Shaun said, 'Go on then. What's he done now?'

'I'm not sure "done" is the right world. It's what he's proposing I do. Look.' Thea picked up her phone and scrolled through her emails so Shaun could read Julian's invitation to a business meeting at The Harborough Hotel. 'What bothers me most is that he didn't want me to talk to you about it.'

Thea ploughed on while Shaun read; determined to give him the whole story before he reacted. She detailed as much as she could remember about the overheard telephone conversation in the pub, about Julian wanting to "manoeuvre the right person into doing the interview" and how whatever it was he was up to had "worked a treat" and that "the production team were very impressed" because he'd had "a private word in the right ear".

'Honestly, Shaun, the man is so slimy.'

Shaun said nothing. He just sat staring at her, making Thea's blood chill as she saw him battling not to get angry. Taking a deep breath, she kept talking, telling him about how Julian had intercepted her outside the campervan before they came home and how, most important of all, she hadn't told Shaun any of this at the time because she didn't want to upset him.

'And, to be frank, I wouldn't trust Julian as far as I could spit and—'

'What text?' Shaun cut across her, his tone sharp.

'Pardon?'

'It says here, in this email, that there was a text.' He paused before reading out Julian's words, '*As you haven't replied to my text, I have had to assume it never reached you.* Well? Did it reach you?'

Thea licked her lips, 'Yes, but I was ignoring it. I didn't want to ruin things. We were having fun, and to be honest—'

'Having fun?' Shaun sighed. 'We were. And yet all the time you were keeping secrets. A phone call you overheard, a text and this email. How much else have you not shared with me, Thea?'

'Nothing!' Guilt knotted within Thea. 'I know I should have told you straightaway, but I didn't want to upset you. I was so afraid of hurting you, and, as I have *no* intention of doing anything for Julian once the show is fully recorded...'

As Shaun's eyes clouded, his countenance drawn, Thea felt an unexpected urge to giggle. He looked just like a Victorian school master, sat in a Victorian drawing room, waiting to tell the parent of an errant pupil what a disappointment they were. She didn't giggle though. Shaun's next words stole the impulse before her lips had even formed into a curve.

'You tell me all this now, *long* after the event, and expect me to believe Julian doesn't fancy you or that you don't fancy him?'

'What? Are you insane? Of course I don't!'

'What other reason would you have for keeping this from me? After the hard time you gave me for not even realising Sophie liked me in Cornwall – now you're being just as blind. Worse! You aren't blind – you're refusing to be honest about his or your feelings.' Shaun's words stayed horribly calm, sadness echoing in every syllable. 'And it's not just me that this affects!' Shaun was on his feet. 'I can't believe you'd do this to Ajay and Andy. After all the AA have done for you. If it hadn't been for them, you'd never have found the fortlet, and this place wouldn't be doing so well.' He raked a hand through his hair, making his fringe stick out at awkward angles.

Thea's mouth dropped open. 'I know that! This is *nothing* to do with that. I was trying to do the right thing! To protect your feelings. I didn't want to freak out anyone about the phone call I overheard until I knew I wasn't getting the wrong end of the stick. You know what half heard conversations are like! It might have been nothing to do with *Landscape Treasures* at all.'

'Oh no you don't!' Shaun was shaking his head. 'Of course it was about *Landscape Treasures*! Don't you remember what Julian said at that meal?' Aware he was shouting, and not wanting to be overheard, Shaun hissed, 'This has got to be about what he was saying about a shake up after *Treasure Hunters* change format!'

The colour drained from Thea's face. 'But it might not. What if I'd told you all what I'd heard and it had become gossip – and I'd been wrong?' Thea felt sick as she regarded Shaun's closed off expression. 'And that call might have had *nothing at all* to do with Julian wanting to talk to me about being a presenter. Which, by the way, I haven't agreed to – nor will I. I like my life here, thank you very much!'

Neither of them spoke. Thea stared across the short space between them on the sofa. It was only half a metre, but it might as well as have been three miles. The scent of chocolate, deliciously heady only moments ago, now turned her stomach. She could hear Helen's words echoing through the back of her mind. '*Tell him before everything gets ruined*'.

Shaun got up. He gave her a long hard stare, before walking away without another word.

Thea sat, frozen, unsure how she'd screwed up their conversation so completely. Fear made her feet move as her brain screamed out unhelpful questions. *Where has Shaun gone? Has he gone gone? Have I just screwed the best thing in my life?*

Running from the room, she took a guess that he'd headed outside and dashed to the backdoor. Glad that Tina and Sam had gone to visit Bert and Mabel, so no one was in the kitchen to ask her what was going on, Thea was in time to see Shaun disappearing into the woods. Without even stopping to put some shoes on, she ran after him.

Her mind raced; she had no idea what to say. She'd hurt him, and she deserved to be shouted at a bit, but not left. Not when all she'd tried to do was spare his feelings.

Thea was almost on his heels, when Shaun stopped moving and swung round to face her. 'Go on then. Explain. Why didn't you tell me about the text and email straight away? And yes, I get why you didn't mention the phone call in front of the AA, as they can be a bit gossipy, but why not tell *me*? We were alone straight after we'd had lunch. Why not say then? I never had you down as someone who enjoys playing games, Thea, so tell me. *Why?*'

'I was trying to!' Suddenly angry, Thea's hands gripped her hips. 'Okay then, how's this for why. I think Julian wants me to replace *you* as the presenter of the show.'

'What?' Shaun sagged back against the nearest tree.

Stepping forward, determined not to soften too fast,

Thea lowered her voice, speaking with quiet determination. 'Look, I'm sorry, Shaun. I have no evidence, just a hunch, and as I'd never rob the man I love of his job in a million years, I didn't want to say anything until I knew it to be a fact. But get this straight – I DO NOT FANCY JULIAN.'

As Shaun's mouth opened, Thea held up her hand. 'And, before you jump in again, I wish I *had* told you straight away. The only reason I didn't was because I did not want to hurt you if my hunch was wrong.' She ran a hand through her hair. 'Something I have well and truly cocked up.'

Shaun said nothing. He just stared at her for so long that eventually Thea was compelled to fill the silence.

'I don't trust Julian. What I overheard him say on the phone could have been him lying to someone. And, while we're at it, if you think for a single second that I'd do a thing to hurt Ajay, Andy or any of the *Landscape Treasures* team, or you, then you can carry on walking without me!'

The sound of the birds chatting to each other in the trees around them suddenly seemed abnormally loud as Thea waited for Shaun to respond. She was cold despite the sunshine that furled through the gaps in the overhanging branches of the mix of oak, pine and ash that dotted the landscape they'd run into. Her sock covered feet were scratched and sore.

Finally, Shaun spoke. 'You said you didn't want to tell me about Julian potentially replacing me with you until you knew it to be a fact.'

'Yes.'

'That implies you were planning to spend time with him to do just that.'

'What? No!' Thea shook her head. 'That isn't what

I meant at all. I wanted to talk to you about what to do and—'

'But you didn't, Thea. Did you?'

Thea watched as Shaun stalked deeper into the trees. This time she didn't follow him.

Thirty-seven

Tuesday April 7th

Helen sat on the side of her bed and listened. Nothing stirred. It had been at least four hours since Tina and Sam had returned from having dinner with Bert and Mabel, and as she hadn't seen Shaun or Thea since lunchtime, she assumed they'd retired to their bedroom on the floor below ages ago.

She couldn't hear any movement from the room next door where, she assumed, Tom and Dylan were fast asleep.

Helen checked her watch. It was three minutes to midnight. Her bag had been packed for an hour, although there were still piles of notes on the chair by the window. If she didn't pack them, perhaps she wasn't really going to leave.

The hands of her watch ticked on another minute.

'If I'm going, I need to go now.'

Helen's mouth was dry and her eyes felt dull with tears long shed, which had dried in streaks across her face. She hadn't bothered rubbing over where they made her skin feel tight.

It had been the picture that had been the final straw. The nudge she'd needed to stop avoiding what was becoming increasingly obvious. She hadn't been reading the signs wrong, no matter how much she wished she hadn't.

All the phone calls Tom had been taking. *They can't all have been work or wedding stuff.* Tom must have claimed they were to save her feelings. He was merely trying to soften the blow before admitting Sue had worn him down and he'd agreed to go back to her for Dylan's sake.

Helen closed her eyes. Dylan's happy face appeared behind her eyelids.

They'd had so much fun wandering around the house and grounds all day; finding egg sized hidey-holes. Dylan had drawn a rough map with lots of little x's on it. Declaring he'd created a treasure map, he'd been making pirate noises with hilarious results, when he'd suddenly got extra excited, run over to where his dad was typing into his laptop and borrowed his phone. Seconds later, Dylan was back, proudly showing Helen a photograph of a painting.

It was obviously Mill Grange. But it was the three figures that had twisted the knife in Helen's gut as Dylan effused about how his painting had pride of place over the art room table.

Mum, dad and son.

Helen still wasn't sure how she'd managed to make all the right noises, telling Dylan how clever he was, before guiding him back to his father with claims of an abrupt headache.

By the time she was in her room, the headache was real, so when Tom put his head around the door an hour later to see if she was alright, she didn't have to lie about feeling a bit rough.

He'd sat next to her for a while, his palm soothing her forehead, his fingers teasing out her fringe. She'd wanted to ask him about the painting, but the words stuck in her throat. She hadn't wanted to hear him tell her about the sacrifice he was going to make for his son.

The hands of her watch clicked on. One minute to midnight.

The sound of Sue's voice talking to Tom nudged itself to the forefront of Helen's mind as she stood up. *I think we owe him some proper family time, don't you?*

She picked up the ring of keys that had sat in the windowsill of her attic room since she'd taken up the offer of staying at Mill Grange for a sabbatical. They undid the front door to her home in Bath.

She weighed them in her hands for a moment, before knocking the paperwork on the chair into a neat pile and sliding it into a waiting carrier bag. Then, ripping the last clean page from her notebook, Helen sat down and began to write.

Wednesday April 8th

The sound of a door closing woke Thea with a start.

'Shaun?'

She looked around, expecting to see him lying in bed next to her, before remembering she wasn't in their bed, and she hadn't seen Shaun since he disappeared through the trees at the back of Mill Grange.

Clutching the blankets she'd borrowed from the laundry store to her chest, Thea sat up on the drawing room sofa. She thought she could hear the faint sound of a vehicle moving. *Is that Shaun? Is he leaving?*

Getting up, she ran on silent feet to the front door, wincing as the bruises she'd gathered from running through the woods without shoes made their presence felt. She was relieved to see the coat he'd been wearing hanging from its usual hook.

I must have imagined the sound of someone going out.

Heading back to the sofa, Thea sank back down. Although she'd managed some sleep, her whole being ached with tiredness and her mind spun with regrets and what ifs.

I should have told him straight away.

He should have accepted you were trying to spare his feelings.

I hurt him.

You were trying not to hurt him – but he wouldn't listen.

He can't honestly believe I fancy Julian!

In that second, she wondered why she was the one sleeping on the sofa, when Shaun had their cosy double bed to himself. Grabbing the moment of indignation like a shield, Thea threw down her blankets. Mumbling to herself as she took the stairs two at a time, Thea made a beeline for her bedroom. 'I'm not losing this relationship because of Julian bloody Blackwood!'

Helen pulled into a layby just outside Upwich and let the tears erupt.

She didn't doubt Tom's feelings for her. Not for a minute. But there was no way she could ask him to choose between her and his son's future happiness, so she'd decided to make it easier for him.

Blowing her nose into a handful of tissues, Helen pushed her shoulders back as she sat behind the wheel. 'I have a job to go to, a home and a life in Bath. I was fine before I went to Mill Grange. I *will* be fine again.'

Not allowing herself to look back at the village sign, Helen restarted her Land Rover's engine and pulled out onto the silent night.

Thea's hand was on the bedroom door before her indignation shrank into anxiety. *What if Shaun doesn't want me in there with him?*

Knowing the longer she left it, the worse she'd build the situation in her mind, Thea twisted the handle of the door and went in.

'You couldn't sleep either then.' Shaun was sat up against the bed's headboard.

'No.' Thea shut the door behind her, not sure if she should come towards the bed or not. 'I'm sorry. I really was trying to do the right thing, but I messed up.'

Shaun patted the side of the bed. 'I know.'

A tiny flicker of hope leapt up in Thea's chest. 'That I was trying to do the right thing or that I messed up?'

'Both.'

Thea limped across the room. 'Fair enough.'

Shaun flicked on the bedside lamp. 'You've hurt yourself?'

'I wasn't wearing shoes when I ran after you.'

'Idiot.'

'Pretty much.' Thea could see his expression was drawn. She wondered if he'd been crying. 'Where did you go?'

'I got as far as the Tarr Steps. Sat on the grass by the water and had a think.'

'A good place for thinking.' Thea threw her clothes off

and grabbing an oversized t-shirt from the chair next to the bed, slipped into bed. 'Can I ask what you thought?'

'That I was wrong when I told you that I wouldn't mind giving up presenting *Landscape Treasures*. Not that I knew that at the time, but back then I wasn't facing it as a real prospect. It certainly hadn't occurred to me that you'd be the one who'd replace me when the time came.'

Thea groaned. 'But I wouldn't. No way would I do that to you. You must know that?'

Shaun's expression caught between a half smile and a grimace. 'Yes. I know that. You don't even want to be a presenter at all, do you?'

'No. I like my life here.' Thea could feel the heat of Shaun's thigh against her. 'I'm not saying I'd never guest present for *Landscape Treasures* again; but I wouldn't for Julian. I wish Phil had never left.'

Shaun snorted. 'Me too.'

As a hush feel between them, Thea asked, 'Can I say something?'

'Only if it isn't about Julian. I can't face more arguments on no sleep.'

A lump formed in Thea's throat. So much for her brief hope that he'd forgiven her. 'I just love you. That's all.'

Shaun switched the light off again and snuggled under the covers. 'I love you too.' He rolled over, so he was facing away from Thea. 'I'm just not sure I trust you, or know what to say to you right now.'

Thirty-eight

Wednesday April 8th

Tina sat at the kitchen table, two large pieces of paper laid out before her. One was a to-do list for the preparation of the house ready for Easter Sunday, in four days' time. The other was covered in hastily scribbled names of everyone she and Sam intended to invite to the wedding.

Taking a sip from her coffee cup, Tina stared at both lists, not sure which to tackle first. Time seemed to be slipping through her fingers like grains of sand.

Her eyes flicked to the box of wedding invites sat to her left. Doodling a flower in the corner of the nearest piece of paper, Tina glanced at the kitchen clock. It was almost nine o'clock. Thea had promised she'd help her this morning, but so far, the only people she'd seen were Tom and Dylan, who'd already had their breakfast, and were weeding the walled garden with Sam. Helen, she suspected, had been up long before her, and was already hard at work on her book in the store room office.

Assuming Thea had overslept, Tina dipped a cookie in her mug and surveyed the kitchen. That was the room that would need the most work before Sunday. Everyone always wanted to see the kitchen, whether it was semi-modernised and in use or not.

'Right. Mabel will be here in a minute to help clean up.' Tina spoke bracingly to the paper in front of her. 'Until then, I'll write wedding invitations.'

Tina felt a surge of happiness as she read the words, "Miss Tina Martin and Mr Sam Philips invite you to their wedding at Mill Grange – two o'clock, May 23rd" which had been printed in gold script across the front of each perfectly square invite.

She'd addressed fifteen envelopes before the familiar pad of Mabel's soft soled shoes walking along the corridor that joined the kitchen with the main door made Tina recheck the time. Half past nine and still no sign of Thea or Shaun. Guessing they were making the most of having a lie in, in a decent sized bed, Tina shuffled the sealed envelopes into a pile, and ticked off the names of the people invited so far from her list.

'Morning, Mabel.' Tina gestured to the kettle. 'I was about to heat some water before cleaning the dresser, would you like a cuppa at the same time?'

'No thanks, dear. Bert and I just had one.' Mabel gestured to the invitations. 'Good to see you've made a start.'

'I wasn't sure what to do first, to be honest. There's so much to get done.'

'It'll all happen, don't worry.' Mabel hooked an apron out of her bag and tied it in place. 'I hope you don't mind, but I asked Diane if she'd like to help out.'

'Not at all. She was brilliant when we were restoring Mill Grange before Sam bought the place. Thanks, Mabel.'

'My pleasure. I knew you'd be okay with it.' Mabel winked. 'Diane will be here at ten.'

Tina laughed. 'You're priceless.'

'So Bert tells me.'

'How is he this morning?'

'Getting better by the day.' Squeezing some washing up liquid into a bowl in the sink, Mabel added some of the hot water from the kettle to the bowl and pulled on her rubber gloves. 'Having the wedding to look forward to has galvanised him. Thanks for asking him to be involved. It means a lot to him. To us.'

'As if we could do it without you!' Tina grinned. 'Tom tells me he has enlisted Bert to help with planning Helen's birthday as well.'

Mabel smiled. 'The old boy was chuffed about that. Certainly plenty to keep his mind occupied while he watches appalling day time television.' Wrinkling her nose against the commonality of turning a television set on before the evening news, Mabel asked, 'Where is Helen anyway, and Thea, come to that?'

'I haven't seen them. Helen's probably working on the book. She wants to squeeze as many words out as she can before she leaves.'

Mabel sighed. 'She is going then?'

'She hasn't said otherwise.'

'But Sam did ask her to stay?'

'He did.' Tina shrugged. 'But we can't offer her anything like the wage the Baths can. And she has her own home in Bath.'

'And Tom and Dylan?'

'I haven't liked to ask.' Tina put the invitations in a drawer out of the way of the cleaning frenzy that was about to begin. 'They seem happy together, but whenever I ask about Tom, she changes the subject.'

'Ah well, early days for them yet.' Mabel spoke sagely. 'Time will tell.'

'I expect you're right.' Tina pulled on a pair of yellow Marigolds. 'I'm not sure where Thea is. I thought she might be having a lie in, but she promised she'd help from nine. It isn't like her to be still in bed at ten, even if Shaun is with her.'

Footsteps in the corridor made the women look at each other.

'That's probably her now.' Mabel plunged her arms into the washing up bowl just as Sam appeared.

'Did I miss the kettle boiling?'

'You did.' Tina held her gloved hands up as if to show she was already in Mrs Mop mode. 'We thought you were Thea. I don't suppose you've seen her this morning?'

'She's in the main garden with Shaun. Looked like they were having a heart to heart.'

'Really?' Tina turned to face the gardens. 'I wonder what that's about?'

Mabel paused in her labours. 'Must be something to do with *Landscape Treasures*. Thea wouldn't be late without good reason.'

'That's true.' Sam turned to Tina, hoping she'd understand that he wanted to talk to her out of earshot of the old lady. 'I don't suppose you could lose the rubber gloves for a second? I wanted to show you something in the walled garden.'

'But I've only just—'

'You carry on, lass.' Mabel flapped her away. 'I'll get the table scrubbed down then I'll put the kettle on for the workers.'

'What is it?' Tina asked as soon as they were outside of the kitchen.

'Someone slept in the drawing room last night.'

'Really? Are you sure?' Tina's eyebrows rose.

'There are blankets in there, and a definite indent in the cushions.' Sam led the way towards the offending sofa.

'Shaun?'

'It would explain the private conversation and why you haven't seen Thea this morning.'

'I hope they're alright.' Tina found herself wondering how the wedding would go if the best man and chief bridesmaid weren't talking to each other. 'They're made for each other.'

'They are,' Sam agreed, 'but right now I think all we can do to help is remove all evidence of this before anyone else sees it and then leave them in peace.'

The spring sunshine dazzled Thea's face as she risked a glance at Shaun out of the corner of her eye. He was looking across the garden towards the fortlet. His body language was closed off and the gap between them on the bench was marked.

Thea tried not to feel bad about not helping Tina and Mabel in the kitchen; telling herself her friends would understand when she explained the reason for her delay.

Feeling the shake in her fingers that always happened when she was stressed, Thea plunged her hands into her pockets as she broke the silence.

'I was waiting until we got back to the Cotswolds to talk to you about Julian's proposition. Stupid as it sounds now, I thought that, as we were having a holiday, work could wait.' She peeped up at him through her fringe, but Shaun was still staring away from her. 'The other archaeologists are on holiday too, so I assumed nothing would change while we had a nice time together. Here. With our friends.'

Shaun kept up his vigil across the landscape. 'Do you honestly think that Julian hasn't been working? That he hasn't been trying to wheedle his way up the next rung of the career ladder while we've been here?'

'But—'

'Men like Julian don't have holidays. They are too afraid to take one in case some other high flyer sneaks above them in the race to the top.'

Thea didn't say anything. She didn't need to. She knew Shaun was right.

After another painfully long silence, Shaun asked, 'His email, did you reply to it?'

'No. I told you I wanted to talk to you first.' Thea exhaled. 'I'm sorry I didn't tell you straightaway. I thought I was doing the right thing. I was wrong. I just wanted us to have a nice time together without Julian ruining it.' She turned to look at him. 'I'm not sure how many more times I can apologise for that.'

Shaun shuffled up on the bench closer to Thea. 'The question is, what do we do about this?'

Thea stiffened. *Does he mean us or Julian?*

She licked her lips, her words coming out as a frightened squeak. 'About us?'

Shaun turned to look at her. 'I meant Julian, but yes, the question of us is there too.'

The warmth from Shaun's leg buffering against her own seeped through her suddenly cold flesh. It gave her a tiny edge of hope. She longed to fling her arms around him, but pride stopped her. *You didn't do anything other than what you thought was best. You were wrong but you admitted that and you said sorry.*

Not knowing what to say, afraid that whatever came out of her mouth would be the wrong thing, Thea looked across the garden. She could see Tina and Sam walking from the kitchen to the walled garden. They had an arm around each other's waist, as they chatted. *We were like that.* Thea battled the urge to cry as she averted her eyes from her friends.

'They look happy, don't they?' Shaun's words took Thea by surprise.

'They are happy.'

'Funny how happiness can be so easily broken.'

'It isn't funny at all.' Thea's shoulders clenched at the implication.

'No, it isn't.' Shaun sighed. 'And to think, if Julian hadn't fancied you, none of this would have happened.'

'What?' The tear on Thea's cheek froze as she turned to face him, anger overtaking her grief. 'You think Julian only wants me to be a presenter because he fancies me, not because I'm any good at it.'

'I didn't say you weren't good at it, but if you didn't press his buttons so much, and always do what he bloody well asks.' Shaun knew he was being unfair, but his bruised ego and sore heart had taken control of his tongue. 'Yes, Julian, certainly Julian… You're like a lovestruck groupie!'

Thea's mouth opened and closed in shock. Clenching her hands into fists, she spoke slowly and deliberately. 'Look, Shaun, my intentions were good but went wrong – it really is that simple. If you truly believe what you just said, then I'd like you to leave me alone – permanently. But if you're prepared to admit you were just talking bollocks and still love me, you know where to find me. Now,' Thea stood up with as much dignity as she could muster, 'if you'll excuse me, I promised Tina I'd help clean the house.'

Thirty-nine

Wednesday April 8th

Tom smiled as he read the text message. Sue had found his dress uniform in a box in her attic. He was contemplating whether Helen might have a thing about uniforms, when he reached the store room door.

'Helen, I—' Tom stopped talking. She wasn't there. Somehow the space felt emptier than normal. The hairs on the back of his neck stood up as he looked around him. Nothing was missing.

Telling himself she'd just popped to the bathroom, Tom was about to leave when he saw a sealed white envelope addressed to Sam and Tina on the desk.

Lifting the envelope, Tom was aware of his heart beating faster. 'Why has she left a letter for…?' His sentence trailed off as a horrible suspicion trickled down his spine.

She hasn't gone. She hasn't.

He ran from the office to the back of the house. There was an empty space where Helen's Land Rover should have been. Tom's pulse accelerated as he spun on the balls of his boots and hurtled around the outside of the house, keeping going until he crashed through the gate of the walled garden.

'Tom?' At the sound of running footsteps, Sam was immediately on the alert. 'What's happened?'

'Helen.' He said nothing else as he thrust the letter in Sam's direction.

Picking up on Tom's unspoken fear, Sam ripped the envelope open, holding the letter so all three of them could see it.

Dear Sam and Tina,

Thank you for allowing me to work in your beautiful home and offering me the chance to stay.

I'm sorry I have messed you around. I promise that was never my intention.

The decision to leave was not an easy one, but it's best for everyone I love that I return to Bath.

Please accept my apologises for missing your wedding. I have left a cheque covering the cost of the dress. Perhaps Mabel knows someone who'd benefit from wearing it.

With love and regret,

Helen xx

Tina removed the cheque from the envelope and held it up to Sam.

Tom stared at them in horror. 'What does she mean, it's

best for everyone she loves?' He glared at the piece of paper as it was an exploded bomb. 'She'd decided to stay, to make a life here. She told me.'

Sam and Tina exchanged glances, neither knowing what to say. But before they could speak, Tom was sprinting from the garden.

He took the main stairs two treads at a time. When he reached her bedroom door he hesitated. She had to be inside. She just had to be. Surely there would have been a letter for him too if she'd really gone.

Her coat and boots were gone. Her rucksack was missing. There were no clothes in her wardrobe, and the chair that had doubled as her desk since Dylan's arrival, held nothing except for a half-used box of tissues.

There was an envelope on the bed.

Tom's hands shook as he picked it up, his forehead creasing into dark lines. How had he messed this up? His mind leapt through every past crime he'd committed in the name of relationships, but he couldn't think of anything he'd done to upset Helen.

His throat dry, his clumsy fingers, Tom undid the envelope.

Dear Tom,

I've gone back to Bath.

As much as I love you, I love Dylan too – so I had to go.

I know you'll understand why.

H xx

He turned the paper over in the hope of there being more, but there was nothing else. She'd written more to Tina and Sam than to him.

The paper curled under his grasp as he read it again.

'No, I bloody well don't understand why!'

Clutching the letter, Tom rushed back to Helen's desk in the store room. There was something he needed to check.

He'd been sure nothing had been removed from her office, but perhaps one thing had gone. And if she'd taken that, then maybe she did love them. Maybe she *had* gone for them – and not because he'd done something wrong. *But why leave? Why not just talk to me?*

Passing a pale-faced Tina in the hallway, Tom dashed on by, not wanting to talk yet. He didn't stop until he was back in the store room.

He sat on Helen's chair and stared at the desk. *You said you'd stay. You said you'd take the job and stay here with me and Dylan.*

The book research and her notebook weren't there, although that hadn't surprised him before. He'd assumed they were in her room. Now he thought they had to be with Helen on her way to Bath. No, in Bath – it only took two hours to get there. His hand automatically went to the car keys in his pocket. He checked the time, he could be there in… *No I can't. Dylan.*

Thinking of his son took him back to the reason he'd rushed back to Helen's desk in the first place.

The stone was gone. The stone Dylan had given Helen. She'd taken it with her.

Massaging his temples, Tom stared at the keys in his hand. 'I don't even know where she lives and I can hardly barge into the Roman Baths and demand to see her. Can I?'

Despite scrubbing her face repeatedly, Thea's complexion remained tight from the tears she'd allowed herself to shed after leaving Shaun on the bench. Heading towards the kitchen, ready to apologise to Tina for being late on clean-up parade, Thea almost collided with her friend in the doorway.

'Oh God, I'm sorry.' Thea was about to explain her absence when she spotted Tina's drawn expression. 'What is it?'

'Helen's gone.'

'What do you mean, gone?' Thea scrubbed at her sore eyes.

'Back to Bath. She left a note for me and Sam and went. God knows when.'

'I heard a door close around midnight.' Thea's hand came to her mouth. 'At first I thought it was Shaun. Then I thought maybe I'd imagined it.'

Tina tilted her head as she regarded her friend. 'You slept on the sofa, not Shaun?'

Blushing, Thea nodded. 'I was hoping no one had found the blankets.'

'Are you alright?' Tina looked at her friend. 'That was a stupid question. I can see you're not. Do you want to talk about it?'

'Yes. No. I don't know.' Thea pushed her shoulders back. 'But my problems can wait. Tell me about Helen? Does Tom know?'

'Yes. He found the note for me and Sam, and then dashed

off again. Presumably to see if she'd left one for him.' Tina passed the letter to Thea. 'Looks like you'll be facing bridesmaid duty solo after all.'

Thea's mouth opened as she read. 'What does she mean, she's gone as it's best for the people she loves?'

'That's what Tom wanted to know. I can only assume she means him and Dylan.' Tina checked to make sure they weren't being overheard. 'While you were away, Helen confided that she was worried about getting together with Tom because it was all happening so quickly.'

'And with a built-in step-son.' Thea groaned. 'Not that Dylan isn't lovely, but—'

'Exactly. From no relationship to a complete family in a few weeks.' Tina headed into the kitchen and poured Thea a glass of water. 'When we were trying on dresses, she was very subdued.'

'Yes, but I just assumed she was out of her comfort zone. Helen is not one for dressing up beyond the requirements of a business suit.'

'And now she'll have to go back to business suits every day.' Tina shook her head. 'I can't imagine Helen behind a desk.'

'If she really has gone to Bath, the team at the Roman Baths will be glad to have her back.' Thea took a sip of water. 'I should have spent more time talking to her. We're good friends, we worked together for years, but since Shaun and I got back from the Cotswolds, there doesn't seem to have been a minute, and now...'

Tina gave Thea a hug, asking gently, 'Where is Shaun?'

'I left him on a bench in the garden. I hoped he'd follow me in, but I haven't seen him so...' Her throat closed in on itself as she mumbled, 'perhaps we aren't a couple anymore either.'

'But that's ridiculous!' Tina suddenly saw her entire wedding party dissolving before her eyes. 'What happened?'

'I'll tell you later. First,' Thea brushed her hands together, 'we find Tom and make sure he's alright. Then we check that Dylan isn't exhausting Mabel, and, well, the house still needs cleaning.'

Sam took a packet of chocolate biscuits out to the table where Dylan and Mabel were enjoying a mid-morning snack.

The boy's eyes lit up. 'Mum says chocolate biscuits are only for when I've been very good.'

'And you have been very good. You've worked hard in the garden this morning. I think you've earned a biscuit.' Sam made eye contact with Mabel, knowing there was no way she wouldn't have picked up on something being wrong from all the running around. 'Would you be a good boy again, Dylan, and stay here while I have a quick chat with Mabel?'

'Okay.' The boy was chomping his way through his biscuit before Mabel had risen to her feet.

As soon as they were out of earshot, Mabel was as no-nonsense as ever. 'Something has happened. In fact, two things have happened.'

'Two things?' Sam frowned.

'Yes.' Mabel nodded. 'Tom first. What's happened there?'

'Helen's gone back to Bath. She left a note, but it didn't explain why she'd gone. Just that it was for the best.'

'And naturally Tom wants to go after her.'

'He hasn't said so, although I'm sure he does, but—'

'He can't leave Dylan.' Mabel looked over her shoulder to the lad munching a second biscuit. 'Tell him to go. Dylan can stay with Bert and me tonight. Or here if you guys think it's best he has his own room.'

'Thanks, Mabel. I hoped you'd say that. I'll go and tell Tom.'

Sam was a few steps away when he turned back. 'You said two things had happened. What's the other thing?'

'Sometimes I think men are born with atmosphere blindness.'

'Sorry?'

'Thea and Shaun. They've been sat over on the bench. Well, they were until Thea headed indoors, probably to have a good cry. The air out here has been heavy with their quiet rowing.'

'Shaun and Thea?'

'Yes.' Mabel looked troubled. 'I think they might have broken up.'

Forty

Tom pulled his old Fiesta onto the inside lane of the motorway. His ears strained to hear the instructions from his sat nav, which, at some point over the past ten miles, he'd managed to knock so that the volume was barely audible.

Thea's hastily jotted "how to find Helen's house" instructions sat on the passenger seat next to him, just in case his mobile battery died or the signal gave out.

Easing off the accelerator, Tom saw the junction to Bath ahead. *What if she slams the door in my face?*

The closer he got to Bath, the more Tom wondered if Tina and Thea were right. They were convinced Helen had gone because she didn't think she was good enough to be a step-parent to Dylan.

But she must know that Dylan adores her?

Squashing down the guilt at abandoning his son, Tom tried to read the sudden barrage of signposts which had come at him after exiting the motorway, while straining to hear the sat nav at the same time.

Turning with the traffic onto London Road, Tom caught sight of a brown tourist sign for the Roman Baths and Bath Abbey out of the corner of his eye. His heart lurched. He might not know where he was, but he knew he was close to where he needed to be.

'I must be the most selfish person in the world.'

Gertrude and Mavis looked up from where they'd been happily pecking at their grain, tilting their necks in Tina's direction.

'Thea and Shaun might have split up and Helen's done a bunk, and I'm stood here worrying about my wedding.'

Gertrude took a half-hearted stab at a slice of pepper with her beak.

'What if Sam and I have to get married with the best man and bridesmaid not talking to each other, and the usher heartbroken because the other bridesmaid is missing?'

A well-timed squawk from Tony Stark, Mill Grange's resident rooster, told Tina to go and talk to her chief bridesmaid.

'But I don't know what to say.' Tina sighed. 'This time yesterday I thought everyone was okay. How can I not have noticed my friends were unhappy?'

Thea had not expected to hear laughter, especially not coming from Shaun. She could hear him and Sam, alongside Dylan's giggling, just beyond the manor's backdoor.

Pausing, her heart thudding, she listened to the sound of happiness that was just out of reach. Thea was about to go and see what they were up to, when something stopped her. *What if my arriving ruins their fun?* The idea that Shaun might stop what he was doing and walk off at the sight of her made her feel sick.

Consumed by misery, Thea didn't hear Tina's footsteps as she emerged from the kitchen.

'I was about to ask if you were okay,' Tina paused, taking in her friend's tired eyes, 'but that would be a stupid question.'

'I should have listened to Helen.' Thea flexed and unflexed her hands, trying to stop them shaking. 'I was trying to do the right thing.'

Not knowing what Thea was talking about, Tina asked, 'But that right thing went wrong?'

'Yes.'

A fresh burst of laughter came from outside. Tina stepped forward to see what was happening. But Thea put her arm out to stop her.

Backing away from the door, Thea muttered, 'If I go out there the fun will be ruined. You go, I'll see you later.'

Tina took a gentle hold of her friend's arm. 'No, we'll go together.'

'But—'

'But nothing. Shaun is a grown up, he won't ruin whatever fun Dylan is having just because you two have had a row.'

Before Thea could protest, she found herself being propelled along in Tina's light, but insistent, grasp.

The scene that met them, made Thea smile despite herself.

Dylan was covered from head to toe in bubbles. Helping Sam and Shaun to wash all the mud and leaves from the driveway had developed into something far more exciting.

Sam, who was adorned with a spattering of stray bubbles, grinned as he saw them. 'I think it's safe to say we used rather too much washing up liquid.'

Tina laughed. 'That's an understatement. What did you do, drop the bottle in the bucket?'

'Yes!' Dylan giggled as he did a little jig. Bubbles flew off him in all directions, making them laugh out loud.

'How on earth did you get so covered, Dylan?' Not ready to acknowledge Shaun, Thea focused on the little boy.

'I was sweeping. My brush hit the buckets and some bubbles flew up and hit my nose.' Dylan could hardly talk for giggling. 'Then I got decorated.'

'Decorated?' Tina raised a questioning eyebrow.

'We decided he looked good in white foam.' Sam winked. 'I think we might have got a bit carried away, Dylan mate.'

'Aww, does that mean I can't be a bubble monster anymore?' He did another jig, sending globules of foam dancing across the air where they landed on his spectators.

'It wouldn't look good if your dad came home to find you with a cold because you'd got all wet helping us clean.' Tina gave him a smile.

'It's a nice day though.' Shaun spoke for the first time. 'Maybe Dylan could play for a little longer, then I'll bundle him into a nice hot shower.'

'Yes!' Dylan immediately stuck both arms into the nearest frothing bucket, pulling them out and walking around like a zombie, his frothy arms dripping as he held them out before him.

As the others pretended to be afraid of the boy, Thea's heart constricted. She knew Shaun wanted children one day, she'd assumed with her. *But now…*

She was pulled out of her depressing thoughts by Tina's hand tapping on her shoulder. 'I think we'd better fetch some bath towels to wrap this lot in.'

Seizing an excuse to be on her own to collect herself, Thea said, 'I'll get them. You stay here and watch the show.'

Taking refuge in the laundry, Thea took her time collecting three bath towels from the store cupboard. She clutched them to her chest, inhaling the newly washed scent. She imagined Shaun holding Dylan's hand as they chatted on their way to the shower, ready to hose him down after his bubble adventure.

'You've been ages. Have you taken root?'

Shaun's voice made her jump.

'I was thinking.' Thea swung round, holding out the towels like an offering. 'You'd better go. I'd hate Dylan to get cold.'

'He's fine. He's running around so much, there is more chance he'll overheat than freeze.'

'Right. Good.'

They looked at each other, or rather, at each other's feet, neither knowing what to say.

Shaun gave up first, spinning around on the soles of his boots. 'I'll take these then.'

'Okay.' Thea let him go.

Helen couldn't settle.

As she'd driven through the night, she hadn't allowed herself to think about anything except getting to the house safely. But ever since pulling the Land Rover onto the drive of her home in Bath just before three o'clock in the morning, her mind had been a mass of regrets. Yet, her resolution that she'd done the right thing, remained firm. Not that knowing that made it any easier.

Helen hadn't been able to sleep in her double bed. There was too much space after so many months in a single. It felt cold and alien, even though the bed, and the room it was in, had been hers for over twenty years.

With no fresh food in the house, and not being able to face the outside world, Helen had eaten nothing since she'd arrived but a pile of fish fingers she'd found in the freezer. For the past two hours she'd paced the house like a caged tiger; disorientated and lost.

Every surface was dusty, but she couldn't face getting the cleaning things out of their cupboard.

Cleaning. 'That's what I'm supposed to be doing at Mill Grange today.'

Helen headed into the bathroom. 'Enough moping, you made your decision. It was hard, but it was the right thing to do. Shower, change and go out. Get some food. Then, pop into the Baths. Tell them you're coming back fractionally before expected.'

They'll ask why.

'I don't have to tell them why. I can say that the remaining work can be done from here.' She thought of the book and its notes. *That, at least, is the truth.*

Forty-one

Wednesday April 8th

Sweat prickled down Tom's neck as he spotted the road he'd been looking for. Thea hadn't been joking when she'd said it was on a steep slope, nor had she exaggerated about how hard it would be to find a parking space.

He spotted Helen's Land Rover as he drove up the narrow road. *At least she's here.* There were no free parking spaces though.

After doing a twenty-three-point turn, Tom eased his car back down the hill. This time he pulled onto Helen's drive. He knew the boot of the Fiesta would overhang the pavement, but as he was far from the only driver to park in that manner, he guessed the local pedestrians were used to having their access encroached.

Sitting where he was, Tom stared at the house. It was just how Helen had described it. A small, well presented terrace that looked as if it could only have been built in Bath. He glanced at each window in turn, but no curtains twitched.

Suddenly nervous, Tom fired off a text to Sam, letting him

know he'd arrived and to check on Dylan. Then, getting out of the car, rubbing his palms down his jeans, he headed for the front door.

Helen had wandered around Waitrose without any real clue what she was throwing into her basket. Now, as she stood in the busy street, she glanced into her two carrier bags. The contents leaned heavily towards the biscuit, chocolate, and easy cook pizza area. There was nothing that made up a proper meal. Her mouth watered at the thought of Mabel's home cooking.

Unable to face more shopping, and telling herself she needed to lose weight anyway, Helen took three paces in the direction of home. Halfway through the fourth step, the idea of being home alone made her stop dead, causing a fellow pedestrian to walk straight into her. In a flurry of apologies, Helen turned towards the Roman Baths.

Her desk was much as she'd left it. The in tray was full and a long overdue to-do list, scribbled on an old envelope, sat next to her computer monitor. Seeing the out of date list reminded Helen how quickly she'd left the Baths; first using the excuse of taking the chance of seeing some rare Roman remains on Exmoor as a reason to take a couple of days off. A trip that turned into a holiday and then a sabbatical. And then…

She shook her head, batting away the pain she kept telling herself she'd get used to and would, eventually, beat. *You have done the right thing. You will feel better in the end.*

Wondering if her coffee machine still worked, or if months of neglect would mean it was clogged and would refuse to serve her in a petty act of revenge, Helen stretched her tired limbs as she headed towards her personal caffeine source.

The coffee machine spat at her; not impressed at being left unused for so long, but begrudgingly dispensing her drink anyway. Fishing a packet of biscuits out of the nearest shopping bag, Helen thought about the delighted surprise on the receptionist's face when she'd arrived in the impressive entrance hall. Then there'd been the friendly wave of the security man as he guarded the door between the museum and the staff offices. Telling them she was back and was popping in to make a start on the hundreds of staff memos she must have missed, Helen had inhaled the familiar aroma of dust, air conditioning and stone that she'd always associate with the Roman Baths. That scent was now infused with the rich blend of Arabica coffee. *I certainly missed the smell of this place.*

Back at her desk, Helen found several months' worth of company bulletins and policy documents staring at her. As uninspiring as they ever were, at least they were largely out of date, and therefore undemanding.

Soon immersed in the pointless correspondence, the ring of her desk phone took her by surprise, its tinny sound echoing around the office.

'Hello... Yes, hello Mike, yes, I'm back in Bath. I thought I'd get my desk backlog sorted before my official restart date.'

Helen could feel herself slipping back into curator mode

as the manager of the museum's board of directors filled her in on a forthcoming exhibition of loaned Roman artefacts. As she took notes, she could hear the relief in his voice that she was back to deal with it for him.

'Week after next you say?' Helen opened her desk diary, causing a waft of dust to float towards her. 'Tuesday arrival, to be opened to the public on following Friday afternoon. Right. What time on the Tuesday?'

Ten minutes later, having been told in no uncertain terms how timely her return was as the new exhibition was rather a last-minute affair, and staff holidays meant there wasn't anyone with as much experience as her to set it up, Mike had gone on to explain how overprotective the owner of the antiquities was, and how careful handling of him as well as the artefacts, would be required.

Glad to have a project to concentrate on, Helen dipped a cookie into her coffee and switched on her PC. The biscuit was part way to her mouth when a knock on the door made her jump. Dropping the cookie into her drink, spraying coffee drops across the desk, Helen swore as brown stains dappled her diary.

The security guard popped his head around the door. 'Sorry to bother you, boss, but could you come to reception. There's a man here who says he knows you.'

'What?' Wiping dots of coffee and biscuit off her cheek, Helen's pulse drummed rapidly in her neck. 'What man?'

'A Mr Harris. Said he'd come from the fortlet where you've been working.'

A trip of heat surged through Helen's chest as her hands went cold. 'Here?'

'Boss?' The security guard, whose name Helen had forgotten, was looking concerned. 'Is he legit, or do I get rid of him?'

'Sorry.' Helen got to her feet. 'I wasn't expecting anyone. Umm…' *What do I do?* She looked at her mug, where the remains of the cookie were floating on the surface of her coffee, slowly decomposing before her eyes. 'I'll come with you.'

Surely Tom understands how painful it would be for me to work alongside him every day and then watch him go home to Sue?

As they passed the fire exit, Helen had a childish urge to run through the door. Only the knowledge that she'd have a hell of a lot of explaining to do if she set off the fire alarms on her first trip back to the office, stopped her.

'Mr Harris, did he have a young boy with him?'

'No, Boss.'

'Thanks.' Helen licked her lips. *You can do this. Just tell him to go home to Dylan.*

Feeling out of breath, even though they'd walked sedately back to reception, Helen nodded her thanks to the security guard as he pushed open the door.

Tom, looking awkward and out of place, was obviously trying hard not to look awkward and out of place. Helen heart constricted.

Remember why you left. This is for Dylan. Remember.

The walk back to her office, with Tom walking behind her, seemed to take six times longer than usual. Helen had felt his presence with each step. His breath on the back of her neck, his hands within touching distance; yet not touching her.

Helen had decided to get in first. To explain herself and then ask him to leave, but the second the door shut behind them Tom pulled the note she'd left him from his pocket, and thrust it out towards her.

'Well?' He sounded angry, but his expression spoke of hurtful incomprehension. 'Perhaps you could start by telling me why you chose to leave this rather than speak to me? Or maybe we should start with you telling me why Sam and Tina got a nice long letter and I got this pathetic excuse for a note? Or how you expected me to tell Dylan that one of his favourite people – that's you – got up in the middle of the night and disappeared without saying goodbye to him?'

Helen's mouth opened, but nothing came out. Her eyes dropped to her coffee cup. The cookie has totally disintegrated and clung in unappealing clumps to the side of her mug.

'Nothing to say?' Tom crossed his arms.

'How's Dylan?' Helen headed back towards the coffee machine.

'If by that you mean, how is he taking you walking out; I haven't told him yet. He is safe at the house with our friends.'

'Right.'

'That's it?' Tom found his resolution not to get angry fading. 'You tell me you're going to stay at Mill Grange, you give my son a gift that he treasures and then, five minutes later, you leave without a word.'

'I told you in the note.' Helen picked up some clean

mugs, glad of the activity as she made two more coffees, even though she'd gone off the idea of drinking anything.

'The note says nothing! Thea and Tina think you've got it into your head that you aren't good enough to help bring up Dylan! Talk about rubbish!'

'What?' Helen cheeks pricked with heat. 'You talked to them about it?'

'Of course I did! They're our friends. I was going out of my mind.'

'Oh.'

'Oh? Seriously? That's it?'

'Coffee?' Helen held up a mug; her head started to thud. She'd been so sure they'd all understand; especially if Dylan had shown them his family painting too.

'I don't want anything other than an explanation.'

Suddenly exasperated; lack of sleep and food catching up with her, on top of the heart she'd broken for herself before Tom could do it for her, Helen sagged onto her desk. 'Are you really going to make me say it, when you know how much it'll hurt me?'

'Say what?' Tom's anger dipped into confusion as he saw unshed tears welling in Helen's eyes.

'The reason behind all the furtive phone calls to Sue, and then... the painting. Dylan's painting.'

'Phone calls?' More confused by the second, Tom said, 'A couple were to Sue, but most weren't. I've been helping Sam and his parents with wedding stuff.'

Helen's pulse raced. 'Wedding stuff?'

'Yes.'

'But you always moved away when you took them, like they were secret?'

'They were – not from you specifically, but I promised Lord Malvern and Sam I'd help keep a few things a surprise until the big day.'

'Oh.' Feeling rather stupid, Helen shrugged. 'Makes no difference anyway, not now.'

'Not now, what?'

'Now you're getting back with Sue.'

Forty-two

Wednesday April 8th

'Getting back with Sue?' Tom was so stunned, not just by what Helen had said but by the certainty with which she'd said it, that he repeated the sentence twice.

'You aren't getting back with her?'

'Not even if Hell froze over!'

'But... Dylan said...' Helen steadied herself against her desk as they confronted each other across the office.

'What did Dylan say?'

'That his mum wanted him to be part of a family again.' Helen felt her head begin to thud. 'And Sue did too. I heard her. She was speaking to you when she said, "I think we owe him some proper family time, don't you?"'

'When did she say that?'

'Just before you went to Sybil's with Dylan for a scone.'

'Did she?' Tom picked up the mug of coffee he hadn't wanted. 'And Dylan? When did he tell you Sue wanted to be a family again?'

'When we were drawing the Easter egg map. What with

that and your furtive calls, and then the painting...' Helen sighed. 'I can't be the person who stops Dylan being with his parents. I love him far too much for that.'

'What are you talking about?' Tom gripped the mug tighter. 'I just told you, the calls were for the wedding. Some were from Lord Malvern and some were Sam asking for help with Bert.'

'Bert?' Helen gave a ringlet of hair that had fallen across her face an agitated tug.

'He needs a new suit, but he's not well enough to go shopping yet. Sam asked me to arrange for a tailor to visit him at home.'

'Oh.'

'I would have told you, but we had Dylan with us all the time, and there's a chance he'd have told Bert in his excitement. Five-year-olds are not the best at keeping secrets.' Tom suddenly strode across the room and put his mug down on the desk next to Helen's. Before he could stop himself, he'd reached out a finger and pushed the ringlet from her eyes. 'I am not, nor will I *ever*, get back together with Sue. Okay?'

'But the painting?'

'The one Dylan did of Mill Grange? What about it?'

'It was of you, Dylan and Sue. I know it's natural for him to paint his parents, but...'

'That wasn't me, Dylan and *Sue*; it was me, Dylan and *you*.' Tom was shaking his head in disbelief. 'Sue was not amused when she saw how proud Dylan was of it. You should have seen her face when Dylan's teacher told us it was to hang on the art room wall at school.'

'*Not* Sue.' Helen's hands gripped the side of the desk.

'Dylan didn't say it was, did he?' Tom pulled up the photograph of the painting on his phone and stared at it. 'Look, he's even got your bouncy hair right.'

Helen looked. 'Kids always paint hair like that, don't they?'

'He didn't paint his or mine like that though, did he?'

'Well, no.' Helen closed her eyes. She could feel the pulse in her fingertips buzz as she tried to make sense of what she was hearing. She'd been so sure it was Sue. 'But what about what Sue said to Dylan about wanting him to be part of a family?'

'Wishful thinking on her part maybe, or perhaps Dylan misunderstood. He's only five.'

Helen didn't know what to say and she looked around her office; her safe space. Somewhere she had intended to recover from her broken heart in private, without anyone knowing she was in pain.

'You must have known I'd come after you.' Tom wrapped a ringlet around his finger.

Not moving, Helen watched as a tiny strand of her hair coiled in his touch. 'I thought I was doing the right thing. Making it easier for all three of you.'

'Easier?' His hand stopped moving, but he didn't release the curl. 'You know how hard it was for me to admit my feelings for you, how much I worried that I was letting you down? If you think having you walk away without explanation was easy…'

'No, I meant…' Helen threw up her hands. 'I have no idea what I mean anymore.'

Reluctantly letting go of her hair, Tom looked at his watch. 'I need to check on Dylan.'

Any reply Helen might have made was cancelled out by a loud unladylike growl from her belly.

While Tom waited for his phone to connect, he gestured to the open packet of biscuits on her desk. 'When was the last time you ate anything that wasn't a cookie?'

'I had some fish fingers last night.'

'Last night?'

'More like just before dawn.' She pointed to her shopping. 'Would you like a biscuit?'

Thea had been relieved when Tina asked if she'd mind making up a batch of soup for the following day's lunch. It had been good to get lost in the unthinking task of peeling, chopping and slicing vegetables.

The stock was beginning to soften the potatoes, carrots and leeks, and a handful of pearl barley and mixed herbs had been thrown in when she became aware of someone watching her. She knew it was Shaun without looking. Her nervous system went into overdrive before either of them had spoken.

'Why do you think I was the one who came to see where you were in the laundry when you went to fetch the bath towels?'

Shaun's opening line had not been the one Thea expected. 'I don't know.'

'Because I wanted to see you. Be alone with you. I wanted to say something to make us better. But when I got there...' Shaun paused, his forehead crinkling as he tried to frame his words, '... you were so closed off. I didn't know how to begin. And Dylan was waiting.'

Thea shuffled her feet against the kitchen floor. 'He really enjoyed being a bubble zombie.'

'Apparently he can't wait to tell Tom, but won't be telling his mum.'

'Really?'

'He said something about Mummy not liking messy games.'

Thea raised her eyebrows. 'Helen wouldn't have minded.'

Shaun gave a half smile. 'Helen would have joined in.'

Taking her phone from her pocket, Thea checked the screen. 'I've sent lots of messages, but I haven't heard anything from her. Have you?'

'Nothing.' Shaun picked an out of date newspaper up off the table and flicked the pages through his fingers without noticing what was written on them. 'I've had an email from Julian though.'

'Oh God.' Thea's entire body went cold. 'What did *he* want?'

Not missing the level of panic in her voice, Shaun stepped towards her as if to give her a hug, but then stopped, the paper forming a flimsy barrier between them. 'To talk to me when I get back.'

'Oh.'

'The email didn't mention the rest of the team. Just me. As production meetings are a group affair, I have to assume this isn't one.'

'Oh.'

'Have you had any more messages from him?'

'No.' Thea stirred the soup a little faster. 'And nor have I replied to the last email.'

'Why not?'

'You mean, apart from the fact it has split us up?'

'You see us as separated?' Shaun laid down the paper, his voice like lead.

Thea grasped the wooden spoon's handle tighter. 'No. Yes. I don't know. I hope not, but well… I did spend the rest of the night in Helen's room after you turned away. Am I staying there?'

'Depends if you're intending to meet Julian, I suppose.'

Battling hard not to snap, Thea said, 'I'm not.'

Shaun licked his lips. He wasn't sure if he wanted to hug her or shout at her. Instead he tiptoed around the issue, asking, 'To be clear, you aren't meeting Julian because you don't want a career in television?'

'No!' This time Thea's groan escaped as a growl as she repeated what she was sure she'd already said a hundred times. 'I never did. And even if I had, I'd never pursue one with Julian. Didn't you listen to anything I said in the garden? I hate to think what the price tag would be for his help.' Thea kept her eyes on the soup. Its comforting aroma was the only thing stopping her from screaming in frustration at going around in conversational circles.

'With Julian, the cost would be very high I imagine.' Shaun swallowed carefully. 'You were on the receiving end of a text, an email and overheard an out of context phone call.'

'And I was foolish not to tell you. We've done this conversation. A lot.' Turning the heat down under the soup, Thea asked, 'Have you heard from Ajay or Andy?'

'Only to confirm they'll see us on the fourteenth of April.'

'Us?' Thea held her breath. She could feel Shaun's breath

on the back of her neck, and silently willed him to put his arms around her.

'You are coming back to the Cotswolds, Thea, aren't you?'

'I don't see that I have much choice. We can't leave the last bits of filming undone.' Thea kept talking. She hated the sound of the brittle practicality in her voice. 'It's as well we have individual campervans. I'll understand if you want me to move mine to the other side of the car park.'

Shaun suddenly shot a hand out and spun Thea around to face him, sending a shower of hot soup across the hob. 'Is that what you think I want?'

'Well, yes.' Thea felt the heat of the Aga against her back. 'I gave you the chance to follow me, to talk to me, but you didn't. You could have at least told me you believed I was being offered the job because I'm good at it rather than because of Julian's alleged feelings for me – but you didn't say that either. And every time we do talk, you ask me the *same* thing, I give you the *same* answer, but you won't believe me. When Sophie fancied you in Cornwall, I hated it, but I listened. I gave you the chance to explain, and I helped you get out of the hole you'd blindly dug yourself into. I trusted you enough to give you the benefit of the doubt. If you don't trust me, then it doesn't matter how much I love you, does it?'

Shaun opened his mouth to protest, but his phone burst into life. 'It's the suit hire people.'

'You'd better answer then.' Thea turned back to the soup as Shaun walked out into the garden. Her appetite had completely gone.

Forty-three

S am woke up to find Tina sat at the little table in the corner of their bedroom. She was bent over her wedding planner notebook, concentration etched on her face.

Opening the bedroom window to its widest setting, Sam took his usual steadying lungful of fresh air on waking. While he saw off the panic that assailed him the second his conscious mind reminded him he was indoors, he asked, 'What's wrong?'

'What makes you think anything's wrong?'

'Because you're tugging on your pigtails as you write.'

Tina smiled. 'Okay. Guilty as charged.'

Hopping back into bed, tapping the space next to him, Sam gestured to the notebook Tina held. 'What have you been working on?'

'You'll laugh.'

'Try me.'

'I figuring out where, as we're having an afternoon tea type buffet after the ceremony, we could ask Thea and

Shaun to sit, so they look like they are still together, while at the same time not having them too close to each other, in case they have a row.'

'Still together?' Sam's eyebrows rose. 'Things aren't that bad between them, are they?'

'Are you kidding?' Tina twisted round so she could see Sam's face. 'Hasn't Shaun told you they've split?'

'I knew they'd had a row, and something wasn't right with the Cotswold dig. Are you sure?'

'Don't men ever talk to each other?' Tina shook her head. 'I've hardly slept worrying about them. And, if I'm honest, the impact on our wedding. I know that's selfish, but we've already lost one bridesmaid. If the best man and chief bridesmaid can't bear to look at one another, as well as the usher being broken hearted...'

Tucking her against his shoulder, Sam let out an exhalation of breath. 'Look, I'm sure Shaun and Thea haven't split. They've just had a major row. They survived when Thea thought Shaun was playing away in Cornwall. It was all a misunderstanding. This is probably the same.'

'I wish it was.'

'Even if they have decided to part, you know they would never let that ruin our day.'

'Not on purpose they wouldn't,' Tina pulled a face, 'but weddings are emotional occasions. What if someone says the wrong thing and sparks them off? What if they are stood side by side in the aisle while we exchange our vows and it gets too much and one of them runs off, what if—?'

'What if I have a word with Shaun and find out what's going on before we jump to conclusions?'

'Would you? Thea hasn't said much. Until she brings up

the subject, I don't like to ask.' Tina sighed. 'Honestly, we just get your parents onside, and now this. Do you think Tom would be best man if Shaun takes off?'

'Why would Shaun take off?'

'I don't know! Why did Helen?' Tina could feel herself becoming panicky. 'I suppose Mabel and Bert could change roles. There's no age limit on being best man and bridesmaid is there?'

Giving her a gentle kiss, Sam shook his head. 'We can't ask Bert to do any more than he's doing, not while he's recovering from pneumonia. And Mabel loves being mother of the bride. We can't take that away from her.'

'I know. But our wedding is any minute now and everyone is falling apart!'

Helen spent a long time staring at Tom's bare back as he slept next to her. She wasn't sure how many hours she'd been awake trying to work out how she'd managed to jump to so many incorrect conclusions.

What do I do now? I told the staff at the Roman Baths I'm back.

Tom gave a hedgehog like snuffle as he rolled over. The view of his naked chest and the memory of how she'd revisited it the night before clouded Helen's judgement for a second.

I shouldn't have slept with him.

She closed her eyes. An image of Dylan asleep in his little bed in Tom's room at Mill Grange flashed through her mind. She'd only been gone a few hours in the grand scheme of things, yet she missed the little boy more than she'd imagined.

Tom grunted, flinging an arm over his head. Helen wondered what he was dreaming about.

The night before they'd gone for their long overdue curry. Helen had steered them to a restaurant she'd never been to before, not ready to go anywhere she'd be recognised. They'd talked for a long time, their meal largely cold before they got around to eating it. Awkward to start with, sticking to the safe ground by conversing about the fort, Tom had eventually got bored of skirting around the issue. He'd told her more about the phone calls he'd been fielding for Sam's father, his attempts to get a tailor for Bert, and about the booking calls he'd taken for Tina while she was in wedding mode.

By the time Helen had been strong enough to address the matter of Sue, she'd felt beyond foolish. Tom had reassured her again that, no matter how much Dylan might want to be a family, being with his ex would not deliver a family atmosphere. It would bring arguments, resentment and a sense of loss that Tom didn't want to live with.

A restful glow hit Helen's chest as she remembered his words, 'Anyone I was with now, who wasn't you, would always be second best. I don't want to settle for second best ever again.'

He loves me. I love him. We both love Dylan. But I told the Roman Baths staff that I'm back and Sam and Tina I'd left. I can't mess them around just because I was an insecure idiot.

Tom turned over again, his arm finding her in his sleep, drawing her close.

As Helen cupped herself into his side, she let out a small gasp of pleasure as his fingers found her right nipple.

Is he awake, or was that an accident?

Not moving, feeling her whole body respond to the tiny movement of his fingertips, Helen closed her eyes.

Perhaps I'll decide what to do later.

Mabel ran a duster around the frame of the nearest painting as Thea, her face drawn, quietly got on with polishing the dining room table. The old lady watched as her friend ran a finger over a section of the mahogany.

'Isn't that's where the Nightjar got in through the window and scratched the table in the summer?'

'In the middle of the night. Scared me to death.' A lump came to her throat. 'It was just after Shaun came to help restore the house. I don't know what I'd have done if he hadn't been here that night.'

'You'd have coped alone.' Mabel sounded very definite on the matter. 'But I'm glad you didn't have to.'

'Umm.' Thea ran her finger over the invisible wound that one of Shaun's furniture restoring friends had fixed for them. 'I was amazed by how much damage one trapped bird could do.'

'Any living thing can act rashly when frightened.' Mabel paused in her labours. 'Do you want to talk about it, Thea?'

Thea shook her head. 'Thanks, Mabel, but there is nothing to say.'

'I doubt that, my dear, but as you like.' Going back to the dusting, Mabel suddenly chuckled. 'Do you remember when you first got here and found me and Diane cleaning things with vinegar? Whatever were we thinking?'

Thea laughed despite herself. 'It took me a while to

discover why Mill Grange smelt like a packet of crisps. We've all learnt so much since then. Changed so much.'

'For the better.'

'Maybe.' Thea laid down her polishing cloth.

'No maybe about it. Sam and Tina are getting married, Mill Grange is in safe hands and fulfilling a life changing purpose, and Bert and I have been given a new lease of life. Not something we take for granted.'

'How is Bert?'

'Same old chap, smiling when it hurts to breathe, smiling wider when it doesn't. He's loving having Dylan here.'

'So is Shaun. He's taken Dylan to Sybil's for breakfast this morning.'

Mabel asked gently, 'You didn't want to go?'

'I wasn't asked.' Picking the buffing cloth back up, Thea put the force of her emotion into polishing the wood. 'Shaun doing things without me is something I'm going to have to get used to.'

Tom stroked a hair from Helen's face. He could feel the slight shake to her body as she came down from the mutual high they'd shared. 'I knew all was not lost because you took the stone Dylan gave you. I knew you still loved us.'

'It was because I love you that I left.'

Tom reached out and picked up the stone from Helen's bedside table. 'But you are coming home now, aren't you?'

'I'm not sure I can.'

'Why?'

Seeing Tom's face fall, Helen gently placed a finger on his lips, 'Not because I don't want to, but because I've left such a mess behind me. Sam and Tina have been amazing friends, but I left their home and their job offer without a word. Plus, I've told my colleagues here I'm back.

'The Baths are short staffed at the moment. I can't disappear again straight away. I've let too many people down lately. You do understand that, Tom, don't you?'

Forty-four

'Not as good as Sybil's brunch, but edible I hope.' Helen served two poached eggs onto Tom's plate as he buttered a mountain of toast. 'It's a miracle I remembered to buy eggs, bread and butter. I wasn't at my best in the supermarket yesterday.'

'I'm sure it'll be delicious.'

A new silence hung over them as they tucked in to their breakfast. Tom had admitted to seeing her point about not wanting to be labelled unreliable; that she had to see the new exhibition through now she'd given her word that she would. Helen could feel the effort it was taking Tom not to say, *"but you said you'd stay with us, and you left anyway"*.

Instead he'd said he understood and they'd been practical, discussing how they'd take turns to drive between Bath and Upwich, work and Dylan allowing. She knew he wasn't happy about her decision to stay in Bath. Neither was she, but now she'd made the move, she felt her hands were tied.

Helen was relieved when Tom's phone rang, cutting through the awkward atmosphere.

The sound of shouting that leaked from the speaker, which caused Tom to hold his mobile away from his ear, filled the kitchen. Sue was not impressed that her son had been left at Mill Grange without his father.

Leaving Tom to cope with his ex's wrath in private, Helen headed upstairs to make her bed. As soon as she saw it however, she knew it had been a mistake to go into that particular room. The aroma of them hung in the air. It smelt of happiness, abandon and desire. Mostly desire. The bed linen, crumpled and half hanging off the mattress, was a stark reminder of what she was giving up. *Not giving up, just not having on a daily basis.*

Helen took a deep breath. 'Space is a good idea. Tom and I got together quickly and I have responsibilities just as he does.'

You promised Tom you'd stay at Mill Grange.

'And now I've promised to do an exhibition for Mike, and I have to draw the line somewhere. This promise has to be kept. Then I'll make a decision about what to do next.' Helen threw the sheets onto the floor, ready to go to the washing machine. 'But first, I'll call Tina and Sam and apologise.'

Helen was still fighting the voice in her head telling her she wanted to wake up to Tom every morning, and that she should do what she wanted for a change – which was only just losing out to her conscience that was yelling that she'd spent months doing what she wanted and it was time she stopped being self-centred – when Tom appeared.

'I can tell by your expression that wasn't fun. Dare I ask what Sue said?'

Leaning his back against the bedroom door, Tom exhaled in frustration. 'Apparently she called Mill Grange last night to say goodnight to Dylan. God knows how she got the landline number. She was not impressed when he told her Daddy had gone away for the night.'

'Oh hell.' Helen didn't know what else to say.

'I'm going to have to go. Sue more or less demanded that I stop at Tiverton on the way home to explain myself and discuss looking after Dylan in the future.'

Helen felt guilt wash over her. 'You don't think she'll use this as an excuse to say you can't see Dylan, do you?'

'Maybe.' Tom's face was grey as he slumped onto the edge of the bed. 'She's used my behaviour with women against me before. To be fair, in some cases she was right to, but this time—'

'It's my fault. If I hadn't taken off...'

Taking Helen's hand, Tom tugged gently so she'd sit next to him. 'Don't blame yourself. Sue has been acting really strange lately, even for her. Every time I think she's developed some maternal instincts she proves me wrong.'

'Surely not being impressed to discover her son was with babysitters and not you *is* maternal instinct? I'd probably have reacted the same way if he was my son.' Helen hoped Tom hadn't noticed her gulp as she spoke. 'You'd better go.'

'I can't persuade you to come with me? You aren't officially back here until Tuesday.'

'I'm not sure Sue would be terribly pleased to see me and...' Helen paused. 'Hang on, did you say she was expecting you to stop at her place in Tiverton?'

'Yes, Sue was very definite about that, she...' Tom suddenly came to the same realisation as Helen. 'She said was going away, didn't she? That's why I have Dylan all week.'

'So, what's she doing in Tiverton?'

Jumping up, Tom kissed Helen hard on the mouth. 'I'm sorry I have to go, but I need to find out what game Sue's playing this time.'

'Good luck.' Wanting to change her mind, and say she'd go with him, Helen forced herself to stay where she was. Even if they were still together at Mill Grange, the conversation Tom and Sue were about to have was for them alone.

Tom was shoving his trainers on and was out of her home before she knew it. Seconds later, Helen was waving his Fiesta drive down the hill at more speed than was sensible; leaving an empty space and empty feeling behind him.

Thea munched a salad sandwich as she flicked through the Job Vacancies page on the *Current Archaeology* website. There were a few that sounded interesting, but they were all abroad.

Getting up from the bed, where she'd been resting her laptop on her knees, she looked out of the attic window and down across the garden. When Thea had arrived at Mill Grange the gardens had been overgrown and the house barely habitable. Now, thanks to a great team of volunteers in the early days, then Sam, Tina, Mabel and Shaun, it was working. Not just working, but providing help for those who needed a fresh start in life.

I don't want to leave.

As she watched, Thea saw Sam, Shaun and Dylan emerge from the gate connecting the woods to the garden. A lump formed in her throat. *Have we drifted too far apart this time to get back to where we were?*

The trees swayed in the light spring breeze, sending light sprays of blossom across the garden. A magnolia petal landed on Sam's head, and she saw him smile as he brushed it to the ground.

Like confetti.

Drawing away from the window, Thea turned off the laptop. There was no way she could leave Mill Grange, and knew in her heart she wouldn't have to. Whatever happened between her and Shaun, he'd be the one to move on. He was only here part of the time anyway. Unless he lost his post with *Landscape Treasures*.

Cradling her mobile, Thea longed to call Tina or Helen to talk, but both her friends had their own problems. The last thing they needed was her offloading about a misunderstanding that had got out of control.

Groaning, Thea sat on the side of the little bed. Walking up the aisle behind Tina, and standing next to Shaun as their best friends exchanged vows, had been something she'd been looking forward to. Now she dreaded it.

I love him, but I have no idea how to fix this. Closing her eyes, Thea conjured an image of the Goddess Minerva she'd kept in her office in Bath. *You helped me before, can you help me now?* Some halfway decent advice would do.

Her mobile burst into life, making Thea's eyes fly back open.

It was Helen.

Tina fired back the final booking confirmation email of the morning. The word was spreading about what Sam was doing at Mill Grange with wounded ex service personnel. Since they'd closed for Easter and the wedding, they'd been an upturn in booking enquiry emails and direct bookings. As she checked the calendar, she smiled. August and September were fully booked. October was almost full as well, and they even had a spattering of bookings for November and the following spring.

She looked around the old scullery that she and Thea used as an office. It wouldn't be the same if Thea left. Not that her friend had mentioned leaving, but Tina knew that the last time Thea had had a relationship fall apart, she'd wanted to move away – have a fresh start. That fresh start had been at Mill Grange. The circumstances were different of course. John had made life so difficult, that Thea had been compelled to leave Bath behind her. Shaun would never do that. So…

Tina's thoughts were interrupted by the ring of her mobile. It was Thea.

'Fancy escaping for a while?'

Tina's eyes automatically flicked to her wedding notebook and the clipboard with today's to-do list. There was so much to do. 'Where did you have in mind?'

'Glastonbury Abbey.'

Forty-five

Thursday April 9th

The words, 'Fancy a catch up as we walk around Glastonbury Abbey', had come out of her mouth before Helen's brain had registered that by offering Thea a day away from Mill Grange she was holding up work at the house and wedding arrangements even further. A crime she'd compounded by asking if Tina would like to come too.

Now, as she climbed into her Land Rover, Helen was relieved to be doing something positive. She'd never be able to relax until she'd apologised to her friends for walking out on them.

As she backed out of her driveway, Helen glanced at her watch. Tom should reach Tiverton in the next forty minutes or so. *I hope he's okay.*

Sam had virtually pushed Tina into Thea's car.

'But there's a wedding to plan! And what about Dylan?'

'Mabel has promised to bake cakes with him this afternoon. Now off you go. Have some fun! And if you can, find out what's going on with our bridesmaids. The wedding will be easier to plan with them as part of it.'

On the drive to Devon, Tom had been determined that he and Sue would manage a whole conversation without him getting exasperated. He'd told himself it was reasonable that she'd be cross, and that if their situations were reversed, he'd have demanded an explanation too. However, hit by a torrent of accusations about not caring for their child, his resolve had fractured approximately thirty seconds after his arrival at Sue's front door.

'Sue!' Tom slid his hands into his pockets. 'Will you just stop shouting and let me speak!'

'You abandoned our son!'

'Says the woman who dumped her child at Mill Grange for longer than planned so she could go away for the week, having just assumed I had no plans of my own, but then came home.' Feeling his temper fraying, Tom snapped, 'Why did you do that? Was it some sort of test to see if I could cope, or is lying to me becoming a hobby?'

'I was away. I'm back now, that's all.'

Sensing a slight softening in Sue's anger, Tom asked, 'Good back now, or been dumped by boyfriend back now?'

'As if you'd care either way.'

'Don't be childish.'

'I had a few days away with friends, that's all.' Sue jutted her chin out, steering the focus away from herself. 'So, why did you leave Dylan alone?'

'For a start, I did no such thing. I left him with people who care for him, and in my defence, the situation I found myself in was unexpected. It was a split-second decision. If Dylan was not in safe hands, I wouldn't have gone.' Tom levelled his eyes on Sue's face. 'You know I wouldn't.'

Resting her back against her front door, Sue uncrossed her arms. 'Okay, yes, I know you wouldn't. It was a shock that's all. I need to know I can trust you with Dylan. It's important.'

'Of course it's important.' Tom frowned. Something about Sue's tone set alarm bells ringing. 'Why didn't you call my mobile last night? Why ring the house?'

Sue averted her gaze to Tom's feet. 'I was looking at the website for Mill Grange, saw the number and thought I'd ring it for a change. I wondered who'd answer, and if, should there be an emergency and I couldn't reach you, it was a good number to use instead.'

'O... kay.' Tom felt his unease rising. 'Who answered?'

'Someone called Thea. Sounded like she'd been crying.'

'Really?'

'Yeah. She said you'd gone to Bath and would be back today, and that Dylan was fine.'

'I spoke to him this morning.' Tom's lips curved upwards. 'Apparently they had a bubble session yesterday. He was being a zombie.'

Sue sighed. 'He'd have enjoyed that.'

Tom was becoming more confused than ever. 'Sue, what's all this about? I mean *really* about. You know I wouldn't endanger Dylan, so your calling me to rant about that was an excuse. What I can't figure out is if you're being awkward for the sake of it, or if you called because you feel guilty about something.'

Sue suddenly looked up from studying her feet. 'Would you like to come in?'

'You're inviting me into your home? You never do that.'

'Some conversations shouldn't happen on the doorstep.'

They'd got as far as the motorway before Tina couldn't hold back from asking the obvious question. 'Have you spoken to Shaun yet?'

'No.' Thea concentrated on overtaking a lorry.

'Um, you will still be my bridesmaid, won't you?'

'Of course!' Thea let out a puff of breath. 'I'm sorry, Tina. Your wedding party is dissolving in front of your eyes, isn't it?'

'It rather is.' Tina shrugged. 'I wish you were all okay though, and not just for selfish wedding reasons.'

'Me too.'

'Did Helen give any clue as to why she ran away?'

'No, but she said Tom had been and gone again and that she'd explain when she saw us.'

'Is it good that he's left already or not, do you think?'

'I've no idea, but he wouldn't leave Dylan at Mill Grange without him for long either way.'

'I suppose not.' Tina watched the world blur through her window as they whizzed along the M5. 'At least, if Tom's back, the boys will get a few more jobs done. I feel ever so guilty not being there.'

Thea sighed. 'I think there's been far too much guilt over

what's been done and not done in and around Mill Grange over the last few days.'

'That's true.' Tina brightened as she told Thea about how many bookings they had over the coming months.

'There you go then. Despite the romantic fallout, Mill Grange is working.' Thea tried an ironic laugh, but it came out as a groan of defeat. 'We've earned a break and Helen needs to talk.'

The sofa he perched on had been designed for appearance rather than comfort. Tom could imagine Sue showing it off to visitors, but he couldn't imagine Dylan playing or sitting comfortably on it.

As Sue came in with a tray of tea and coffee, Tom wondered if she'd been crying but dismissed the thought as a trick of the light.

'You told me that Sam had no money, but I've seen the website. He's loaded. He has to be.'

This was not the opening Tom had been expecting, but it was very "Sue". 'And I explained that buying the house and doing it up took all of his money and that it still needs a lot of work. The business is new. So far there is enough income to pay the staff and no more. Any weird ideas you have about titles and land equalling ready cash can be forgotten right now. This is Mill Grange not Downton Abbey.'

'I don't believe you.'

'I can't help that.' Tom picked up his mug of coffee. 'I also don't see why we are talking about it. Sam's financial status is none of our business.'

'Your wages will be good though. You could easily afford to look after Dylan, couldn't you?'

'My wages are only a fraction above minimum wage and after maintenance there is nothing left. You know that.' Leaning forward, Tom said, 'Can you please just tell me what all this is leading up to?'

Taking a deep breath, Sue put down her tea and looked Tom straight in the eye. 'I have a new partner. It was him I went away with. He wants me to move to Australia. I came home early so I could have space alone to think about what to do.'

Forty-six

Helen pulled into Glastonbury Abbey car park as the church bells chimed two o'clock. She couldn't see Thea's car.

They'll come. They haven't changed their minds.

She picked up her mobile hoping to see a text from Tom. There wasn't one.

Of course he hasn't texted. He'll be talking to Sue. Sorting out whatever she wants this time.

Telling herself to stop over-thinking everything before it became a habit she couldn't break, Helen went off to tackle the unnecessarily complex parking pay machine. She was just tapping in her registration number when Thea's car pulled up behind the Land Rover

Tom stared at Sue. He knew his mouth was open, but as hard as he tried, the words he was trying to say wouldn't form.

'Say something!'

'You can't go. I—'

Sue pursued her lips. 'I can do what the hell I like, Tom. And if you think you can stop me, then you're very much mistaken.'

'No, I meant...' Too winded to raise his voice, Tom shook his head. 'Dylan, he's happy here.'

'Yes.' Sue's hostility faded. 'He is.'

'So how can you even—'

Sue raised a hand. 'Please, Tom, just listen for a minute.'

Tom could feel his pulse thudding in his neck as he watched his ex get up off her armchair, grab a whisky bottle from the sideboard and pour herself a half measure.

'His name's Nathan. He's my boss at the supermarket. There's a new store opening in a large town near Sydney. Nathan is going to be the manager.'

Tom's head reeled. To think that Helen had got it into her head that Sue was after a family reconciliation with him and Dylan. The family she must have been referring to when she'd spoken to Dylan didn't include him at all. It didn't even include living in England. There'd be no visits to Dylan. No picking him up from school. No nativity play trips with Helen to see his son as a shepherd or a wise man.

Is that why she dropped him with me for a week, to give us time together before she takes Dylan away forever?

'Say something.' Sue gripped her glass, staring into the autumnal liquid. 'Do you want one of these? I assumed, what with you driving...' She trailed off as she saw the agony on his face.

Tom tried to think of something to say, but nothing came. He felt sick.

'It seems a nice place. Abbotsford it's called. I've been on Google Maps. Some of the houses we're looking at buying are amazing.'

Closing his eyes, Tom took a long slow breath. 'How could you do this to Dylan? He's just settled. He's happy.' *And so was I, just for a while.*

Rather than yell at him, Sue shifted uncomfortably in her seat and sipped some of the whiskey. 'My move would give him stability, a chance to be part of a family. Even if... even if it meant that one of his parents was far away.'

'Far away!' Tom found his voice rising this time. 'You're talking about New South Wales Sue! That's the other side of the bloody world!'

'There's Skype and Zoom and Facetime and—'

'And no cuddles. No comforting him when he cries. No building dens or exploring. No pulling off his wellies when they get stuck. No helping with homework. No anything!'

'There are holidays.'

'On our wages? Come off it, Sue. Get real.' Tom sank back, the uncomfortable sofa digging into his spine. 'I honestly thought you'd changed. It really looked, just for a minute, that you were putting Dylan first.'

A single tear trickled down Sue's cheek. 'I didn't mean to fall in love, Tom.'

Momentarily stunned, the concept of love and Sue not fitting neatly together in his mind, Tom found himself thinking of Helen. He hadn't intended to fall for her either, and yet he had. He'd been powerless to stop it.

'Perhaps you'd better tell me about Nathan.'

*

Helen had started apologising as soon as Tina got out of the car, and had repeated herself twice as they moved through Glastonbury Abbey's pay station, and again as they passed onto the lime green grass which led towards the abbey's stunning skeletal remains.

'It's alright.' Tina tried to reassure her friend. 'We all do things we regret, but what I don't understand is why. It's not like you not to face things head on.'

'No, it isn't, is it?' Pointing to a picnic bench near the café, Helen stared up at the architectural splendour. 'Coffee before we explore?'

'Always.' Thea and Tina spoke in unison, making Helen realise how much she was going to miss working with them.

Helen fiddled with her car keys as she apologised to Thea for not letting on about her relationship with Tom. 'I should have said. It's not as if our attempts to keep it secret worked!'

Tina grinned. 'You both looked so loved up, it was blatant.'

Helen sighed as she went on to explain about Dylan's painting, how he'd mentioned Sue wanting him to be part of a real family, and her assumption that – combined with what she'd overheard Sue say – that had meant Sue wanting to try again with Tom.

'And you didn't want to be the one who stopped Dylan being with his parents.' Tina nodded. 'That I get.'

'I panicked. The thought of Tom being around and not being with him.' Helen laid the keys on the table, and looked across at the abbey where King Arthur and Guinevere were reputed to have been laid to rest after a life time of love. 'As

I had a home and job in Bath to return to... well, it was a bolthole and I bolted.'

As she picked up a menu, Thea asked, 'But now you've spoken to Tom? Is that what's happening? Is he getting back with Sue?'

'No. I got it wrong, so I can add feeling a total idiot to my list of achievements this week.'

Thea patted her friend's shoulder. 'Coffee all round? And cake?'

'Please,' Tina patted her waist, 'although only a little slice. Now I've got the wedding dress, I don't want to have to go on a last-minute crash diet.'

'There's nothing of you!' Thea winked as she headed to the café counter, the chocolate and orange cake she'd seen mentioned on the menu firmly in her sights.

As Thea disappeared, Tina asked, 'Are you staying in Bath then, Helen? You can still come back you know.'

'But I messed you and Sam about big time and—'

'And nothing. If you want to come back, you can. But once we're married and the guests start to come back, we'll have to know for sure, because if you aren't coming back, we'll need to employ someone else.'

'Of course you will.' Helen thought of the fortlet and how much work she'd put into it already. The idea of someone else taking over made her sad. 'I'd love to come back, but I can't. Do you think my successor should write the book on the site?' She sighed rather more loudly than she intended. 'I'll get the notes to you.'

'Why wouldn't you be able to come back?' Tina was puzzled. 'I thought you and Tom had sorted yourselves out.'

'We have, but in the few hours between my arrival in Bath and him following me, I went back to the Baths, and found myself straight back into the fray. There's an exhibition they need organising, and no one's free to do it.'

Thea arrived back at the table, her tray laden with cups and cake. 'An exhibition? Makes sense they'd want you to sort that out. You were always the best at that.'

Helen gave a half smile. 'I gave my word you see, that I'd get it sorted.'

'So you won't be returning to Mill Grange?' Tina looked disappointed as she forgot about her no cake eating policy and stuck a fork into the gooey chocolate orange filling.

Thea sat down, pulling her plate towards her. 'You want to though, don't you? Return to Mill Grange I mean.'

'Yes, but I've let so many people down lately. I can't do it again.'

'And Tom? How did he take it when you told him you weren't returning to Upwich with him?'

'Stoically.'

'Is that good or bad?' Tina pushed a bowl of sugar cubes in Helen's direction.

'I haven't a clue. Sue called and he dashed off before we could talk.'

'What did Sue want?' A cloud crossed Thea's face. 'She called the house last night.'

'I know. That's why Tom's gone to see her. She was not impressed at him leaving Dylan alone.'

'Hell, I didn't think. I should have pretended Tom was too busy to come to the phone.'

Helen shook her head. 'Tom wouldn't want you to lie for him.'

Thea stabbed her fork at her cake. 'But you're still together as a couple?'

'Yes.' Helen was thoughtful. 'Ironic, really, as my eventual return to Bath was one of the reasons we took so long to get together in the first place. Tom doesn't like long distance relationships.'

Thea found herself thinking of all the months Shaun had been away on excavation since they got together. Over half their relationship had been spent over the phone. 'I can understand that. But it's only Bath, and you could meet here. Dylan would love it!'

Helen grinned, already picturing the boy in one of the suits of armour dressing up kits hanging up in the café's shop window. 'He'd be battling dragons for King Arthur in no time.'

Tina hardly dare ask the next question, but the need to know was burning a hole in her tongue. 'You will be coming to the wedding now, won't you?'

Thea pounced on the opening. 'Oh yes, please, Helen. Apart from the fact that Tom *has* to see you in that dress, I can't stand there on my own. Especially now.'

Helen didn't miss the slump of Thea's shoulders as she stared at her cake, her fork playing with it rather than scooping it up. 'What do you mean, especially now?'

Shaun stood in the doorway of the room he'd shared with Thea. It hadn't taken long for her pile of clothes to disappear from their haphazard heap on the chair in the corner. Apart from a couple of novels and a hairbrush, there was no sign she'd ever been there. With a resigned groan he tugged his rucksack out from under the bed.

Feeling bad about upping and leaving so soon after Helen had gone, Shaun consoled himself with the fact he wasn't doing a flit. He had to go. His job may depend on it.

Cramming all he could into his bag, Shaun left the suit he'd bought to be best man in, hanging in its plastic overcoat on the wardrobe door. A silent message to Thea, that he was coming back.

Forty-seven

Friday April 10th

Thea sat on a bench in the garden, a thick jumper shielding her arms against the early morning air.

Sam had delivered the message as soon as Thea and Tina had arrived back at the manor the previous evening. The smiles on their faces were immediately extinguished by the news that Shaun had been summoned to the Cotswolds.

'He's gone too.' Tina had paled at the thought of another member of her wedding party disappearing.

'He'll be back for the wedding.' Sam looked at a silent Thea. 'I'm sorry.'

Breathing slowly, Thea had asked, 'Did Shaun say why he was summoned?'

'Just that he needed to speak to Julian.'

As she watched the sun rise, Thea wondered if Julian had really summoned Shaun, or if he'd simply decided to go and talk to the producer.

At least I slept. As the dawn mist floated across the garden, Thea muttered a word of thanks to Minerva for small mercies. Tucking her knees under her chin, her feet resting on the edge of the bench, Thea realised she hadn't been surprised he'd gone. Part of her had even been relieved. If he wasn't there, then she didn't have to wonder what to say all the time, wonder how to act, wonder how to simply be.

'Doesn't stop me loving him though, does it?'

You've explained all you can. All you can do is wait now.

'That's so hard. Doing nothing is hard.'

Sometimes it's the only thing you can do.

'What will Julian say to him?'

The Goddess sent a shrug across the astral plain. *Whatever is in Julian's own best interests.*

Hugging herself tighter, Thea thought over her conversation with Tina and Helen. It had been good to lay it all out, to share the confusion that had been running around her head.

She and Shaun hadn't had the smoothest ride in their relationship. It had taken a while for her to allow herself to like him, let alone date him. Then, not so long ago, Shaun had been the romantic target of a student archaeologist in Cornwall, and Thea had wondered if she'd lose him to her. 'I gave him the benefit of the doubt. I listened to him.'

And you don't think he's paid you the same courtesy.

'I made a mistake and said sorry. That should be enough.'

Perhaps you need to find out why that isn't enough.

Thea sat up straight. 'Hurt pride? No, not Shaun – he'd admit to that. So why? Why won't he talk to me?'

Fighting the urge to pick up her mobile and call him to ask that very question, as it wasn't even six o'clock in the morning, and there was a good chance he wouldn't answer the call even if he was awake, Thea stared into the woods before her.

'What you're saying, Minerva, is that I just have to wait.'

And while you wait, be there for your friends.

Thea got up and headed back to the house. In two days' time the place would be overrun with Easter egg hunters and in just over a month her best friend was getting married. Somewhere there would be a whole heap of to-do lists.

Tom looked down at the figure asleep in his arms. Dylan had been a ball of sugar-fuelled energy when he'd got back to house the previous evening. Too shell-shocked to talk, he'd taken Dylan on a night time walk, hoping it would both excite and exhaust him.

Running a gentle hand over his son's hair, not wanting to wake him, but at the same time, wanting to commit his touch to memory, Tom fought the urge to cry. He wondered if Dylan would develop an Australian accent.

Picking his phone up off the chair next to the bed, Tom re-read the text he'd received from Helen last night. He was glad she'd gone to Glastonbury to meet her friends. At least she could stop worrying about Tina and Sam being angry at her departure. He hadn't told her about Sue's bombshell yet, but he would today. This was too big for him to handle alone. He'd needed Helen's help if he was going to cope without Dylan.

I suppose I could move to Bath now. We could be together there and not here.

Tom looked down as Dylan wriggled in his sleep, his robot pyjamas all twisted around his legs and arms.

But if I leave, Sam and Tina will have lost me, Helen and Shaun in one week. I can't do that to them.

He smiled as he recalled Dylan stalking owls in the woods last night. He'd tried so hard to be quiet, but had still managed to sound like a herd of elephants.

Realising he hadn't asked Sue when they were leaving, Tom closed his eyes. 'Before that time comes, we are going to have lots of adventures Dylan, I promise.'

Tina found Thea, Mabel and Diane blitzing the drawing room. A tour de force of dusters and furniture polish; they were making short work of any spider's web or dust that dared to have settled since the room was last cleaned.

Thea dropped the cloth she was using to wipe the window sill for a moment. 'We thought we'd crack on. It's like old times getting the house ready for the public.'

'Thanks everyone.' Tina gave Thea an appraising look. She hadn't expected to see her. She'd also expected puffy eyes and signs of strain. 'Are you okay, Thea?'

Getting closer to her friend, Thea muttered, 'Nope, but I'm tired of moping. So, I'm getting on with what needs getting on with – if you see what I mean.'

'I do indeed.' Tina inhaled the scent of beeswax polish that now hung around the room. 'Weather forecast is good for the weekend, so looking positive for hiding the eggs outside.'

'Dylan is looking forward to hiding them all,' Mabel mused. 'He was going to do it with Helen, but…'

'I'm sure he'll have fun anyway.' Thea exchanged a look with Tina. 'In the meantime, it's all systems go for Easter

Sunday, and, with the wedding just over a month away, it's all systems go for that too. Both bridesmaids and the best man are detailed to be back here on the day.'

'The best man?' Mabel paused in the act of dusting.

'Shaun's had to go back to the Cotswolds ready for the next part of the dig.' Thea hoped she sounded breezy. 'I have to go back on Tuesday as well, but we'll be here for the wedding.'

Diane was almost jumping up and down. 'It's so exciting! Where are you going on honeymoon, Tina?'

'We aren't.' Tina's smile weakened. She'd been trying very hard not to think about that. 'With Sam's claustrophobia, hotels and unknown places are out so we thought we'd save the money and have a holiday in a few years' time, when Sam's a bit better.'

Tom swept his phone from the side of the dig as soon it rang. He expected it to be either Sue or Helen. He licked his lips, ready for either a row or a difficult conversation – but it was a number he didn't recognise.

'Hello. Tom Harris speaking.'

'Mr Harris, forgive the interruption, it's Charles Phillips. I hope you don't mind, but I wondered if you could do me a favour...'

Forty-eight

Sunday April 12th

Helen yawned as she pulled the Land Rover up the drive at Mill Grange. It was only eight in the morning, but she'd promised Dylan she'd be there for the whole day so, not wanting to risk getting caught up in the Easter Sunday traffic, she'd left Bath just before six.

She was surprised at how quiet it was. She'd expected the Easter egg hunt signs to already be up, and Dylan running around with armfuls of chocolate.

Feeling a little like she was trespassing, Helen wasn't sure if she should just stroll on in as she always had, or if she should go to the front door and knock. She headed to the kitchen door anyway, hooking her overnight bag on her shoulder as she went.

As soon as she crossed the threshold, she knew why the drive was deserted. Everyone was in the kitchen. The chatter and laughter floating along the corridor knocked away a little of the strangeness she felt at not knowing

363

which bedroom she was supposed to leave her stuff in. *I can't share with Tom, he's with Dylan.*

Dylan. She couldn't believe what Tom had told her. No; that wasn't true. She could believe it – she just didn't want to. The thought of Mill Grange without Dylan…

Don't think about that now. This is Dylan's day. It is him you are here for. Nothing else.

Taking a deep breath Helen called out, 'Hello! Is it okay to come in?'

The response was instant. Dylan shot out of the kitchen, closely followed by Tom and Thea.

'Can I say it first, Dad, can I?'

'Say what?' Helen hooked Dylan up into her arms, and held him tight.

'Happy Birthday!'

Helen cuddled him closer, inhaling the scent of his freshly washed hair. Her reply of 'Thank you, Dylan' was lost as a mumble in his shoulder, before he started to wriggle like a jumping cracker.

Letting him drop to the floor, Helen found her hand engulfed in his as she was tugged into the kitchen. She looked at Tom, who mouthed 'Happy birthday, darling,' as she was towed forwards.

'Surprise!' Mabel, Thea, Tom, Sam, Tina and Bert chorused, as Dylan pushed Helen onto a seat and climbed onto her lap.

The kitchen table was heaped with more birthday presents than Helen had had in the last decade's birthdays combined. A bunch of six balloons sat as a centre piece and a large lemon cake with four lit candles was positioned at the end.

'I-I don't know what to say,' Helen stuttered. 'Thank you.'

'No need for thanks, lass.' Bert waved from his seat at the head of the table. 'Your birthday gave me an excellent excuse to leave the house. Thought I was going to be stuck on that sofa forever!'

'It's so good to see you, Bert. You look well.'

'I am well. Just slow. Darn slow... hate that!'

Dylan giggled. 'Bert said a bad thing, Dad!'

Tom rolled his eyes. 'And I'm sure Bert is very sorry. Aren't you, Bert?'

'Whoops, yes. Very sorry.' Bert winked at Dylan. 'Now come on lass, open these pressies. We've got an Easter egg hunt to prepare!'

An hour later, stuffed with lemon cake, her cards all lined up on the table before her, a mountain of wrapping paper at her feet Helen was overwhelmed and incredibly happy.

When she'd woken up that morning, her first thought had been that Tom wasn't there. Her second had been that she was forty years old. This second thought had made the first infinitely worse.

Deciding she'd done enough wallowing over the past week for a lifetime, Helen pushed down her feelings about waking up alone on her fortieth birthday, and focused on the day ahead. It hadn't occurred to her that her friends would remember her birthday, not with the Easter egg hunt, the wedding, Bert being unwell and now Dylan's imminent departure.

Deep down though, she'd hoped someone would

remember. And most of all, she'd hoped that someone would be Tom.

'Do you like it?' Dylan had wanted her to save his present until last, and now, as Helen held up the A4 sized notebook with a cartoon dinosaur on the front, complete with a dinosaur pen and pencil case, she knew that, if someone didn't rescue her soon, she'd burst into tears.

'It is the most perfect gift of all, Dylan, thank you.' She gave his cheek a kiss, making him grimace and wipe it off with his sleeve, which, in turn, made everyone laugh. 'What shall I write in it?'

'Stories!' Dylan started to bounce around the room, making Helen wonder how much of the sugar he'd had off the top of the lemon cake. 'The stories you do me at bedtime. My stories.'

'That's a great idea.' Helen slipped her new pen into the pencil case. She had no idea how to write a children's story, but suspected she was about to learn.

Mabel, who'd been keeping a careful eye on the time, stood up. 'I hate to break up the party, but we have two hours until the Easter egg hunt starts.'

Tina nodded. 'Best get busy then. Sorry, Helen.'

'Sorry?' Helen shook her head. 'How can you be sorry? I've never been spoilt like this, ever. And I'm looking forward to the hunt.' She turned to Dylan. 'Got that map ready for hiding the goods?'

Tom had been relatively quiet as his friends and his son fussed over Helen, asking about Bath and her plans; making sure she knew this would always be a second home, even if she didn't come back permanently. Now, as the party broke up, he caught her eye. 'Do you have time for a quick word before you are covered in chocolate?'

'As soon as I've helped clear up this lot.'

Batted away from having to tidy up by both Tina and Thea, as Sam steered Dylan towards the egg mountain in the drawing room, Helen found herself in the scullery turned office with Tom.

Something's happened. Sue must have told him when Dylan's leaving. Helen found her pulse racing, and suddenly her euphoria turned to nausea.

'I wanted to say Happy Birthday privately.'

Feeling her rush of anxiety lessen as Tom's lips met hers, Helen leaned into his arms.

'Did you like all your gifts?'

'Loved them.' Helen smiled. 'The mini dustpan and brush set from Mabel might have made us all chuckle, but actually, it will come in very useful.'

'Here.' Tom fished a small box, all wrapped in gold paper, form his pocket. 'From me. I wanted to give it to you alone.'

'But I've had your present.'

'The notebook? That was from Dylan.'

Her fingers suddenly clumsy, Helen unpeeled the sticky tape to relieve a small jewellery box. Hesitating, she glanced at Tom.

'Go on. It won't bite.'

Angling back the lid, Helen gasped at the delicate silver chain sat on a square of velvet. It was a pendant of a small silver trowel.

'It's beautiful. Wherever did you find it?'

'That doesn't matter. I'm just relieved you like it. I wasn't sure, with your incredible hair colouring, if silver or gold would be best.'

'I love it.' Helen was already lifting it from the box to fasten it around her neck. 'Thank you.'

Tom admired how the trowel pendant sat neatly just above the dive of her cleavage. 'Looks good. A bit too good actually, I don't think I'd better let my eyes linger.'

Laughing, Helen held him close. 'I love it and I love you, but now it's Mill Grange's turn to be showered with attention. Ready for the chocolate onslaught?'

'As I'll ever be. Dylan has already had a visit from the Easter Bunny. It'll be a miracle if he isn't sick by teatime.'

Thea had lost count of how many empty tea and coffee cups she'd carried back to the kitchen. She was sure the whole of Upwich had come to see how the manor had changed since it was last opened to the public, just before Sam bought the house. *When Shaun and I got together.*

As she stacked the dishwasher, Thea tried and failed to stop the next logical thought. *And this time it's when Shaun and I split up.*

She hadn't heard from him since he returned to the dig site. Thea had lost count of the number of times she'd almost called him, almost texted, almost emailed. But as he'd walked out on her, and he hadn't been in touch, she resisted temptation so far.

When she wasn't thinking about Shaun, she was worrying about what Julian might be saying to him. *Had he lost his job? Would any change at Landscape Treasures mean trouble for the AA as well?*

Thea had almost called Ajay, but knowing how much he liked to gossip, she hadn't dare.

Glad that there was so much to do at Mill Grange, Thea checked her watch. She had ten minutes before she was due to give a tour of the house. Just time to run up to the attic and stuff a few clothes into her rucksack.

Tomorrow she had to return to the Cotswolds, whether she wanted to or not. However things were with Shaun and Julian, she was determined to be professional and return to finish the additional filming they wanted to do over the mosaic.

Besides, she thought as she stuffed her cosiest pyjamas into her packing, *I helped to find that mosaic. I'd like to see it again.*

Flinging a pair of boots onto the bed, Thea checked the time and ran down the servant stairs, before stopping. As she paused to gather herself, she heard Dylan and Helen chatting happily about how fast the eggs were being found. Sticking on the fake smile that she seemed to have worn as a constant mask over the past few days, Thea headed to the main door, where her next group of guests would be gathering.

Forty-nine

Monday April 13th

The back of the Land Rover was full of balloons. Helen hadn't wanted to leave Mill Grange – but this time there were no tears, just a sense that she was doing the right thing, even if it had turned out to be for the wrong reasons.

The bonfire Sam and Tina had organised for her last night, with jacket potatoes and slightly too much Prosecco, had been the perfect end to a successful day.

The Easter egg hunt had pulled in so many people that Tina and Tom had to do an emergency run to the village shop to buy up all of their leftover eggs, and even then, all but four had been hunted down by the eager locals and passing tourists.

As she swung out of the village, Helen allowed her mind to drift over the night with Tom. Every time they were together it was better than the time before. She couldn't believe how her body responded to his touch, and marvelled that he found her Rubenesque curves so exhilarating.

'I'm forty, but I'm not alone and I'm not lonely.'

A cloud passed over her thoughts as she considered how Tom would cope without Dylan within hugging distance. She'd have to be there for him. 'I will be.'

Goodness knows how Mabel and Bert will take the news when Tom tells them.

Thea didn't allow herself to look at the signposts stating how far she was from Stow-on-the-Wold as she drove her car along the Fosse Way. The hotel she and Shaun had stayed at before Easter could only be a few miles away, and she couldn't prevent herself from reflecting on how different the drive from the dig to Stow had been to her return trip.

She'd never imagined that when she went back to the Cotswolds, she'd be alone. Her palms were sweaty against the wheel, her nerves coming from thoughts about what sort of reception she and Shaun would get from their colleagues now they were separated, rather than any anxiety about appearing in front of the cameras again. *Will Ajay and Andy still talk to me? After all, they've been Shaun's friends for years. I'm just the girlfriend – ex girlfriend. At least, I think I am.*

Unsure if it would be easier to accept they were apart if one of them had actually said the words, or if it would have just made it worse, Thea snapped at herself, 'We're grownups for goodness sake, we don't need to spell out the obvious.'

Thea pushed her shoulders back in a way she'd seen Mabel do when she was trying not to worry about Bert. 'Minerva, I know I neglected you while I was with Shaun, but any wisdom you could throw my way right now would be welcome.'

Keeping her eyes on the road, looking ahead for a garden centre she was sure she remembered being along this stretch of the Fosse Way, so she could pop in and compose herself over a coffee before arriving at Birdlip, Thea tried to focus on the reason for her journey.

Tina hummed happily as she scattered some feed into the chicken run. For the first time in weeks she relaxed. The wedding plans were on schedule, and although Shaun was currently AWOL, she was sure that, whatever the situation with Thea, he wouldn't let them down. And, if he did, Sam had assured him that Tom would step up to the role of best man, with no hard feelings about not being asked to do the job in the first place.

She couldn't wait to see Dylan dressed in a little suit of his own; he'd been so excited when they'd asked him if he'd like to be Shaun's right hand man, and be in charge of the wedding rings. 'Looks like I'll have both bridesmaids, the best man, the ring bearer and the usher all in place after all, Gertrude.' Tina dropped a slice of apple at her favourite hen's feet. 'I do wish Thea and Shaun were alright though.'

As Gertrude gave the chicken equivalent of an unhelpful shrug, Tina laughed. 'Maybe I shouldn't leave them to sort things of themselves? Maybe I should give them a helping hand.'

A blunt cluck seemed to warn Tina against interfering.

'You think I should let them get on with things themselves and not interfere?' Tina tugged at her right pigtail as she watched Betty and Mavis home in on Gertrude's apple slice. 'I tell you what, I'll give them until the wedding. If they haven't swallowed their mutual pride and come to their senses, I'll sit them down and make them talk to each other.'

All three hens looked at her.

'You think that's a bad idea.' Tina wondered if they were right. Perhaps there wasn't any going back for Thea and Shaun this time.

The campervan she'd used before was just where she'd left it. As were Shaun's, Ajay's, Andy's and three others, which Thea presumed belonged to Hilda, who did their makeup and hair, and a camera and sound man. Otherwise, the field behind the pub was empty. All of *Landscape Treasures* regular diggers, and the local archaeology team diggers, had gone.

Thea threw her rucksack into the camper, and turned to the pub. If she knew anything about archaeologists, that's where they'd be if they weren't digging. Not waiting to ask herself if she was ready to see Shaun or not, Thea strode towards The Carthorse.

Andy and Ajay were huddled over two pints of beer and a plate of sandwiches. There was no side of Shaun or, thankfully, Julian.

With a deep breath she approached the table. 'Hi, boys.'

'Thea!' Ajay stood up as she came towards them. 'It's great to see you.'

There was something about his tone that made her uneasy. 'You sound surprised to see me.'

'Well, yes. I mean, after what happened...' Ajay's sentence petered out as he got up. 'Can I get you a drink?'

'Coffee please.'

As Ajay left, Thea looked at Andy expectantly, 'How do you mean, "after what happened?" What did Shaun say to make you think I wasn't coming back to finish the job properly?'

'Shaun didn't say anything. It was Julian. He said you'd decided television wasn't for you, so we'd be finishing up with just Shaun on camera.'

'He did what?' Thea got back to her feet, her hands suddenly shaky. 'I said no such thing. Julian knew damn well I was coming back to finish up opening the mosaic and help with the voiceover work. He made it an order rather than a request!'

'Woah!' Andy put a hand out and gently pulled Thea back to her seat.

'Where is Shaun anyway?'

'In a meeting with Julian.' Andy looked worried, as he gestured towards the function room. 'They've been ages.'

Thea went cold. 'Do you know what they're talking about?'

'No.' Andy's frown deepened. 'Don't you?'

Thea didn't answer. 'Has any of the extra filming happened with the mosaic yet?'

'Not yet.' Andy glanced up at Ajay as he placed a coffee cup before Thea. 'The cameraman only arrived this morning. Hilda isn't due until after lunch.'

Torn between relief that Shaun hadn't started without her, and guilt that she thought he might have, Thea asked, 'When did Julian tell you I wasn't coming back?' *And why has Shaun been here all this time? What's he been doing?*

'This morning, when we got here.' Ajay shifted in his seat.

'He told us that you'd been offered the chance to stay but had turned it down in favour of your work at Mill Grange.'

'What did Shaun say?'

'Not a lot.' The AA exchanged puzzled glances. 'Mumbled something about it not being like you to be so unprofessional, but Julian either didn't hear him, or didn't want to hear him.'

'The latter more likely.' Ajay's eyebrows knotted together. 'We'll know more when Shaun comes back. We'd only just arrived when Julian spirited him away.'

They don't know about Shaun and me.

Sipping her coffee, Thea embraced the cup, its heat helping to ease the shake to her fingers. 'And you've no idea what Julian is up to?'

'Nothing beyond a suspicion that this is about *Treasure Hunters* going up in the world.'

Thea took another sip of coffee while she considered if she should tell them about the overheard phone call and Julian asking her to work for him in the future. She'd just decided she should, when the door to the function room opened, and a grave-faced Shaun appeared.

Fifty

Monday April 13th

Dylan stuck his tongue out of the corner of his mouth as he concentrated. Tom watched as his son worked hard, trying not to colour over the lines of the picture of St George fighting the dragon, from a colouring book Helen had bought in Glastonbury.

'That's good.' Tom sat down at the kitchen table. 'You'll have to show your mum when you get back.'

'I'll show Harriet too. She likes dragons.'

'Does she?' Tom wondered if Harriet knew about Dylan's forthcoming change in circumstance. 'You're fond of Harriet, aren't you?'

'She's fun. Like Helen.'

'I'm glad your mum found her. You're lucky to have a childminder you like. I remember my babysitter. She was scary.'

Without looking up, Dylan selected a dark green pencil. 'Did Nan and Grandad *really* leave you with someone scary?'

Hearing the surprise in his son's voice, Tom was taken aback. He hadn't thought about it before. His parents were always going to the pub, frequently leaving him with the sharp-tongued old lady next door. 'Things were different back then. Harriet's a daughter of your mum's friend though, isn't she? So she's bound to be nice.'

'Mum's special friend.' Dylan swapped the dark green crayon for a bright red one to colour the plume sprouting from St George's helmet.

Tom's pulse thudded as he leaned closer to Dylan. 'Special friend? Like a best friend you mean?'

'Sort of.' Dylan added an extra stroke to the page and turned to look at his dad. 'Can boys and girls be best friends? My friend Davy says not, but he's a bit silly sometimes.'

'Of course they can. I'm very good friends with Thea and Tina, aren't I?'

'And Helen. I think Helen is your best friend.'

Tom ruffled his son's hair, wishing Helen was with him now that Dylan had given him the perfect opening to share their news. *But she isn't going to be here that often. They'll be lots of things I have to tell Dylan alone. Until he's gone.*

'Yes. Helen is my best friend. You like her too, don't you?'

'She got me this.' Dylan smoothed a hand over his work of art before choosing a grey pencil and addressing his concentration to St George's armour.

'Can you stop colouring for a minute while I tell you something?'

Dylan paused, his pencil ready to return to work the moment his dad stopped talking. 'You know that sometimes we have special friends. Like girlfriends and boyfriends?'

'Yeahhhh.' Dylan pulled a face. 'They do kissing and huggy stuff.'

Tom laughed. 'Sometimes, but mostly they just care for each other a lot. Even more than best friends. Love each other. Like Sam and Tina.'

'They're getting married.'

'Yes. Are you looking forward to it?'

Dylan wrinkled his nose. 'I think so.'

Knowing it would be easy to drop the subject, Tom knew that would be the coward's way out, so he said, 'Well Helen is my girlfriend. Is that okay with you?'

'Are you getting married then?' Dylan asked. 'I like Helen. I could wear my new suit again.'

Tom scooped Dylan up and hugged him until he squirmed.

'Dad!'

'Sorry.'

Dylan picked his pencil back up. 'Can I colour in now?'

'Sure.' Tom watched. 'So, are you okay with it, Helen being my girlfriend? She wanted to be here when we asked you, really.'

'Helen has to work in Bath now. You should know that if she's your girlfriend, Dad!'

'So I should.' Tom smiled. 'I'm going to phone her in a minute. I'll tell her you don't mind.'

Dylan kept his eyes on the pencil tracing around the outside of the armour. 'Harriet said she's lucky that mum and her dad are special friends, cos she gets me as a brother.'

'Harriet is Nathan's daughter?' The words had come out

of Tom's mouth before he'd considered if Dylan knew Sue's partner's name.

'Yes.' Dylan's forehead creased into two puzzled lines. 'Didn't Mum say?'

'No. No she didn't. How old is Harriet?'

'Eighteen.'

Tom watched his son settle back to his art. *How old is this Nathan if he has an eighteen-year-old daughter?* 'If you're okay, Dylan, I'm going to call Helen.'

'Don't forget to tell her about my suit in case you want to get married too.'

'We've only just got together, Dylan.'

'That's a shame. Mum says I grow so fast my suit won't fit for long.'

Thea clutched her coffee cup tighter. She wasn't sure if she should stay sitting down or go to Shaun's side as he emerged from his meeting with Julian.

She could feel the AA were watching her, but her eyes stayed on Shaun as he rested against the door he'd closed behind him.

Ajay beckoned him forward. 'Don't keep us in suspense!'

'You look like you need this.' Andy pointed to the pint he'd already got in for Shaun to drink. 'Or can't you move from the door because your guarding Julian's brutally murdered corpse?'

'In which case,' Ajay grinned, 'I'll go and get a wheelbarrow and we'll all start work on a hole to put him in.'

Appreciating the AA's attempt to lighten the atmosphere,

Thea licked her lips. 'Can you say what he told you, or have you been asked to keep quiet?'

Not missing the reference to Julian having told Thea not to share what he'd told her, Shaun confirmed, 'He said he would rather I kept quiet about our conversation.'

'I bet he did.' Ajay growled. 'And are you going to, stay quiet, that is?'

Shaun kept his eyes on Thea. She could see regret shining in his eyes. *But is that for us or because of what Julian has just told him?*

'No, I'm not.' Shaun pulled himself away from the door, glancing back over his shoulder, making sure Julian wasn't right behind him. 'But it has to go no further than the four of us.' He fixed his gaze on the AA. 'I mean that, boys. None of your tittle-tattle.'

'As if we would!' Ajay feigned hurt, but his eyes remained serious. 'So, what's going on?'

Trying not to mind that Shaun hadn't even said hello, Thea put her cup down, and plunged her hands into her pockets. Shaun would know they were shaking, but she didn't want the AA to pick up on her anxiety as she waited for him to speak. When he did, he took her by surprise.

'Julian wants to speak to you now, Thea. That's why he hasn't come out. He wanted me to send you in to him.'

'What? How did he know I was here?'

'You were due today, weren't you? By midday. You're never late. We knew you'd be here.'

'But he told you guys I wasn't coming back, so...' Thea shook her head, tired of trying to work out what game

Julian was playing. She looked towards the door. 'What does he want?'

'You know what he wants.' The reply was blunt. If Ajay and Andy hadn't already worked out all was not well between their co-hosts, they knew now.

'Can you tell me what he said to you first?'

Shaun grunted into his pint. 'And keep him waiting?'

'Until Hell freezes over if necessary,' Thea snapped back.

'Woah!' Andy held up his hands. 'What's with you two?'

Ajay's eyes narrowed. 'I'd put money on Julian. He's put his oar in here, hasn't he?'

'Please, Shaun.' Thea looked straight at him. 'Just tell us.'

Shaun put his pint down. 'Sorry. He just winds me up the wrong way. He's so damn smarmy.'

'Agreed.' Ajay picked a sandwich up from the plate in the middle of the table. 'So, what's he done?'

'Thea. Tell them what Julian asked of you.' Shaun hurried on before she could object. 'It's relevant, I promise.'

As Thea explained about the overheard phone call and Julian's emails and invitation to guide her into the world of television properly, she spoke fast, apologising every second sentence for not telling them before.

Andy brushed her apologies away. 'Man like that, you don't know what to trust. Why tell us something that could be a pack of lies?'

Ajay agreed. 'Or manipulation.'

Thea looked at Shaun as she replied, 'I'm glad you two can see that.'

As a frosty silence descended, Ajay looked straight at

Shaun. 'Let me guess, you still think he fancies Thea? Well, I wouldn't blame him if he did. Thea is a fine-looking woman, intelligent, funny and excellent on camera. Of course he's attracted to her. That does not mean she's attracted to him. So, with all due respect Shaun, wake up and smell the roses, and for God's sake tell us what is going on before Julian comes out to collect Thea himself!'

Taken aback, Shaun caught Thea's eye. She didn't look triumphant, she just looked tired.

'Okay. Okay.' He cradled his pint as he spoke. 'What Thea overheard is, sadly, in line with what Julian mentioned at that meal he held for us. *Treasure Hunters* have succeeded in getting a better timeslot on a more mainstream channel. One of the reasons for this is their presenter has been dumped.'

Ajay groaned. 'Please tell they don't have a brain-dead celebrity with no archaeological experience and no passion for the subject beyond increasing their profile.'

'I have no idea who it is, but it has rattled our lords and masters' cages.'

'Including Julian's?' Thea wasn't sure why she asked such an obvious question.

'He was surprisingly smooth about the situation, but he's made it crystal that a change of presenter here is bound to follow.'

Andy turned to Thea. 'He wants you to do it, doesn't he.'

Shaun looked directly at her too. 'Well, has he asked you to do it?'

'You know he hasn't. But the implication was there. I told you that when we were at Mill Grange.'

'Hang on.' Andy waved his sandwich as he spoke. 'What

exactly did Julian say to you Shaun? Have you lost your job as our presenter? Is the show being re-commissioned next year?'

'All I got was a lecture on the need to increase viewing figures, the changes in the viewing demographic, and how shows need young female presenters these days.'

'In other words, he said nothing at all.' Ajay rolled his eyes. 'Just wanted to get you worried and second guessing about your future as our presenter – what with you *not* being female.'

'Or young,' Andy added.

'*Young* women.' Thea mentally counted to ten so she didn't explode. 'Well that rules me out then, so perhaps you could get that particular bee out of your bonnet Shaun. And, while we are at it, you know full well that I do not want a television career, and I particularly dislike anyone – male or female – getting a job based on their gender alone. All jobs should go to the candidate best suited for it. Equality is supposed to work both ways. God…' She paused, realising she was talking rather louder than she'd intended to, and that the AA were looking at her in an odd way. 'You know I hate that sort of thing.'

After a second's awkward silence, Shaun nodded.

'And, as I've said more times than I care to mention, I'd never take your job away from you. Right,' Thea stood up, her hands tingling within her jeans pockets, 'I'd better find out what I can.'

She'd only taken one step when the door to the function room opened, and Julian, his laptop bag in his hand, his designer jacket slung over his shoulder, waved at her. 'There you are, Thea. Come on, we've lots to discuss.'

'Come on where?' Thea glanced at Shaun.

'The Harborough Hotel. I told you in the email.' Without looking at the *Landscape Treasures* team he kept on walking. 'I'll meet you by my car.'

Thea knocked back the dregs of her coffee, getting ready to leave, when Ajay placed a hand on her arm.

'Before you go, I've had an idea…'

Fifty-one

Monday April 13th

Having told Julian she'd follow him in her own car, Thea found herself waiting in the hotel's lobby while the producer spoke to the receptionist.

The modern furnishings and tinny music that leaked through a speaker in the corner of the room felt at odds with the age of the building; jarringly out of keeping with the rest of the Cotswolds. Ignoring the stainless-steel tables and chairs, Thea watched Julian sweet talk the young woman behind the counter. With a wave to Thea to sit down and wait, Julian disappeared with the receptionist down a corridor.

Now what? Thea perched apprehensively on the edge of an uncomfortable metal seat.

She hadn't wanted to come, but the AA, furious at whatever their producer was planning – before they even knew what it was – had convinced her to at least try and discover what was going on. *It's their futures too – not just Shaun's.*

The receptionist returned to her desk, but there was no sign of Julian.

Five minutes later, the receptionist came over to Thea. 'Mr Blackwood apologises, he has to take a call. He won't be long. Can I get you a drink while you wait?'

'No, thank you.' Shifting in the hard seat, Thea closed her eyes. Shaun had looked awful. He obviously hadn't slept and his anger at being messed about by Julian was etched into every tired line on his face.

He didn't look at me.

Glancing at her watch, Thea got up. She was waiting to see a man she didn't like and didn't trust. Someone who had driven a wedge between her and the man she loved. She'd had enough.

Picking up her handbag, Thea went over to the receptionist. 'Can you point me in Mr Blackwood's direction please? I don't have time to wait any longer.'

'The Oakwood suite. The door's labelled. Fourth room after you go through the glass door at the end of the corridor.'

'Thank you.'

'Would you like me to phone ahead?'

'No, thank you.'

With her mobile phone in her hand, Thea knocked on the door to the Oakwood Suite and waited. Hearing no reply, she pushed it open. Julian was still on the phone. He was looking out of the window, his back to the door, which was at least six metres from where she stood. He was completely oblivious to her presence.

This wasn't a conference room as his messages had claimed, but a palatial suite, made up of a lounge and bedroom and, presumably, a bathroom. A double bed sat next to where Julian stood. He wore a dressing gown, and quite possibly nothing else.

OMG. Shaun was right!

Thea was about to back out, when Julian raised his voice down the phone. His words froze her feet to the floor.

'I told you I had it covered!'

Had what covered? Thea took a step backwards, hoping the door wouldn't creak as it closed.

'I know she doesn't fit the age range you specified, but she looks a damn sight younger than she is and, frankly, we need someone who knows what they're talking about. This isn't a sports show where people can fake enthusiasm when they need to. This is skilled stuff.'

With her foot keeping the door ajar so she could escape when she needed to, cold crept over Thea as she listened.

'Cowlson's influence over her is fading fast. He was like the proverbial bear with a sore head when I saw him. Give me an hour and the deal will be done...' Julian laughed at whatever was being suggested down the other end of the line '... a perk of the job...'

Shaun's influence? Whoever Julian was talking to, it was her they were talking about. *If he thinks I'm perking anything... Bastard.*

Resisting the renewed urge to run, Thea held her ground. The more she heard Julian incriminate himself the better.

As Julian began to close the conversation, Thea gripped the open door tighter, the airy corridor behind her reassuring. She lifted her phone higher, knowing that despite everything, if she called Shaun, he'd come.

'Okay mate, I'll email when things are signed and sealed, if you see what I mean.'

Thea tensed. She had a horrible idea she saw exactly what he meant by signed and sealed as her eyes strayed from Julian's robe clad back to the bed and back again.

His mobile made a light thump as he threw it onto the duvet behind him. Julian stretched his arms above his head as he stared across the countryside beyond the window. His robe slipped up in the process, revealing over-toned calves to Thea's unimpressed eyes.

'Now all I've got to do is persuade her.' Julian spoke to the view in general, spinning around at speed as Thea, her heart in her mouth, replied.

'Persuade who exactly?'

'Thea?' A flash of panic crossed Julian's face, only to be extinguished by a half smile. 'How long have you been there?'

'Long enough.' She held out her phone. 'You have ten seconds to tell me who you were talking about and what your intentions for her are before I call Shaun, and ask him to report you to the production company.'

'I don't think that would be a wise move for your future, Thea.' Julian patted the bed as he sat down. 'Why don't we talk about it like civilised adults?'

'How about you put your clothes back on and we talk about it in the bar, in public, like civilised adults?'

'But I've gone to so much trouble for you.'

The snorting laugh that escaped Thea's lips came out before she could stop it. 'You told me this was a meeting room. That we were to have a conversation about my future. Unless I'm very much mistaken, such meetings normally take place while fully dressed, with tea and coffee to hand, not in dressing gowns with champagne already on ice.' Thea pointed to the ice bucket she'd just spotted on the opposite side of the room. 'Rather pre-emptive of you. Or backwards thinking even – this isn't the 1970s!'

'I prefer forward thinking.'

'I bet you do! Either way, that's a waste of champagne.' Thea marvelled at how steady her voice was. 'Are you going to tell me what this is all in aid of, or do I call Shaun?'

'You two broke up.' Julian sounded satisfied by the fact.

'I thought you and I were here to have a professional discussion. Shaun is a professional and so am I, and for your information I love him very much. Now, tell me, who were you talking to?'

'The person who could make you a household name.'

'Like Cadbury's or Harpic?'

'Don't be flippant, Thea. I'm serious!'

'Serious! You are acting like a 1960's film producer trying to seduce a young actress. What's wrong with you!? The world has changed! Or have you been too busy smarming your way up the greasy pole to notice?'

Finally accepting that he'd gauged Thea all wrong, Julian got back up and gave her a curt nod. 'I'll see you in the bar in five minutes. It'll be worth your while, I promise.'

The sun shone behind Shaun as he beamed into the camera, highlighting both him and the work of art at his feet. Only Thea and Hilda knew just how much makeup had been applied to stop him looking like he hadn't slept for weeks.

'This, one of the finest villa mosaics in England, possibly

the world, is a stunning example of local craftsmanship.' Shaun knelt down and extended an arm, sweeping across the Roman tesserae to underline his words. 'The way each and every tile has been cut, to fit precisely into its given space, is a testament to the devotion of the mosaic makers of the age. The Gloucester school of mosaic makers, who must surely have been responsible for this work of art, should be justly proud.'

Thea crouched besides Shaun, her trowel to hand and she looked into the camera. 'We can only wonder what they'd think, to know that here we are, almost two thousand years later, marvelling at their skill, and opening up this bath house floor to be admired by future generations.'

'Cut!' Julian lowered his hand as Thea's closing words were delivered faultlessly into the camera. 'We'll do a check through for sound quality, but I suspect we are finally done here. If you could wait in the pub, I'll confirm completion as soon as I have it.'

As Julian strode towards the camera and sound men, Shaun growled under his voice. 'That's it then. No, "thanks for coming back to finish off" no, "sorry to inconvenience you" just, oh, we're done now, off you go and play!'

'Shaun!' Thea snapped in exasperation. This wasn't the Shaun Cowlson she had first met, fuelled by exuberance and full of love and passion for his job and his life. He was lost. Thea battled the urge to shake him back into his usual optimistic self. She spoke softly, her hand brushing his arm. 'What the hell has happened? Please, talk to me.'

'Talk about what? Top tips on how to be the lead presenter on *Landscape Treasures* perhaps? You've been back from the hotel with him for three hours, and you've said nothing about what you got up to there. And knowing him I—'

'Right. That is it!' Thea threw down her trowel in exasperation. 'That is officially it! Have you any idea what I have been through today? Have you? No, you haven't a clue, because I came straight back from the hotel with that creep and got on with what we are here for. Not because I'm trying to show Julian how suitable I am for your job – which, for the millionth time, *I DO NOT WANT*, but because I'm a professional. *We* are professionals. Or we're supposed to be.

'There was no time to talk to you about my meeting. I was not putting it off. Nor was I hiding anything from you. And if you can tell me exactly when I was supposed to have filled you in on my meeting, then I'd be very interested to know when that moment was!'

Fifty-two

Monday April 13th

Taking three big gulps of air, Thea's hands shook as she checked her phone. Whatever app it was that Ajay had installed to record her conversation with Julian, had left a notification on her screen, so she presumed it had worked. She didn't dare play back the conversation for fear of accidentally deleting it.

Now, as she stood in The Carthorse beer garden, grateful that no one was around to see her as she gathered herself, Thea knew that what she was about to do was probably in breach of data protection and possibly illegal.

Thea had felt uneasy when Ajay had suggested recording her meeting with Julian. She had a feeling Ajay was intending some sort of mild blackmail, but as an image of Julian in his bathrobe floated through her mind, it squashed down her guilt. He'd been underhand with her; she was simply returning the compliment.

With a deep breath she headed to the bar. Ajay and Andy were in the corner of the room, bent over their laptops, making sure all the geophysics graphics for the broadcast were in order, so they too could go home.

Here goes nothing.

Sam hung up the phone, turning to Tina as she broke eggs into her lemon cake mix.

'All sorted. The marquees will go up on the afternoon before the wedding. I've offered mine and Tom's services as labour, so that will cut costs a bit. One will be in the walled garden for the ceremony, and then two others will go on the main lawn for the reception.'

'That's great.' Tina squeezed some vanilla essence into the mix. 'Sybil confirmed this morning that she'll provide afternoon tea for forty, to be served under a marquee in the main garden. My dress is sorted, and we have two bridesmaids primed and dresses sorted – thank goodness!'

Sam wrapped his arms around her as Tina stirred a spoon through the bowl. 'I can't believe I'm in a kitchen, *inside*, with the woman I love, soon to get married. I never dared dream that one day...' Sam broke off, suddenly unable to finish his sentence.

'It's okay, I know.' She kissed him gently. 'I can't believe my luck either. Not only do I get to marry the kindest man in the world, I get to see him in a suit.' She winked playfully. 'Even more of a miracle perhaps.'

'Cheek!' Sam pulled playfully at her pigtails. 'And I can report that the suit is, finally, in the process of being sorted. Tom found someone who'll come to us, rather than me to them. He's going to sort Bert as well. I'll be relying on you to sidetrack Mabel, so Bert and I can tackle the tailor without her well-meaning help.'

'I'll do my best, but I'm promising nothing!' She gestured a floury hand towards the clock. 'I was just wondering how Thea was getting on with Shaun. I know they've both promised to still be best man and chief bridesmaid, but it would be a hell of a lot nicer for everyone if they had sorted themselves out before the wedding.'

'Got back together you mean.' Sam rubbed at his stubbly chin. 'I'm wondering if that will be one miracle too far.'

'But they love each other.' Tina dropped her spoon with a clatter against the side of the bowl. 'If they'd just get off their high horses and talk to each other.'

'You can't manufacture happy endings for everyone you know.' Sam kissed the top of her head.

'I could try though, couldn't I?'

She'd almost called Tina. A chat to her best friend for some advice would be more than welcome, but as she didn't know how much time she had before Julian turned up, Thea headed to the AA.

The moment Ajay spotted her, he pulled out a chair and patted it conspiratorially. 'What happened? Did it work?'

'I have no idea. I don't dare check in case I press the wrong thing and mess it up.'

Andy looked surprised. 'You can work an app, surely?'

'Of course I can, but this is important, and not just to *Landscape Treasures*.' Thea lowered her eyes. 'The mosaic filming is finished. Julian's checking the last few bits to camera now.'

'So where's Shaun?' Ajay glanced towards the door. 'He's usually first through the door for a post episode pint.'

'I left him on site.' Not particularly wanting to replay the one-sided row they'd just had, Thea laid her mobile on the table. 'How do we play this back?'

'I think first,' Ajay picked up the phone, 'if you have no objection Thea, I will back up the recording onto the computer.'

Feeling as if she'd fallen into a spy movie, Thea said, 'Whatever you think best.'

Andy leaned forward, his expression eager. 'What did he want anyway? Was Shaun right about you being in the frame for his job?'

A sound behind them made Thea jump. She spun around, guilt etched all over her face, expecting to see Julian. Instead, Shaun stood with his hands deep in his pockets. He looked utterly defeated. 'Well Thea, was I right?'

Mabel finished grating a pile of cheese ready to make lasagne to stock up Mill Grange's freezers. She approved of Tina's plan to make sure Shaun and Thea were manoeuvred together, so they had no choice but to talk, but she couldn't see how it could work.

'Surely, by the time they're back here, they'll either be back together or completely apart. Anything we do will come too late.'

Tina sighed. 'Thea plans to come straight back here after they've finished filming. Tomorrow, hopefully. There wasn't much left to do.'

'And Shaun?'

'He told Sam he'd be back before the wedding.'

Mabel took a large pan from the cupboard, and drizzled in some olive oil, ready to fry some mince. 'So he might not arrive until the day before the wedding?'

Tina's resolve faltered a little. 'I'd assumed he'd come back here after filming too. I mean, where else would he go?'

'Where did he go between filming before he met Thea?'

'Hotels I think.' Tina passed Mabel a spatula from a tub behind her. 'He's never mentioned a place of his own.'

Thoughtful as she adjusted the flame beneath the pan, Mabel added some pre-chopped onions to the oil. 'With any luck, they'll be mended again before they get home, but if they aren't, then perhaps…'

'Perhaps?' Tina smiled as she saw a calculating expression cross the old lady's face.

'I was just thinking. Weddings are very emotional occasions. They make one think.' She sprinkled some garlic into the pan. 'Yes…' she muttered to herself as she watched the mix begin to caramelise… 'Yes, that might work.'

'What might?' Tina asked as Mabel stirred.

'Best you leave it to me, Tina. It's your wedding day, time to worry about yourself and Sam and let your mother-of-the-bride play fairy godmother.'

Bert couldn't stop chuckling as Dylan ran around the room with a tape measure, fully endorsed by the tailor, James, who was obviously used to being helped by his client's offspring.

Sam had been somewhat surprised to find the itinerant tailor was not an aging man in a well-cut suit, but a chap in his twenties in smart jeans and a shirt.

'I can't believe you arranged this for me, Sam.' Bert held out an arm so that James could measure his underarm. 'I was a bit concerned about letting you and Tina down.'

'You could never do that.'

Bert chuckled. 'You haven't seen my original suit.'

'I'm sure it wasn't that bad.' Sam smiled as James ducked under Bert's arm and tackled his back.

'Oh the suit's fine, it's me. I've shrunk! I'm sure it's the fabric that is supposed to shrink in the wash and not the wearer, but there you go. That's old age for you.'

Dylan sat on the sofa and looked up at his friend, his eyes wide. 'Dad says you aren't old, you just sat still and lots of life happened.'

Bert burst out laughing. 'Did he now! Well, your dad might well be right. Where is Tom, by the way?'

'Fetching his suit.' Sam watched James as he moved around Bert, able to work as they chatted, being present but apart.

'It's at my house.' Dylan twirled the tape measure around his wrist. 'Mum had it in the attic.'

'There.' James jotted his last measurement into his tablet, and gestured for Bert to sit down. 'All done, Mr Hastings. So, father of the bride. A proud moment.'

'You have no idea.' Bert's eyes filled with tears, but he ignored them. 'I'm in your hands, James. What colour would suit my suit?'

Shaun stared at the phone. He was finding it hard not to comment as he listened, but he'd promised the others he would keep his mouth shut until he'd heard the whole recording. Anyway, it was compelling listening. If he spoke, he might miss Julian digging himself deeper into a hole.

His urge to say "I told you so" to Thea when she'd explained, prior to Ajay playing the recording, that the promised business room had turned out to be an executive suite, with champagne laid on, had only been curtailed by the desolate expression on Thea's face. For the first time, he noticed she was hurting as much as he was.

Shaun felt a stirring of remorse as he listened to Thea on the recording, telling Julian that it was him she loved. He risked a glimpse at her now, sat opposite him, her hands holding each other to hide the mild shake he knew would be there.

As they reached the end of the first part of the recording where Thea left for the bar, Ajay pressed pause. Silence coated the table for a moment, before Andy said, 'This could end his career. His behaviour's more prehistoric than any dig I've ever covered.'

Ajay nodded, but Thea just stared at the mobile on the table before them. She could feel the seconds ticking past as she waited for Shaun to say something.

When he did speak, Thea's heart dropped lower. 'I was right then. He does fancy you.'

The AA exchanged glances, before Ajay said, 'No offence to Thea, but I don't think so mate. He was just after being able to blackmail her, or buy her by getting his leg over. Not really the same thing.'

'Arrogant git,' Andy hissed, shifting in his seat as the atmosphere between Thea and Shaun thicken. 'Maybe we should hear the rest?'

As Andy reached forward to press play, Thea realised

she didn't want to hear it. She didn't want to see Shaun's reaction to what came next. If, after listening, he wanted to find her, then fine, but even if he finally believed that she had done nothing to encourage Julian, it was going to take more than a sorry and a hug to sort them out.

She put her hand over her phone. 'You've got the recording on your laptop haven't you, Ajay?'

'Sure.'

'Then if you don't mind, I'm very tired. I'm going to have a rest. If Julian needs more filming, give me a call.'

Then, without giving them time to reply, Thea left the pub, her heart thudding, but her head held high.

Fifty-three

Friday May 22nd

Tina had been up since five. The chickens had been cleaned and given strict instructions not to mess their coop up before tomorrow's wedding. The kitchen had been scrubbed to within an inch of its life, and Sybil had been and gone, delivering a glut of double cream and jam, ready to accompany the scones she'd make the following day.

As the kitchen clock chimed ten o'clock, Mabel could be heard humming to herself as she made up some of the main guest bedroom, so that Sam's parents had a place to change in once they arrived in the morning. The bathrooms had been cleaned, and the banister to the main staircase shone, giving out a deliciously comforting aroma of beeswax.

Filling a large teapot with boiling water, Tina experienced a sense of happy satisfaction. She was getting married tomorrow. Everyone who made up the wedding party was either there, or due by early morning. The weather forecast, although not foretelling bright sunshine, was claiming a dry spring day for the morrow.

Tom had taken charge of Bert and Dylan's suits, which hung in the downstairs bedroom Tina usually shared with Sam. Her own dress, still at the boutique, would be collected by Thea that afternoon, along with the bridesmaid's dresses; while Mabel had her mother-of-the-bride outfit under control.

Pouring some milk into a jug, Tina placed it and some cups onto a tray, before adding some cake plates. Today might be a preparation day, but she was determined to make it as much a part of the wedding celebration as she could.

'Shall I grab the cake?' Thea, her arms full of clean tea towels from the laundry, came in.

'Thanks. I'll never be able to carry all this outside in one go.'

'Has Helen arrived?' Thea dropped the clean linen into a drawer, and hooked the cake tin from the cupboard.

'Not yet. She's due around eleven, so we'd better save her some cake. Sue's bringing Dylan over first thing in the morning, so he gets a decent night's sleep at home, and so Tom doesn't have to worry about him while they have a mini stag night tonight. Bert and Mabel are here though, as are Diane and Bill and Derek – you remember them from when we restored the house?'

'Of course. How wonderful.'

Tina watched her friend as she fetched some sugar for Bert's tea, her eyes were cloudy. 'Let's sit down a minute.'

'Isn't the tea ready?'

'It can wait.' Tina twirled a pigtail around a finger. 'You know it's weird. I thought when the wedding got this close, I'd be ball of panic, but I feel really calm.'

'That's good.' Thea picked a teaspoon off the tray and played it between her fingers. 'Anyway, you have nothing to be nervous of. Sam's a good man. You have a great home and a good future.'

Tina knew Thea was sincere, but she didn't miss the wistfulness in her friend's voice. 'I am very lucky. And to think, I almost shunned him because he has a ponytail.'

Thea chuckled. 'You went out with some awful blokes before Sam.'

Tina rolled her eyes. 'I wish I could claim otherwise. Remember Leon!'

'The Silver Fox!' Thea grinned, but suddenly she became serious. 'You just wanted security back and thought older men with money could give you that. Perhaps the right one might have in time, but I'm glad you met Sam.'

'So am I!' Tina hesitated. 'You can talk to me you know. Just because I'm getting married tomorrow, doesn't mean you can't offload if you need to.'

'Thank you, but in all honesty there's nothing to offload, because I have no idea where I stand where Shaun is concerned.'

'You haven't heard anything from him?'

'Not a word since he heard the recording of Julian talking to me in that hotel last month. Perhaps I should have stayed and watched him listen to the rest of it, but at the time, I couldn't face it.'

'And you assumed he'd come and find you once he'd heard the recording.'

'Yes.' Thea sighed. 'I imagined him coming to talk to me in private. But he didn't.'

'I'm sorry, hun.'

'The last thing I know about Shaun for sure came from Ajay. He knocked on my campervan door to let me know

I wasn't needed for any more filming and that Shaun had already left. Last seen heading for the television studio in Bristol to talk to the board that controls *Landscape Treasures*. Apparently, he didn't react at all to what he heard Julian say to me in the bar via the mobile recording. He simply asked Ajay to email him the recording and took off.'

'What did he say in the bar?'

'It was all along the lines of how, if I played my cards right, then the television world would be my oyster. He talked about me presenting, not just archaeology shows, but game shows too. Or, if I didn't want to do anything too common, he was sure a pretty face like mine could get her own historical documentary series. Apparently if I "played the game his way", I'd become the most sought-after celebrity on television.'

'Is this guy for real?' Tina rolled her eyes.

'Sadly, yes.'

Tina reached a hand across the table and gave Thea's a squeeze. 'Do you still love Shaun?'

'It would be a damn sight easier if I didn't.'

'Sam had a call from him yesterday. Shaun will be here this afternoon.'

'Okay.' Thea stared at the sugar cubes. 'Forewarned is forearmed. Don't worry, I won't let you down.'

'I didn't think you would.'

Thea licked her lips. 'I suppose it's more that I desperately don't want to let myself down by dissolving into a puddle of tears the minute I see him.'

'You won't.' Tina observed her friend's tired face. 'The old Thea might have done. The one who came to Mill Grange in the first place. The one whose life was stuck in a rut, with an annoying ex and limited self-confidence. She might have gone to pieces, but look at you now! I know you were a successful historian before you came here, but since you arrived here you've helped establish a retreat, an excavation and you've been a television presenter!'

'All because of Shaun.'

'No. Not because of Shaun.' Tina shook her head. 'Some of the opportunities perhaps, especially when it came being part of *Landscape Treasures*, came via Shaun, but you still had to have the guts to do all those things. If you were no good at it, you would not have lasted five minutes. Television isn't a world known for charity. You stood in front of the cameras and did what was asked of you.'

'With help from Hilda and Ajay and—'

Tina waved her friend's words away. 'You know what I mean. And don't forget, you stood up to Mabel when you first got here. No mean feat! And then there's this situation now.'

'How do you mean?'

'The Thea Thomas who first came to Mill Grange would have pretended she didn't mind that her partner didn't listen to her, or that he could even imagine she'd steal his job.'

Thea shrugged. 'So I grew some backbone. Long overdue.'

'If Shaun can't take you for who you are now, then, however much it hurts, he isn't the one for you.'

'That's what I keep telling myself.' Thea got up and flicked the kettle back on. 'I think I'll have coffee rather than tea.'

Tina gestured to the teapot. 'I should get this outside before it's stewed.'

'It's the not knowing that's getting to me. Logic tells me that we're over. I haven't heard from Shaun for ages. When I last saw him, he hardly said a word, and yet an annoying part of my brain keeps telling me it doesn't *feel* over. Something in me won't let go of that nagging hope that he still loves me.'

'I suspect he does. But he's dug himself into a hole so deep that he can't see a way out.'

Thea picked up her mug of coffee and the cake tin. 'Come on, enough self-pity. This is your special weekend. Let's go and eat some cake.'

'Always a good plan.' Tina smiled. 'We need enough to line our stomachs. Mini hen party tonight.'

'I love that you and Sam are referring to your stag and hen evenings as "mini" events.'

'Well, we don't want to get drunk and go through tomorrow with hangovers, so they will end at 10 p.m. sharp, and sober.'

Thea laughed. 'You're the boss.'

It was a relief to get out of her Land Rover. The traffic on the motorway south had been a nightmare. At one point, having driven just one mile in an hour, Helen had begun to believe she'd be better off walking to Mill Grange

'Four and a half hours! Oh well, at least I'm here in time to have a wash and change before the hen do!' Brushing her hands down her jeans. Helen hooked her holdall over her shoulder, and headed straight to the back garden, bypassing the house, in favour of following the bustle of activity she could hear going on behind it.

Tom, who'd been keeping an eye out for her ever since she'd sent a sneaky text while stationery in a traffic jam to warn she was running late, stopped what he was doing, and came to her side.

'It's looking good.' Helen nodded to the marquees that were already erected. 'I see I interrupted chair positioning duty.'

Tom hugged her. 'I'm glad of the break. Chairs lose their fascination after a while.'

'I can imagine.' She gestured towards the marquee furthest from them. 'What's Sam doing? Looks like he's wrestling something.'

'A stubborn patio heater. We've ordered a couple for each marquee in case the spring weather delivers less than the hoped-for sunshine tomorrow.'

'Sensible.' Helen's gestured towards the kitchen. 'Any chance of some grub? I'm famished.'

'Come on, let's find your lunch. Mabel saved you some sandwiches and a slice of cake.'

'That would be great.' Helen lay a hand on his arm. 'Before we join the others though, any word from Sue about her trip?'

Tom's smile faded. 'She sent a text this morning. September. No exact date has been given. There are visas and things to sort.'

'September.' *Three and a half months before we lose Dylan.* 'Does he know yet?'

'No. Sue doesn't want to worry him until she has to, and for once, I'm in agreement with her.'

Fifty-four

Although Thea had enjoyed helping Tina get Mill Grange ready for the wedding, and it was great to have Helen there, she felt detached from everything that was going on. As if she was a voyeur watching the fun rather than being a part of it. She'd lost count of the number of times she'd looked towards the door, the main gateway, or the drive.

It made no difference. Shaun hadn't arrived. As the hours ticked by, she was increasingly convinced that he wasn't coming.

'He won't let Sam down.' She threw some grain into the chicken run. 'I know he told Sam and Tina he'd be here after lunch and it's nearly five, but he's a good man, Gertrude. His friends are important to him.'

The hen tilted her head as if to ask, 'Why isn't he here then?'

'Held up in traffic like Helen was, maybe. A last-minute meeting with Julian, perhaps – although I hope not.' Thea looked over to the wedding marquee. It was deserted now after a few frantic hours of chair placement and planning where they'd put the flowers in the morning.

She closed her eyes. 'Minerva, am I being a fool here? Should I give up hope with Shaun?'

The goddess of wisdom was unhelpfully quiet as she dropped some pepper slices into the coop and took her leave. She had a hen party to get ready for. Thea didn't think she'd ever felt less like partying in her whole life.

Sam engulfed Tina in a massive hug as the friends split off into two halves. Thea watched as they said goodbye as if it would be years until they saw each other again, not just one night.

Before leaving the manor, the last job had been to make sure Tina had left nothing she might need the following day in the downstairs bedroom, and move it to the bedroom she was using upstairs. Her dress, dutifully collected, was already awaiting her on the wardrobe door.

As the future bride and groom said goodnight, the group peeled off, with Sam, Tom and Bert making a beeline for Moira's finest ale in the Stag and Hound, while Tina, Thea, Helen and Mabel headed towards Sybil's.

Shaun's absence had not been mentioned.

'Welcome!' Sybil threw open the door to her tearoom. 'May the after-hours' shenanigans begin! Bucks Fizz anyone?'

Tina was giggling uncontrollably as Sybil finished telling stories about some of the things she'd got up in her youth.

'And there we were thinking you were such a good girl! I'm shocked!'

Sybil winked. 'I'm nothing compared to Mabel here! Right heartbreaker she was!'

Mabel didn't deny the accusation as she lifted up the jug of orange juice, ready to dilute the champagne she'd already poured into her glass.

Helen, who'd been drinking her champagne unadulterated for the last hour, reached for the juice after Mabel. 'I'd better go easy, or I'll be walking backwards down the aisle.'

Tina giggled. 'You will be anyway.'

'I will?'

'I saw Tom in his wedding clobber today. You aren't going to want to take your eyes off him, and the usher stands at the back of the marquee.'

'I would be lying if I said I wasn't looking forward to seeing him in a suit.' Helen's blush spread down her neck as her mind leapt to Tom's potential reaction to her bridesmaid's dress. 'And Dylan of course. I bet he looks fantastic.'

Mabel raised her glass. 'Like a mini Tom Cruise.'

'Not that mini.' Sybil nudged Mabel's elbow, almost sending her drink flying. 'Tom Cruise is on the short side I believe.'

Tina smiled as Mabel's eyes rolled again. 'I think you need something to soak that champagne up, Sybil, or you'll be buttering the jam and creaming the tea pot tomorrow.'

'Don't you worry about me. Lead lined stomach.' Sybil tapped her waist. 'Anyway, I remember your orders. No drinking after 10 p.m., and tea and coffee on standby to round off the evening. Gone are the days of strippers and tying folk to lampposts.'

'I thought it was the stag that got stripped naked and tied to a lamp post.' Helen got up to look out of the window. 'Nope, you're okay Tina, not a single naked man with a ponytail in sight.'

Tina laughed. 'How about naked men without ponytails?'

'At least three, possibly four.'

Thea lowered the glass of orange juice she'd been sipping. 'I haven't seen you like this for ages, Helen. I'd forgotten about your post-alcohol silly side.'

'Out of practice.' Helen twirled a curl of hair around her fingers. 'I don't think I'd better have any more, though!'

'It wasn't a criticism.' Thea felt bad for commenting. 'I just meant that it's lovely to see you so relaxed.'

Mabel raised her glass which was already almost empty. 'Love of a good man that is.' She hiccupped, making everyone burst out laughing.

'Okay!' Sybil got to her feet, 'if Mabel is at the hiccupping stage, we need cake!'

'Scones!' Helen and Tina chorused.

'But you'll be having scones tomorrow at the wedding.' Sybil shook her head, 'Surely you don't want them now as well?'

'Don't be daft, woman.' Mabel got up, swaying slightly as she did so. 'I'll give you a hand. We could eat your scones all day every day forever.'

As they tottered towards the kitchen, Sybil chuckled. 'I think most of you already do.'

Watching them leave, Tina said, 'I believe Mabel is tipsy. I never thought I'd see the day.'

'She told me she can take Bucks Fizz like its lemonade when we chatted earlier.' Thea smiled affectionately. 'I suspect she could, once upon a time. I'm damn sure Sybil was right about her being a heartbreaker.'

Tina tapped the side of her nose with a wink. 'When Bert was in the hospital, he told us how he'd fallen for Mabel the second he saw her red hair. It was love at first sight.'

'A red head.' Thea looked towards the kitchen, from where the clatter of plates being none to gently stacked, could be heard. 'That figures. Saucy lot the red heads.' She winked at Helen, who blushed again.

Tina drained her glass, before gesturing to Thea's half full one. 'Have you had anything to drink at all?'

'Orange juice.' Thea winked. 'One of us has to make sure the bride gets home in one piece.'

'That's why we have the curfew and coffee.' Tina held up the champagne bottle. 'Can't I tempt you to one?'

'No thanks.' Thea turned to see Sybil and Mabel tottering across the tearoom with a steaming pile of cheese scones. 'And now I'm even better!'

'It'll be a miracle if any of us fit into our dresses tomorrow,' Thea muttered to herself as she hit the fresh air.

Sybil, having run out of orange juice, and not wanting to be responsible for a bride with a hangover, despite Tina's earlier good intentions, had asked Thea to fetch some from Moira in the pub.

It was good to be away for a moment. Although she'd begun to relax with the arrival of the scones, and had certainly laughed alongside her friends as they'd chatted through butter heavy mouthfuls, Thea still felt as if she was experiencing life through the wrong end of a telescope.

She checked her watch. It was already nine thirty. If Tina really did want them all to be good girls and back to Mill Grange at ten, she was going to have to confiscate the last two bottles of champagne Sybil had lined up in ice buckets.

Despite it being packed, Thea could hear Bert laughing as she weaved her way through the pub garden. He, Sam and Tom, were sat at a patio table, swathed in coats to keep off the evening chill, with a suspiciously large number of empty glasses in front of them, and nothing more nourishing than some packets of crisps to fend off the hangovers they'd promised Tina not to have.

Waving as she headed to the bar, Thea called to Moira, who was serving at least three people at once, with her usual good humour. 'Sybil's out of orange juice. Any chance?'

'She warned me that might happen. I put a few cartons in the back room. Can you help yourself?' Moira added a straw to a cola, while pulling a pint. 'Tell Sybil we'll sort the money out on Monday.'

Giving the landlady a thumbs up, Thea sidled past the bar and down a narrow corridor to a room she'd been to twice before. Her palms tingled as she remembered how she'd had a meal with Shaun there, during what they'd since labelled their first 'non-date'. The second time she'd been there, she'd run away. Having been tricked into thinking she was having a meal with Shaun, she had been greeted with the prospect of dinner by her former boyfriend, John.

'Well, this time, you are simply fetching orange juice, so stop panicking and get back to the girls.'

As soon as she pushed the door open, the inevitability of it hit her. 'Seriously!'

Shaun jumped up from the sofa. He looked guilty. 'Hi,

Thea. Sorry for the cloak and dagger bit, but I didn't think you'd come if I'd asked.'

Thea's pulse galloped as she stood in the open doorway, her arms crossed. 'Sybil lied about the orange juice.'

'Possibly. She may have run out.'

Thea frowned. 'Moira had some lined up anyway.' She could see the promised cartons on the room's dining table.

'There was a genuine possibility Sybil would run out. Mabel knocks it back, according to Bert.'

'That, at least, is true.' Thea marched to the table and picked up two cartons. 'And if I don't get back, the mother of the bride could be nine sheets to the wind by ten.'

'Stay. Please.' Shaun pointed to the sofa.

'We're in the middle of our best friends' hen and stag night!' Thea's forehead creased as she said, 'Sam does know you're here, doesn't he? Tom was beginning to think he'd be stepping in for you.'

'Of course he does. I'd never let him or Tina down.'

Thea clutched the juice to her chest. 'I'll go and tell Tina. Unless she knows as well.'

'I doubt it. I haven't been here long.' Shaun tried again, 'Please Thea, we need to talk. Will you sit down?'

'Give me one good reason why I should.'

'Actually, I can give you three.'

Fifty-five

Friday May 22nd

'Three reasons? I'm honoured.' Thea leaned against the side of the table, the juice still in her hands.

Shaun ran a hand through his hair, his eyes on the boxes of juice. 'I listened to the recording.'

'I know. I was there.'

'I mean, I heard it again. All of it. Several times, especially the conversation in the hotel bar. The part you didn't stay to rehear.'

'Can you blame me?'

'Not really. Although I wished you'd stayed.'

'Then you should have said.'

'Would you have, if I'd asked you to?'

'Yes.'

'Oh.' Shaun stared at the untouched pint of beer on the table next to the sofa. 'I assumed you'd tell me to piss off. I wouldn't have blamed you.'

'Yes, you would.' Thea sighed. 'At the time, you would.'

Grimacing, Shaun reluctantly admitted, 'Maybe. I wasn't thinking straight.'

'You don't say.' Thea waved a carton of juice at him. 'I really have to go.'

'Sybil never runs out of anything.'

'What?'

'She knows I'm here. I texted.'

Thea put the cartons back on the table and took some steadying breaths. 'Sybil?'

'I didn't want to ask any of the others to conspire with me in case you got the hump with them. There is a wedding tomorrow after all.'

'So you admit to conspiring then?' Thea shook her head. 'And what if I fell out with Sybil?'

'No chance of that. Your cheese scone source would be cut off.'

Thea saw a smile hit his eyes. *Don't smile back. He doesn't deserve it.* 'You said there were three reasons why I should stay.'

'Yes.' He patted the sofa again. 'Won't you sit down?'

'Depends on the three reasons.'

'Okay.' Shaun took a swift gulp of beer and twisted around so he was looking straight at Thea. 'The first is obvious. I love you.'

'Obvious? I would say that's some way off the mark.' Thea pushed her hands into her pockets.

'Fair enough, but I do.'

Resisting the urge to tell him she loved him too, Thea asked, 'Second reason?'

'Because I am sure you'd like to hear what happened when I caught up with Julian after hearing the recording.'

Thea's eyebrows rose. 'You met Julian again? Ajay said you'd gone straight to the television studios. I assumed it was to play the board the recording.'

'I did. But not to play the recording. I didn't want to come across as a blackmailer.'

'So, what did you plan to do?'

'Tell them that a rumour had reached me about *Treasure Hunters* changing presenter, see if they were aware of that, and ask if it had implications for us as a series moving forward.'

'Sounds reasonable.'

'Unfortunately, I wasn't feeling reasonable. It's probably a good thing I didn't get to see the board. Not then anyway.'

Suddenly very tired, Thea sank onto the sofa, leaving a gap between her and Shaun. 'So you went to the television studios, but you *didn't* speak to the board?'

'I was in reception, queuing to see if the head guy had time to see me, when Julian came in looking flustered.' Shaun scowled. 'You should have seen his expression when he saw me.'

'I can imagine.' Thea gave a sad shake of her head. 'Did he know he'd been recorded? I didn't tell him.'

'No, but he was looking spooked. I guessed he was there to talk to the board too. In his case, for damage limitation purposes. After all, you'd just accused him of sexual harassment.'

'No I didn't. I could have, but he didn't do anything beyond making some presumptions about his own attractiveness and its power to help him get what he wants.'

'You accused him of acting as if he was in the 60s or 70s. That amounts to the same thing these days.'

'I suppose it does.' She fidgeted with her fingers. 'It was rather creepy. Julian in a bathrobe was not on my list of things to see before I die.'

'Shame you didn't video him as well as record him. More proof!'

'Proof? Hardly. I don't want to be thought of as someone who'd stoop to blackmail either. That's Julian's level, not ours.'

'You said ours.' Shaun looked hopeful.

'Figure of speech.' Thea kept her eyes focused on her hands. 'Talk to me, Shaun. Just tell me everything that has been going on. Then we'll see if there is any "ours" or not.'

'You remember when I was in Cornwall and you were jealous of Sophie?' Shaun sounded resigned as he rested back against the sofa.

Taken by surprise by his opening, Thea sat up straighter. 'I wasn't jealous. I was suspicious of her and baffled that you could be so naive as to not notice she fancied you.'

'Okay,' Shaun's shoulders sagged as he cradled his pint between his palms, 'well, you might not have been jealous of Sophie, but I *was* jealous of Julian. I didn't like him from the second I saw him, and all my instincts told me not to trust him.'

'But why be jealous of him? I told you repeatedly that I didn't like him.'

'That's where the being stupid bit came in.'

'Go on.'

'You remember the meal we had with Julian and the AA?'

'Engraved on my memory.'

'Looking back, that's when I started to lose my perspective. He was laying out a future where I wasn't part of *Landscape Treasures*, albeit simply because of a change in status for *Treasure Hunters*. I know I said to you that I was cool with moving on after the show, that I knew it couldn't last forever. No presenting job does. But, it wasn't you I was trying to convince. It was me.'

Thea closed her eyes as she listened to Shaun explain how he'd been seized by panic that the career he loved was about to be taken from him, and although he did have Mill Grange to work at, and there'd be a lifetime of talks and books to write ahead of him if he wanted it, he hadn't been ready to let go.

Then, with Julian giving Thea more and more screen time, combined with the fact she'd heard him talking on the phone about a change in personnel – and had kept that knowledge to herself – Shaun had become convinced that, not only was he for the chop, but that he'd be replaced by the woman he loved.

Shaun looked at her imploringly. 'I told myself I was paranoid. That you'd never do that to me and that Julian was just the producer. He doesn't get to make those sorts of decisions, so it was all fine.'

'But then you discovered Julian had invited me to a hotel to discuss my future on screen.' Thea groaned. 'I really am sorry I didn't tell you straightaway.'

'I know, and if I'd been thinking logically, I'd have accepted your reasons for not wanting to worry me or disturb our break at Mill Grange. But the insecurities about my future had taken hold, and common sense had flown out of the window. I couldn't stop wondering what I'd be without *Landscape Treasures*. I didn't want to be someone who resented my partner.' Shaun took another mouthful of beer. 'I can't say I've liked myself very much lately.'

Thea said nothing, afraid that if she spoke now it would break the spell and Shaun would clam up again.

'Ajay and Andy have given me a hell of an ear bashing.' He gave a puff of exasperation. She smiled, but still said nothing, hoping he'd get to the point

'Anyway, then I heard the recording. I couldn't believe it at first, and then I could. Only Julian could think such tactics were still acceptable.'

A silence fell over the room for a moment. Thea checked her watch. 'Are you going to tell me why you walked out on Mill Grange, what happened when you saw Julian when you got back to the Cotswolds before me, and, more to the point, what happened when you saw him at the telly studios? If not, I must get going. I promised Tina I'd have her home around ten. I'm already late.'

Shaun sat up. 'Sorry, yes. So, short version, I left Mill Grange in a huff because I was a stupid idiot with hurt pride and an imagined looming career crisis. When I got back to the Cotswolds prior to your arrival at the request of the Cotswold Archaeology folk – via a message from Julian, I went to consolidate the paperwork for the site in general, so it could be handed over to the locals for the remainder of the excavation.

'Julian only returned to the area a few hours before you did. He found me and the AA in the pub, and that's when he took me through to the function room and dropped the bombshell. He told me that he'd heard you and I were estranged and that he trusted I had no objection to him asking you out as well as offering you my job.'

'He said what?' Thea jumped off the sofa, about to demand to know how Shaun could even consider that she'd agree to go out with Julian, when a thought stopped her. 'Hang on, how did he know about our situation? I'm not even sure what it is.'

'Andy. He rang me to apologise afterwards. Apparently, Julian was going on about you being wasted on me, and he snapped, telling Julian he should be proud of himself for breaking us up.'

'Oh.' Thea's words came out as a whisper. 'You told Andy we'd split up.'

'Not in so many words, but I assumed you'd left me.'

'*You* left *me*!' Thea was furious. 'I gave you the chance to talk and you walked away.'

'I already said I was an idiot for doing that!'

'This is ridiculous. We're going around in circles. Again!' Thea thumped back onto the sofa. 'So, Julian had just told you he wanted to ask me out when you found me in the pub with the AA. We did our onscreen bit, and then you heard the recordings I'd taken of Julian being creepy. So, now skip to the bit where you disappear without a word, again, and go to the television studio.'

Draining his pint, Shaun grunted. 'I didn't go straight to Bristol. I knew I wasn't thinking straight, so I decided to use my common sense. I waited, booked into a pub in Cirencester for a few nights to cool off and sort a few final things out with the folks in the museum about the mosaic. It was a few days later that I went to Bristol and spoke to Julian.'

'But not the board?'

'No. I might still do that though.'

'What did Julian say?'

'You should have seen his face when he realised I had a recording of your conversation. I told him that, unless he told me exactly what was going on, I would take it to the board.'

'Did he tell you?'

'Eventually.' Shaun gave Thea a hopeful half smile. 'We were both wrong. Julian never had any intention of replacing me on *Landscape Treasures*.'

'He hadn't?' Thea leaned nearer to Shaun. 'But everything he said was—'

'Intended to undermine us.'

'It worked.' Thea's forehead crinkled into wrinkles.

'Hopefully not irrevocably.'

'What *was* he planning then?'

'Julian Blackwood is – or will be if I don't expose him – the producer of the new look *Treasure Hunters*. It was *that* show he had you in the frame to present.'

Fifty-six

Friday May 22nd

Having abandoned her no alcohol policy in light of what she'd just learned, Thea drank a glass of Pinot with rather more speed than was wise.

Treasure Hunters? She could see why Julian was keen to become their producer. They were in the process of moving from being a second-rate series to an up and coming show. He'd relish the challenge of trying to make more popular than *Landscape Treasures*. But why try and destroy her and Shaun's happiness in the process?

Lost in their own thoughts, not knowing what to say to each other, Shaun and Thea sat either end of a sofa, coming to terms with how they'd both been played.

'The thing is,' Thea said, suddenly awkward, 'Julian didn't do that much damage to us at all. We did it to ourselves.'

Shaun knew she was right. 'He enjoyed watching us unravel. Or, hearing about it at least. During that bit on the recording where he said he'd almost broken us, his voice oozed triumph.' Swirling whiskey around in his glass, having decided he needed something stronger than beer, Shaun added, 'Would be good wouldn't it, from a publicity point of view, to have two rival shows hosted by real life rivals. Real life exes.'

'We wouldn't be rivals. Even if we aren't together, that wouldn't happen.'

'I know that, but Julian thinks as if he's living in a soap opera.' Shaun took another sip of the amber liquid circling his glass. 'His mind works like a tabloid newspaper. I'd put money on him already having *The Sun* on standby, with headlines all typed up and ready to go. "Treasure Trowels Drawn at Dawn", or something equally tacky.'

Thea shivered at the thought. 'At least we've deprived him of that. I made it very clear I had no interest in working with him on any level. And as for anything else. Ug! No thank you!'

'At least we know he's leaving *Landscape Treasures*.'

'Is he? That's fantastic!'

Relieved to see a genuine smile on Thea's lips, Shaun nodded. 'Assuming we're re-commissioned for a new series, it'll be under another new producer.'

'They can't be worse than Julian.' Thea peered into her wine glass, the weight of what hadn't yet been said hanging over her. 'Do Ajay and Andy know about Julian and *Treasure Hunters*?'

'Not yet. I wanted to talk to you first.'

'Thanks.' Thea drained her glass and looked at the time. It was almost midnight. 'Been the bane of our lives hasn't it, *Treasure Hunters*? What with Sophie messing with them to try and keep *Landscape Treasures*, or you, rather, in Cornwall last autumn, and now this.'

Shaun sighed. 'They're a good team, or they were. Goodness knows what it'll be like once Julian has finished with them.'

'Well, we know it'll be a female presenter under thirty-five, probably blonde.'

Shaun snorted. 'Maybe we should call all the female archaeologists we know and warn them!'

'Not a bad plan.' Thea looked back at the orange juice cartons. 'I have to go. In a few minutes it'll be our best friend's wedding day. I ought to be at the house in case Tina's having last minute jitters.'

Shaun's expression was sad but accepting. 'Do you think she'll be in a panic?'

'Honestly, no. Tina has been amazingly calm since her wedding party stopped running away from each other and generally acting like children.'

'Point taken. I'm sorry I went away.' Not giving Thea time to respond, Shaun got to his feet. 'Would you like me to walk you home?'

'Surely you're going that way anyway?'

'I've got a room here.' Shaun waved a hand towards the door to the bar. 'I wasn't sure, you know, about us... It didn't feel right to sleep at Mill Grange.'

'Oh.' Not sure if she was disappointed or relieved, Thea headed to the door. 'I'll be fine walking up on my own. This is Upwich not London.'

Shaun let her get as far as the door. 'Actually, if you wouldn't mind the company, I think I'll come with you anyway.'

'There's no need. Really.'

'There's every need.' Shaun gave her a rueful look. 'Three reasons, remember? Number one, even if things have been odd lately, I still love you. Two, because you needed to know what Julian was planning and then there's number three.'

'And number three is?' Thea's heart beat faster as she hovered by the door, uncertain if she should hug him or hold back.

'Three is obvious! I've been an idiot, and I intend to try, somehow, to make it up to you.' He moved to the door, pushing it open for them both. 'And I shall start by acting like an old-fashioned gent, and see you safely home.'

Mabel gave a satisfied nod as she watched from her cottage's bedroom window. Shaun and Thea may not be walking arm in arm as they made their way from the pub to the manor, but nor were they arguing.

Reassured her suggestion that Shaun talk to Sybil about ways to get Thea on her own had worked, she changed for bed. The sound of Bert's snoring, rather more breathless than it used to be, echoed around the room.

Brushing her hands down her full-length night shirt, Mabel ran an approving eye over Bert's suit and her own wedding outfit. 'Mother and father of the bride.' A single tear suddenly trickled down her wrinkled face. 'Sam, Tina, I'm not sure you'll ever truly understand how much this means to us.'

Tom had been keeping a vigil at the attic window. 'It's alright, Thea's back. Shaun's just walking her up the drive.'

'They're together?' Helen felt a rush of relief. 'Thank goodness for that!'

'Not sure *together* is the word, but they're talking at least.'

'No kiss on the doorstep then? He hasn't come in with her?' Helen's newly discovered romantic streak was disappointed.

'Hang on.' Tom craned forward to try and see the door below him. 'Nope. Shaun's heading back to the pub, so presumably Thea is now climbing the stairs this way.' Tom turned to look at Helen. 'Okay if I stop spying on our friends now?'

'It's not spying if we're worried about them.'

Tom laughed. 'I'll remember to tell the lads that on our next forces reunion. They'll love that.'

Helen stuck her tongue out at him. 'Alright. You know what I mean though.'

'I do.' Tom slid back into bed. 'But if you're expecting them to turn up tomorrow all lovey-dovey, then I fear you're going to be disappointed.'

Sam had seen Thea and Shaun walk up the drive together. As he watched Shaun head off down the driveway again, he almost got up from where he was sat, on the picnic bench near the dig site, to see how his friend was, but something stopped him.

There had been no raised voices. No body language that suggested a row. But nor had there been any form of good night kiss or hug.

'It's enough for now though.' Sam gazed across the garden and into the woods. 'Hopefully, if they stay here a while, they'll heal. This place is good at healing people.'

Getting up, he readied himself to walk through the kitchen door, towards his last night's sleep as a single man.

Tina heard the click of heeled boots on the stairs and immediately got out of bed. She paused by the bedroom door and listened. One pair of feet was ascending the staircase, not two. She pushed opened her door and poked her head out. 'Thea?'

'Tina?' Thea started in the quiet. 'What are you doing up? You should be resting before tomorrow.'

'Too excited to sleep. Anyway,' Tina tilted her head as she regarded her friend, 'I wanted to see how you were. How did it go with Shaun?'

'Sybil told you about setting me up then?'

'Apparently Shaun badly wanted to talk to you.' Tina looked sheepish. 'Did it work?'

Too tired to go through it all again, Thea simply said, 'I know what Julian was up to. Shaun's job is safe. I was never in the frame for it. Beyond that, Shaun and I are friends again.'

'Just friends?'

'He told me he loved me and that he'd been an idiot. Apparently, he wants to make it up to me.' Thea gave a brave smile. 'Now, stop worrying about me and Shaun. In a few hours you, Miss Tina Martin, will become Mrs Tina Philips, daughter-in-law to the earl of Malvern no less!'

Fifty-seven

Saturday May 23rd

Tom checked his mobile. The wedding was in two hours and Sue still hadn't arrived. He looked at his outfit for the day, hung on the back of the bedroom door. He didn't dare put it on until the last minute in case he was needed to do something outside or in the kitchen. Anyway, he'd imagined helping Dylan and Bert into their suits before putting on his own.

'Where the hell are you?' He checked the time again. He was due to be at the cottage to help Bert get ready in thirty minutes. 'You promised! You *promised* not to be late today.'

Calling Sue's mobile again, hoping the reason she didn't answer was because she was driving, Tom ran outside. There was no sign of them.

What if they've had an accident?

He squashed the thought flat. This was Sue scoring points in whatever weird game was going on in her head this time.

Turning round, Tom headed to the marquee where he knew he'd find Sam and Shaun helping Sybil lay out plates and cutlery for the late lunch come afternoon tea style reception. He'd only gone two paces when the sound of a car pulling in behind him sent a mutter of relief shooting from his lips. Relief that was extinguished when he saw Sam's parents' Bentley rather than Sue's Mini.

Bea rolled down the window as they came level with the usher. 'Tom, how wonderful. A sunny day for it too. Where will we find Tina and Sam?'

'Tina's inside getting ready with Thea and Helen. They're using the bedroom opposite the main guest suite. Sam's in the back garden sorting cake forks.'

Charles laughed. 'Nothing more unnecessary than a groom in the final hours before his wedding. Might as well put the chap to use!'

'I'll see you at the house.' Tom gestured ahead. 'Then, as usher of this parish, I'll show you to your room.'

'Shouldn't you be flapping just a little bit?'

Helen marvelled as a serene Tina sat in the middle of the bedroom, a chaos of makeup, hairbrushes, lingerie and packets of biscuits all around her.

'No need. Sam's here, the dress is ready and all my friends are on hand to help share our day. What is there to worry about?'

Thea laughed as she lounged in the doorway. 'You have to be the most relaxed bride in history. I was convinced you'd be anxious this morning.'

'Nothing to be anxious about,' Tina picked up the nearest hairbrush, 'although if I don't start getting ready Mabel will tell me off. The wedding day list on her clipboard states I should be having my hair done at ten and it's almost five past. We'll get told off if we are behind schedule!'

'This is the bit where I wish you'd arranged a professional hairdresser.' Thea took the hairbrush from Tina. 'What if I mess it up?'

'You won't!'

As Tina brushed biscuit crumbs off her baggy shirt and moved to the chair in front of the dressing table and mirror, Helen peered out of the window. 'Sam's folks are here. Tom's with them'

'Excellent!' Tina beamed. 'Is that everyone present and correct then?'

'I think so.' Helen headed to the door. 'Sue said she'd deliver Dylan at nine-thirty sharp. Tom planned to take him to Bert's until we were ready for him, so I assume he's there. I'll go and fetch Bea. She's bound to want to come up.'

The moment she saw Tom, Helen knew something was wrong. His smile was in place, he was saying all the right things to Sam and his parents as they chatted by the front door, yet she wasn't fooled.

Greeting Bea, Helen offered to help take her vanity case and wedding outfit, while Tom took Charles's suit, so Sam could take his parents to see how the walled garden had been prepared for the ceremony.

As soon as they were out of earshot, Helen asked, 'What's wrong?'

'Sue hasn't arrived with Dylan.'

'What!?' Helen looked over her shoulder, as if she expected to see Dylan running towards her. 'Are you sure?'

'Of course I'm sure!'

'Sorry, it was a silly question.' Helen frowned. 'Does Sam know?'

'No. I didn't want to worry him.'

'I assumed he was already with Bert.'

'He ought to be.'

'We'll have to tell the others soon.' Panic tugged at Helen. 'He was so excited about being in charge of the rings.'

'I'll kill Sue when they get here.'

Helen checked her watch. 'I'm supposed to be getting changed. What shall we do? Do I tell Tina?'

Tom bit his lip. 'Not until you have to. If Sue hasn't turned up by eleven, I'll tell Sam.'

Helen read her watch again. 'We could go and fetch Dylan. If we drove to Tiverton and back non-stop, we could get him and be back in time.'

Tom was already moving towards his car, when he stopped suddenly. 'I could. Not you. If I'm delayed, the wedding can still start without me, but Tina needs you. She'll already be wondering why you aren't upstairs.' He lifted up Charles suit. 'Can you manage to carry this as well?'

'Yes, but...' Helen her arms laden, stuttered as she spoke the fear that had struck her. 'What if... what if they aren't there?'

'Not in Tiverton? Where else would... oh. No, no, no... She wouldn't. Not even Sue would...'

Helen watched the colour drain from Tom's face.

'If she has taken him to Australia, now, without saying goodbye, I'll...'

Her hands full, Helen was helpless to follow him as Tom,

running at full pelt, disappeared around the corner of the house.

'Have you spoken to Shaun today?'

Tina relaxed back as Thea smoothed the brush through her long blonde hair while the curling tongs next to her sent out faint wafts of hot steam.

'No, but I know he's around. Mabel's ticked his arrival off on her list.'

Tina watched Thea's reflection in the mirror. 'Are you alright?'

'I am actually. I slept well for the first time in ages, although only briefly as Mabel's schedule had me up at seven. Now I've heard what Shaun had to say, it's like I've stopped waiting for the axe to fall.'

'He said he loves you.' Tina looked at Thea more closely. 'Do you still love him?'

'Yes, but...'

'But?'

'He thought me capable of stealing his job and didn't believe me when I told him otherwise. Things won't be the same now.'

'I am sure they won't. But,' Tina ventured, 'perhaps, just maybe, they could be better.'

Mabel, clipboard to hand, waved as Helen, her arms full of Bea and Charles's wedding clothes, walked gingerly along the corridor to the stairs, afraid of dropping or creasing the garments.

'Is that everyone here then?'

Not wanting to panic Mabel, Helen mentally crossed her fingers. 'As far as I know. Sam is showing his parents the garden and I'm off to change.'

'Excellent.' Mabel gestured to her tightly tided apron. 'I'll just check the kitchen is all set for Sybil to find anything she needs, should she need it. Then I'll lose this and get ready myself.'

Giving Mabel what she hoped was a reassuring look, Helen started to move faster before her fingers cramped under the weight of too many coat hangers. Her pulse thudded in her chest as she took each stair. *I ought to get ready, but if Tom needs me, then...*

Helen's thoughts were cut dead by the sight of Tina coming out of the bedroom. Her hair was curled in relaxed ringlets around her shoulders, and her eyes shone with happiness.

'Just nipping to the loo before I tackle the makeup.' She paused. 'You okay, Helen?'

'Yes. These are just heavy. You look fantastic.'

Tina laughed as she pulled at her old shirt. 'Maybe I'll get married in this. It's cosier than the dress. Dylan said it was silly dressing up and being uncomfortable. I'm wondering if he was right!'

As Tina disappeared into the bathroom, Helen all but ran into the guest suite and dropped the outfits and vanity bag on the bed.

She's going to be so disappointed if Dylan can't come. Helen shivered. The thought that she might not see the lad in his little suit clawed at her heart. But not as much as the thought that neither she, nor Tom, might get to see Dylan without flying to the other side of the world.

Fifty-eight

Saturday May 23rd

'**W**ow!'
Bea voiced her approval as Helen and Thea lined up to have their bodice laces pulled in as tight as they could go.

'You look incredible!' Sam's mum looked effortlessly immaculate in a flowing silk dress dotted with a rainbow of flowers. 'Shaun and Tom are lucky boys.'

As Tina's future mother-in-law left to check on the bride in the next room, Thea let out an exhalation of breath.

Helen picked up a hairbrush and pointlessly swept it through her bouncing curls. 'Are you having trouble breathing in you dress, or was it the "lucky boys" comment that has you sighing?'

'A little of both.' Thea adjusted her cleavage with an unladylike prod. 'Although I feel a bit less at sea since I spoke to Shaun, I can't help thinking that only a little while ago we were a couple who were planning to walk down the aisle together as best man and bridesmaid. I even wondered if, maybe, one day... And now...' She shrugged. 'Well, at least we're friends.'

'More than friends, surely?' Helen pushed back a strand of hair that had fallen across her eyes.

Determined not to let a wave of uncertainty claim her, Thea gave her friend a bracing smile. 'It'll work out if it's supposed to. How about you? Your smile's looking a bit forced too. You and Tom okay?'

'Very okay. It's Dylan.' Helen moved to the door and closed it behind her, suddenly desperate to share her concerns. 'He isn't here.'

'What?'

'Sue never turned up. Tom's gone to fetch him.'

'Gone to Tiverton? But the wedding's in an hour.' Thea went pale as she sat on the side of the bed, then instantly got up again. 'Damn, these are difficult to sit in.'

'I wish he hadn't gone.' Helen headed to the window, wishing she could see Tom and Dylan running across the lawn. 'Tom could drive past Sue and not notice, or they might not even be there because...' Helen's voice broke, her words sticking in her throat.

Thea's face clouded as her friend pushed a tear away, smudging the mascara they'd only just applied. 'Helen?'

Helen dabbed at her eyes with a tissue. 'I promised I wouldn't say. Tom's so cut up about it, although he's pretending he isn't. Dylan doesn't even know yet.'

'Doesn't know what?'

'Sue has a new partner. They're moving to Australia.'

'Oh my God!' Thea stared at her friend in horror. 'Poor Tom.' Speechless for a moment, Thea whispered, 'Bert and Mabel will be devastated.'

'There's a lot of that going on.'

'I'm so sorry, Helen.' Thea glanced at her watch. 'Sue didn't say they were leaving today did she?'

'She said September. But...'

'Right.' Thea sucked her lip, feeling the lipstick she'd applied dissolving. 'Won't they need visas and stuff? Have they got those sorted?'

Helen spun round, 'No. No they haven't, so they can't have just gone. I'm so silly. I just panicked, I... So where *are* they?'

Thea checked the time. 'Well, whatever Sue's doing, we have an hour before the ceremony, and half an hour before pre-wedding photographs outside.'

Helen checked her phone. There were no messages. 'Do we tell Tina and Sam that their ring bearer and possibly their usher might not be coming?'

'I don't know.' Thea lifted her lipstick off the side. 'But I do know we don't have long to get every trace of worry off our faces, retouch our damaged makeup, and get outside.'

Having shown both the photographer and the registrar the way to the walled garden, Mabel stood with Sybil at the entrance to the reception marquee. The women nodded in mutual satisfaction. A few of the village guests had arrived, and were milling around the grounds, muttering murmurs of appreciation.

The glasses, some prefilled with Bucks Fizz, champagne or orange juice sat on a table ready for the guests to sip pre and post ceremony, shone in the late morning sunshine. Two large jugs of ice water waited next to a huge variety of platters, laden with scones, tucked under cotton clothes, ready to be revealed once the guests were seated at the reception.

'There are forty tubs of clotted cream in the fridge, and glass bowls of jam are waiting on trays in the kitchen.' Sybil spoke with the confidence of a good job already well done. 'As soon as they say "I do", I'll slip away and get everything uncovered.'

Mabel held up her clipboard. Only three boxes were left to tick. 'What time are your waitresses getting here to help?'

'Twelve.' Sybil held up a teaspoon to make sure it was polished to perfection. 'They are going to dish out the butter. Not something I want to do yet, as this sunshine will melt it too fast.'

Placing a tick next to 'Food and Drink', Mabel smiled. 'Just Bert to arrive with Dylan, and the men and bridesmaid's pre-wedding photographs to do, and we're almost there.' She handed the clipboard to Sybil. 'I'm trusting you with this now. I need to fetch Tina.'

'Shouldn't Bert do that?' Sybil took the clipboard, understanding the trust involved and the seriousness with which Mabel took such things.

'Normally yes, but we agreed there were too many stairs for him at the moment. His breath still isn't quite right. He'll meet Tina in the drawing room, before we kick off.'

As Mabel moved towards the manor, Sybil called out, 'I didn't say, you look amazing Mabel. The Queen herself would envy that purple.'

★

Lord Malvern stood next to his son, a look of pride on his face that Sam had never dreamed he'd see directed at him.

'Good choice, son.' Charles straightened his own jacket as Sam brushed down his. 'Tina will be as proud of you, as are your mother and I.'

'Thank you.' Sam stared in the mirror. He'd almost cut off his ponytail as an extra wedding present for Tina, but at the last minute, he'd simply tucked it inside his collar.

'Almost time to go over the top.' Folding his handkerchief into his top pocket, Charles headed to the door. 'I promised your mother I'd make sure Mr Hastings was alright. Check his speech over and that sort of thing.'

'You can call him Bert, Father, and don't worry, he won't say anything inappropriate. Mabel would kill him if he did, plus Dylan will be with him, so it'll be family friendly.'

'And the rings are safe?'

'Shaun has them. He'll pass them to Dylan, who will pass them to me on the registrar's say so.'

'All systems go then.' Charles tugged his pocket watch from his waistcoat pocket. 'By my reckoning, we should be getting outside. Pre wedding photographs with the best man, usher and pageboy are in ten minutes.'

Tina lifted the photograph of her parents off the table by the bed and held it to her chest. Her friends were wonderful, but that didn't mean she didn't wish life had been different. One twist of fate, due to one careless driver, and suddenly she'd had no parents.

'I think you'd like Sam.' She spoke to her mum and dad,

smoothing a finger around their glass covered faces. 'He'd have liked you too.'

As the door behind her opened, Tina placed the photograph on the dressing table.

Mabel followed the direction of Tina's gaze. 'They look fine people.'

'They were.' Tina didn't look round. 'I know it's daft, but I wanted them with me as I got ready, so I brought the picture through from my room.'

'Not daft at all. Why don't we take them with us?' Mabel opened her palatial handbag. 'They could watch from the signing table. There's plenty of time for me to get their frame polished and in place before the wedding starts.'

Without waiting for a debate, Mabel popped the photograph in her bag. 'Now then. Let's have a look at you.'

Shaun saw his mobile light up a second before it buzzed into life.

'Tom? You okay? Need help with getting Bert ready? I was just going to call, you've been…'

Thirty seconds later, Shaun, dragging his suit jacket over his back, making sure the wedding rings were safely stowed in his inside pocket, picked up his car keys and dashed down the backstairs to the driveway.

Stopping to text Sam to say he was off to provide an extra pair of hands at Bert's, and that they may be a touch behind schedule, but not to worry, Shaun drove to Upwich as fast as the speed limit and narrow lanes would allow.

Less than ten minutes later, he was with an anxious looking Bert, who was stood on the doorstep.

'Shaun? Aren't you supposed to be doing photos with Sam?' Bert gave a hoarse cough. Shaking it off, he asked, 'Where's Tom and young Dylan?'

'Now that, Bert, is the question.'

Fifty-nine

Saturday May 23rd

Thea and Helen stood back to back, their widest smiles on their faces, as the photographer took a picture of them beneath the apple tree.

As blossom fell around them like tiny dry snowflakes, Helen tried to concentrate on holding her posy of flowers and looking happy, rather than worrying that there was no sign of Tom or Dylan. Meanwhile, Thea, also worrying about Tom and Dylan, was trying not to wonder if Shaun would want to expand on the conversation they'd had the previous evening, or if, after a night's sleep, he'd decided enough was enough, and they'd be better off as friends.

When the photographer had finally finished with them, both bridesmaids made a dive for the mobile phones they'd hidden under the table Mabel had insisted they set up for the empty glasses people were bound to accidentally carry through from the main garden to the walled one.

'Anything?' Thea asked as Helen studied her screen.

'Nothing.' Helen looked across to where Sam and his parents were chatting by the chicken coop. 'I'm going to have to tell Sam, aren't I?'

'Maybe.' Thea was about to put her phone down, when a text vibrated in her hand. 'It's Shaun.'

'You okay?' Helen saw her friend's eyes cloud for a split second, before she let out a deep breath.

'Shaun's with Bert, apparently he nodded off and there'll be a short delay. They'll be here as soon as possible.'

'Oh thank goodness!' Helen looked anxiously towards the house. 'That gives Tom at least another fifteen minutes to get here.'

'He might be with Bert.'

Helen shook her head. 'Shaun would have said.'

Thea spotted Mabel coming through the gate to the garden. 'We'd better go and tell her. I bet she's already twitching that the best man photos haven't started yet.'

'Thanks for doing that, Bert.'

'Not at all.' Bert held out his right arm so Shaun could help him into his jacket. 'Mabel will easily believe I dropped off. Better she gives me an earful later than stresses now and worries Sam and Tina.'

Shaun looked at his phone. There was still nothing new from Tom. 'Well, if we dawdle for another ten minutes, and then drive over to the house, we should buy Tom a bit more time.'

A shadow cast over Bert's face. 'I hope Dylan's alright.'

*

Mabel was beginning to run out of things to say as the minutes ticked by on the drawing room clock, when Thea put her head around the door.

'Helen just had a text from Tom, they got a bit delayed, but they're on their way.'

Tina puffed out an exhalation of air. 'I was getting worried. I mean, I know weddings often run late, but I feel like I've been pacing in here for hours.'

'I know, I'm sorry.' Thea pulled a face. 'Why don't you sit down?'

'I don't want to crease my dress before the ceremony.' Tina stroked her skirt. 'Is that silly?'

'Not at all.' Thea smiled, as a memory of pre-Mill Grange Tina, who'd loved dressing up in pretty clothes, popped through her mind. 'Fear not though, everyone is happy out there. The drink is flowing, although Sybil is making sure the alcohol consumption is low! And better still, you have a visitor.'

Thea opened the door and Bert came in.

With a nod to Thea, Mabel gave her husband her seal of approval. 'Very smart, my boy, very smart indeed. We'll be outside waiting. As soon as Dylan is here, we'll begin.'

As the door shut behind his wife, Bert took a step forward and held out both his hands for Tina to take. 'Beautiful. Just beautiful. No other word will do.'

Suddenly choked, Bert, a glaze of tears over his eyes, held Tina's palms tightly. Her fitting ecru dress flattered her slim figure, the bodice neatly tied, allowing her just enough room to breathe. A slim panel of lace along the top of the bodice was twinned with the lace detail in the short veil that sat, pushed back, over her golden ringlets.

'I know I'm not your father, but I do know that if he were here, he'd be as bowled over as I am. This is an honour and a privilege.'

'Thank you.' Tina's eyes shone with gratitude. 'Not just for this, but for always being there for me and Sam. Really, Bert, I don't know what we'd do without you.'

'You'd muddle along just fine!'

Throwing caution to the wind, and risking a crease or two, Tina gave Bert a big hug. 'Have you seen Sam? Is he okay?'

'He's just fine. With his parents at the moment. That's a good family you're marrying into.'

Tina laughed. 'Can't get much better than an earl and countess.'

Bert chuckled, 'Oh that's just window dressing lass. I meant, they are nice people. Now then,' he stretched his arms out, 'let me sit down and look at you properly until that young Dylan arrives to look after both of us.'

Tom spotted Sue's Mini in a layby ten miles out of Upwich. He could see Sue, sat by herself, on the bonnet of the car. She was playing with a mobile phone in her hand. He couldn't see Dylan.

Relief sent sweat trickling down his back. They must have broken down. Sue can't have a phone signal. It's okay. Dylan is okay.

Pulling into the small space left, Tom checked his watch. It was a quarter to twelve. Whatever he did, there was no way he'd be back before the wedding started.

'Tom.' Sue sounded resigned.

'Where's Dylan? Has the car broken down?'

'Asleep in the back.' She tilted her head to the car behind her. 'And no, we haven't broken down.'

'Then what on earth…?' Tom reined in his temper. 'Sue, I have to take Dylan to get ready. He's the ring bearer! The wedding is either going to run late or he'll miss out on his big moment. All because of you!'

Sue looked up at Tom, meeting his eyes for the first time. 'I needed to think, so I went for a drive. Dylan fell asleep.'

'A drive? Sue, you're impossible! Tina and Sam are getting married at twelve! Dylan is important to the ceremony. They'll want him in the pre-wedding photographs.'

Sue looked at her watch. 'Sorry. Lost track of time. I was thinking.'

'Thinking?' Not sure what to say, and knowing there was no time for a row, Tom bit his lip. 'Is it okay if I take Dylan then?'

'What?'

Tom stared at Sue. 'Is it alright if I take Dylan to the manor? I'm not having you turn round and accuse me of kidnapping him or something!'

Now Tom looked closely, he could see that Sue had been crying. He wondered if she'd slept. 'Are you alright?' He shifted awkwardly. 'Look, if you wanted to come too, I'm sure Tina and Sam wouldn't mind. As long as we don't argue at their wedding.'

'Thanks, but I'll pass.' She paused as she unlocked the car. 'I'd like a photograph though, if that's okay. One of Dylan in his suit.'

'I've already pre-ordered you one.'

'Oh.' Sue seemed to rally as she opened the back of the

car and smoothed her sleeping son's fringe. 'I'll collect him at four o'clock. On the dot.'

'On the dot? Really? Does that mean Dylan and I can look forward to an hour or two sitting in the driveway waiting for you, or does it mean four o'clock?'

'Don't be petty.'

Biting his lip, Tom went to the Mini and opened the door. Dylan was sound asleep in his car seat, oblivious to his father's arrival or his location. 'Right. Four o'clock.'

'Thank you.' Sue pushed her hair from her eyes. 'I'll get his bag. He wanted to bring his new dinosaur toy to show Helen. Harriet gave it to him.'

Tom's eyebrows rose in wary surprise. 'Did Dylan tell you about Helen?'

'I'd worked it out.'

'Oh.' Tom watched Dylan's chest rise and fall gently in his sleep. 'I was going to tell you about us, but after your news I—'

'Neither of us have been exactly forthcoming lately. Look,' Sue passed Tom Dylan's rucksack, 'at four, do you think you'll have time to talk? There's so much to sort out.'

'I'm not sure.' Tom unclipped Dylan from his seat, lifting his sleeping form out of the Mini. 'If Sam and Tina don't need me, maybe.'

'Thanks.'

'Right.' Tom was suddenly worried about Sue, a sensation that was entirely new to him. 'You are okay, aren't you?'

'Not really.' Sue glanced at her watch. 'Look, could I come after all? Do you think anyone would mind?'

An image of Helen flashed through his mind. 'If you

promise – and I mean promise – to keep a civil tongue in your head.'

'I just want to see Dylan do his thing. Then maybe I'll slope off to that café we went to.'

'Get in, we'll talk as we drive.'

Two minutes later, driving much faster than he normally would, Tom said, 'Sybil's Tea Rooms will be closed. Everyone's at the wedding.'

'The whole village?'

'Yes. Sam and Tina are popular.' Tom sighed. 'They are also extremely kind, and I have no doubt they'll make room for you. It will mean you meeting Helen, are you up to that today? You look like you haven't slept.'

'I haven't.'

Tom glanced in the rear-view mirror. Dylan, despite moving from car to car, was still asleep. 'Sue, come on, tell me what's wrong.'

'I…'

Tom's voice became gentle. 'Are you ill? Are your parents alright?'

Sue gave an overtired giggle. 'I'm fine health wise, although I can see why guilt might kill people.'

'Guilt?' Tom was puzzled. 'Look Sue, I am interested and despite everything I do care. If I can help I will, but do you think you could do me a favour before I listen to you?'

'Sure.'

'Can you call Shaun? His number is open on my phone. Tell him that I am half an hour away, and that if they want to go ahead with the wedding we'll understand.'

★

Shaun ran across the gravel drive to where Thea and Helen were talking to Mabel and Sybil.

'What is it?' Thea's eyes rested on the phone in Shaun's hand. 'Tom?'

'Yes.' He looked at Helen. 'Well, sort of. I think it was Sue.'

Mabel's eyes narrowed. 'The woman who was so rude in your tearoom, Sybil.'

'The one who doesn't eat scones.' Sybil's forehead creased. 'Are Tom and Dylan alright? I've got Dylan a strawberry milkshake to try today.'

'All she said was that they are half an hour away, that she's very sorry for the delay, that it is all her fault, and that Tom said to go ahead without them if we like, but they are coming.'

'They?' Helen looked at Thea. 'They? As in, Tom and Dylan are coming *with* Sue?'

Sixty

Bert put out an arm for Tina to take. 'Best foot forward?'
'It's time?'

'Mabel just gave me a thumbs up through the window, so it's time.'

Looping her arm through Bert's, Tina confessed, 'I've got a bit nervous.'

'It's all the waiting, it can do that.' Bert patted her hand. 'You'll be fine, and in thirty minutes you'll be Mrs Tina Philips.'

'And in forty minutes I'll be eating a scone. I'm starving!' Tina patted her dress. 'I know Mabel offered us some food, but I didn't dare eat in case I spilt something down my front.'

Bert chuckled. 'I promise you, lass, the minute you get to the head of the aisle, the time will pass in seconds, and you'll have a plate full of jam and cream before you know it.'

449

Mabel walked with determined purpose towards the walled garden. Pushing through the gate she made a beeline for the marquee. Then, with slightly more force than necessary, banged her reclaimed clipboard against one of its metal struts. 'Ladies and gentleman!'

Everyone swung round to face her.

'Please take your places. The bride is on her way!'

As Mabel tucked her bag under her chair at the front of the makeshift aisle, her eyes met Bea's. Exchanging an emotional nod, as one they turned to Sam, who with Shaun and Dylan by his side, moved to stand before the registrar.

Helen and Thea lightly hugged Tina and Bert as they arrived at their side.

'Ready girls?' Bert adjusted his jacket, making the medals Sam had insisted he place over his breast pocket jangle.

'Ready.' Tina beamed.

'Good stuff.' He winked. 'Don't forget to say hello to the chickens as you go past, or Gertrude will sulk.'

Giggling as they went, Tina took her posy of freshly picked garden flowers from Thea, and peered ahead through the garden. Apple blossom and magnolia petals fluttered in the breeze as they walked; her best friends behind her, a man she respected more than any other to her side, and the man she loved ahead of her.

As they passed the chickens and reached the head of the aisle that had been made beneath the marquee, Tina's breath caught in her throat and her pace slowed. She wasn't sure if she'd made a noise or not, but Helen had made one behind her.

There was no doubt that Tom looked handsome in his army dress uniform, and judging by the expression on his face as he watched their approach, he was equally approving of Helen's outfit. But it was Sam who took Tina's breath away. He'd told her he'd ordered a suit. She wondered what he'd put himself through before he'd been able to put it on. She wasn't sure how she wasn't crying.

Speaking so only Tina could hear as they moved forward, Bert tapped his medals. 'Sam asked me to wear these on my new suit. He said it was time we embraced our past, rather than being ashamed of it.' The old man paused, emotion heavy in his voice. 'He's healing, and that's largely thanks to you.'

'And you.' Tina wanted to say more, but they'd reached the head of the aisle and suddenly she was standing next to her future husband and was being eased from Bert's gentle care.

Sam had seen Tina falter when she saw his outfit, and knew in that moment it had been the right thing to wear. His parents and Bert had reassured him that it was, but that hadn't stopped Sam ordering a standard morning suit as well in case his nerve went, or he had a panic attack as he'd put the uniform on.

As he watched her approach, his pulse beating fast, Sam marvelled that the incredible woman walking in his direction, a huge smile on her face, was actually going to marry *him*. Only a year ago his claustrophobia had been so bad he couldn't enter the house he now owned. Tina had sacrificed her own comfort and lived in a tent in the garden with him, even though she was often freezing – and now she was going to be his wife.

As Shaun nudged his arm, indicating he should step forward to greet Bert and Tina, Sam felt as if he truly was the luckiest man in the world.

Helen had told herself she would not try and spot Sue among the guests. Nor would she speculate about the reason for her presence and their lateness. *Look where that sort of over thinking got you last time.*

Now, however, as she gazed at Tom, his uniform making him look more gorgeous than ever, Helen found herself wondering if Sue was staring at him in the same way she was.

Thea had promised herself she wouldn't look at Shaun any more often than she did any other member of the wedding party. But as the registrar began to speak, and she witnessed a look of love pass between Tina and Sam, she couldn't help herself.

He looked great in a suit, and as he stood, Dylan's little hand in his, Thea's heart started to ache. *Not now! You've been so strong. Hang on!*

Wishing her bodice gave her room for a really deep breath, Thea gave an internal sigh. *Minerva, if ever I needed your help, now is the time.*

*

Glad he had Dylan to keep an eye on, Tom fought not to turn to look at Helen. *God she's magnificent in that dress.* He swallowed slowly as Sue's presence dampened his thoughts. He was still reeling from what she'd told him. The memory of her face as she explained what was wrong, made him reach out to Dylan and lay a hand on his shoulder.

As the registrar raised a finger in his direction, Shaun opened his palm to reveal two gold rings, which he passed to Dylan.

He could feel the congregation behind him mutter with pleasure as the little boy stepped forward and, with a toothy grin, held the first ring to Sam, who placed it on Tina's outstretched finger as they exchanged their vows.

As Dylan passed Tina the ring destined for Sam's finger, Shaun couldn't help himself. Peering over his shoulder, his eyes met Thea's as he mouthed, 'I'm sorry.'

'Did I do alright, Dad?' Dylan slipped his hand into his father's. 'I didn't drop the rings.'

'You were brilliant.' Tom launched Dylan up into his arms so he could see Sam and Tina, now man and wife, signing the register. 'Your mum, Helen and I are very proud of you.'

Dylan hugged his dad as he turned to Helen, who was

stood just behind him. 'I've got a new dinosaur. I've called him Harold.'

'An excellent name for a dinosaur.' Helen met Tom's eyes, mentally asking if he was alright.

'Harold's a Stegosaurus. They were herbivores.'

'Indeed they were.' Helen smiled. 'I look forward to meeting him.' She was about to tell Dylan how smart he looked, when she saw Tina and Sam turn for a photograph of them signing the registrar. 'They're nearly done. Ready to be in lots of photos, Dylan?'

'Do I have to?'

'Yes.' Tom and Helen spoke in unison, before Tom said, 'I tell you what, why not go and say hello to the chickens? You've done your bit for now. I'll fetch you when it's time to say cheese. Just no noise okay?'

As Dylan scooted off, Tom grabbed hold of Helen's hand. 'There's lots to tell you later, but for now, I have to say, you look incredibly sexy in that dress.'

Shaun stood next to Thea as they watched Sam and Tina pose for the traditional signing of the marriage certificate photograph. 'I meant it, I'm sorry.'

'Me too.' Thea kept looking at his friends. 'What do we do now though?'

Shaun gingerly reached out, offering her a palm. 'Maybe we could hold hands for a while?'

Thea's fingertips met his. 'A good place to start.'

*

The scones had all gone. Sybil had likened it to witnessing a flock of starving vultures hit a zebra carcass. The speeches, which had been heartfelt and mercifully short, were over and Tina was dying for the chance to relax her smile muscles. Holding Sam's hand as they moved around the marquee, chatting to their guests, she was relieved when Bea and Charles beckoned them to their table.

As he sat down, Tina muttered, 'Do you think anyone would notice if I kicked off my shoes? My feet are killing me.'

Bea laughed. 'Mine have been off for almost an hour!'

'Well done, Mum.' Sam sank down, keeping Tina's hand in his. 'Having a good day?'

'Wonderful!' Bea clapped. 'Great weather, lovely people, amazing food and we've seen our son marry a fabulous girl. What more could we ask for?'

Tina blushed her thanks as Charles raised his glass in their direction, before adding, 'And a fabulous location. We're sorry if we caused you some anxiety about the venue.'

'Forget it.' Sam waved the point away. 'You're here, and even the chickens got to watch.'

Bea smiled. 'The walled garden is beautiful.'

Tina rubbed her right foot as she said, 'It'll look even better later. We've rigged some fairy lights up over the remains of the greenhouse. When it's just us, family and close friends here for supper, then we'll light it up.'

'Talking of the greenhouse,' Charles exchanged a nod with his wife, 'brings us to the reason we beckoned you over. Your wedding gift. We want, if you'll allow us, to pay for the greenhouse to be restored.'

Sam's mouth fell open as his father continued.

'We're sorry we couldn't work out a way to get it done up as a surprise before the wedding. But we wondered if this might help out instead?'

Tina shuffled close to Sam as he opened the blue Basildon Bond envelope that Charles passed to them.

'That should cover it, son. If there's any left over, then it could go towards something else. Architect's plans for converting the mill into flats or something.'

'But, Dad...' Sam's eyes met his father's. They both knew he hadn't referred to his father as "dad" for a very long time. 'I mean, both of you, this is a fortune, we can't...'

As Tina saw the amount written on the cheque, her hand came to her mouth. 'We can't take that, it's too much, it's—'

'It's about what we paid to help Sam's brothers set up homes abroad and for the honeymoons we treated them to.' Bea took hold of Tina's hand. 'Anyway, you make my son happy, there's no price anyone can put on that.'

Sixty-one

Saturday May 23rd

'They look so happy.' Thea perched on the edge of the bench nearest the fortlet.

'They really do.' Shaun peered into the woodland before them. The new spring buds on the tree's branches were bursting into life. 'We were too, weren't we? Happy, I mean?'

'I thought so.' Thea undid the top lace of her bodice and gave a ragged breath. 'Just so you know, I'm not trying to seduce you, I just can't breathe.'

'Shame.' Shaun gave a weak smile. 'I wouldn't have resisted.'

Knowing she wouldn't stop him if he helped ease the pressure off her lungs a little more, Thea made herself focus. 'Why did you walk away when I apologised?'

'Stupid, plain, boring idiotic pride.' Shaun placed his palms on his knees and stood up, pacing in front of Thea and the bench. 'I was so busy feeling sorry for myself after thinking that you could keep anything from me, that I didn't listen – didn't want to hear the truth when I heard it,

I suppose. If I had a pound for every second I wish I'd got up and followed you into the manor to talk...'

'Does that make us equal then?' Thea allowed herself to face Shaun. 'I wish I'd told you about Julian's offer and the overheard pub conversation straight away, and you wish you'd spoken to me straight away once I'd issued one in a long line of ignored apologies.'

'Pretty much sums it up.' Shaun reached out a hand, relieved when Thea took it. 'When I finished the excavation in Cornwall in the autumn, when I was blind to Sophie's infatuation, I promised I'd never be so stupid again.'

'You did promise.'

'I broke the promise, didn't I?'

'Big time.' Thea shook her head. 'I never considered Julian's offer, you know. Not for a moment.'

Shaun took her other hand. 'If I'm honest, it wasn't that he was after you to work for him that got to me, it was the idea that I might be past it career-wise.'

'You're still good at your job.'

'And I love it.' He shrugged. 'I know it won't last forever, but if a new series is commissioned, I hope I'm part of it.'

'It will be, and you will be.' Thea freed a hand to wipe a stray hair from his forehead. 'Julian used our feelings to help his cause. A ploy that seriously backfired on him. We shouldn't let it ruin what we have.'

'I think this is the bit where I hold you tight and tell you I love you. You hug me back and say the same, then we both promise each other not to be so stupid ever again.'

'Okay.' Thea buried herself into Shaun's shoulder. 'That works for me.'

'Good, because your untethered bodice is doing things

to me that would mean I'd have to walk away at speed otherwise.'

'Shaun?' Thea wrapped her arms around his waist. 'Two things.'

'Tell me.'

'If anything like this happens again, we talk first, rather than act like children. Agreed?'

'Agreed.' Shaun inhaled the scent of Thea's hair. He'd begun to think he'd never relax against the gentle aroma of shea butter and coconut again. 'And second?'

'During the reception I took a leap of faith and booked two nights at that hotel in Stow-on-the-Wold on my phone. They only had a luxury suite with a king-sized bed left. I hope that's alright.'

Mabel sat next to Bert and placed her lilac hat ceremoniously on the table in front of them. 'You did them proud.'

Bert grinned at his wife as he placed his palm over hers. 'As did you, old girl.'

They sat quietly, holding hands, both knowing that they were thinking the same thing. *We never had a son or a daughter to see happily married. We never thought we'd have a day like this. Yet, here we are. Aren't we lucky?*

Tom watched as Dylan climbed onto his mother's lap, cuddling Harold the Stegosaurus to his chest. He was still in shock after what Sue had told him and badly wanted to talk to Helen before Sue took an overexcited Dylan home.

He could see Helen, arms full of empty plates, stacking them into the crates that Sybil and her team had brought over from the tearoom. Tom collected up a handful of glasses, and headed in her direction.

'Do these go in a crate too?'

'That one over there.' Helen pointed to a foam lined box to the right. 'How are you doing?'

'I'll be better when we've had a chat. Do you have time now, do you think?'

Looking over her shoulder, reassured that Sybil's waitresses had the clear-up under control, Helen nodded. 'My old office?'

The stone walls of the store room come office felt soothing after the heat of the spring sunshine. Helen shivered as they entered her old work space. Tom took off his jacket and placed it over her shoulders.

Helen smiled. 'Thank you. Although don't stand too close, or I might have to seduce you. I'm sure you've been told you look good in uniform a million times, but hell, you look good in a uniform.'

Tom gently coiled a curl that hung across Helen's fringe between his fingers. 'Hold that thought. For now, I need to tell you why I was so late.'

Although it hadn't taken long for Tom to share his news, Helen had to repeat it back to him several times before it sank in.

Sue was still going to move to Australia with Nathan, but

Dylan was not going with them. Her partner wanted a new start in a new country with no ties. And that meant leaving both Harriet and Dylan behind.

'But how could Sue... I mean...'

Tom grimaced. 'That's why she was late. Her conscience isn't letting her sleep. Apparently, she's been drumming up the courage to tell me for ages that she thinks Dylan will be better off with me full time.'

'But, he's her son!'

'Yes,' Tom slipped his arm around Helen's waist, 'and he's mine. And although I am delighted I won't be losing him to the other side of the world, I can't help wondering how his mum leaving him is going to affect him.'

A trickle of fear ran down Helen's spine as she asked, 'What will you do?'

'I'll have to live in Tiverton. No way am I going to move Dylan now he's settled at school.' He licked his lips. 'That's why Sue was going on about Sam having loads of money and assuming I got paid heaps. She was making herself feel better about leaving me to care for Dylan full time. The thing is,' Tom looked anxiously at Helen, 'how do you feel about it? I mean, I know you love Dylan and he loves you, but you'll be like a mum to him with Sue gone. That's what Sue was getting at with all the family stuff, I think. Dylan being part of a family with me – us.'

Tears gathered in Helen's eyes.

'Helen?' Tom felt panic grip him, 'You aren't going to run away again, are you?'

She smiled as she shook her head. 'No, never. I was just wondering how we'd tell Dylan his mum was leaving him.'

'Not our problem. We'll have to pick up the pieces

though.' Tom sighed. 'At least there's Zoom and Skype and all that, so we can make sure he talks to his mum every day.'

'Maybe we can record the school nativity and that sort of stuff?' Helen shifted on the hard seat. 'I suppose we could rent Sue's house. Just get the landlord to adjust the contract?'

'We?'

'Yes, of course.' Helen paused. 'Although, I'm not sure I want to live where Sue did, so...'

'But you live in Bath.' Tom curled a spiral of her hair around a finger.

'I had a surprise for you. I wasn't going to say until you got back to Bath with me, but, maybe now's a good time.'

'If it's good news, then now is the perfect time.'

'I've been given permission to work from home three days a week. I thought I'd work from here. Tina already knows and said it was okay, but if we had a home that was big enough in Tiverton, then, I could work from there instead.'

Tom grabbed hold of Helen and held her close. 'Live with me and Dylan?'

'If you'll have me?'

'Are you kidding? Of course we will.' Tom held her by the waist, his face serious. 'It'll be tough sometimes. Dylan is going to miss Sue.'

'I know.' A wave of nervous happiness hit Helen. 'But we'll muddle through. The three of us.' She stood up, her heart pounding hard in her chest. 'Now, come on, we have a little boy to say goodbye to and our friends' wedding to get back to.'

Epilogue

Saturday May 23rd

'**W**here is everyone?'

Tina looked around the deserted kitchen. Now she'd stopped moving for a moment, she realised the whole house had an empty feel, as if she and Sam were the only ones there.

'They're probably in their rooms, taking ten minutes before we meet in the walled garden. Bet everyone's exhausted.' Sam wrapped his arms around her. 'We could go to ours too.'

Seeing the look in her husband's eyes, Tina smirked. 'There's nothing I'd like more, but…'

'We are the hosts. I'll just have to wait to examine how that incredible dress is staying up. Something, I should warn you, I intend to take a great deal of time doing.'

'I'm glad to hear it.' Kissing him hard, Tina pulled back. 'It's been an amazing day.'

'It has. Come on then, Mrs Philips, if no one's here, they must all be adhering to Mabel's schedule. It's ten past six.

Her list stated everyone should be assembled in the walled garden for a quiet drink and chat by fairy light ten minutes ago.'

'I'm looking forward to handing out the thank you presents.' Tina smiled as she thought of the gift they'd got for Dylan. 'Mabel assures me she has the gifts all hidden beneath the registrar's table, even the one for her, bless her.'

'I hope she remembered to do those rounds of sandwiches she talked about as well. Goodness knows there isn't a scone or scrap of cream and jam left in the place. And as for beer and wine... you can forget it.'

'Actually, Sam, I'd rather have a cup of tea.'

'I have a confession.' Sam kissed the top of her head. 'I asked Mabel to make up the onsite thermos flasks. There will be tea and coffee.'

Flinging her arms around Sam, Tina laughed. 'That's why I married you then! I knew there must be some reason!'

As they approached the garden, Sam slowed. 'Why's it so quiet? I can usually hear Bert laughing a mile off.'

Speeding up, they moved into the garden. The fairy lights shone across the skeleton of the greenhouse, making it look enchanted. There was not a soul to be seen.

'They aren't all hiding, are they?' Tina peered about. 'I'll jump a mile if they all shout boo!'

'Nowhere to hide. Unless they've squeezed in with the chickens.'

Pointing ahead, Tina saw something on the table where they'd signed the register. 'What's that?'

'The thermos I asked for with,' Sam frowned, 'a large envelope propped against it.'

Dashing forwards Tina picked it up. It had *Don't Panic, everyone is fine*, written on it.

Sam smiled. 'Our friends are up to something. I think I like it.'

'Like it?'

'We're on our own on a romantic spring evening on the best day of our lives.' He slid his hands around her waist. 'Let's open the envelope. See what our friends have done this time.'

Dear Mr and Mrs Philips,

As you aren't able to go away for a honeymoon, we thought we'd bring the honeymoon to you, here, at Mill Grange.

We have all moved out for a week. You have seven peaceful days of just yourselves and the chickens!

Our wedding present is a full freezer and cupboards stocked with food and drink. A Chinese takeaway is due to be delivered to you at 7 p.m. tomorrow night. As for this evening, Moira from the Stag and Hound has been given a key, and will pop in with a three-course meal at eight. She has instructions to put it in the Aga/fridge, and not disturb you.

We all wish you the best honeymoon and look forward to seeing you next weekend.

Lots of love,

Thea, Shaun, Tom, Helen, Dylan, Sybil, Bert and Mabel.

xx

PS – thank you for the beautiful presents. We all loved them – especially Dylan, who can't believe he owns his own archaeologist's trowel. He's so proud! (Love, Thea xx)

Tina looked at Sam, her mouth open. 'A honeymoon at home.'

'With no one here but us.'

Tina felt choked as she re-read the letter. 'We have the best friends.'

'We do.' Sam led her to a row of chairs beneath the marquee, as he whispered, 'Now then, tell me, Mrs Philips, exactly which of these dress fastenings is the best one to open first?'

Acknowledgements

When I first created the characters for Midsummer Dream at Mill Grange, I never dreamt that I'd be lucky enough to write a whole series for them. Writing the adventures of Thea, Tina, Shaun and Sam – not forgetting Mabel and Bert – has been an absolute joy, and I'd like to thank a few people who've helped me along the way.

First, the team at Aria (Head of Zeus), especially Hannah and Rhea, who have both been so supportive and passionate about Spring Blossoms at Mill Grange.

Also, to my agent, Kiran; many thanks for your guidance and encouragement.

The Mill Grange series would never have come to life if it hadn't been for Tammy Nicholson, who welcomes me and my colleague, Alison Knight (along with many of our Imagine students), to Northmoor House – the inspiration for Mill Grange - on Exmoor every year, for our Imagine writing retreats.

Finally, to my family and friends, who support my constant need to write with regular deliveries of coffee, chocolate, and kind encouragement.

About the Author

JENNY KANE is the bestselling author of several romantic fiction series. Her first novel, Another Cup of Coffee (Accent Press), was a Kindle bestseller. The final novel in this series, Another Glass of Champagne, was released in June 2016. Jenny Kane's Cornish romance, Abi's House, hit No.1 in the Amazon Romance, Contemporary Fiction, and Women's Fiction charts, and was followed by a sequel, Abi's Neighbour, Jenny's seventh novel.

Hello from Aria

We hope you enjoyed this book! If you did let us know, we'd love to hear from you.

We are Aria, a dynamic digital-first fiction imprint from award-winning independent publishers Head of Zeus. At heart, we're committed to publishing fantastic commercial fiction – from romance and sagas to crime, thrillers and historical fiction. Visit us online and discover a community of like-minded fiction fans!

We're also on the look out for tomorrow's superstar authors. So, if you're a budding writer looking for a publisher, we'd love to hear from you.
You can submit your book online at ariafiction.com/ we-want-read-your-book

You can find us at:
Email: aria@headofzeus.com
Website: www.ariafiction.com
Submissions: www.ariafiction.com/ we-want-read-your-book

 @ariafiction
 @Aria_Fiction
 @ariafiction